Your Face Tomorrow

ALSO BY JAVIER MARÍAS,
AVAILABLE FROM NEW DIRECTIONS

A Heart So White
All Souls
Dark Back of Time
The Man of Feeling
Tomorrow in the Battle Think on Me
When I Was Mortal
Written Lives
Your Face Tomorrow, Volume One: Fever and Spear

FORTHCOMING

Your Face Tomorrow, Volume Three

JAVIER MARÍAS

YOUR

FACE

TOMORROW

Volume Two
Dance and Dream

Translated from the Spanish by Margaret Jull Costa

A NEW DIRECTIONS BOOK

First published in Spain in 2004 as *Tu rostro mañana, 2, Baile y sueño* by Alfaguara, Grupo Santillana de Ediciones, S.A.

Published by arrangement with Mercedes Casanovas Agencia Literaria, Barcelona, and in association with Chatto & Windus, The Random House Group UK.

Acknowledgments:
The translator would like to thank Javier Marías, Annella McDermott, Palmira Sullivan, and Ben Sherriff for all their help and advice.
Grateful acknowledgment is made to Random House, Inc., for permission to reprint from *The Selected Poetry of Rainer Maria Rilke* the lines from the first "Duino Elegy," copyright © 1989 by Stephen Mitchell. The Eliot lines are quoted from "The Love Song of J. Alfred Prufrock," copyright 1917 by T.S. Eliot.

This book was made possible in part by an investment from the Literary Ventures Fund: *investing in literature one book at a time, providing a foundation for writers around the globe.*

The publication of this book has been assisted with a translation subvention from the Director of Books, Archives, and Libraries of the Cultural Ministry of Spain.

Manufactured in the United States of America
New Directions Books are printed on acid-free paper.
First published clothbound in 2006
Design by Semadar Megged

Library of Congress Cataloging-in-Publication Data

Marías, Javier.
[Tu rostro mañana. English]
Your face tomorrow : fever and spear / Javier Marías ; translated from the Spanish by Margaret Jull Costa. p. cm.
Volume I, Fever and Spear ISBN-13: 978-0-8112-1612-8
ISBN-10: 0-8112-1612-8
Volume II, Dance and Dream ISBN-13: 978-0-8112-1656-2
ISBN-10: 0-8112-1656-X
(alk. paper)
I. Costa, Margaret Jull. II. Title.
PQ6663.A7218T8313 2005
863'.64—dc22
2005000992

New Directions Books are published for James Laughlin
by New Directions Publishing Corporation
80 Eighth Avenue, New York 10011

Your Face

Tomorrow

For Carmen López M,
who will, I hope, want
to go on listening to me

And for Sir Peter Russell,
to whom this book is indebted
for his long shadow,
and the author,
for his far-reaching friendship

3
Dance

Let us hope that no one ever asks us for anything, or even enquires, no advice or favour or loan, not even the loan of our attention, let us hope that others do not ask us to listen to them, to their wretched problems and their painful predicaments so like our own, to their incomprehensible doubts and their paltry stories which are so often interchangeable and have all been written before (the range of stories that can be told is not that wide), or to what used to be called their travails, who doesn't have them or, if he doesn't, brings them upon himself, 'unhappiness is an invention', I often repeat to myself, and these words hold true for misfortunes that come from inside not outside and always assuming they are not misfortunes which are, objectively speaking, unavoidable, a catastrophe, an accident, a death, a defeat, a dismissal, a plague, a famine, or the vicious persecution of some blameless person, History is full of them, as is our own, by which I mean these unfinished times of ours (there are even dismissals and defeats and deaths that are self-inflicted or deserved or, indeed, invented). Let us hope that no one comes to us and says 'Please', or 'Listen'—the words that always precede all or almost all requests: 'Listen, do you know?', 'Listen, could you tell me?', 'Listen, have you got?', 'Listen, I wanted to ask you: for a recommendation, a piece of information, an opinion, a hand, some money, a favourable word, a consolation, a kindness, to keep this secret for me or to change for my sake and be someone else, or to betray and to lie or to keep silent for me and save me.' People ask and ask for all kinds of things, for everything, the reasonable and the crazy, the fair, the outrageous and the imaginary—the moon, as people always used to say, and which was promised by so many people everywhere precisely because it continues to be an imaginary place; people close to us ask, as do strangers, people who are in difficulties and those who caused those difficulties, the needy and the well-to-do, who, in this one respect, are indistinguishable: no one ever seems to have enough of anything, no one is ever contented, no one ever stops, as if they have all been told: 'Ask, just open your mouth and keep asking.' When, in fact, no one is ever told that.

And then, of course, more often than not you listen, feeling fearful sometimes and sometimes gratified too; nothing, in principle, is as flattering as being in a position to concede or refuse something, nothing—as also soon becomes clear—is as sticky and unpleasant: knowing, thinking that one can say 'Yes' or 'No' or 'We'll see'; and 'Perhaps', 'I'll think about it', 'I'll give you an answer tomorrow' or 'I'll want this in exchange', depending on your mood and entirely at your discretion, depending on whether you're at loose ends, feeling generous or bored, or, on the contrary, in an enormous hurry and lacking patience and time, depending on how you're feeling or on whether you want to have someone in your debt or to keep them dangling or on whether you want to commit yourself, because when you concede or refuse something—in both cases, even if you have merely lent an ear—you become involved with the supplicant, and you're caught, enmeshed perhaps.

If, one day, you give some money to a local beggar, the following morning it will be harder not to give, because he will expect it (nothing has changed, he is just as poor, I am not as yet any less rich, and why give nothing today when I gave something yesterday) and in a sense you have contracted an obligation with him: by helping him to reach this new day, you have a responsibility not to let this day turn sour on him, not to let it be the day of his final suffering or condemnation or death, and to create a bridge for him to traverse it safely, and so it goes on, one day after another, perhaps indefinitely, there is nothing

4

so very strange or arbitrary about the law found among certain primitive—or perhaps simply more logical—peoples where anyone who saves another person's life becomes that person's guardian and is deemed for ever responsible (unless, one day, the person they saved saves their life and then they can be at peace with each other and go their separate ways), as if the saved person had been empowered to say to his saviour: 'I'm alive today because you wanted me to be; it's as if you had caused me to be born again, therefore you must protect and care for me and keep me safe, because if it wasn't for you, I would be beyond all evil and beyond all harm, or safe more or less in one-eyed, uncertain oblivion.'

And if, on the contrary, you deny alms to your local beggar on that first day, on the second day you will be left with a feeling of indebtedness, an impression that might increase on the third and fourth and fifth days, for if the beggar has negotiated and survived those dates without my help, how can I but commend him and thank him for the money I've saved up until now? And with each morning that passes—each night that he lives through—this idea will put down still deeper roots in us, the idea that we should contribute, that it is our turn. (This, of course, only affects people who notice the ragged; most simply pass them by, adopt an opaque gaze and see them as mere bundles of clothes.)

You have only to listen to the beggar who approaches you in the street and you are already involved; you listen to the foreigner or to someone who is lost asking you for directions and sometimes, if you're taking that route yourself, you end up showing them the way, and then the two of you fall into step and you become each other's insistent parallel being which, nevertheless, no one sees as a bad omen or as a nuisance or an obstacle, because you have chosen to walk along together, even though you don't know each other and may not even speak during that time, as the two of you progress (it is the stranger or the person who is lost who can always be led to another place, into a trap, an ambush, to a piece of waste ground, into a snare);

and you listen to the stranger who appears at the door persuading or selling or evangelising, trying always to persuade us and always talking very quickly, and just by opening the door to him you are caught; and you listen to the friend on the phone speaking in an urgent, hysterical or mellifluous voice—no, it's definitely hysterical—imploring or demanding or suddenly threatening, and you're already enmeshed; and you listen to your wife and your children who know of almost no other way of talking to you, at least this—asking I mean—is the only way they know of talking to you now, given the growing distance and diffuseness, and then you have to take out a knife or a blade to cut the bond that will eventually tighten around you: you caused them to be born, these children who are not yet beyond all evil or beyond all harm and who never will be, and you caused them to be born to their mother as well, who is like them still because she is now unimaginable without children—they form a nucleus from which none is ever excluded—and they are inconceivable without that figure who is still so necessary to them, so much so that you have no option but to protect her and care for her and keep her safe—you still see this as your task—even though Luisa is not fully aware of it, or not consciously, and even though she is far away in space and moving away from me in time too, date by date and with each day that passes. Even though each night that I negotiate and traverse and survive casts an ever denser cloud over me, and still I cannot see her, do not see her.

Luisa did not get caught or entangled, but she did, once, become involved because of a request and a gift of alms and she involved me a little in both of those things too, this was before we separated and before I left for England, when we had not yet foreseen the deepening rift or our backs so firmly turned on each other, at least I had not, for it is only later on that you realise you have lost the trust you had in someone or that others have lost the trust they had in you—if, that is, you ever do realise, which I don't really think you do; I mean, that only afterwards, when the present is already the past and is thus so changeable and uncertain that it can easily be told (and can be retold a thousand times more, with no two versions agreeing), do we realise that we also knew it when the present was still present and had not yet been rejected or become muddied or shadowy, how else would we be able to put a date to it, because the fact is we can, oh yes, we can date it afterwards with alarming precision: 'It was that day when . . .' we say or remember, as people do in novels (which are always heading towards a specific moment: the plot points to it, dictates it; except that not all novels know how they're going to end), sometimes when we are alone or in company, two people summing things up out loud: 'It was those words you came out with so casually on your birthday that first put me on my guard or began to distance me.' 'Your reaction disappointed me, it made me wonder if perhaps I was wrong about you, but that meant I'd been wrong about you for years, so perhaps you had simply changed.' 'I just couldn't stand the way you kept criticising me, it was so unfair that I thought maybe it was simply a ploy of yours, a way to freeze me out, and frozen out was how I felt.' Yes, we usually know when something breaks or breaks down or begins to grow weary. But we always hope that it will sort itself out or mend or recover—by itself sometimes, as if by magic—and that what we know will not be confirmed; or if we see that it is something far simpler, that there is something about us that annoys or displeases or repels, we make valiant efforts to change ourselves. These attempts, however, are made in a theoretical, skeptical spirit. In reality, we know that we won't succeed, or that things no longer depend on what we do or don't do. It is the same feeling that the ancients had when an expression came to their lips or their minds, an expression which our time has forgotten or, rather, rejected, but which they recognised: 'The die is cast.' And although the phrase has been more or less abolished, the feeling still persists and we still know it. 'There's nothing to be done about it' is what I sometimes say to myself.

A young woman—very young—had posted herself at the door of the hypermarket or supermarket or pseudomarket where Luisa used to do the shopping, she was not only very young, she was also foreign and a mother and was both these things twice over: for she had two children, one only a few months old sitting in a battered stroller and another, who was older, but still very small, two or three perhaps (or so Luisa thought, she had noticed that he was still wearing nappies under his short trousers), and who guarded the stroller like a soldier, a tiny unarmed member of the Praetorian guard; and the young woman was not only Rumanian or Bosnian, or possibly Hungarian—although that is less likely, there are far fewer of them in Spain—she also appeared to be a gypsy. She couldn't have been more than twenty, and on the days when she begged there (it wasn't every day, or perhaps Luisa simply didn't happen to see her), she was always with her two children, not so much because she wanted to inspire pity—this was Luisa's inter-pretation—as because she clearly had nowhere else to leave them or no one else to leave them with. They were part of her, as much a part of her as her arms. They were her prolongation, they were *with her* just as the dog was *without a leg*, according to Alan Marriott's vision when he decided, in his imagination, to link his dog with that other young gypsy woman, so that together they formed for him a horrific couple.

The Rumanian woman would spend hours standing at the door of the supermarket, sometimes she would sit on the steps at the entrance and push the stroller back and forth on the pavement, with her older son on guard. The reason Luisa noticed her was not because of this tableau vivant, this picture, which is both effective and fairly commonplace, even though it's now forbidden to use children when begging—and Luisa isn't the kind of person who takes pity on just anyone, nor am I, or perhaps we are, but not to the point of her putting her hand in her purse, or, in my case, of me putting my hand in my pocket, every time we come across an indigent, we couldn't afford it in Madrid, we don't earn enough for such extravagance, and our crude and callous officials are constantly transferring to the big city, and releasing onto its streets, wave upon wave of illegal immigrants who know nothing of the language, the country or the customs—people who have just slipped in via Andalusia or the Canaries, or via Catalonia and the Balearics if they're coming from the East, the officials wouldn't even know which country to send them back to—and they are left to get by somehow without papers and without money, with the number of poor people always on the increase, poor people who are disoriented, lost, peripatetic, unintelligible, nameless. Luisa, then, did not notice this little group, one of many, because they struck her as being unusually deserving of pity; she singled them out as individuals, she noted the young Bosnian woman and her child sentinel, I mean that she saw them as *them*, they did not seem to her indistinguishable or interchangeable as objects of compassion, she saw beyond their condition and their function and their needs, so widespread and so widely shared. She did not see a poor mother with her two children, she saw that particular mother and those particular children, especially the older child.

'He's got such a bright, lively little face,' she told me. 'And what touches me most is his readiness to help, to look after his little brother, to be of some use. That child doesn't want to be a burden, although he can't help but be one because he can't yet do anything on his own. But small though he is, he wants to take part, to contribute, and he's so affectionate with the baby and so alert to what might happen and to what is happening. He spends hours and hours there, with no means of entertaining himself, he goes up and down the steps, he swings on the handrail, he tries to push the stroller back and forth, but he's not really strong enough yet for that. Those are his main distractions. But he never strays far from his mother, not because he's not adventurous (as I say, you can see that he's really bright), but as if he were aware that this would just be another worry for her, and you can tell that he's trying to make things as easy as possible for her, well, insofar as he's able to, which isn't very much. And sometimes he strokes the young woman's cheek or his little brother's cheek. He keeps looking around and about him, he's very alert, I'm sure those quick eyes of his don't miss a single passer-by, and some he must remember from one visit to the next, he probably remembers me already. I find it so touching, that terribly responsible, industrious, participatory attitude, that enormous desire to be useful. He's too young for that.' She paused and then added: 'It's so absurd. A moment ago, he didn't even exist and now he's full of anxieties he doesn't even understand. Perhaps that's why they don't weigh on him, he seems quite happy, and his mother adores him. But it's not just absurd, it's unfair too.' She thought for a few seconds, stroking her knees with her two hands, she had sat down on the edge of the sofa to my right, she had just come in and had still not taken off her raincoat, the shopping bags were on the floor, she hadn't gone straight to the kitchen. I've always liked her knees, with or without tights, and fortunately, since she usually wore a skirt, they were nearly always visible to me. Then she said: 'He reminds me a bit of Guillermo when he was small. I used to find it touching in him too, it's not just because they're poor. Seeing him so impatient to participate in the world or in responsibilities and tasks, so eager to find out about everything and to help, so aware of my struggles and my difficulties. And, even more intuitively—or more deductively—aware of yours too, if you remember, even though he saw you much less.'

She wasn't asking me, she was merely reminding me or confirming my memory. And I did still remember, even when I was in London, when I didn't see the boy and was beginning to fear for him; he was very patient and protective towards his sister and often shared or gave in too much, like someone who knows that the noble, upright thing is for the strong always to give in to the non-tyrannical, non-abusive weak, a rather old-fashioned principle nowadays, since now the strong tend to be heartless and the weak despotic; he was even protective of his mother and, who knows, possibly of me, now that he felt that I was exiled and alone and far away, an orphan in his eyes and understanding; those who act as a shield suffer greatly in life, as do the vigilant, their ears and eyes always alert. And those who want at all costs to play fair, even when they are fighting and what is at risk is their survival or that of their most indispensable loved ones, without whom it is impossible to live, or almost.

'And Guillermo hasn't changed,' I said to Luisa. 'I hope he doesn't, but then again, sometimes I hope he does. He's bound to lose, given the way the world is going. I thought he'd learn to take better care of himself when he went to school and experienced the dangers for himself, but the years have gone by, and that doesn't seem to have happened. Sometimes I wonder if I'm being a bad father by not training him, not teaching him what he needs to know: tricks, cunning arguments, intimidation, caution, complaints; and more egotism. One should, I think, prepare one's children. But it's not easy to instil in them what they need to know, if you don't yourself like it. And he's a better person than I am, for now at any rate.'

'Well, it might have been a waste of time in his case anyway,' answered Luisa. And she got up as if she were in a hurry. 'I'm going out again before they leave,' she said. That was why she hadn't yet taken off her raincoat or unpacked the bags: she knew she hadn't quite come home. 'I usually give her a bit of money when I go in, she's got a box you can throw coins into, and I gave her some today. But on my way out, she asked me for something, it's the first time she's ever asked me for anything, in words I mean, in a very strange, limited Spanish, I couldn't make out the accent, and she used the occasional Italian expression as well. She asked me to buy her some of those baby wipes that are so useful for keeping children clean, you know, the sort you can just pull out of a box. I said no, that she should buy them herself and that I'd already given her some money. And she said: "No, money no, money no." I've been going over and over it in my head and I think I've just understood what she meant. She must be collecting money for her husband or for her brothers or her father, I don't know, for the men in her life. She wouldn't dare touch any of that money without their permission, she wouldn't be able to decide, on her own, to spend it on something, she must have to hand it over and then they buy whatever they think should be bought, perhaps attending to their own needs first. They would think baby wipes were superfluous, a luxury, they wouldn't give her money for something like that, and she'd just have to put up with it. But I know they're not a luxury, those children spend hours on end there, and they must get really sore and chafed if she can't clean them up now and then. So I'm going to buy them for her. I hadn't realized until now, she can't do what she likes with what she earns, not a single penny of it, that's why she asked me for the thing itself and why the money was of no use to her. I'll be right back.'

When she returned shortly afterwards, she took off her raincoat. I had unpacked the bags meanwhile, and everything was in its place.

'Did you get there in time?' I asked. She had aroused my curiosity.

'Yes, they obviously stay there until the shop closes. I went in, bought the wipes and gave them to her. You should have seen the look of joy and gratitude on her face. I mean she's always very grateful anyway and always gives me a big smile whenever I give her any money. But this time it was different, it was something for her, for her use and for the children, it wasn't part of the common pot, money, then, is all the same and once it's mixed up you can't tell whose is whose. And the little boy was happy too, just to see her happy. He had such a celebratory look on his face, even though he didn't really know what it was he was celebrating. He's so quick, so bright, he notices everything. If things don't go too badly for him in life, he'll be a great optimist. Let's hope he's lucky.'

I knew that Luisa was already involved by that request for help, which she had answered belatedly and, therefore, after some thought. She wasn't caught or entangled, but she was involved. Whenever she went back to the supermarket and saw the young Hungarian woman and her little optimist, she would wonder if the wipes had run out, for the children's need for them would not, of course—nor would it for a long time. And if the woman wasn't there, she would wonder about her, about them, not in a worried or, far less, an interfering way (Luisa is not one to draw attention to herself, nor does she go poking about in other people's lives), but I knew she was involved because, from then on, without my ever having seen them, I myself would sometimes ask about them and wait for my wife to bring me news, if there was any.

A few weeks later, when people were avidly buying things for the fast-approaching Christmas season, she told me that the Rumanian mother had again specifically asked her for something. 'Hello, *carina*,' the young woman had said, which made us think that before arriving in Spain she must have spent some time in Italy, from where perhaps she had been unceremoniously expelled by the brutal, xenophobic, pseudo-Lombardic authorities, who are even coarser and more oafish than our own contemptuous, pseudo-*madrileño* ones. 'If you don't want you tell me no, but I ask you one thing,' had been her polite preamble, for courtesy partly consists in stating the obvious, which is never out of place when employed in its service. 'The boy wants a cake. I cannot buy. Can you buy for him? Only if you want. It is there, *detralángolo*,' and she pointed around the corner, and Luisa immediately knew which shop she meant, a very good, expensive pâtisserie which she also frequented. 'If you don't want, then no,' the woman had insisted, as if she knew perfectly well that the request was a mere fancy. Yet because it was her son's fancy it was worth asking.

'This time, the boy understood everything,' Luisa said. 'She was giving expression to something he wanted, and he knew it. Well, the look of suspense on his face left no room for doubt, the poor little thing was waiting with bated breath for my Yes or No, his eyes like saucers.' ('Just like a defendant awaiting the verdict,' I thought, though without interrupting her, 'an optimistic defendant.') 'Anyway, I didn't know what exactly she meant by "a cake", and, besides, they seemed to know precisely which one and it was that and no other that they wanted, and so the four of us had to go over to the pâtisserie so that they could show me. I went in first so that the people in the shop could see that they were with me, and even then a lot of customers instinctively moved away in disgust, they made way for us as if to avoid contagion, I don't think she noticed, or perhaps she's used to it and it doesn't affect her any more, but it did me. It was the little boy who, very excitedly, pointed out the cake to me in a display case, a birthday cake, not very big, and the young woman nodded. I told her that they should go back to the steps outside the supermarket—the pâtisserie was packed and even more so with us and the stroller and everything—while I stood in the line, bought the cake and had them wrap it up, then I'd bring it over to her. What with one thing and another, it took me a quarter of an hour or thereabouts, and I had to laugh when I came round the corner, carrying the package, and saw the little boy, his eyes fixed on that spot and with a look of such expectation on his face, I'm sure he hadn't taken his eyes off that corner for a second since returning to his place, waiting for me to appear, bearing the treasure: as if he'd been mentally running all that time, out of pure impatience, pure longing. For once, he left his mother's side and ran to meet me, even though she called to him: "No, Emil! Emil, come here!" He ran round and round me like a puppy.' Luisa sat thinking, a smile on her lips, amused by this recent memory. Then she added: 'And that was that.'

'And now that you've done what she asked, won't she always be asking you for more things?' I said.

'No, I don't think she's the sort to take advantage. I've seen her several times since I bought her the baby wipes, and this was the first time that she's expressly asked me for something else. One day, I saw her menfolk hanging around there, I suppose one of them was her husband, although none of them behaved any differently towards her or the children. They may well have been her brothers or cousins or uncles, some relation or other, there were four or five of them standing near her, talking, but without including her in their discussions, and then they left.'

'They probably act as a kind of mafia and carry out checks to make sure other beggars don't take her place. A lot of beggars pay a form of rent for a particularly good spot, there's a lot of competition even in the world of begging. And it's no bad thing, I mean, she probably wouldn't be able to hold on to it if she didn't have some kind of protection. What were the men like?'

'A rough lot. I'm afraid that, in their case, I, too, would have moved out of their way as if to avoid contagion. Nasty-looking men. Tetchy. Bossy. Cheating. Dirty. Oh, and they all had cell phones and wore lots of rings. And some of them sported vests.'

'Ah,' I thought, 'the reaction of the other customers in the pâtisserie; it really did affect her, she won't forget it, she'll be very conscious of it the next time she goes in there alone or with our own well-to-do, non-mendicant children: she obviously felt it very deeply. She's involved. But it's nothing serious and won't become so. Doubtless I'm involved too.'

I found out to what extent I was involved during my time in London. Because even there, far from Luisa and from our children, I would sometimes remember the young Bosnian woman and her two children, the small, responsible, stateless optimist and his brother in the old stroller, none of whom I had seen and whom I had only heard about from Luisa. And when they came into my mind, what I wondered most was not how they would be getting on or if they had had any luck, but—perhaps strangely, perhaps not—whether they were still in the world, as if, only then, would it be worth devoting a brief, vague, insubstantial thought to them. And yet that wasn't the case: even if they had left the world because of some misfortune or some dreadful mistake, because of some injustice or accident or murderous act, they had already joined the stories I had heard and incorporated, they were yet one more accumulated image, and our capacity for absorbing these is infinite (they are constantly being added to and never subtracted from), the real and the imagined as well as the false and the factual, and as we progress, we are constantly being exposed to new stories and to a million further episodes, and to the memory of beings who have never existed or trodden the earth or traversed the world, or who did, but who are now safe more or less in their own blessed insignificance or in blissful unmemorability. Emil had reminded Luisa of our son Guillermo in the past, when he was two or three years old, and now this growing son of ours, in turn, reminded me or us—for our children are always in our thoughts—of the small insignificant Hungarian boy, when he might well already have moved on and, in his enforced nomadic state, left for another country or might not even exist in time, expelled from it early on by some unfortunate incident or encounter, as often happens to those who are in a hurry to participate in the world and its tasks and benefits and sorrows.

Sometimes, I would wake in the middle of the night, or so I thought, bathed in sweat sometimes and always agitated, and, while still inside my dream or clumsily and belatedly only just emerging from it, I would ask myself: 'Are they still in the world? Are my children still in the world? What is happening to them on this distant night, at this very moment in this remote space of mine, what is happening to them right now? I have no way of knowing, I can't go into their rooms to see if they're still breathing or if they're whimpering in their sleep, did the phone ring to warn me of some evil or was it just ringing in my murky dream? To warn me that they no longer exist, but have been expelled from time, what can have happened and how can I be sure that, at this very moment, Luisa isn't dialling my number to tell me about the tragedy of which I have just had a premonition? Or else she wouldn't be able to speak for sobbing and I would say to her: "Calm down, calm down, and tell me what happened, it'll be all right." But she would never calm down or be able to explain because there are some things that cannot be explained and will never be all right, and sorrows that can never be calmed.' And when my disquiet gradually ebbed away—the back of my neck still damp with sweat—and I realised that it was all to do with distance and anxiety and sleep and the curse of not being able to see—the back of the neck never sees, nor do exiled eyes—then, by association, the other question would formulate itself, pointless and bearable: 'Are those two Rumanian children on the supermarket steps still in the world, and is their young gypsy mother? I have no way of knowing and it doesn't really concern me. I have no way of knowing tonight, of course, and tomorrow I will forget to ask Luisa if she happens to phone me or I her (it isn't our usual time) because, by day, I won't care so much if she does or doesn't know what has become of them, not here in faraway London, that's where I am, yes, now I remember, now I understand, this window and its sky, the curving whistle of the wind, the bustling murmur of trees which is never indifferent or languid like the murmur of the river, I'm the one who moved to another country, not the little boy (he may still be wandering my streets), in a few hours I will go to work in this city and Tupra will be waiting for me, Tupra, who always wants more, Bertram Tupra, who is always waiting and insatiable, who sees no limits in anyone and asks more and more of us, of me, Mulryan, Pérez Nuix, and Rendel, and of any of the other faces that might join him tomorrow, including ours when they are no longer recognisable, because they have grown so treacherous or so worn.'

Asking, asking, almost no one holds back and almost everyone tries; who doesn't? They might say no—that is the reasoning that goes on inside every head, even those that do not reason—but if I don't ask, I won't receive, that's for sure; and what do I lose by asking, if I can manage to do so without hoping for too much. 'I'm here, too, because of a request, originally and in part,' I was thinking as I lay, halfasleep, halfawake, in London, 'it was Luisa who asked me to go, to leave the field clear and to move out of the house and to make things easier for her, and to leave the way open to whoever might come, and then we would both be able to see more clearly, without cramping each other's style. I did as she asked, I obeyed, I listened: I left and set off, I moved away and kept walking, until I arrived here, and I have still not gone back. I don't even know yet if I've stopped walking. Perhaps I won't go back, perhaps I will never go back unless another request is made, which might be this: "I was so wrong about you before, come here. Sit down here beside me again, somehow I just couldn't see you clearly before. Come here. Come to me. Come back. And stay for ever." But another night has passed, and I have still not heard that request.'

Young Pérez Nuix was about to make a request too, after thinking long and hard before doing so. She wanted something, possibly something she did not deserve given that she had followed me for far too long, unable to make up her mind to approach me, in that heavy night rain and, what's more, dragging or being dragged along by a poor, drenched dog. I didn't have to think about it, I knew as soon as I recognised her voice over the intercom and when I buzzed the door downstairs so that she could come up and talk to me, as she had already announced: 'I know it's a bit late, but I must talk to you. It'll only take a moment' (she had said this in my language and had called me 'Jaime', as Luisa would have done had she come to my door). And I knew it as I heard her walking unhurriedly up the stairs, one step at a time, along with her dog, a very wet pointer, and when I heard the latter shaking himself dry, under cover at last and at last with some obvious direction (without the incomprehensible, insistent sky continuing to hurl down more rain upon him): she paused on the false landings or turns in the stairs, which had no angles only curves and were adorned, as almost all English staircases are, with a carpet to absorb the water that falls from us when we shake ourselves dry—so many days and even more nights of rain; and I heard Pérez Nuix strike the air with her closed umbrella, it would no longer conceal her face, and perhaps she took advantage of each brief pause and each time the dog shook himself to glance for a second in a hand mirror—eyes, chin, skin or lips—and tidy her hair a little, because hair always gets damp even if you protect it from the rain (I had still not seen whether it was covered with a hat or a scarf or a cap or a kitschy little beret worn at an angle, I had never perhaps even seen her head outside the office and outside our building with no name). And I had known it, even when I did not know it was her or who she was, when she was just a woman, strange or mercenary or lost or eccentric, helpless or blind, in the empty streets, with her raincoat and boots and with that agreeable thigh of which I had caught a momentary glimpse (or was that my imagination, the incorrigible desideratum of a lifetime, deeply entrenched ever since adolescence and which never fades and, as I am discovering, never goes away) when she crouched down to stroke the dog and speak softly to him. 'Let her come to me,' I had thought when I stopped abruptly and turned to look at her, 'if she wants something from me or if she's following me. That's her problem. She must have a reason, assuming she was following me or still is, it can't be in order *not* to talk to me.' And there had, in fact, been a reason, she wanted to talk to me and to ask me for something.

I looked at the clock, I looked around me to make sure that the apartment wasn't too untidy, not that any apartment I've ever lived in has been (but that is why we tidy people always check for untidiness whenever anyone comes to see us). It was rather late for England, but not for Spain—there, lots of people would just be going out to supper or wondering where to eat, in Madrid the night was just beginning, and Nuix was half-Spanish or perhaps less—Luisa might be going out right now for a long night with her putative, partying suitor who would want nothing to do with my children and would never step over the threshold (nor—bless him—would he ever occupy my place). That's her problem, I had thought beneath the endless spears of water, and I repeated these words to myself while I held the door open waiting for her arrival, she was panting a little as she came up the stairs, she had walked quite a long way, I could hear them both panting, her and not just the dog, the same thing had happened to me shortly before, when I came up the stairs and even after I had arrived—two minutes to catch my breath—I had walked a long way across squares and down empty streets and past monuments. That's her problem, one thinks mistakenly or incompletely, or that's his problem, when someone is preparing to ask us something. It's my problem too, we should always add or should I say include. It would doubtless be my problem once the request had left her lips or her throat and once I had heard it. Once we had both heard it, for that is how the person making the request knows his or her message has traversed the air and cannot be ignored, because once it's in the air, it has reached its destination.

Initially, she talked non-stop and filled the air, young Pérez Nuix—a way of postponing what one has come to say, the important part—while she was taking off her raincoat and proffering me her umbrella as if she were surrendering her sword, and while she was asking me what she should do with the dog, who was still spraying drops of water everywhere whenever he shook himself.

'Shall I put him in the kitchen?' she asked, still in Spanish. 'He'll make everything wet if I don't.'

I looked at the poor, resigned pointer, he did not look like the kind of dog to raise any objections.

'No, leave him. He deserves a bit of consideration. He'll be better off with us. The carpet will help him dry off, it's pretty *batallada* anyway.' I realised at once that this was an odd expression, neither proper Spanish nor an adaptation of some English expression, maybe both my languages were becoming not so much confused as unreliable, because I spoke the latter almost all the time and thought in the former when I was alone. Perhaps I was losing my confidence in both, because, unlike Pérez Nuix, I had not been bilingual since childhood. I added: 'I mean very *sufrida*.' I wasn't sure, though, that *sufrida* was the right word either, my mother had used it in a different sense, referring more to the colour of a fabric than to its ability to stand up to wear and tear. My mother spoke excellent Spanish, much better than my contaminated version.

And that was about all I did say while my visitor apologised: forgive me for turning up here at this late hour, forgive me for not warning you first, forgive me for being so wet and for bringing with me an even wetter dog, but he desperately needed a walk, would you mind very much lending me a towel for a moment, don't worry, it's for me, not the dog, do you mind if I just take my boots off, they're supposed to be water-proof, but nothing's proof against rain like this, and my feet are frozen. She said all this and more in a kind of torrent, but she didn't take her boots off—a remnant of discretion perhaps—she merely unzipped them both and, later, zipped them up again, in fact, she fiddled with them a little, zipping and unzipping them, while she was sitting down, although only a couple of times while I was actually there, because I had insisted she take a seat while I deposited her now dispensable items of clothing in the kitchen along with my now dry ones, for I had stood for a while looking out of the window, and she had hung about, undecided, once she had ascertained where I lived, I mean before ringing the bell and announcing herself without actually using her name. However, I found it hard to believe that, doing our kind of work and with files so easily to hand, she hadn't known my address already, she could have waited for me outside my front door and thus avoided having to trail me through the disagreeable night, or waited in still more comfort in the foyer of the hotel opposite, from where she would have seen me arrive or would have noticed my lights on (although, during the hours that I'm away, there is always at least one light on day and night), and she could then simply have crossed the square and barely got wet at all. I asked if she would like some-thing to drink, something hot, alcoholic, or water perhaps, but she didn't want anything just then, she lit a cigarette, we all smoked in our office despite the regulations, apart from Mulryan who was trying to give it up, and she continued talking quickly and volubly in order not to get to the point or to the one thing that she was obliged to tell me—what a night, it feels as if it were raining all over the world, no, she didn't say that, but something similar with the same trivial meaning, if one pretends there is nothing extraordinary about one's extraordinary behaviour it can end up not seeming extraordinary at all, this very dumb trick works with the dozy, passive majority and there's nothing more useful than liberties taken and left unchecked, but neither she nor I, Tupra or Wheeler belonged to the majority, rather, we were the sort who never let go of our prey, are never dazzled and never entirely lose the thread or lose sight of our objective, or only in part or apparently. She did not cross her legs until a little while later, as if her indecisiveness about the zippers on her boots were only possible while her legs remained parallel and at a right angle, nor did she use the towel I quickly handed her to dry her legs (she was wearing dusky stockings, not dark or transparent; I noticed a loose thread which would soon become a run, even though they were winter tights), she applied it to her face, hands, throat and neck, not this time to her sides or armpits or breasts, none of those was visible. Her thigh was the one I had glimpsed before when the skirt of her raincoat fell open, in the street, at a distance, except that now I could see both thighs, in their entirety, as one usually does, a good reason to look at the dog lying at her feet, an even better reason to lean forward and pat the dog, I remembered De la Garza at Wheeler's cold buffet supper making himself dwarfishly small by sitting on a very low pouffe in order to inspect Beryl Tupra's uninhibited thighs beneath her very short skirt (although hardly beneath, rather, outside her skirt, although it may not have been her thighs for which he was watching and waiting). Pérez Nuix's skirt wasn't anywhere near as short, although it did ride up slightly or quite a lot when she sat down; and I, of course, would never stoop to such puerile tricks, for a start, spying isn't my style, at least not with an ulterior motive, which there clearly was in this instance—a remnant of discretion on my part perhaps.

'What a night, it feels as if it were raining all over the world,' she said again, well, either that or her more prosaic equivalent, and this meant that she had done with all the preambles and diversionary manoeuvres and her dilatory fiddling with the zippers on her boots (they were zipped now, although not fully) and with the towel, which she still held scrunched up in the hand that was now resting on the sofa, like someone keeping hold of a used handkerchief which they might need again at any moment, with sneezes one never knows if another one is on the way. She was showing quite a lot of leg and she must have been aware of just how much, but nothing in her attitude indicated that she knew—it wasn't at all obvious—and when it comes to things that are not entirely manifest, you must always allow room for doubt, however clearly you think you can see them. 'She's very intelligent in that respect,' I thought. 'So much so that she can't possibly not be aware of what she's showing, but, at the same time, her utter naturalness—she's not immodest or an exhibitionist—gives the lie to any such awareness, indeed, gives the lie to its importance, like that morning in her office when she didn't bother to cover herself up for several seconds— not that long really, but long enough—and I saw that she had not entirely ruled me out: nothing more than that, I didn't start getting ideas, I don't think I'm that big-headed, and there's a great gulf between feeling desire and not entirely rejecting some-one, between affirmation and the unknown, between willingness and the simple absence of any plan, between a "Yes" and a "Possibly", between a "Fine" and a "We'll see" or even less than that, an "Anyway" or a "Hmm, right" or something which doesn't even formulate itself as a thought, a limbo, a space, a void, it's not something I've ever considered, it hadn't even occurred to me, it hadn't even crossed my mind. But in this job I'm learning to fear everything that passes through the mind and even what the mind does not as yet know, because I have noticed that, in almost every case, everything was already there, somewhere, before it even reached or penetrated the mind. I'm learning to fear, therefore, not only what is thought—the idea— but also what precedes it or comes before, and which is neither vision nor consciousness. And thus you are your own pain and fever or can be, and then . . . and then, who knows, one day you might hear a "Yes" regarding something or spoken by someone who has not yet been ruled out: depending on the threat or the vulnerability or the insecurity or the favour asked or the hurt, or the interests involved or the revelations, one sometimes makes late discoveries, sometimes after a surprising and prolonged semi-lascivious dream or, while awake, after a few flattering words, indeed, one does not even have to be the object of passion oneself, it is still more treacherous then: someone finally explains himself or herself and gets our attention and, seeing that person speaking with such vehemence and feeling, we start to wonder about that mouth from which those thoughts or arguments or that story are emerging and consider kissing it; who has not experienced the sensuality of intelligence, even fools are susceptible, and not a few unexpectedly surrender to it even though they cannot put a name to it or recognise it. And at other times we realise that we can no longer do without someone who, before, seemed to us totally expendable, or that we are prepared to take whatever steps are necessary to reach someone towards whom, for half a lifetime, we took not a single step, because, before, he or she had always made the effort to cover that distance, which is why each day they were always so close at hand. Until, suddenly, one day, they grow weary of the journey or else spite gets the better of them or their strength fails them or they are dying, and then we panic and rush off to find them, worried to death and shorn of any pretence or reserve, the sudden slaves of those who once were ours without our ever wondering about their other desires and believing that being our slave was their one conscious desire. "You never felt for me what I felt for you, nor wanted to; you kept me at a distance, not even caring if we never saw each other again, and I do not reproach you with that in the least; but you will regret my going and you will regret my death, because it pleases and contents one to know that one is loved." I often quote these words or repeat them to myself, wondering whose going I will unexpectedly regret and who, to their surprise, will regret my death; I quote it inaccurately and very freely, the farewell letter written more than two hundred years ago by an old blind woman to a superficial foreigner, still young and good-looking.'

'She doesn't rule me out, but that's as far as it goes,' I thought. 'Her legs reveal themselves unthinkingly and in doing so do not exclude me, nothing more, that's all, I am the one who notices and bears it in mind. In reality, though, it is nothing.'

And then I took advantage of her repetition of the phrase and the ensuing silence, because she was aware that she had repeated herself and was slightly thrown. It was up to her to say why she had come, but when she stopped short, I felt obliged to remind her:

'What was it you wanted to talk to me about? What is it you want to say?'

She had merely been delaying it, perhaps that is necessary before any kind of transaction can take place, one can rarely come straight to the point right from the start without causing offence or sounding like a mafioso or a bluff, scornful multi-millionaire, and even they, like the ancient kings, have their ceremonies (as one famous, anxious king in Shakespeare once pointed out and underlined), at least those of the old school did, whether Italian or not, although from what I know and have even seen in London, the present-day ones bother with them less. She had delayed it, but was certainly not going to run away from it, she wasn't going to back out after taking all those steps, she had turned up at my house unannounced and at night, despite having been with me a few hours earlier and despite the fact that she would see me at work again a few hours later, therefore her inevitable doubts must have been left downstairs in the street in the rain, cast out for ever from the moment she rang my bell and uttered one of my names, Jaime. Nor did her character seem to allow for such a thing: hesitation, yes, in abundance—or, rather, deliberation, or the slow process of getting herself used to what is imminent or to a decision already taken, or the condensation of an event so that it actually becomes an event, when it is just about to happen, but is still not as yet either past or an event because an event cannot be present until it occurs; but certainly not retreat. She must have thought about it a lot, walking along with her dog and seeing my back in the distance, and before that too, that same morning in our building with no name or who knows for how many mornings, plus, possibly, their corresponding afternoons and evenings.

She smiled warmly as she usually did, but also as if my question couched in two tenses had relieved her a little of the responsibility. I noticed how, whenever she spoke to me, there was a brief gathering of energy before she uttered the first phrase: it was as if she mentally constructed it and structured it and memorised the whole thing before pronouncing it, and that she had to gather momentum or take a run-up so that once she had started she would be unable to stop or make emendations, and thus never be the victim of premature regrets as she was speaking. However, this time I saw no hint of a blush, perhaps she had been through the blushing stage already out in the street and had left it behind her there. Her smile was, rather, one of shy amusement, as if she were mocking herself a little to find herself in the position of having to explain or justify herself to a colleague she saw on a daily basis and whom she had, quite naturally, met that very day on the neutral territory where they never had to seek each other out, unlike now, for young Pérez Nuix was seeking me out, requiring my presence, and had followed me through the deluged city with its hidden inhabitants. It was clear, therefore, that our usual common ground was unsuitable for talking about whatever it was she was going to talk to me about; it might, indeed, be the worst possible place, the least appropriate, entirely inadvisable place, too many ears and the occasional sharp eye. Her smile had in it, then, a hint of mockery, probably aimed at herself; there was nothing flirtatious about it, perhaps only a desire to please and to soothe; it was saying: 'All right, now I'm going to come out with it, I'm going to tell you, don't be impatient, and don't worry, I'm not going to waste any more of your time. I'm a nuisance, I know, or I'm being a nuisance, but that's just part of setting the scene, you've noticed that, you can see that, you've realised that already, you're not stupid, just new.'

'I wanted to ask you a favour,' she said. 'It's a big favour as far as I'm concerned, but less so for you.'

'Ah, so she's asking me for something,' I thought. 'She's not proposing or offering, she could have done either, but she hasn't. She's not unburdening herself, or confessing, or even telling me something, although every request contains some story. If I let her continue, I will already be involved; afterwards, possibly caught and even entangled. It's always the same, even if I refuse her the favour and do nothing, there is always some bond. How does she know that it's less of a favour for me? That is something no one can know, neither she nor I, until the favour has been granted and time has passed and accounts have been drawn up or time has ended. But with that one phrase she has involved me, she has casually injected me with a sense of obligation or indebtedness, when I have no obligations to her nor, as I recall, any debts. Perhaps I should simply say straight out: "What makes you think you have the right to ask me a favour, any favour at all? Because you don't, when you think about it, no one has the right to ask anyone, even the return of a thousand favours received is entirely voluntary, there's no law that demands it, at least no written law." But we never dare say such things, not even to the stranger who approaches us and whom we do not like and who makes us feel uneasy. It seems ridiculous, but, in the first instance, there is usually no escape, and I have no escape from young Pérez Nuix: she's a colleague; she has come to my house on a night so foul that even a dog shouldn't be out in it; she's a half-compatriot; I let her in; she speaks my language; she is quite disinterestedly showing me her thighs, and very nice thighs they are; she's smiling at me; and I am more of a foreigner here than she is. Yes, I'm new.'

'How can you possibly know what something will cost someone else?' I said, trying to rebel at least against that assumption, against that one part, trying, with that reply, to dissuade her subtly and politely—too much politeness and too much subtlety for someone who really wants something and has already started asking for it. I was seduced, too, by curiosity (not much yet, just the unavoidable minimum; but that is all it takes) and, perhaps, by flattery; discovering that one is capable of helping someone or granting them something, let alone of saving them, usually heralds complications, possible upsets, all disguised as simple satisfactions. It was because of that sense of being flattered that I was about to add: 'What can I do for you?' But I stopped myself: that would have meant the immediate cancellation of my mild attempt at dissuasion or timid rebellion. Given that I was going to surrender, I must at least go down fighting, even if I fired only warning shots. There would be no shortage of ammunition.

'Yes, you're right, forgive me.' She was cautious, as I knew, she wasn't going to challenge anything I said until she had asked me for whatever it was she wanted from me, nor would she contradict me or fall out with me, not before, although possibly afterwards, in order to persuade me or to frighten me if I dug my heels in or proved stubborn. 'You're quite right, it's a baseless supposition. To me it seems like a really big favour, and that makes me think that for the other person, in contrast, it won't be that difficult. Although I genuinely believe it wouldn't be difficult for you. But perhaps, on second thoughts, I shouldn't ask you. It's true, one never knows.' And when she said this, she sat up on the sofa and straightened her neck like an alert animal, nothing more than that, like someone acting as if she were just beginning to consider the very vague possibility of maybe thinking about perhaps leaving. Oh no, she wasn't going to leave, no way, not like that, absolutely not, she had put in a lot of effort, she had pondered the matter, she had expended both time and indecision on me. She would only leave with a 'Yes' or a 'No'. Although she would probably make do with an 'I'll see what I can do, I'll do my best', or 'But I'll want this in exchange', one can always make a promise and then go back on one's word, it happens often enough. 'Well, it depends', however, would definitely not be good enough.

'No, no, really, just tell me what it is. Please, tell me.' It did not take me long to cancel my attempted rebellion, it did not take me long to surrender. Politeness is a poison, it's our undoing. I didn't want to go to bed in the early hours without having something sorted out. I stroked the dog, he was obviously tired from the weight of water pressing down on his almost aerial walk, tis tis tis, he was gradually drying off. He wasn't particularly young. He was dozing now. I patted his back, he straightened his neck as his mistress had, just for a second, when he felt my friendly hand; he rather haughtily allowed himself to be patted, then lowered his head and took no further notice of me, I was, after all, just a passing stranger. He really wasn't up to getting a soaking like that.

'The day after tomorrow or the day after that, I think, or next week at the latest,' Pérez Nuix began, after all, she had been given the green light and wasn't going to miss the opportunity, 'you'll be asked to interpret someone I know, probably in person and possibly on video too. I want to ask you not to spoil his chances, not to let Bertie rule him out, I mean, not to let Tupra just dismiss him or give a bad, overall final report either because he doesn't trust him or because he trusts him too much. He'd have no reason to do so: I know this acquaintance of mine is not the deceitful sort, I know that, I know him. But Bertie can be very arbitrary at times, or else when he does see something very clearly, he sometimes goes against that clarity, precisely because he sees it so clearly. I mean, oh, I don't know, but anyway.' She herself noticed how lacking in clarity her own last sentence was. I realised that, despite the long build-up, what Pérez Nuix did not as yet know was in which order to expound, tell, persuade, ask. Hardly anyone knows that, and so they fail. Even those who write. But she carried on, she wasn't going to start all over again. 'I've seen someone make such a horrendous impression on him that he's decided, out of hand, to help him and to offer him some incredible opportunity; and vice versa too, with someone who had everything to recommend him, I've seen him refuse to have anything to do with him or even to accept his help, again completely out of hand. He doesn't like things too clear or too simple, or anything that is apparently unmixed, because he's convinced that there is always some admixture and that the only reason we cannot see it is because of some very clever concealment or because of some momentary laziness on the part of our own perspicacity. And so if he isn't offered any doubts, he creates them himself. When we're the ones who lack the doubts—Rendel, Mulryan, you, me, the out-of-house people, Jane Treves, Branshaw, or whoever—he provides them. He sets them out for us, invents them. He so distrusts the indubitable that he modifies his verdict accordingly, contrary to his own certainty, not to mention ours. It doesn't happen very often because such total conviction is so rare, and he would never put his hand in the fire for any human being. Tupra knows very well that no one is as straight as an arrow, that no one is consistently the person he is or even was, not even the person he aspires to be and has not yet been for a single day. "It's the way of the world," he says and then he moves on, he expects nothing and nothing surprises him.'—'It's the way of the world', yes, I, too, had heard him say it a couple of times.—'But when he thinks he can affirm something with utter conviction, then he denies or suspends that affirmation, which is precisely what we are not allowed to do. That's what he's there for, to introduce an objection, a suspicion, to contradict us and contradict himself and, where necessary, to correct. Certainty in him is very rare, but it has occasionally happened: and if someone strikes him as utterly decent and trustworthy, in practice, he probably treats him like a scoundrel on the make and advises whoever has requested the report not to trust him. And the other way round too: if he finds someone to be irremediably, almost constitutionally disloyal, shall we say, he might well suggest using him at least once, just to try him out. That is, he warns the client: once and once only, just to see, in some minor deal that involves no major risks.'

Young Pérez Nuix had launched into her request but had immediately left it vaguely floating, without completing it or focusing on it, then she had gone on postponing it or measuring it out or preparing me for it, so that talking to me would not take only 'a moment' as she had announced from the street. Or was it simply that other thing, that she didn't know in what order to approach the topic, and the sentences all crowded into her head, and then branched off and diverged, causing isolated, preliminary questions to arise in my mind relative to what she was saying? I was struck by various things she mentioned without intending to mention them or unaware that I did not know about them. The conversation would be even less brief if I was to linger over all of them.

'Jane . . . Treves, Branshaw?' was my first question. I lingered over those names, I couldn't just let them pass.

'Yes, t-r-e-v-e-s,' she replied, perhaps judging by my brief pause that I had not quite caught the names, and she automatically spelled them out in English, spelling in Spanish came less naturally to her: '*ti, ar, i, vi, i, es*', that's how it would sound to a Spaniard (and I had, in fact, assumed that it would be written as Trevis or Travis). Biographically, she was quite a lot more than half-English. She spoke my language as fluently as I did or just a touch more slowly, and she had a good, even literary vocabulary, but from time to time she slipped in some odd word or expression or used an Anglicism or was drawn into an English pronunciation; her *c* or *z* was softer than the norm, as it is with Catalans when they speak Castilian Spanish, as was her *g* or her *j*; fortunately, her *t* was not fully alveolar nor her *k* as plosive as it is among the English, because that would have made her diction in Spanish unbearably affected, almost irritating in someone with such a mastery of the language. However, it was the other surname, Branshaw, that had amused me, although I wasn't going to start enquiring about him nor explain my interest, it wasn't the moment, one must always be careful with talk, a second's distraction and it can become infinite, like an unstoppable arrow that never reaches its target and continues flying until the end of time, never slackening its pace. I did not, therefore, insist, I did not linger any longer, that has to be avoided, opening up more and more subjects or parentheses that never close, each one containing its own thousands of digressions. 'They're people Bertie uses, occasional informants, from outside, more or less specialised in certain areas, certain fields. Oh, that's right, you haven't come across them yet,' she added as if the penny had just dropped and, judging the matter to be closed, she didn't want to spend any more time on it, and nor did I. She kept calling Tupra 'Bertie', then correcting herself and slipping up again, that was doubtless how she thought of him, that is how he presented himself to her in her mind, even though at work she addressed him as Bertram, at least in my presence, still friendly but more formal, it would be equivalent in my language to a respectful use of the familiar '*tú*'. He had not yet given me permission to go that far, that would come later, and at his urging not mine.

'What do you mean "whoever has requested the report"?' That was my second preliminary question. 'What do you mean by "client"? I thought there was only one and that it was always the same one, albeit with different faces, I don't know, the navy, the army, such-and-such a ministry or one of the embassies, or Scotland Yard or the judiciary or Parliament, or, I don't know, the Bank of England or even Buckingham Palace. I mean the Government.' I had been about to say 'the Secret Service, MI6, MI5', but that would have sounded too ridiculous on my lips, and so I avoided it and replaced it as I went with: 'Or the Crown. The State.'

It seemed to me that young Pérez Nuix did not want to spend time on this subject either, she had launched into the first part of her speech and had not reckoned on the possible side effects of my curiosity. Perhaps she was formulating her request in calculated stages, perhaps she was getting me accustomed to it first, getting me used to the idea in several phases (the main drift of the request was already clear); or its nature—but she would not want to lose her way among unexpected matters of procedure, in preambles and long explanations.

'Well, yes, generally speaking, that's so, at least as I understand it, but there are exceptions. We don't often know who exactly we're reporting to, or who our interpretations, our judgements, are intended for. We certainly don't, but Tupra, I imagine, must always know or deduce who it is. Or perhaps not, some commissions probably reach him through the intermediaries of other intermediaries, and he doesn't ask questions unless he can do so without arousing suspicions or causing upset. And he has a very precise idea of when it's safe to do so; he spends his whole life calculating such things. But he'll have some idea, I suppose, of where each commission comes from. He can see through walls. He can sniff out where things come from. He's very bright.'

'Does that mean that we sometimes work for . . . private individuals, if I can put it like that?'

Young Pérez Nuix pursed her lips in a gesture that was half mild annoyance and half self-imposed patience, as if she were unresistingly accepting the irritating fact of having, after all, to discuss the matter, *velis nolis* or doubtless *nolis*, much against her will. I had the advantage of directing the conversation, of abbreviating it or delaying it or diverting it or interrupting it as long as her request remained incomplete, or at one remove, as long as it had been neither accepted nor rejected. Yes, until the eternal or eternalised 'We'll see', until the 'Yes' or 'No' had been pronounced, she would be pretty much prohibited from contradicting me in any way. This is one of the ephemeral powers of the person doing the granting or refusing, the most immediate compensation for finding oneself involved, but one pays the price for this too, later on. And this is why, often, in order to make that power last, the reply or decision are delayed, and sometimes never even arrive at all. She uncrossed her legs and crossed them again the other way, I saw the run in her stockings begin on one thigh, she would not discover it for quite some time, I thought (she was not looking where I was looking), and by then the size of the run might make her blush. But I wasn't going to tell her about it now, that would have been an impertinence or so it seemed to me just then. What little of her thigh that was revealed, however, was of a very pleasing colour.

'Does it really matter?' she asked, not defensively, but as if she had never thought about it and was therefore asking herself the question too. 'We're always working for Tupra, aren't we? I mean, he hires us, he pays us. He's the one we answer to and the one to whom we give our work, on the understanding that he'll make the best use of it, well, that at least is what I assume, I suppose. Or perhaps, I don't know, perhaps I just think that it's not my concern. Is it the concern of a car worker what happens to the screws he puts in or the engine he builds along with his co-workers, for example, if it's going to be an ambulance or a tank, or, if it is a tank, whose hands the tank will end up in?'

'I really don't think the two things are comparable,' I said and said no more. I wanted her to go on arguing, I was the one in charge just as Peter Wheeler was in charge when he and I were talking, or Tupra when he urged me on or questioned me or forced me to see more and then wormed things out of me.

'Well, what do you want me to say?'—*Bueno, cómo me quieres que diga*, she had said. Yes, there was definitely something strange or half-English sometimes about her turns of phrase in Spanish, yet they were almost never merely incorrect.—'Going further than that would be like a novelist worrying not about the publisher to whom he hands over his novel so that the former can find as wide a public for it as possible, but about the potential buyers of what the publisher produces under his imprint. There would be no way of selecting or controlling or meeting those buyers, and, besides, that wouldn't be the novelist's concern. He puts stories, plots and ideas into his book. Bad ideas, temptations if you like. But surely what arises out of them, what they unleash, is neither his business nor his responsibility.' She paused for a moment. 'Or do you think it would be?'

She seemed sincere—or genuine—I mean that she seemed to be thinking what she was saying while she was formulating it, somewhat uncertainly, hesitantly, with a sense of spontaneity and of effort too (the effort of really thinking, nothing more, but which is something that is becoming less and less common in the world, as if the whole world nearly always resorts to a few set pieces available to everyone, even to the most unlettered, a kind of infection of the air).

'I'm not even sure the comparison works,' I replied, and now I joined her in her effort, 'because our reports aren't, as I understand it, public but more or less secret; at any rate, they're not available to be read by anyone nor are they sold in shops; besides, they're about people, real people whom no one has invented and who cannot, therefore, be made to disappear or be dropped in the next chapter, and for whom I have no idea whether what we say has much or little importance, if it causes them great harm or brings them great benefit, if what it withholds from or grants them is crucial to them, if it makes their plans possible or completely sinks them, plans which, as far as they're concerned, are important, possibly vital. If it resolves or ruins their future, or, at the very least, their immediate future (but then the distant future depends on the immediate future, and so everything else ends up depending on it too). Anyway, I don't believe it is the same thing, reporting to the Crown or the State and reporting to a private individual.'

'Ah, you don't believe that,' she said. Not with irony (she could not as yet allow herself that), but perhaps with surprise. 'And what do you see as the fundamental difference?'

Ah, yes, what did I see? Her question made me feel suddenly ingenuous, absurdly much younger or less experienced (I was, as she said, new), and it suddenly became a very hard question to answer without appearing a complete idiot, a novice. I had no option but to try, though; after all, I had come out with the remark, and I couldn't simply allow it to fall at the first fence, I couldn't just give in like that and say: 'Yes, you're right. There is, as far as I can see, no difference at all.'

'At least in theory,' I said protecting myself as best I could, 'the State safeguards the common interest, the interests of its citizens, that should be its sole concern. At least in theory,' I said again: I didn't really believe what I was saying, even as I was saying it, and that is why it emerged only slowly; she would be bound to notice this, 'it's just an intermediary, an interpreter. And its components, which are always circumstantial, are not subject to personal, individual or private passions, either base or elevated. How can I put it, they are representatives, a part of the whole, and nothing more, and they are replaceable, inter-changeable. They have been chosen, in places where that's usual, as is the case, up to a point, in both our countries. One assumes they're working for the general good. According to their own lights, of course. True, they can make mistakes, and even pretend to make mistakes in order to disguise as error any personal, selfish gain. That inevitably happens in practice, possibly frequently. Possibly all the time and everywhere, from the sewers up to the palace. But we have to assume their theoretical good faith, otherwise we would never be able to live in peace. There can be no peace without the assumption that our governments are legitimate, even honest, because our states are too. (Or you can dispense with that illusion, if you like.) And so you work for them based on that theoretical good faith, which also touches or enfolds or protects you in your mission, your job, or even in your mere acquiescence. On the other hand, you wouldn't work for any private individual without first finding out exactly who he is, what he does, what he proposes, if he's a criminal or an honest man. And to what aims our efforts will contribute.'

'You said it. In theory,' agreed young Pérez Nuix, and she uncrossed her legs and lit a cigarette, one of mine, she took it without asking, as if, in this respect, she were a pure-bred Spaniard. They weren't Rameses II, just Karelias from the Peloponnese, far from cheap, but not that rare either, I never skimp on cigarettes. With that movement, the run in her stockings advanced a little further, but she still didn't see or feel it. (Or perhaps she didn't care.) (Or perhaps she was offering it to me: a minimal, insignificant, progressive nakedness; no, that I didn't believe.) 'Look, in all the years I've been here, I've never seen anyone who wasn't a private individual.'—That 'here' I took to mean 'working here'; as far as I knew, she had spent most of her life in her mother's country.—'Not even in the army, which is mostly about obeying orders and very little about taking decisions, a machine they call it. But it isn't, nothing is. It doesn't matter what posts people occupy, or whom they represent, whether they have high responsibilities or are mere errand-boys, whether they've been elected or chosen arbitrarily, it doesn't matter where their authority, however large or small, comes from, or whether their sense of the State is great or non-existent, their loyalty is beside the point, as are their venality and their proclivity for changing sides. It doesn't matter if the money that passes through their hands belongs to the Treasury and that not a penny piece of it is theirs. It doesn't matter, they will handle huge amounts of money, never mind insignificant sums, as if they were their own. I'm not saying that they keep the money, not all of them, or not necessarily; but they distribute it according to their whim or convenience and only afterwards find reasons for that distribution, never before. There are, as you know, always reasons *a posteriori* for any action, even for the most gratuitous and most unspeakable actions, reasons can always be found, ridiculous, improbable and ill-founded sometimes and which deceive no one or only the person who invents them. But you can always find a reason. And sometimes those reasons are good and convincing, impeccable; in fact, it's easier to find a reason for some thing that has happened than for plans and intentions, for proposals or decisions. What has already happened provides a very strong, solid starting point: it's irreversible, and that provides a standard, a guide. It's something to hold on to. Or more than that, something to adhere to, because it binds and obliges, and so half your work is done for you. It's far easier to give reasons to explain something that is past (or, which comes to the same thing, to find them or even, why not, provide them) than to justify beforehand what you want to happen, what you're trying to achieve. Anyone in politics knows that, as does anyone in diplomacy. As do wet gamblers, or criminals when they decide to eliminate someone and do eliminate them, knowing that they will deal later on with any previous considerations and with examining the pros and cons when they meet them as consequences; but the eliminee has been eliminated, you see, and there's nothing anyone can do about it, and there's nearly always gain, not pain. And everyone who occupies some post of responsibility knows this, even if they're the last policeman in the last village in the remotest of shires.'— 'She didn't use our Spanish word *condado*,' I thought, 'but then it isn't much used nowadays.' After all, it was her language too. And she had used the English term 'wet gamblers' too, an expression I had never heard and didn't understand, perhaps it had no real equivalent in Spanish, given that she had not even attempted to find one: it meant literally *jugadores húmedos*, or *tahúres mojados*, I had a sudden anachronistic image of waistcoats on Mississippi riverboats.—'And they're all private individuals, I can assure you, under the uniforms and outside of their offices, and inside too, when they're alone.'—I remembered Rosa Klebb, SMERSH's ruthless murderess in *From Russia with Love*, who, according to that novel, might have killed Andrés Nin; I remembered the description of her that I had read in Wheeler's house, on that night of improvised, feverish study by the river of calm continuity: 'She would be difficult to get out of her warm, hoggish bed in the morning. Her private habits would be slovenly, even dirty. It would not be pleasant . . . to look into the intimate side of her life, when she relaxed, out of uniform . . .' And there was still time for this thought to cross my mind: 'Few people are exactly appealing when they get out of or into their warm bed, when they relax or let themselves go or lower their guard; but I know that Luisa is, and this young woman seems as if she would be; or perhaps neither of them ever does lower her guard, despite that ever-growing run in her stockings.'—'To a greater or lesser degree everyone allows themselves to be led by their impulses, they are oriented, guided by their sympathies and antipathies, by their fears, their ambitions, their conjectures and their obsessions; by their

preferences and their grudges, biographical or social. So I don't
see the difference, Jaime. But then it's better for me that you do
see the difference, because that means you won't mind so much
doing me the favour I'm asking. Because this commission
comes from private individuals and not from the State, that
much I know. I mean that it comes from private private
individuals.'

I said nothing for a moment, neither of us did. I was aware
that young Nuix had still not asked me the favour, not strictly
speaking, not entirely, not completely. And she had not, therefore, contradicted or disagreed with me at any point, she had
merely set out her point of view, based on her experience,
which appeared much greater than seemed possible given her
youth, at what age did she start, at what age would she have left
behind that youth which she preserved only when she remained
silent or when she laughed, not, of course, when she argued or
held forth, nor when, in the building with no name, she
interpreted people with such discernment, she would long since
have plumbed my depths, she would already have turned me
inside out? Unless there were still times when she saw me as an
enigma, as did the person who had written my report, the one
about me. Unless she considered me 'a lost cause' upon whom
it would be pointless squandering thought, as, according to that
text, I myself did. ('He knows he doesn't understand himself
and that he never will,' the writer of the report had said of me.
'And so he doesn't waste his time trying to do so.')

I wondered to what extent Tupra was speaking through her;
some of her arguments sounded like him to me, or rather (I
hadn't actually heard him use them) they sounded like his way
of being in the world, as if he might have silently inculcated her
with them during their many years of proximity or, perhaps,
intimacy. 'So I don't see the difference, Jaime,' she had said, for
example, doubtless in order not to upset me, instead of 'I don't
agree with you, Jaime', or 'You're wrong, Jaime', or 'You really
haven't thought it through, try again', or 'You have no idea'. I
had several questions troubling me, but if I gave voice to them

all, we would never end. 'What do you know about criminals?', 'Who are these "wet gamblers"?' and 'Who do I have to lie or keep silent about in order to please you?' and 'You still haven't asked me the favour, I still don't know what it is exactly', and 'How long have you been working here, how old were you when you started, who were you or what were you like before?' and 'Which private private individuals do you mean, and how is it that this time you know so much about this particular commission, its origin and provenance?' In fact, I could have asked all these questions, one after the other, I was in charge of the conversation, that was my privilege. There was no way now that it would take only the 'moment' that she had promised, everything immediately grows longer or becomes tangled or adhesive, as if every action carries within itself its own prolongation and every phrase leaves a thread of glue hanging in the air, a thread that can never be cut without something else becoming sticky too. It often astonishes me that there should always be an answer for everything or that an answer can always be attempted, not just for questions and mysteries, but for assertions and things known, for the irrefutable and the certain, as well as for doubts and looks and even for gestures. Everything persists and continues on its own, even if you yourself decide to withdraw. This was definitely not going to take a 'moment', nothing is brief unless cut short. But it clearly depended on me now as to whether it became a whole night plus its ensuing dawn, or the drunken loquacity of a shared insomnia.

'You still haven't properly asked me the favour, I still don't know what it is exactly. And which private individuals do you mean, which private private individuals?'—And as I repeated the young woman's words, I could not help remembering Wheeler and his recitation about kings and private individuals: 'What infinite heart's ease must kings neglect that private men enjoy! And what have kings that privates have not too, save ceremony, save general ceremony?' Those lines had sprung effortlessly from his memory, while I, on the other hand, still did not know their provenance.

I ended up asking her only two questions, postponing the others. But when you postpone something you never know if you are, in fact, renouncing it, because at any time—that is, always—there may not be a tomorrow or an afterwards or a later, yes, that is possible at any time. But no, that's not true: there is always more to come, there is always a little more, one minute, the spear, one second, fever, another second, sleep and dreams—spear, fever, my pain, words, sleep and dreams—and then, of course, there is interminable time that does not even pause or slow its pace after our final end, but continues to make additions and to speak, to murmur, to ask questions and to tell tales, even though we can no longer hear and have fallen silent. To fall silent, yes, silent, is the great ambition that no one achieves. No one, not even after death. It is as if nothing had stopped resonating since the very beginning, not even when we can no longer recognise or trace the living, who are perhaps still alive, we live alert to and troubled by innumerable voices whose origin we do not know, they are so distant and muffled, or have they just been dug down too deep? Perhaps they are the feeble echoes of unrecorded lives, whose cries have been seething in their impatient minds since yesterday or for centuries now: 'We were born at such a place,' they exclaim out of their infinite waiting, 'and we died at such a place.' And far worse things too.

Sometimes four or five of us would go out together, and occasionally six or seven, when Tupra invited Jane Treves or Branshaw or both, for I did eventually meet them, or even, depending on the situation or the place, some other sporadic outside informant or guide. These were times, I think, when Tupra felt festive and convivial and in need of accompaniment, not so much company as accompaniment, in need of an escort, a retinue or perhaps a herd, as if he wanted to experience a feeling of belonging, to have a tangible, noisy sense of forming part, with us, of a team or a group or a body, and being able to say that word 'us' often. On several such nights and days my sense was, rather, of being part of a gang, or of a matador's *cuadrilla*. I guessed that this gregarious inclination corresponded with times when he was fleeing from Beryl or she from him, if it was Beryl. Not that it mattered *who* exactly: it corresponded with times when no particular woman was allowing herself to be sufficiently monopolised by him or, consequently, when there was no woman to distract him during his freer or more sociable or diplomatic or preparatory moments from his realms and his manoeuvres, or else when he was avoiding the threat of some woman becoming all too particular.

These were only guesses on my part. Tupra did not tend to talk much about his private life, at least not directly or in narrative form (he very rarely told stories, or even anecdotes; on the other hand, he was more than ready to listen to them), he did so only through vague remarks and hints and occasional comments, which, apparently unintentionally, alluded to past experiences from which he liked to extract laws and deductions, or, rather, inductions and possible rules of behaviour and character, or, rather, cast-iron, set-in-stone rules, according to his absorbent and appreciative eyes which could take in at a single glance a whole area or a place packed with people, a restaurant, a disco, a casino, a pool hall, an elegant reception room, the foyer of a grand hotel, a royal function, an opera, a pub, a boxing match, a racetrack and, were it not a flagrant exaggeration, I would even say a football stadium, Chelsea's Stamford Bridge. His pale eyes did not merely take in something as tiny as the scene at a buffet supper, they penetrated and analysed and drained it in an instant (me included)—it was child's play to him.

These, however, were my intuitions, suppositions, and imaginings; for his part, he exposed fragments and revealed isolated flashes of his past life in the form of maxims and adages or, sometimes, unintended aphorisms, almost proverbs of his own making. And thus one gradually tied up loose ends, which, however, always came undone again, however firmly one had tied them and with however perfect a knot, as if, in his case, the areas of shadow grew still larger whenever one managed to glimpse the glowing ember of some isolated period or insignificant episode of his existence, or as if each tiny revelation served only to make one appreciate the vastness of what remained dark or opaque or murky or even distorted, just as his long eyelashes, the envy of many women, always rendered murky or opaque the ultimate intention of his meditations, which were so prolonged they seemed almost insubstantial, and the true meaning of his looks, which were, it is true, clear and flattering and warm, but very hard to decipher. It was not surprising, then, that we men should be suspicious of eyes that were both so welcoming and so elaborately adorned.

We might, for example, be at a performance by a nightclub singer, sitting round a table near the dance floor or the stage in one of those splendid but antiquated clubs to which he sometimes liked to take us in order to soothe our dazed minds and offer us a leisurely transition period before finally sending us home, those, that is, who could take it, the night-owls, or those he kept closest by his side. And pointing his dense eyelashes in the direction of the artiste, Tupra would suddenly murmur: 'Women who sing in public are very exposed and are always the victims of those who guide them; she would collapse on the spot, like an old sack, if the man who steers her steps each night and leads her up onto the stage were to turn his back on her and walk away, never mind if he were to spurn her. All it would take would be one malign breath from him and she would fall to the floor and wish never to rise again.' For a few seconds, I wasn't sure if he was speaking from personal knowledge, if perhaps he knew about the suicidal dependence of that woman on someone whose face or name were also known to him (a bag of flour, a bag of meat, that's what they use to practise sticking in bayonets or spears, in one there is pain and sleep and in the other nothing). And if I dared to test him out ('Do you know them, Mr Tupra, that woman and that man?' Or perhaps, by that time, I was calling him Bertram), then he would make it quite clear that this was not the case or not necessarily so, and that he was merely applying to the present what the past had taught him: 'I don't need to know them personally,' he would reply, keeping his eyelashes trained on the singer, that is, with his face still in profile, without turning round, and in a tone of slight or purely theoretical regret, 'I know exactly what this particular man and woman are like, I've seen dozens of them everywhere, from Bethnal Green to Cairo.'

That would give me an idea, or several ideas, the most obvious being that he knew Bethnal Green, that depressed east London neighbourhood, quite well and that he had been in Egypt, probably not as a tourist. I couldn't help wondering either if he hadn't, at some point, acted as agent for a female artiste and was referring to himself and to his submissive former protégée. However, I rejected this hypothesis at once, he didn't strike me as the protective, vigilant, or even dominant type, that is, with the permanent responsibilities which all those qualities imply. 'He was probably witness to that drama or outline of a drama,' I thought, 'even if only on two occasions: in Bethnal Green and in Cairo.' I sensed or knew (I sensed it first and knew it later on) that if I asked him a direct question or tried to make him focus on a particular event, he would ignore me and avoid the subject, not so much in order to appear mysterious as because reminiscing bored him, he would doubtless not have understood those people who love to speak about their experiences, experiences that they know inside out, including how they ended, and still less those narcissistic writers of diaries who can never quite free themselves from their past, and repeat it with embellishments.

For that reason I did not try to worm out of him or to draw from him any *a posteriori* explanations for his rulings, there was no point, if they came, they came of their own accord and possibly several nights later, and, at most, I would allow myself a little joke at his expense: 'And what about women who *dance* in public, Bertram? Are they equally exposed?' Tupra had a sense of humour or, at least, tolerated mine. He would shoot me a rapid sideways glance, bite the inside of one cheek so as not to allow so much as a half-smile to escape him, and then would pick up my comment, or so it seemed to me, because nothing in him was transparent or sure or to be taken for granted: 'No, Jack, dancers are far less exposed; bear in mind that keeping on the move always provides protection, it's much more dangerous to stay still, it makes you more vulnerable. Those who run away or hide often forget this, they allow fear to take advantage of them, instead of themselves taking advantage of fear.' He had a way of linking sentences so that the second diverged from the first, the third from the second and so on until he wearied of them all and preferred to remain silent for a while. With him, therefore, it was difficult to go into any subject in depth, unless he was the one asking the questions, the one wanting to reach the bottom of something. 'In what way can one take advantage of fear?' I asked once, seduced by one of his divergent sentences: 'I assume you mean one's own fear.' To which he replied: 'Fear is the greatest force that exists, as long as you can adapt to it and feel at home and live on good terms with it, and not waste energy battling to ward it off. Because you can never entirely win that battle; even in moments of apparent victory, you're already anticipating its return, you live under constant threat, and then you become paralysed, and fear immediately takes advantage of that. If, on the other hand, you accept fear (that is, if you adjust to it, if you get used to it being there), that gives you incomparable strength and you can then take advantage of that strength and use it. Its possibilities are infinite, far greater than those inherent in hatred, ambition, unconditionality, love, the desire for revenge; they're all unknown quantities. Take someone in whom fear has taken deep roots, in whom fear remains active, an everyday kind of fear that has been incorporated into normal life, that person will be capable of truly superhuman exploits. Mothers with small children know this, or most do. As does anyone who's been in a war. But you haven't, have you, Jack? You've been lucky. But that also means that your education will be forever incomplete. They should send mothers into battle with their children nearby, within sight, to hand, because mothers carry their fear with them, it's a permanent fixture; there could be no fiercer combatants.' If I asked him what wars he had known or taken part in, he certainly wouldn't tell me and wouldn't name them; and if I asked him to expand on his thoughts about the perfect education for a man or about the ferocity of mothers with young children, he would almost certainly bring the conversation to a close. There always came a point when his divergences would fail to find another path, would run into scrub or sand or swamp. He might even put his finger to his lips and then point that same finger at the singer with a look of implicit reproach at my chatter, as if demanding for her art the respect which he himself had denied it only moments before, when he had first spoken, albeit in a murmur and without once taking his eyes off her.

At the start of every sociable period (these usually lasted two or three weeks), he would invite us out, on some work pretext, to suppers or to evenings of itinerant partying. 'I'd like you all to come with me to an important meeting,' he would say or, rather, command, in his semi-authoritarian way. 'I want to give the impression to some people I'm doing a deal with that we form a compact, almost intimidating group.' 'I want you to be particularly attentive to our guests tonight, make them feel comfortable, make sure they have a good time, but keep a close eye on them, because I'll ask you about them later, the more views we have the better.' He didn't usually explain further, or say why he wanted to create that impression or what the deal was or who exactly they were, these individuals with whom we were mingling, mostly British with the occasional foreigner, although, when I think about it and if I include Americans, foreigners weren't so very infrequent. Sometimes, however, it was absolutely clear what or who they were, either from the way the conversation developed, or because they were famous, as famous, almost, as Dick Dearlove. Tupra had an incredibly varied acquaintanceship for one man, if, that is, he was just one man, because I heard him called by different names or, rather, surnames, depending on the place and the company and the circumstances. The first time the maître d' of some expensive restaurant addressed him in my presence as 'Mr Dundas', he saw that my surprise might give him away and so, after that, he always warned us or me whenever he was not going to be wholly himself. 'I'm Mr Dundas here,' he would tell us. 'Here, I'm Mr Reresby, remember that.' 'They think of me in this place as Mr Ure.' I had to ask him to spell this last name, just hearing it pronounced wasn't enough for me to catch it, that is, to imagine it written down, on his lips it sounded like 'Iuah', I couldn't even guess at its spelling. They were all unusual surnames, slightly antiquated, odd (perhaps vaguely aristocratic or, to my ear, approximately Scottish), as if

Tupra, having given up his own name, was not prepared also to do without the originality of name that had accompanied him since birth, without that Finnish, Russian, Czech, Turkish or Armenian Tupra, always assuming he had, as Wheeler believed, borne that name for a long time. He would have found it extremely galling to be called, even if only for a while, something dull or something that might be confused with something else, as most people, in principle, would, when choosing a false name: I don't know, Gray, Green, Grant, or Graham, excluding, of course, such threadbare possibilities as Brown, Smith and Jones.

Generally speaking, he wanted us to behave perfectly naturally in social situations, and only on special occasions did he give us any more precise instructions than to be studious and to remain fully alert, asking us, for example, to probe or delve into a certain area; but then he didn't usually take all four or more of us along, only the most appropriate people for the task, or even only one, me, Pérez Nuix, Mulryan or Rendel, I went out with him on my own a few times and even on a couple of trips abroad, but I imagine that happened to all of us from time to time. He might ask us to be especially solicitous towards, or to flatter and almost woo, one particular person, he would appoint Rendel or me for these toadying operations when it was women who showed signs of boredom or complaint (burdensome wives or flighty mistresses, Mulryan never perfomed very well with them), or Pérez Nuix or Jane Treves if what was required was to enliven the mood or gaze of one of those men who get depressed and even sulk when there is no female presence at the table or on the dance floor (I mean a female presence they have met already and with whom they are on familiar terms and before whom they can preen themselves).

Once, it fell to me to dance attendance on and to flatter an Italian lady who was bidding farewell to her youth only very slowly, not to say kicking and screaming, meanwhile nurturing a multitude of minor caprices, if she had any major ones it did not, fortunately, fall to me to witness them or to deny or satisfy them. She was the wife of a compatriot (of hers) called Manoia, with whom, as far as I could make out from what they were saying, Tupra was deep in conversation about politics and money. The truth is I felt so little curiosity that I rarely managed to take much interest in whatever matters my transitory boss had in hand; and so I hardly ever paid much attention *motu proprio*, and often discovered, when he did require my attention, that his possible intrigues, assignments, explorations or barterings left me completely cold. Perhaps, too, it was because I was never really that well informed, and it's hard to feel involved in things that are so piecemeal and hazy and outside our influence. (I noticed that young Pérez Nuix did keep a much closer eye on all these goings-on and their meanderings, and that she tried hard to do so; Mulryan had no option, since he was the one—at least this was my impression—who kept, how can I put it, the diary, accounts and inventory of all matters left unresolved, untamed or unfinished; as for Rendel, it would be difficult to say, for he tended to remain silent for long periods or else, when he was drinking or perhaps smoking—my cigarettes were not the only ones filling our office with smoke—he would suddenly start lecturing or telling a whole string of jokes which he himself would greet with loud guffaws, until he returned to his usual mute state, both modes of being framed by a kind of uneasy cloud or cumulus of smoke.) The only reason I took in anything on that particular night was because the English spoken by the Italian husband was rather less intelligible than he himself thought, and Tupra would call on me (asking for help with a rapid movement of his fingers or of those eyebrows like two black smudges) to help him out and translate a few phrases or some key word when he and Manoia got themselves into a prolonged tangle and ran the grave risk of understanding entirely the opposite of what they were reciprocally proposing or agreeing, or were prepared to accept.

The surname Manoia sounded southern to me, more by

intuition than knowledge, as did the man's accent in Italian (he converted unvoiced consonants into voiced, so that what one heard him say was, in fact, *ho gabido* instead of *ho capito*), but he had more the look of a Roman—or, rather, Vatican—mafioso than of a Sicilian or Calabrian or Neapolitan one. The large glasses—the glasses of a rapist or a hard-working civil servant, or both, for they are not mutually exclusive types—which he kept pushing up with his thumb even when they had not slipped down, and his gaze, almost invisible due to reflected light and his incessantly shifting, lustreless eyes (the colour more or less of milky coffee), as if he found it hard to keep them still for more than a few seconds, or else could not stand people examining them. He spoke in a low, but doubtless powerful, voice, it would be strident if raised, which is perhaps why he moderated it, resting one hand on the other, but without leaning his elbows on the table, not even one, so that they remained there, unsupported, a position which, after a few minutes, must inevitably have caused some discomfort, or perhaps it was the small voluntary, commemorative mortification of a Catholic of the greatest integrity or, possibly, intensity, from the obscurest and most legionary wing of the Church. He seemed, in the first instance, mild and anodyne, apart from having too long a chin (not, however, to the point of prognathism) which would doubtless have led him to nurse stubborn feelings of resentment—that is, with no one target— during adolescence and perhaps childhood, even if that childhood had been only a moderately introverted or burden-some one; and in the way he had of drawing in that chin, of gnawing at the inside of his cheek, one sensed a mixture of deep-seated, never-banished embarrassment and a general readiness to take reprisals, which he probably did, I would guess, at the slightest provocation or on the least excuse or even with no need for either, as vengeful people—or at least the more subjective of them—do. An irascible man, then, although he would doubtless be considered, rather, as measured, because he would almost never give vent to that anger and would be the only person who knew about it and discussed it, if that verb can be applied to something that would take place only in his own overheated interior. The few occasions when his rage surfaced would doubtless be terrifying and best not witnessed.

His wife might possibly have done so, but she would certainly not have been its object, how else explain her impulsiveness or her ease: she must have known, in advance, that she had been granted a plenary indulgence or a full papal bull. And yet, for all that, she seemed so full of new insecurities—every age takes us by surprise; each one takes a long time to come into effect inside us, or, perhaps, to catch us up—that it was very hard not to feel affectionate towards her despite the fact that she required a great deal of work, especially from me, her entertainer and plaything for the evening. Her husband doubtless loved her, and that would be of some help, but as far as certain unstoppable advances or retreats are concerned there is no help. I had engaged her in inconsequential chatter throughout our supper at Vong's—a restaurant almost next door to the Berkeley Hotel—or, to be more precise, it was she who had engaged me in chatter; she was not a shy woman and very talkative, and thus little effort was required from me in that department; however, now and then, she would stop and fold her arms, thus providing a frame for her nautical neckline—by which I mean that she was wearing a top with a boat neck or, in her particular case, more of a Viking longship or canoe neck—and would sit looking at me, a friendly smile on her lips, and then, with a gesture not without charm— an imitation, shall we say, of a justified reproach—give voice to one of her favourite or more persistent requests: '*Mi dica qualcosa di tenero, va, su, signor Deza,*' she would say, without any transitional phrase or preamble, even though in that exotic restaurant we hadn't yet danced together and were not even on familiar terms. (In fact, she called me 'Detsa', which is how she pronounced my name.) '*Su, signor Deza, no sia così serioso, così antipatico, così scontroso, così noioso, mi dica qualcosa di carino,*' and this desire to be fussed over would last for a while. And thus she would put me in the awkward position of having to come up with something sweet or charming to say to her, without, however, being bold or offensive, something Tupra had earnestly warned against when he had described her to me and lectured me about her the day before in his office, with his retrospective, and also terrifyingly accurate, eye for the ladies. He had said very little about Manoia, or only obliquely, the odd key characteristic, but a great deal about his dear lady wife Flavia, because he, Reresby—the name Tupra was using that night, perhaps it was the one he normally used for Italy, or for the Vatican—was not going to be available to distract her and keep her happy.

'Grant her every whim, Jack, whatever she wants,' he had said. 'But be careful. From what I know and from what I've seen of her, she won't want anything more than flattery. At her time of life, she needs that by the truckload, but a generous, skilfully applied dose of it will be enough for her to go to sleep feeling calmer and more contented than when she woke up, and it's the same for her every night and every morning; because after each nocturnal triumph she will wake with the same diurnal anxiety, thinking: "Last night, I was fine, but will I be all right today? I'm another day older." And if you had to keep her company for two evenings in a row (don't worry, I'm not expecting that to happen), you would have to start the compliments and the hard work all over again from zero, she's reached a time in her life which is insatiable but non-cumulative, you see, continually forgetting what has been gained. But be quite clear, she herself is insatiable only in that one respect, for endless blarney and sweet talk, for reinforcement, but nothing more. Not even if it seems to you crystal clear that she is asking you for more with every look and every gesture, by the way she touches you and turns to you and by what she says. You must not give way or be taken in. Theirs is a marriage . . . well, let's say it's a Catholic marriage, and doubtless very strict in that respect, although not in any other, I'm pretty sure they ignore all the other precepts, in fact, some I know they do ignore. Manoia wants her to be happy and that's what matters, at least, that's what matters to me tomorrow. But he would, I believe, despite his tepid appearance, be capable of stabbing anyone who went too far, even if only verbally. So keep your wits about you and, please, study the line—his, not yours—between good and bad taste very carefully, we don't want any stupid complications. You could misjudge her, you see. Well, don't. Heap attentions on her, but if in doubt, remember, less is definitely more, less we can do something about, but not more. That's why I'd rather take you than Rendel, although he's better suited to a jolly, fun-loving woman like Mrs Manoia. He doesn't always know when to apply the brakes.'

There was always something surprising to me about the way in which Tupra referred to the people he dealt with, studied, interpreted or investigated, perhaps he never merely 'dealt with' anyone. Even though there were so many of them and they came and went in rapid succession, for him they were all *someone*, he clearly never saw them as simple or inter-changeable, mere types. Even though he would never see them again (or had never seen them in the flesh, if all we had was video footage), even if he formed and gave us a poor opinion of them, he did not reduce them to outline sketches or dismiss them as ordinary, as if he were always very conscious that even among the most commonplace of people, no two are alike. Another man might have summed Flavia Manoia up thus: 'She's your typical reluctantly menopausal woman, so just put up with all her boring chatter and make her believe that she can still knock men out, including you, that's the way to win her over. Not that you'll find that so hard to believe, because she probably did knock them out a few years ago—by the dozen. Take a good look at her legs, which she keeps in excellent shape and quite rightly shows off, and you'll see what I mean.

She's even got a wiggle when she walks,' such a man would add, a man with only a very vague idea of where the line between good and bad taste lies.

Tupra, on the other hand—or was he already Reresby when we were on our way to the restaurant in the Aston Martin that he drove on nights when the aim was to make a good impression or to toady up to someone—went into long, complex disquisitions on the lady which went beyond her and her insignificant case (on the lips of the thoughtful Reresby she no longer seemed quite so insignificant). It was when I heard such subtleties from him that I saw the influence of Toby Rylands, of whom, according to Peter Wheeler, he had been a disciple, and then I would see again how linked their characters were, or was it merely that ability, or that shared gift which they also attributed to me (in all other respects, Tupra was completely different): 'Bear in mind that, deep down, what fills Mrs Manoia with horror,' he remarked as we waited at a red light, 'is not her own imminent physical decay, against which she is struggling as best she can, but the troubling intuition that her world is about to disappear and is already dying. Some of her oldest friends have died in recent years, a few very unexpectedly, it's been a bad time; in some cases, her friends have retired, in others, there are people who would like to speed them on their way to retirement. It's no longer easy for her to find companions to go out on the town with every night of the week, and nowhere will you find proper parties with hosts and everything on a daily basis, still less in Rome, which that killjoy Berlusconi and his maladroit ways have transformed into one long yawn' (I translated the rather literary word 'maladroit' to myself as *mala sombra*, it doesn't mean quite the same thing, but never mind, and 'killjoy', which I'd never heard before, I took to mean *ceniza* or, perhaps *aguafiestas*). 'I mean companions in the old sense, the traditional sense. There are some younger people following in their footsteps, they want to find favour with Manoia, because, in his field, he has no intention as yet of stepping aside.' Here I noticed the school of Sir Peter Wheeler: just as Wheeler had taken ages to explain to me what exactly Tupra's 'line of work' was, Tupra was now nonchalantly mentioning Manoia's 'field', in order not to have to say anything more about it. Not that I really cared. 'But she feels slightly lost among all these apprentices, too much of a veteran. That's the worst that can happen to someone who has been young for far too long, whether because she entered the adult world too soon, or because she made one too many pacts with the devil (that's just a manner of speaking, of course, such pacts are purely a matter of chance). Then, because she didn't have children, she continues to be the little girl of the house, and that brings with it a lot of bad habits, she pays dearly for the contrast as soon as she steps out into the street, and in any disco she finds to her horror that she is suddenly competing for the title of oldest person there; it's very corrosive to the soul, that moving between two worlds. She'd be better off at the casinos.'

I was surprised to hear not the slightest hint of irony in his use of the word 'soul', which is not to say that no irony was intended. The car started off again, but he kept talking. With him it was impossible to tell when he knew something for sure, with facts to back him up, and when he was offering a purely personal interpretation of what he saw, whether he was up to date on the Manoias' precise circumstances or was merely making conjectures—or, in his case, decisions— -based on other occasions when he had met them (or perhaps, who knows, only the one occasion): 'Can you imagine a world in which you hardly know anyone any more and, even more humiliating, in which no one knows you, or only from hearsay? That is what she is beginning to see happening, without as yet admitting as much to herself, of course, without actually putting it into words, possibly without the slightest awareness that it is this, above all, that is making her feel more embittered and terrified with each day that passes. But now and then I've seen in her the same look of precariousness and surprise that enters the eyes of the old when they drag their feet and live longer than expected, outlive almost all their contemporaries and even the odd descendant, it's even happening to Peter Wheeler, and he's in the fortunate position of having his replacements ready, which is the privilege of people who are admired by those who are going to replace them and who do replace them, or of the great maestros. But what hope is there for a nice lady who was once very pretty and still is if you like, who is fond of parties and celebrations, and whose greatest merit was that she made life around her a little brighter, superficially at least?' Just as, in cars in England, I never got used to sitting in what was to me the driver's seat and not having the steering wheel in front of me, so I could never be quite certain what was intentional and what accidental—meaningful or superfluous—in each sentence spoken by Tupra: there was always a doubt in my mind as to whether I should simply listen to them or note them down with my retentive faculties at full power, paying close attention to every word and not taking a single syllable for granted. Sometimes I adopted the latter strategy and it was terribly exhausting being under such constant tension. 'Which is no small thing, of course, when you've been around some very unpleasant lives,' added Tupra or Reresby and started instinctively looking for a parking place, only to realise at once or pretend to realise: 'Ah, the staff at the restaurant will park it for us.'

'When the time comes for finding replacements or spares, what hope is there for anyone,' I thought, as we got out of the Aston Martin, and Tupra gave the valet the keys along with a list of detailed, not to say obsessive, instructions. 'Both the admired and the unadmired or the despised, the maestros and their followers, Tupra or me or that jolly lady, what aspirations can we have?' I said to myself, not listening to him now, since he wasn't speaking for my benefit. 'You content yourself with whatever comes your way and are even grateful that something or, above all, someone does come your way, even if they're only diluted versions of what has been suppressed or interrupted or of those you miss; it's hard, very hard indeed to replace the missing figures from our life, and you choose a few or none at all, it takes an effort of will to cover the vacancies, and how painful it is to accept any reduction in the cast of characters without whom we cannot survive, can barely sustain ourselves, and yet if we don't die or, at least, not very quickly, it is always reducing down, you don't even have to reach old age or maturity, all it takes is to have behind you some dead beloved person or some beloved person who ceased to be beloved and became instead a hated omission, our most loathed erasure, or for us to become that for someone else who turned against us or expelled us from their time, removed us from their side and suddenly refused to acknowledge us, a shrug of the shoulders when tomorrow they see our face or when they hear our name which, only the day before yesterday, their lips still softly whispered. Without actually saying as much, without formulating the idea in our minds, we understand how difficult this business of replacement is, just as, at the same time, we all offer ourselves up to occupy vicariously the empty places that others assign to us, because we understand and are part of the universal, continual, substitutional mechanism or movement of resignation and decline, or, sometimes, of mere caprice, and which, being everyone's lot, is also ours; and we accept our condition as poor imitations and accept that we live ever more surrounded by them ourselves. Who knows who is replacing us and whom we are replacing, we only know that we are someone's replacement and that we ourselves are always being replaced, at all times and in all circumstances and in any endeavour and everywhere, in love and in friendship, in work and in influence, in domination, and in the hatred that will also tire of us tomorrow, or the day after or the next or the next. All of you and all of us are just like snow on somebody's shoulders, slippery and docile, and the snow always stops. Neither you nor we are like a drop of blood or a bloodstain, with its resistant rim that sticks so obstinately to the porcelain or to the floor, making it harder for them to be denied or glossed over or forgotten; it's their inadequate, ingenuous way of saying "I was here" or "I'm still here, therefore I must have been here before". No, none of you, none of us, is like blood, besides, blood, too, ultimately loses its battle or its strength or its defiance, and, in the end, leaves no trace. It simply took longer to erase, and made the drive to annihilation work harder too.'

And so in the disco, when Mrs Manoia had drunk moderately during supper and moderately while she watched, longingly and with foot tapping, the crowded, heaving dance floor—two moderations can, after all, make an excess—and she was already calling me, in Italian, Jacopo or Giacomo, with the stress on the first syllable, and was, of course, addressing me as '*tu*' and urging me to address her likewise, she took advantage of a truce or a change of register in the music on one of the two dance floors to insist on dancing a few slow, or perhaps only semi-slow, dances, first with her husband, who took off his glasses, breathed on them, polished them with a cloth and gave her a myopic look declining her offer, then with Tupra, who raised one open hand to indicate his unfinished duties of hospitality and business towards her unwilling spouse (it was too noisy for anyone to be able to talk except by shouting directly into someone's ear, or else by signs alone), and lastly with me, who had no option but to say yes. I was struck by the fact that, despite the foreseeable results of her initial attempts and despite my having been the one who had been looking after her throughout the evening and although she was, by then, professing for me as much warmth as I was beginning to feel affection for her—transitory emotions which, by the next morning, we would be unable even to recall, without any feelings of guilt on either side—she had respected the hierarchy even when asking for a partner, which indicated a strong, deep-rooted sense of respect.

And perhaps that was why, having offered each of us three

men, in the correct order, the opportunity to dance with her, she then felt she had been given permission to wrap herself around her enforced *partenaire* in the most tempestuous and even somewhat immodest manner, by which I mean that she pressed herself furiously, indeed almost painfully, against me. Not that she intended to hurt me, it was, I think, simply that she was not entirely in control of her true volume (just as backpackers are unaware of the amount of space they take up, because, however hard they try, they cannot feel the beloved burden or limpet on their back as part of their own body), nor could she have realised the impact on my breast of her two breasts, which were as hard as logs and as pointed as stakes—her bust must have been made out of the densest wood or, possibly, granite. The woman had gone too far, she had lost all sense of proportion in her zeal to fortify and shore them up, probably in so many stages that her memory deceived her as regards the date of the last time and the number of stages in total. They were delightful to look at, and her canoe or gondola neckline doubt-less flattered them, but, when one thought about it, there was absolutely nothing nautical about that particular promontory. What could the jolly Mrs Manoia have had stuck, embedded, placed, propelled, injected or built inside herself—marble, a citadel, iron, two pantheons, anthracite, steel, it was like being impaled on two stout stalactites, or two pointed irons minus the flat part, as sharp-prowed as an iron but entirely round. It seemed to me a degenerate form of a contemporary madness, and an abuse too; I could understand why her husband might avoid being assailed by such twin bulwarks, and Tupra, I imagined, who had a quicker, better eye than mine, would have calculated at a glance the risks of any full-frontal collision (I refer to the collision of the male with those horizontal pyramids or, perhaps, giant rubies, for the blouse or top with the boat neck-line was a slightly watered-down shade of wine red, and in the neurotic disco lights it flashed and even glowed iridescent).

It was, however, very hard to get angry with Flavia Manoia, or to slight her, knowing that one so easily could: she was too affectionate, cheerful and vulnerable, all three things at once, and only one of those things would have been enough to stop me brusquely rejecting her or even moving discreetly away. And so I withstood the pressure of those two horn-like cones, trusting that she would be the one to put air and distance between us, although the word 'trusting' is far too weak, for the truth is, I was desperate for her to do so. Reresby would have been right, as he almost always was, to commend her legs, if he had ever got round to doing so; and one had to acknowledge that the lady knew exactly the right length of skirt for her build and stature, three inches above the knee; if you saw her from a distance, with her lithe, swaying sensuality, her firm, robust bust, her shapely, rather hard calves and thighs, as well as that eminently screwable ass, as a man with no time for good taste might have put it, she could give precisely the impression she intended every night and thus oblige her husband—as I saw immediately with a slight sense of unease—to put on his now clean glasses and keep watch out of the corner of one eye on her every step and every embrace. The devil does not always demand exaggeration or at least not from everyone, and he doubtless makes pacts of infinite gradations as regards appearances, and is perhaps very exact about distances: sometimes he is kind to a body or a face far off in the shadows, but will condemn and destroy it in the light and from close up (he does not normally allow the opposite to happen). This was not exactly the case here—Mrs Manoia's features had, in Vong's restaurant, seemed extremely pleasant, although not tempting, definitely not that—but in exuberant motion and with a man in her arms she looked far more attractive than when in repose and gulping down or, rather, sucking at bits of crab: sufficiently attractive anyway for someone leaning at a bar, some metres or yards away, to stand up and scan and sniff the dance floor and, more than that, to begin to wave both hands histrionically when he recognised the individual she was clutching to her with practised fanaticism, otherwise known as her dance partner.

I, on the other hand, did not, at first, recognise him. Mrs

Manoia made me perform so many turns—she wasn't so much doing a semi-slow dance as a semi-fast one, and I was dancing to her tune and to her commands—that I could not fix my eyes on any one point for more than a few tenths of a second, it was worse than being on a carousel. So much so that I took him for a black man, due to the poor visibility and my own precipitate movements and because he was wearing a very pale jacket, several sizes too large and with massive shoulder pads, and the only people I have known who dared wear such an item of clothing, loose but structured, cut very straight, were certain members of that race, especially well-built, nouveau-riche types belonging, loosely, to the world of show business: athletes, boxers, TV celebrities, dandified rappers. For a few seconds, I thought he must be one of them, because in his left ear gleamed an earring, a hoop rather than a stud it seemed to me, which was too large and loose for the taste of the modern, ultra-hip scene of the time, although I don't know about now (I don't go out so much), as if a gypsy had lent it to him or as if he had stolen it from a pirate of the sort that hasn't existed for two hundred years, not at least in the West. Luckily, he wasn't wearing a hat with a brim broad or narrow, or a scarf tied in a knot at the back of his head buccaneer-style, bandanas they call them now (he might have decided to go for that had he wanted a coordinated look), he wore his hair greased or smoothed or, rather, pulled back, so much so that for a second, confused moment I feared that he might have secured it with something worse still, namely, a black hairnet like those worn by Goya's *majos* or, perhaps, as unashamedly sported by the period bullfighters I've seen depicted in engravings and paintings, again by Goya. If I say luckily, this is not just because those who wear hats nowadays, never mind people who wear them indoors, strike me as pathetic individuals, not to say enormous phoneys (they have pretensions not so much to originality in style of dress as to some kind of biographical-artistic originality, men and women alike, although in the latter this seems not only more affected, but completely unforgivable, and women who wear berets, either straight or at a rakish angle, deserve to be shot), but because when I finally realised the identity of the dude or groover or guy, black or otherwise, standing at the bar (this was in a brief moment of stillness allowed me by my Vatican spinning top: she stopped turning for about ten seconds and I got a clear, ungiddy view of the figure waving his hands in the air), it occurred to me that had he been wearing a gypsy violinist's hat or a pirate headscarf I would not have been able to bear it, the mere sight of him, I mean, and still less his company in the presence of people who knew me, I would have found it unbearable to have anyone associate me with that man, even if only as a fellow Spaniard: I would have denied myself in order to keep him at a safe distance, I would have invented another name (Ure or Dundas would do, since those names were free that night), I would have pretended to be a complete stranger and, of course, British or Canadian through and through, I would have said to him in a heavy fake accent: '*Mi no comprender*. No Spanish.' And confronted by his probable, barbarous attempts at English, I would have closed ranks entirely: 'No Spanglish either, *hombre*.'

So when I recognised him, and saw that he was not wearing any horrifying headgear (at least that was something), I felt only disbelief in my martyred bosom, that is, I managed to think the following thoughts in the midst of my frenzied dancing: 'My God, it's not possible. The attaché De la Garza hangs out in London discothèques dressed like a dandified black rapper, or perhaps like the black proxy of a black boxer. At this hour, he himself may well believe he's black.' And I added to myself: 'What a dickhead, and white to boot.' He was clearly a man who had no time for good taste, or in whom bad taste was so pervasive that it crossed all frontiers, the clear and the blurred; more than that, he was someone capable of taking a lascivious interest in almost any female being—a rather smutty interest, verging on the merely evacuative—at Sir Peter Wheeler's party, he had been capable of taking a fancy, and quite a large fancy at that, to the not-quite-venerable reverend widow or Deaness

Wadman, with her soft, straining décolletage and her precious stone necklace of orange segments. (I mean, of course, an interest any female *human* being, I would not like to insinuate things I know nothing about and of which I have no proof.) Flavia Manoia, who was of a similar age, but with considerably more style and dash (a dash of her former beauty, I mean), could easily turn his head after the couple of drinks he already had inside him or was planning to drink in the next few minutes. Instantaneous associative memory made me glance around, quite illogically, for the not-quite-ancient Lord Rymer, the famous and maleficent Flask of Oxford with whom De la Garza had shared so many toasts at the buffet supper and who infallibly incited anyone who placed themselves within reach of his bottle (or flask, it comes to the same thing) to drink like the proverbial fish. But his fame and his clumsy manoeuvrings were now confined to strictly Oxonian territory since his retirement from the House and the consequent abandonment of his legendary intrigues in the cities of Strasbourg, Brussels, Geneva and, of course, London (perhaps he wasn't a life peer, but it was rumoured that the increasingly intoxicated wisdom of his interventions in the Lords—a never-satisfied wisdom—made it advisable, in the end, for him to give up his seat prematurely); and with his convex silhouette and his unpredictable feet he would never have ventured into the brutal world of discos, not even if chaired there by De la Garza and one other person.

I trusted that Rafita de la Garza would be accompanied by that other person or by several, by someone at any rate, or so I thought with a modicum of relief (again, at least it was something) when I saw that he was also waving or, rather, making gestures calling for patience and forbearance from a group of four or five people sitting at a table not far from that occupied by Tupra and Manoia, all, or most, of them self-evidently Spanish, given their shrill voices and their loud, attention-seeking laughter (besides, one of them—a complete idiot—was apparently so moved by the idiotic music that he was wearing the incongruous expression of someone listening to the purest and most painful of flamenco songs, of the kind that would never be played there in a million years, not even in an adulterated, jazzed-up version): it was a very exclusive place of din and deafening clamour, the most idiotically chic place of the season for those who, while not so very young, were nevertheless extremely wealthy, a place chosen by Tupra perhaps to please Flavia Manoia, or so that the only ear that could hear what he said would be that to which his lips were pressed.

'Fucking hell, Deza, where did you get your hands on this piece of pussy?' Those were the great dickhead Rafita's first, repellent and even depressing words to me in Spanish when he could contain himself no longer and swayed onto the dance floor in a terrible pastiche—for that was what it was— of a cocky black man, the semi-slow number was still unfinished, as, therefore, was our semi-fast dance. 'Come on, introduce me, come on, you pig, don't be so selfish. Is she with you or did you pick her up here?' He obviously assumed that Mrs Manoia was English and so, once more, felt invulnerable in his own language, he probably spent his whole stupid life in London feeling exactly that, one day he would put his foot right in it and someone would make mincemeat of him or beat him to a pulp. I was still busily executing turns and he was spinning in my wake (behind me, I mean), addressing the back of my neck with perfect aplomb, entirely unabashed and unembarrassed: I recalled that he specialised in repeatedly interrupting other people's conversations until they imploded, so there was nothing surprising about the fact that he should sidle his way into other people's dances and pulverise those as well. 'I'll bet you a first edition of Lorca that you've pinched her off some idiot here. When we're off the dance floor, you'd better watch out, eh?'

These small comments of his so enraged me—the puerile rather than, as he probably thought, crude nature of the last; the pedantic wager of this would-be bibliophile; the groundless conceit of his patriotic vulgarity ('we' had to mean 'we Spaniards')—that despite my determination to respond to him in obscure English—for a reason I give below—and to stick with all the resolve of a prisoner of war to my identity as Ure or Dundas, I could not control myself and managed to hurl a few shouted words at him, with my head slightly turned, although not my captive torso:

'You haven't got a first edition of Lorca, Garza Ladra, not even a stolen one.' He probably failed to catch the insulting operatic allusion, but I didn't care, just having made it was reward enough for me. He certainly didn't pick up on it until later, and in a very slow-witted way; initially, though, he opted for a rather snooty, argumentative tone:

'That's where you're wrong, bright boy,' he said, and wagged one absurd, be-ringed finger: he obviously donned his disco gear complete with all the accessories whenever he went out to do some serious partying, or perhaps to play the would-be black; but what could not be explained in such a context (and this is the reason I mention above, the one that should have made me decide to play dumb, and in which aim I immediately failed) was the black Goyaesque hairnet that De la Garza actually and impossibly was wearing to keep his hair in place or for some other cretinous motive, and so my confused vision of that second moment turned out to be right. Now, on the other hand, I couldn't believe it, despite my vision being blindingly clear now. The net did not even have a bob or a ponytail to fill it, its content was pure nothingness; given that he had had the nerve to wear such an anachronistic item, the choice of a sick mind, he could at least have hired a hairpiece, in order, within the awful twisted logic of the idea, to give it meaning and weight and some justification ('meaning' is a manner of speaking, as is 'justification', as is 'mind'). It occurred to me that he might have been sold or given a first-edition Lorca by the former director of the National Library of Spain, who was, I understand, a friend of his and who had, it would seem, taken full advantage of his post—now he was making the most of a still higher post—to squeeze ridiculous prices out of the finest antiquarian booksellers, claiming that he was acquiring the rare, expensive volume in question for that public institution, which was often, moreover, closed to Spanish citizens (appealing, in short, to the patriotic or, in this case, the most easily duped side of each seller), when, in fact, those books flew direct, with no official stopover, to his own private collection, which was still in a phase of rapid expansion.

I chose not to enquire just then why I was a bright boy and why I was wrong. I noticed that Mrs Manoia was beginning to get annoyed. It was completely unacceptable that, in the middle of a dance, her dance, some ridiculous and possibly already rather inebriated man should clumsily join us on the dance floor, position himself behind her partner and begin loudly berating the back of the latter's neck; it had been even more discourteous on my part, I realised, to reply to this erratic individual, even if only with a single, angry phrase, instead of stopping him literally in his tracks and sending him packing back to the bar, or even further off if I was really trying. Nevertheless, I wasn't sure if her annoyance was due to my momentary neglect, to De la Garza's pure, simple and unprecedented intrusion, or to the fact that I had not immediately suggested a halt to the dancing in order to introduce them formally. It seemed to me she felt some curiosity about Rafita the nightbird in his unintelligible get-up, but it was hard to tell, it might just have been complete bewilderment: as she danced, she must have been seeing two faces juxtaposed, which would have put her off pressing still more closely to my breast or concentrating on and enjoying her steps; I saw, too, how, irresistibly, she kept glancing up at the person behind me, she was understandably distracted by the sight of that accessory more suited to a matador or to an eighteenth-century *majo*, she could probably not quite make out what it was or its improbable significance, its hermetic symbolism. Or perhaps she had sensed from the very first that, regardless of the string bag with which he had chosen to adorn his hair, regardless of the fortune-teller's earring with which he had encumbered his ear, this second Spaniard would be for her a certain, possibly inexhaustible, source of flattery. The idea came to me anyway, and in a fit of irresponsibility and egotism, it occurred to me that it would be no bad thing to let the attaché join us for a while, he would keep her supplied with a variety of glowing words and compliments (albeit indecipherable), and put on a brave front (the phrase was never more apt) and withstand the stakes or logs if she insisted on more dances. (I was, I feared, being more meagre with my words of praise than I was expected to be, not because I was being excessively prudent or because I found it hard to flatter such a spirited and receptive woman, who was, basically, very easily contented, except that no amount of contentment lasted her for very long and she required constant nourishment, but because I get so bored with expressions such as *carine* or *tenere*, and their monotonous nature soon cloys, even if I happen to read them in a novel or hear them in a film, even if I say them in real life or someone addresses them to me.) Whatever the truth of the matter, it took only four words from Flavia Manoia for me to convince myself that the current situation was unsustainable and that I should, without further delay, proceed to the introductions. And I felt quite certain of this when I saw out of the corner of my eye that Manoia, into whose ear Tupra was insinuating long, whispered arguments or propositions, had shot a couple of interrogative, not to say inquisitorial, glances at the dance floor since De la Garza had been pestering us, a total stranger, in his eyes, who showed every sign of being a troublemaker and who might even be taken for a debauchee.

'*Mah*,' was Flavia's first word, and it is a word of great ambiguity in the Italian language, it can indicate consent, vexation, slight interest, slight irritation, confusion, doubt, or it may merely announce a full stop and the start of a new topic. And then she added: '*Che sarebbe, lui?*' This was enough for me to interrupt the dance and disimpale myself very gently and carefully from the palisade, but she asked me one other thing before I pronounced the names: '*E cosa vuol dire* pussy?' She must have understood almost nothing of what had been spoken by that disgrace to the Peninsula (although nowadays there are so many similar disgraces that they almost constitute the norm, and so can hardly be termed a disgrace), but perhaps she had sensed that this memorable term was intended for her, that it had been applied to her, and in pretty brazen tones.

'Rafael de la Garza, from the Spanish embassy in London. Mrs Flavia Manoia, a delightful Italian friend of mine.' I used Italian to introduce them, and took the opportunity to insert an adulatory word; then I added in Spanish, that is, purely for Rafita's benefit and in order to warn him off or to contain him (possibly a naive endeavour): 'That's her husband over there, he has a lot of influence in the Vatican.' I was hoping to impress him. 'On the same table as Mr Reresby, you remember Mr Reresby, don't you? At Sir Peter's party?' Of one thing I was sure, he would not remember that in Wheeler's house Tupra's surname had been Tupra.

'Oh, but he's so young, your ambassador,' she replied still in Italian, while they shook hands. 'And he's so modern too, so daring in the way he dresses, don't you think? Your country is clearly so very up to date in every respect. Oh, yes, in every respect.' Then she asked me again about 'pussy', she was determined to know. 'Tell me what "pussy" means, go on, tell me.'

De la Garza was talking to me at the same time (each of them bellowing in one of my ears and each in his or her own language), keeping the lady's hand clasped in his for far too long, that is, holding it prisoner while he unleashed a long string of insults and obscenities which the sight and recollection of Reresby caused to spill from his mouth as soon as he spotted him, and which I wasn't entirely able to follow, but from which I picked out the following words, fractured phrases and concepts: 'bastard', 'ringlets', 'big tall bitch', 'an absolute whore', 'showing me her panties', 'they cleared off', 'great lump of lard', 'flabbing up against her', 'fucking sofa', 'did you get them off her', 'pretence', 'goddamn gypsy', 'bitch', 'oh, purr-lease', and a final question: 'Did you have a dash in the bloomers yourself?' After this torrent of words, he brought himself back for a moment to the present:

'What did you say before about *ladra*? You mean this gorgeous specimen of a woman? Fucking hell, look at those bazoomas.' His vocabulary was often at its most schoolboyish or antiquated when he was trying his best to be crude. He had, however, seen that any approach might be problematic. He had not, on the other hand, even considered the matter of their obvious artificiality (the work of man), he was not a person for fine distinctions or for getting lost in petty details. Then, for an instant, he adopted an unctuous tone to address and flatter Flavia: 'It is an enormous pleasure to meet you, madam, and may I assure you of my equally enormous admiration.' This she did understand, it would have been crystal clear to any Italian.

Otherwise, he was just as foul-mouthed or, indeed, even more so (nights of dissipation, especially nights of arduous hunting, only encourage this), although I had never heard the expression 'to have a dash in the bloomers' (that old-fashioned use of 'bloomers' was odd). It was extremely crude as a euphemism, but it doubtless was one—a euphemism, that is—and one should, I suppose, be grateful for small mercies. Fortunately none of the people I was with would understand any of these brutal, vulgar expressions.

I was half regretting my egotistical weakness (I should have denied us both, him or me or the two of us, 'You've never seen me, I don't know who you are, you don't know me, you've never spoken to me and I've never said a word to you, as far as I'm concerned, you have no face, no voice, no breath, no name, just as for you I do not even have a back') when Tupra beckoned me over to the table, he had so many things to explain to Manoia that he was bound to need me as interpreter at some point—that much was plain—to help them past some blockage. I wasn't sure whether to take Mrs Manoia with me, and therefore Rafita too, who would not be shaken off that easily, he did tend to the adhesive. But that might really annoy Tupra, I thought, if I were to land him with that rude expert in belles-lettres (who, moreover, he already knew) right in the middle of his negotiations (and, what's more, laden with jewellery and wearing a fishing net); and so I opted for leaving Flavia in the provisional care of De la Garza—a disquieting thought—I could see he was more than ready to enlighten her with his learned witticisms or to stultify her with dances more primitive than mine, but which would not, however, be unwelcome. Before absenting myself, I whispered or, rather, yelled in her ear, so that she would not bear me a grudge for failing to give her an answer:

'"Pussy" means "beauty".'

'Really? But how? Where does it come from? It's such a odd word.'

'Well, it's an affectionate, colloquial term from Madrid, prison slang.' I threw in that last part, I don't know why—as decoration. 'He considers you a great beauty, as each and all of us do.' Well, that's how I said it in Italian, more or less verbatim. 'That's what he said.'

'But surely the ambassador hasn't been to prison?' she asked, startled. There was in her voice not so much shock (she must have grown used to seeing friends and acquaintances ending up in the clink) as an absurd degree of pity and alarm about the monstrous *majo*'s police record and his possible past misfortunes (personally, I would have packed him off to the pokey for a good long time, with or without a trial). She was concerned, I suppose, because of his youth.

'No, no, at least not as far as I know. The word started off as prison slang, but words go forth, travel, fly, expand; they're free, are they not, and no bars or walls can imprison them. They have a kind of terrible strength.'

'*Temibile*,' put in De la Garza, who had been listening in and had understood random words in my Spanish-tinged Italian (he was simply guessing, there was no way he spoke Italian; guessing, I mean, at the one adjective he had contributed).

He was a real ace at that, at butting in with some irrelevant comment, with no idea what the topic of conversation was, and entirely uninvited, and even, sometimes, when he had been firmly and plainly rebuffed.

'There's no need, *quindi*,' I went on, 'to go to prison to find them, I mean, the words that were born or invented there. And, by the way, he's not the ambassador; he's just part of his team. But I'm sure he will be some day. Indeed, I think he will rise still higher if, as seems inevitable, he continues in his present vein: they'll make him Secretary of State, *anzi* minister.' There is no exact equivalent in Spanish for those two words, *anzi* and *quindi*.

'Minister? But minister of what?'

'*Beh*. Culture probably; that's his field, he's knows all there is to know.' I said this quite spontaneously: *beh* is another ambiguous word in Italian, perhaps I simply didn't like to be found wanting in the use of indefinable vernacular interjections. And I added, moving a little away from her, with the intention of making it easier for De la Garza to hear and to catch more than just a few random words: 'No one knows more about world literary fantasy, including the medieval and the palaeo-Christian. Oh yes, he knows a hell of a lot.' This I translated with unforgivable literalness, quoting what he had said at Wheeler's party. '*Sa un inferno*,' I said brazenly, knowing that the expression doesn't exist and is, therefore, incomprehensible. 'Which, as well as being valuable and useful, is also tremendously chic, you know.'

'Tremendously chic,' commented Rafita, who had understood very little despite my very clear enunciation. His words were slightly, very slightly, slurred, it might pass off quickly if he eased up on the drinking or if lust restored his clarity of speech; this time, he didn't even repeat his one attempt at an Italian word. He was looking at Mrs Manoia with fixed, glassy desire, by which I mean that he was staring in near stupefaction at her two silicone menhirs.

'Really? *Addirittura*.' Another expression for which there is no exact Spanish equivalent.

'Now, if you'll excuse me, dearest, most delightful Flavia'—I was at least piling on the superlatives, which are more common in Italian—'I must leave you for a few moments in the very best and most chic of company. Our friends are calling me.'

There I left her, beneath the hooves of the dark horses and in the faux-black mouth of the wolf and before the menacing maw of the crocodiles, hoping that her husband and Tupra would not keep me long, I felt responsible for the lady's evening, for her well-being and contentment, I wanted her ten bracelets to continue tinkling. As I walked back to rejoin Tupra and Mr Manoia, I saw that De la Garza was, for the moment, avoiding dancing with Flavia and was, instead, leading her over to his table, not far from ours, and to his noisy, mainly Spanish friends, and this reassured me a little because we could see them from our table and he could not so easily heap her with compliments there as he could when they were alone and dancing. (There were a couple of women in the group, and many of my female compatriots dislike any kind of competition, even when it's purely imaginary and there's not so much as a hint of it because basically there *is* no competition: they were both about twenty years younger than Mrs Manoia, who would, however, have given them a run for their money had she met them without that two decades' age difference—'Luisa isn't like that,' I thought, 'she doesn't compete with anyone, and if someone does try to challenge her, she just moves away, perhaps because she's sure of herself, or because she's happy being the way she is, perhaps I'm the same.') I noticed that the idiotic music lover and poseur was now very quietly clapping, holding his, cautiously clapping hands close to his ear, his eyes tight shut, fully aware of his intense pose, and even wailing softly to himself (given the tortured, ecstatic look on his face, like that of a willing martyr, it must have been a formidably painful piece of flamenco), absorbed in music that was ill-suited to such depths of grief, perhaps he was following another tune in his head with incredible concentration and constancy, or perhaps he really was listening to it—and therefore deaf to the disco music around him—through tiny hidden headphones, like the ones my dancing neighbour opposite must use in his prancings. His face looked familiar, rather peasant-like despite the baroque ringlets that sought to soften or even deny it, his hair furiously dyed a demented black; I got the feeling that he was a very important, very famous writer, he might have given a talk at the Cervantes Institute that evening, brought *ex profeso* from the Peninsula by De la Garza, and I would have missed it, a magisterial reading, a magical recitation, how stupid of me. He seemed to me a complete fool and, immersed as he was in his mournful clapping, he, of course, failed to notice Flavia's arrival at the table; the others did not even get up when Rafita made the introductions, with the exception of one man who was perhaps British, given his appearance and his preservation of certain manners; the British are taking a little longer to perceive all manners as entirely dispensable. With a despotic gesture, the attaché ordered the others to move up to make room for them, I saw them sit down rather close together (their legs would be touching, Mrs Manoia's skirt had ridden up a little—a little too much, I mean—perhaps that would arouse her knight-flatterer) just before I did the same, only not quite so cosily, on a chair to Reresby's left, he preferred people to sit on that side if possible, I imagined that he heard better with that ear and saw better with his right eye.

He immediately asked me what the Italian was for the four or five words which he had taken the precaution of noting down on his coaster and on which Manoia's English, being rather sparse in vocabulary, would have foundered. One of them, oddly enough, was 'vows', or to be more precise 'to take vows'; another was 'toadstool', equally strange, and in another sphere entirely; a third was 'nipples', which did not help me in my deductions. It was understandable that Manoia would not know these words, less so that Tupra had not resorted to alternatives or approximations to explain them, even, in the last instance, to gestures (perhaps, despite his surname, he was too English for that). Fortunately, I had read or heard them before and could find equivalents (*pronunciare i voti*, there I was guided by the Spanish; *funghi, piuttosto quelli velenosi*, here I had to explain; *capezzoli*, I ventured: I seemed to remember that the stress fell on the antepenultimate syllable, but I wasn't sure). Luckily, too, my curiosity was not aroused. I trusted, however, that the *capezzoli* or nipples in question were not Mrs Manoia's, I would have found any reference to them embarrassing (even though any reference would have been purely medical or, shall we say, pathological), having been impaled on them as if by two darts and still conscious of the impression they had left on my chest. I was about to go back to her side, having fulfilled my task as walking dictionary, when Tupra stopped me with a gesture, he showed me the flat of his hand as if warning me: 'Wait, we might still need you.' Manoia took advantage of the pause provided by these consultations (he only reacted to the third, and then very soberly: '*Ah, gabezzoli,*' he repeated in his non-Roman accent, an accent that came from further south) to lift his long, bluish chin and look across, with his glasses pushed well up on the bridge of his nose and held there with his thumb, at the table that had welcomed his wife with such very Spanish indifference.

'Who are they?' he asked me in his own language, in a tone of scorn and distrust, or almost displeasure.

'Spaniards; writers, diplomats,' I replied, realising that I had no idea who they were and knew none of their names, although the name of the famous, important writer doing the clapping was on the tip of my tongue (though I still couldn't think what it was). 'That young man works at the Spanish embassy, Mr Reresby knows him too.' And I turned to Tupra and said in English, to get him involved and make him take some share of the responsibility, purely as a preventive measure. 'You remember young De la Garza, don't you? He was at that supper in Oxford, he's the son of Pablo de la Garza, who did such a lot of good work here in the war and, afterwards, was, for many years, Spanish ambassador to various African countries.' It seemed to me—quite absurdly—that this snippet of family background would reassure them. 'He's a good lad, very thoughtful.' And I repeated this last comment in Italian to Manoia, to see if he believed me (*'Un bravo ragazzo, molto premuroso'*), while in Spanish I could not stop myself thinking: 'The great schmuck, the numbskull, the pest.'

Despite the light glinting on Manoia's glasses, I managed for a moment to see his fugitive gaze because he held it for a little longer than usual, trained on Rafita and his gang. I saw in it mockery, malice, and also a touch of anger, as if he had recognised in them a class of people on whom he had sworn vengeance many years before. Yes, he seemed a man capable of feeling fury even in response to minor provocations, but if he let it out, it would doubtless be with no warning at all, with no way of foreseeing it, still less of stopping it. A tepid rage, controlled by him, and rationed out—he could stop it, even once unleashed—most disconcerting for other people. That was what he was like. That was what he carried around inside him. But Tupra was doubtless right: he could also give vent to that anger.

'What's he got on his head, a mantilla?' asked Manoia, openly scornful now. 'Is he thinking of going to early-morning mass?'

'Oh, you know what young people are like nowadays, when they go out they love to dress themselves up in strange outfits, they like to be original, to look different.' It was a cruel irony that I should find myself obliged to justify both his fakery and his foolishness. 'It's a very ancient piece of headgear, but very Spanish; bullfighters used to wear it; it dates from the eighteenth century, I believe, or possibly earlier.' I gazed rancorously at Rafita. From a distance, he reminded me of Luis Meléndez's self-portrait in the Louvre, albeit in degraded and debauched form; and what the painter is wearing on his head is hardly comparable: a knotted scarf if I remember rightly, like a crown of laurels or intended to achieve the same effect. Rafita was talking loudly and animatedly, he was pontificating or telling jokes (one or the other), Mrs Manoia wouldn't understand half of it, but he was addressing the others at the table too, especially a blondish young woman with a look on her face of permanent disgust, it's an expression you often find on the faces of certain rather dim and unappealing Spanish women from wealthy families; a Spanish man requires a strong stomach if he is to marry a Spanish woman purely for money. I imagined that Rafita was destined for just such a marriage; he wouldn't be in a hurry, though: he was still impatient, inexpert, acquisitive, he would still have to pass through many terrible beds occupied by incontinent, female lookalikes of that unforgettable actor Robert Morley or by women who resembled Peter Lorre's dissolute twin, whom he would have desired in a drunken, nocturnal moment of surrender only to awake to crapulous morning satiety, horrified at himself and at them. 'In short,' I added, weary of all this pussyfooting around, 'he's a good lad, but a bit of a numbskull, a *mameluco*.' The Spanish word had been circling around in my head; I tried it out to see if it existed in Italian as well, with sister languages everything is possible and you never can tell.

'*Un po*'? Eh. *Mammalucco totale. Eh. Questo si vede, eh,*' Manoia said, correcting me, and I had to agree: Rafita was a total, utter, complete numbskull. Although what actually emerged from Manoia's lips was '*Mammalugo dodale*', he seemed incapable of emending his blurred, abbreviated vowels or his invariably voiced consonants, I wondered if he would speak in the same drawl to the delicate members of the Roman Curia, I had got it into my head that the couple were both citizens of the Vatican, there must be some who were not cardinals or bishops or chaplains, or acolytes or nephews of the Pope. 'Is not so very young for such foolishness,' he said, shifting into his slightly undigested English so as not to exclude Reresby from our comments. 'This idiot must be thirty at least, no, Reresby?'

'Thirty-one,' replied Tupra, as if he knew this for a fact. And he added, to dissociate or detach himself from what I had implied: 'I've never actually spoken to the man, I only know him by sight, from that supper at Oxford. He gets overexcited when there are women about, that much I've gleaned.' I wasn't sure whether he was warning me with this remark, so that I would remain alert, or warning the husband so that he could rescue Flavia at once and not expose her to whatever this retarded adolescent might do, things tend to turn nasty in the wee hours.

Then Tupra once more claimed Manoia's attention. He again pressed his fleshy lips to the latter's ear and continued explaining or persuading or pleading or urging. I didn't bother to listen, I kept one watchful eye on the Spanish table, and kept glancing with the other at Manoia and Tupra in case they should need me, now and then I caught scraps of their conversation, whenever the music abated slightly or when one or other of them spoke more loudly, occasional words and the odd name. I had no doubt that Tupra would end up getting out of Manoia whatever it was he wanted from him, a commitment, a promise of help, an alliance, a secret, a purchase, a sale, a privilege, a plan, a denunciation, or some work, be it dirty or clean. I always saw him as the most persuasive person in the world and had had experience of this myself, and personal experience always has an excessive influence on the formation of our beliefs. But beyond my own partial impressions, it was clear that his postponed vehemence, that flattering and permanent state of alert, the sense of intelligence and warmth which, when it suited him, he transmitted to those he spoke to, the sense that not a single word you said was ever ignored or wasted and was, therefore, never spent or spoken in vain; that strange reserve of tension, which never got in the way socially (one always felt very comfortable with him, very much at ease if you like) but which was always there beneath the surface of his minor vanities and his quiet, gentle ironies, more like a promise of intensity and significance than any kind of threat of conflict or turbulence; it was clear that all his effervescence, kept in a chamber in a state of endless waiting, or perhaps subterranean or captive, managed to infect even the most reluctant and suspicious, and persuaded them if not to come over to his side, at least to put themselves in his shoes, to see things from his perspective, or perhaps simply on his level, which was that of the man himself. Which is the proper and inescapable level.

So there he was, murmuring away in the midst of the hubbub, minute by minute earning the ear of his guest, like an argumentative, diaphanous Yago or Iago, one whose good word would remain safe until the curtain fell and even after that, in the echo of his speeches when he returned home (good words and bad faith can go hand in hand and be perfectly compatible, the former takes care of resources and the latter of the objective, or the means and the end, if you prefer more political terms); it was as if he did not have much need for subterfuges and tricks nor even for simple deceptions, or for the surreptitious infusion of poisons and germs to divert or direct minds and to obtain oaths, surrenders, renunciations and near-unconditional support. Tupra would never have to think or say or propose to himself the very ugly words spoken by the Moor's standard-bearer: 'I'll pour this pestilence in his ear', because he persuaded purely by dint of persuasion and would rarely hatch any plot based on false information or lies, or so it seemed to me: his reasonings reasoned, his enthusiasms enthused and his dissuasions really did dissuade, and he needed nothing more, apart from, very occasionally, his silence, which doubtless silenced those with whom he kept silent. But, on the other hand, he might often have to think or say to himself those other troubling words of Iago's: 'I am not what I am.' For me it was difficult to know what he was, despite the supposed gift that I shared with him, or despite the undoubted curse which was perhaps mine alone. Nor would it be easy to know what he was not.

'The Sismi', that was one of the names which, on more than one occasion, left his mouth or Manoia's, and when it was the latter, it sounded, in that predominantly English context, like 'the sea's me', too unlikely a name even for a boat or a racehorse (although I remembered myself on that feverish night of reading at Wheeler's house beside the River Cherwell, when I thought as I went to bed: 'I am the river'), which is why I assumed it must be an acronym, that of some organisation or institution or order, of a Vatican faction or fraternity (like the 'ndrangheta or the Camorra in the South). I also caught five surnames, at least they were the ones I remembered, because they were repeated during that part of the conversation and because I have an excellent memory that files away any names that my eyes see or my ears hear: Pollari, Martini, Letta, Saltamerenda, Navarro, especially the first three. (They went well with Incompara, the false Italian and semi-false Briton of whom young Pérez Nuix had spoken to me on the night of her rain-drenched visit and whom she wanted us to protect and to favour, selfishly and without anyone noticing.) Partly to combat the habitual inconstancy or slackness of my curiosity and partly because I found the fourth name extremely funny, I decided that I would look them up later in a recent edition of *Who's Who in Italy*, although such catalogues tend to feature only people of a certain public merit, such as Sir Peter Wheeler in the United Kingdom, and there was no reason to think that these individuals were anything other than obscure private citizens, like Tupra and like me; but who knows. (It was perhaps more likely that they would appear in the old files in the building with no name; as would Manoia too, along with his delightful wife.)

I was getting more and more worried, with De la Garza on the verbal hunt for Flavia (he had not as yet, I trusted, embarked upon a tactile or fingertip search), and with Flavia defenceless against any darts which that great, mannered, vulgar brute might spit at her: at the moment, she was laughing (a good or a bad sign depending on who was doing the looking), I did my best not to lose sight of them for more than a few seconds at a time, when I should really have been listening and looking at my companions at table. Tupra had been quite right when he prevented me from leaving them, because my support was needed again, this time by Manoia to help with a few words or phrases in English, I remember he asked me about *invaghirsi*, about *sfregio*, and about *bazza*, all three of which put me in a tight spot. I didn't know the first at all, and so, after trying to gain time by pretending to check that he hadn't said *invanirsi*, I translated it intuitively in two different ways, as 'to inebriate' and 'to swoon' or 'faint' (this was the fault partly of the Italian word's phonetic proximity to the Spanish word *vahído*, meaning a dizzy spell), which while they were not, of course, synonyms could at least happen consecutively, and were therefore not, in that order, impossible. Anyway, I didn't think my infidelity would be that important or give rise to any grave misunderstandings, the gentleman had a liking for unusual words I realised (even regional ones), or perhaps he was simply testing me in order to make me look stupid. I didn't know the second word either, this was terrible, nor could I connect it with any other words I knew; Manoia grew impatient with my vacillations, and started rudely badgering me ('*Uno sfregio! Sfregio, dai! Uno sfregio!*'), at the same time running one thumbnail down his cheek from top to bottom; but since it didn't occur to me that the word could possibly mean scar or *cicatriz*, after all, Italian has the word *cicatrice*, I foolishly opted for something halfway between sound and gesture, that is, for the Spanish *estrago*, which I converted into the English 'damage' or 'havoc'. Later on, when I consulted a dictionary, I wondered if Manoia had threatened to make just such a scar on the face of some fellow human being tomorrow, and then my translation would not have been entirely absurd, or did it, I wondered, form part of a description of some mafioso or monsignor, for example, and in that case I would have excelled myself, given that the term corresponded more or less to 'scratch' or 'mark'. As for the third word, that put me in an even worse predicament, because I knew that it had two very different meanings, I had read it or heard it during a stay in Tuscany years before, and my sharp memory had stored it away. I hesitated again, paralysed, because one of its meanings was 'long chin' or 'prominent jaw', precisely the feature that Manoia could not conceal and which, during his childhood in Italy, would doubtless have led to him being dubbed a *bazzone*: I had heard that mocking augmentative in an old film starring Alberto Sordi (who, of course, I best remembered in the buck-toothed role of a *dentone*), or, more likely, applied to that marvellous comic actor, the great Totò, because, all things considered, no one could possibly have beaten him in the *bazzone* stakes. The other meanings, related etymologically to the Spanish *baza* or 'trick' in card games, were 'a stroke of luck' and 'a bargain'. Since I was not in on the conversation and since it was, anyway, barely audible, when Manoia asked me that question (*'Come si dice bazza?'*, or, rather, *'Gome si dishe?'*, the *ch* sound became *sh* in that irrepressible accent of his), I hadn't the faintest idea what they were talking about: I didn't know if he was still describing a hitman or a prelate—whoever it was would certainly be a sight to behold with scars on his cheeks and huge mandibles—or was merely hoping for good luck in their shared projects, or if he was trying to persuade Reresby that the price of his services or of his consent constituted a real bargain. If *bazza* referred to the latter and I translated it only as 'pointed chin', I risked Manoia thinking that I was making some irrelevant and scornful allusion to his most striking feature, and I had realised, right from the start, that the size of his jawbone had clearly played its part in the shaping of his character, which was at best suspicious, at worst vengeful, no, not at worst, for I sensed in him the potentiality for far worse things. If it was the other way round, my translation would make no sense at all, but it would at least not offend him, unless he attributed my avoidance of the correct word to the presence at the table of that chin of his which was, after all, far from prognathous, even under the shifting coloured lights that distorted it and made him look a little like Fagin. Perhaps I was being excessively punctilious, perhaps I hesitated too long, and that made him grow still more impatient:

'*Ma gosa sushede, eh. Non gabishi bene l'idaliano?*'—He had from the outset addressed me as '*tu*' and had clearly not even considered doing otherwise, and he had unhesitatingly called me Jack, following Tupra's example, as if he knew me as well as Tupra did, or as if he had instantaneously inherited that same familiarity (the prerogative of equals or of those who give the orders). His tone now was one of implicit attack, by which I mean that it sounded like one of those demands that you fail to meet at your peril. '*Bazza, bazza, gome si dishe in inglese bazza, eh? No lo sai?*'

And so, without further delay, I opted for 'bargain', all in all, it seemed to me more likely that in a conversation about politics or money, or about benefits or even indulgences, he would be talking about money.

'A bargain,' I said. And, just in case, I added: 'Or a stroke of luck.'

But I didn't like the man's second irritable outburst at all. It wasn't that I felt affronted or bullied. Well, I did, but that didn't matter, I was not what I was ('I am not what I am,' I would sometimes repeat to myself, 'not entirely,' I would think, 'not exactly') when I went out with Reresby or with Ure or Dundas, not even when I accompanied Tupra, alone or with the others; in a sense, I simply played the role of subaltern or subordinate—which, at bottom, I was, given the circumstances and certainly as long as I remained tied to my paid activities and kept my nameless post—or the role perhaps of escort or acolyte—which I never was in any way at all—and I did not take personally any slights to which my character might occasionally be subject, because I received them—how can I put it—on behalf of the whole group and as a mere part of it, the most recent and belated and insignificant part; and the entire group seemed to me, in turn, fictitious, or, rather, devoted to fictions, perhaps that would be more exact. And the fact that almost everything happened in a foreign language only emphasised the artificial, unreal, make-believe nature of what was said and done: in another language you cannot help but feel that you are always acting or even translating (however well you know the language), as if the words you pronounce and hear belonged to some absent person, to a single author who invented and dictated them and had already distributed the parts, and then nothing that anyone says to you makes much of a mark. How much more difficult it is, on the other hand, to bear the reproaches and humiliations and insults that we hear in our own language, which are so much more real. (Maybe they are the only real slights, which is why it would be best to nip in the bud any possible slights Pérez Nuix might deal out; to prevent their even being born so that they would not grieve me and so that I could not store them away. Like those I had received from Luisa, which still resonated, possibly because now there was almost nothing to dissipate or soften them, and she was ever more taciturn with me when we spoke on the phone.)

Besides, that night would eventually end, and I would more than likely never see Manoia again, and so I didn't mind if my 'I' of that evening or of any other spent in the service of Tupra—myself as Jack, let's say—should feel momentarily, and as it were vicariously, discomfited. My 'I' of before that and after was not Jack, but Jacques or Jacobo or Jaime, and that 'I' was stricter and prouder and also more vengeful, while the former could not help but see all the events he witnessed or took part in as slightly pointless and false, as if they did not really concern Jacques or did not happen to him, and as if he were protected from them. The reason I so disliked Manoia's reaction was because it alarmed me sufficiently to feel suddenly implicated, at least in my role as Jack, as a negligent and possibly even failed *chevalier servant*. I realised that his rudeness must have some other cause than my slowness and my hesitancy (or my incompetence, if I was wrong about the stroke of luck and the bargain). It was doubtless to do with Mrs Manoia, and at that precise moment I glanced over at the Spanish table, after an interval of no more than twenty seconds, and De la Garza and Flavia were no longer there.

I looked anxiously around. I had missed the moment when they had left the table, the others were all there, including the trite writer (clapping more furiously now, and looking even more the stereotypical flamenco artiste) and the lacklustre heiress with the invariable expression on her face of someone being forced to breathe the foul odours of some very slow-moving effluvia, which meant that neither the group nor even a part of the group had decamped to somewhere more amusing, only my lady and the attaché had absented themselves. The disco was a big place and I could see only a small part of it, they could have moved to any of the many bars, or gone on to the more distant and more frenetic dance floors; but they might also have become shadows in some dark corner or—although I refused even to imagine this—abandoned the club, together, with unnatural urgency and without saying goodbye. 'No, that's impossible,' I thought, not as yet seriously worried; 'Tupra said that all she wanted were compliments and gallant remarks, and that, however eager she might seem to follow a particular path to its end, she would not take that one first poisoned step forwards, and Tupra is rarely wrong. Tonight, however, the lady, it is true, has had a number of drinks, and it would be best not even to begin to calculate De la Garza's liquid intake. And who has not taken such a step at some point in their existence, in the company of an idiot or a criminal or a monster, no one is safe. But Rafita. With his hairnet. With his enormous pale jacket. With his earring like something a female Cuban singer or a Puerto Rican dancer would wear. As if he were Rita Moreno in *West Side Story*. With his failed Negroid air. So much poison would be suicide, and surely no one would botch his own suicide with such a display of bad taste.' My feelings of apprehension grew, however, when I remembered in my own lifetime certain ineffable couplings I had witnessed, as well as being reliably informed of other aberrant temporary pairings ('one-night stands' they're called in English, a term that has its origins in the theatre and denotes, in my view, a mixture of narcissism and exhibitionism).

Reresby and Manoia immediately noticed my unease. The latter shot a rapid glance at the empty space left by the vanished couple, he remained impassive and did not even touch his glasses, but I felt him grow suddenly dark, he raised his hands as was his custom, holding them in that uncomfortable suspended position reminiscent of certain pious poses, one hand on top of the other in the air, elbows or forearms resting on nothing; I found those hands threatening, bony, rigid—his fingers like yellowing piano keys—as if they were gathering strength or perhaps calm; as if they were preparing themselves or holding back or mutually keeping each other down. Tupra, however, never showed such visible signs of religiosity or piety in any unconscious gesture or posture, not a trace, not even in the cruel form that religiosity often adopts. There was nothing about him of the poseur or even the dissembler, he wasn't like that: if he often seemed opaque and indecipherable it was not because of any non-existent posturings, but simply because it was impossible to know all his codes. (I hoped that he had much the same experience with me, more or less: it would be better for me if he did.) Tupra could tolerate silence all too well, his own, that is, any silence that depended solely on him, any voluntary silence, and anyone who is happy to remain silent wreaks havoc on the impatient and the loquacious, and on his adversaries. That is why I hoped he would speak soon and dissemble a little when he did so (a little and badly, and only for a moment). He hooked one thumb in the chest pocket of his vest in order to appear relaxed: although this was not an unfamiliar gesture in him and resembled one of Wheeler's gestures too, perhaps he had copied the latter, in fact, the more usual pose in both was to hook one thumb under one armpit as if they were carrying a riding crop and resting the whole weight of their chest on it, that, at least, was the impression. And then, half turning towards me, he said in a rapid murmur (and it was clear to me that the reason he spoke to me in this way, swiftly and under his breath, was to prevent his guest from hearing his words):

'First of all, Jack, if you wouldn't mind, take a look in the toilets, both the Ladies and the Gents. Oh, and in the toilet for cripples as well, which tends to be free. Be so kind as to find her and bring her back here.' He used the polite formulae I had learned to dread in him, they were usually a bad omen, a prelude to a rebuke or a reprimand if you didn't shape up and do as he asked. They constituted one of his few interpretable signs, at least as far as I was concerned. 'Don't linger or delay. Bring her back here.' At least, I think that's what he said in English, or perhaps he said something else, perhaps he said 'loiter' or 'dally', but I don't think so. Of one thing I am sure, the expression 'Hurry up' never left his lips. He was as conscious as I was of what is easy and difficult in languages, and those two words, 'Hurry up', were all too recognisable. He knew that Manoia would have understood them at once, even if mumbled and in the midst of all that clamour, or with his mouth obscured by darkness.

No, you are never what you are—not entirely, not exactly—when you're alone and living abroad and ceaselessly speaking a language not your own or not your first language. However prolonged the absence and however unforeseeable its conclusion, because no time limit was set at the beginning or because that limit has become vague or unlikely to be met, and when there is no reason to think that its conclusion and your subsequent return home will one day arrive or hove into view (a return to a before that will not, meanwhile, have waited for you), and thus the word 'absence' loses meaning, depth and force with each hour that passes and that you pass far away from home—and then the expression 'far away' also loses meaning, depth, and force—the time of our absence accumulates gradually like a strange parenthesis that does not really count and which shelters us only as it might commutable, insubstantial ghosts, and for which, therefore, we need render an account to no one, not even to ourselves (not, at any rate, a detailed or complete account). To some degree you feel no responsibility for what you do or see, as if it all belonged to a provisional existence, parallel, alien, or borrowed, fictitious or almost dreamed—or, perhaps, merely theoretical, like my whole life, according to the unsigned report about me which I found in an old filing cabinet; as if everything could be relegated to the sphere of the purely imaginary and, of course, to the sphere of the involuntary; everything thrown into the bag of illusions and suspicions and hypotheses, and, even, of mere foolish dreams, about which, unusually, there has been almost permanent and universal consensus throughout the centuries of which any memory remains, be it conjectural or historical, invented or true: dreams do not depend on the intentions of the dreamer, and the dreamer can never be blamed for the contents of his dreams.

'What can I do, I don't choose them and I can't avoid them,' we say after each murky dream which, once we are awake, seems to us improper or illicit or which, we feel, it would have been better not to have dreamedt at all and certainly not remembered. 'I didn't want to feel that anomalous desire or that baseless resentment,' we think, 'that temptation or that sense of panic, that unknown threat or that surprising curse, that aversion or that longing which now sit heavy on my soul each night, the feeling of disgust or embarrassment which I myself provoke, those dead faces, forever fixed, that made a pact with me that there would be no more tomorrows (yes, that is the pact we make with all those who fall silent) and which now come and whisper dreadful, unexpected words to me, words that are perhaps inappropriate, or perhaps not, while I am asleep and have dropped my guard: I have laid down my shield and my spear on the grass.' Any idea that emerges from the dream-world is often dismissed or invalidated for that very reason, because of its dark, uncertain provenance, because such ideas seem to emerge out of a dream smokescreen, but do not always disappear once consciousness returns, indeed consciousness takes them up and sometimes even feeds them, and thus consciousness coexists with things it did not itself engender; it welcomes them into its bosom and nurtures them and gives them a face and even a name, and incorporates them into its safe, diurnal world even if that means relegating them to a lower category, labelling them as merely venial and gazing upon them paternally, as if every dream that survives the night must inevitably provoke the kind of ironic comment Sir Peter Wheeler made when he finally went to bed, up the stairs and to the left, on the night of that Saturday buffet supper: 'What nonsense,' he said and added, scornfully repeating my words: 'An excellent idea, indeed.' But despite this condescending attitude towards such dream non-sense, I have learned to fear anything that passes through the mind and even what the mind does not as yet know, because I have noticed that, in almost every case, everything was already there, somewhere, before it even reached or penetrated the mind. I have learned to fear, therefore, not only what is thought—the idea—but also what precedes it or comes before.

We perceive and experience the parenthetical time of our absence and all that it involves in much the same way as we do simulacra and fantasies: our deeds or crimes, our own actions and those of others; not only those we commit or endure, but also those we witness or provoke, either unwittingly or deliberately; and during that time nothing is ever truly serious, or so we believe. How right he was, the great playwright and counterfeiter, the poet-spy and blasphemer Marlowe about whose obscure death so little is known, except that it was violent and has become the stuff of legends and has been recon-structed numerous times with impossible exactitude, which is to say that it has been entirely imagined, with the gaze of the imaginer turned towards the dark back of time: he was stabbed to death in a tavern before he reached thirty, at the hands, as has lately been discovered, of one Ingram Frizer, who proved quicker or more vicious or more skilful with a dagger on that May 30th more than four hundred years ago, in Deptford, near the River Thames, which is how the Isis is known in every other place and time apart from when it passes through Oxford, that foreign city which, ages ago now, seemed to be or was my city too and where they call it the River Isis, which is why that is what my memory calls it, the River Isis. How right he was the great poet-traitor, so quick to quarrel, and who never ran away from a fight and who had travelled abroad and who was speaking from his own experience when he had a character from one of his tragedies say: 'Thou hast committed forni-cation: but that was in another country, and besides, the wench is dead.' And for once there is no doubt that here 'country' does not mean '*patria*' or 'fatherland'.

Yes, whatever happens in another country grows immediately faded and faint the moment you return to your own, if not at the very moment when the events themselves are taking place, as if our extreme transience deprived them of all gravity and substance, or as if they hadn't really happened, or had not fallen and weighed upon the world or become etched upon it, or only on the tortuous smokescreens of dreams, from which, afterwards, it is so easy to emerge and which are so easily disowned ('Oh, no, it had nothing to do with me'). And if, moreover, those involved are dead, then what happened becomes even less substantial and less poignant, more ghostly and more preterite, almost as much as the things you read about in novels or see in films, and sometimes you cannot tell the two things apart or distinguish them from what we experience in the nightmares that overwhelm us or from the delirium brought on by pain and fever. Unless, of course, you were the person who killed those dead people or were the cause of their expulsion from the earth and of their definitive silence, whether direct or indirect, unwitting or deliberate, although perhaps the expression 'indirect cause' is meaningless anyway or is merely an acceptable contradiction in terms.

And then there is what Wheeler said about dreams too, and which goes entirely against all that: of the laughter and voices that we hear in dreams, as intense and vivid as those we hear when awake, indeed, often more so, because they are prolonged or repeated and can last all night without their presence fading or without our growing weary—with no rivals in our waking hours and, indeed, unique if they belong to people who have died and who, like the second wife of the blind, widowed poet John Milton, only speak to us again and take on face and form while we sleep—of that laughter and those voices and their words, never before spoken, certainly never while alive, Wheeler said: 'One thing is certain, they are inside us, not somewhere outside . . . They are in *our* dreams, the dead; we are the ones dreaming them, our sleeping consciousness brings them to us and no one else can hear them.' And he went on: 'It is more like an impersonation than a supposed visitation or warning from beyond the grave.' ('It's like an unopposed usurpation with no risks attached,' I myself thought later on, 'since those dead have vacated their place and abandoned the field.') And then, if he was right, I thought, in that idiotically chic disco, while what was about to happen was already happening, if he was right, the will or the lack of it barely matters, just as it doesn't matter if something was deliberate or not, it doesn't matter what happened or did not happen, what was only thought or feared or desired, mere deliberations or longings, the more impossible the better, for we can bask in the tranquillity that their absolute impossibility affords us; it makes no difference if such thoughts get no further than apprehension or suspicion, than failed or sterile or never-formulated instigations or persuasions, than the abortive words of an Iago which, over a lifetime, all of us have tasted or will taste in the mouth, whether seeking our own advantage or survival, or bringing down harm and calamity on others: 'all of this is inside us, not somewhere outside'.

And thus we reach a domain in which what matters least is whether things do or do not exist, because they can always be talked about, just as all dreams, even the most involved and absurd of dreams, can be recounted after a fashion, in fits and starts, recounted to ourselves at least, and not always grammatically; and to that extent whatever has passed through our thoughts has existed; and whatever preceded it or came before, that too has existed. What is the use, then, of the faint, nebulous nature of what happens and what we do when abroad or far away, in another city, in another country, in that unexpected existence that seems not to belong to us, in the theoretical, parenthetical life we seem to be leading and which, up to a point, encourages us, in subterranean fashion, to think, without actually thinking it, that nothing contained by that time is irreversible and that everything can be cancelled, reversed, cured; that it has only half happened and without our full consent? What is the use, if something that even a judge considers not to have happened—a murder, say—if all we did was plan it; a betrayal, if we were merely tempted by it; a calumny or denunciation or deceit, if we only imagined both them and their annihilating effects without actually circulating them or giving them free rein: any judge who saw this would say: 'Overruled, case dismissed'—but what is the use if we feel that something did happen and that we contributed to it and feel responsible for it? All the more if one's job involves making frivolous bets and forecasts, looking and listening and inter-preting and noticing, taking notes and observing and selecting, inveigling, making connections, dressing things up, translating, telling stories and coming up with ideas and persuading others of those ideas, responding to and satisfying the insatiable, exhausting demand: 'What else, what else do you see, what else did you see?' although sometimes there is no 'else' and you have to force your visions or perhaps forge them out of your own inventive powers and memory, which is to say with that infallible mixture which can either condemn or save people and which forces us to announce our prejudices or pre-judgements, or perhaps they are merely our pre-verdicts. All the more if you are like me or like Tupra, like Pérez Nuix or Mulryan or Rendel, like Sir Peter Wheeler or like Toby Rylands, if you possess that not particularly extraordinary gift, one indeed that only others will see in you or which they will teach you to assume that you have, and thus come to believe in its existence.

I did make haste, although Tupra had not explicitly told me to, at least not in those exact words. Moving my chair slightly to one side, I got up, apparently full of resolve. I felt that there was no need to make my excuses, after all Manoia would not miss me, he didn't pay me much attention and was dissatisfied with my work; perhaps he would pay me more attention now and, with his glasses firmly positioned on the bridge of his nose and held in place there, would follow my steps until I had vanished from his field of vision, he would sense or understand or know that I was going off in search of his wife in order to bring her back, regardless of whether or not he had understood what Reresby had said; this exploit of mine, and, still more, its result, would certainly interest him, and he would even feel unease and impatience and would ask after me if I took a while to return from my trip: if I lingered, despite Tupra's urgings—or, rather, orders—if, contrary to his instructions, I loitered or delayed, if I played the fool or failed. All these things could happen if I did not find them soon, if they were hidden away in some corner of the club invisible to me but known to De la Garza because he would already have tried it out on another night with some other desperate menopausal case—I doubted there would be a darkened room where people could crawl around in anonymity—or if they had, in fact, swiftly left the premises—but that was unthinkable—not even stopping to pick up their coats—but that was unimaginable, Flavia would never abandon a Mourmanski fur coat—then, I would have to go out into the street and scan the pavements in both directions, and then run after them, if, that is, I spotted them—I didn't even want to think what the implications would be for us if we were to lose them, or if we already had.

I got to my feet with an overwhelming feeling of heaviness, which can be brought on by various combinations: by fright and haste, by distaste for the cold-blooded act of retaliation we are obliged to carry out, by an overwhelming sense of helplessness in a threatening situation. I didn't really think anything like that had happened, it seemed unlikely to me that Mrs Manoia could have been so very taken with De la Garza, and so rashly too, with her husband only a few steps away negotiating deals with foreigners. In Rafita's case, almost any kind of assault was perfectly possible, from the crassest of propositions to the most fatuous of passes—five fingers, both hands. It seemed to me that the only reason they would enter a toilet together would be maternal compassion, by which I mean that the attaché might, without warning, have felt deathly ill and had a sudden need to go and disgorge everything he had ingested, via the same route or entry point through which he had gorged himself (with Mrs Manoia supporting his pitching forehead, making sure, with all those convulsions and retchings, that his hairnet did not become a noose and hang him). No, I didn't believe in any dramatic change or grave event, not with my more sensible thoughts; but nevertheless I felt a weight in my thighs, a tight knot at the back of my neck, a burden on my shoulders, as if I foresaw (but, no, it wasn't prescience) that because of this whole episode, something was about to go badly wrong, something that would blight us possibly for ever or, at least, for a long time, and I realised at once, then, that the origin of that presentiment had more to do with Tupra, with his dissemblings and his furtive mutterings—which had been far too prompt for his usual contrary and reluctant self—than with Manoia or De la Garza or Flavia, or the rowdy group of Spaniards with their singer of deeply felt songs, or with the situation itself, which as yet entailed no great affront or anomaly. Or with myself, of course, although the feeling was obviously mine alone as I stood up to begin the search. The malaise, the pinprick, the sense of menace or of some impending misfortune, the held breath—or perhaps it was the stealthy breathing of someone preparing to deal a blow, or of something that sat heavy on my awakened soul—all of this emanated from Tupra, it was as if he had crossed a frontier or quickly drawn a line and immediately jumped over it, not so much in his mind as in his spirit, and had already settled on a punishment, regardless of what might happen from then on.

Perhaps he was the sort who does not issue any warning, at least not always, the sort who takes remote decisions for barely identifiable reasons, or without waiting for a link of cause and effect to establish itself between actions and motives, still less for any proof that such actions have been committed. He did not need proof, on those occasions, whether arbitrary or well founded—who could say—when without the slightest warning or indication, he would lash out with his sabre; indeed, on such occasions, he did not even require the actions or events or deeds to have occurred. Perhaps for him it was enough that he knew precisely what would happen in the world if no pressure or brake were imposed on what he perceived to be people's certain capabilities, and knew, too, that if those capabilities were never fully deployed it was only because someone—himself, for example—had prevented or impeded them, rather than because those people lacked the desire or the guts, he took all that for granted. Perhaps for him to adopt the punitive measures which he deemed necessary, he simply had to convince himself of what would happen in each case if he or another sentinel—the authorities or the law, instinct, the moon, fear, the invisible watchers—did not put a stop to it. 'It's the way of the world,' he would say, and he would say this about many of the complex situations described or related or experienced or foreseen during the sessions when we were called upon to give our interpretations and reports (he alone made the decisions and these came later); he applied these words to betrayals and acts of loyalty, to anxieties and quickened pulses, to unexpected reversals, to anxieties and doubts and torments, to the scratch and the pain and the fever and the festering wound, to griefs and the infinite steps which we all take in the belief that we are being guided by our will, or that our will does at least play a part in them. To him, all this seemed perfectly normal and even, sometimes, routine, he knew all too well that the earth is full of passions and affections and of ill will and malice, and that sometimes individuals can avoid neither and, indeed, choose not to, because they are the fuse and the fuel of their own combustion, as well as their reason and their igniting spark. And they do not require a motive or a goal for any of this, neither aim nor cause, gratitude or insult, or at least not always, or as Wheeler said: 'They carry their probabilities in their veins, and time, temptation, and circumstance will lead them at last to their fulfilment.' And for Tupra this very radical attitude—or perhaps it was simply a very practical one, a consequence of his clear, confident, unshakeable opinions—was doubtless just another facet of that way of the world in which words like 'distrust', 'friendship', 'enmity', and 'trust' were mere pretence and ornament and, possibly, a quite unnecessary torment, at least as far as he was concerned; that unreflecting, resolute stance (or one based perhaps on a single thought, the first), also formed part of a style that remained unchanged throughout time and regardless of space, and there was, therefore, no reason to question it, just as there is no need to question wakefulness and sleep, or hearing and sight, or breathing and speech, or any of the other things about which one knows: 'that is how it is and will always be'.

This was not, however, a preventative attitude, not exactly and exclusively, but, rather, and depending on the case and the person, punitive or compensatory, for Tupra saw and judged when dry, with no need to get himself wet—to use Don Quixote's words when he announces to Sancho Panza the mad feats he will perform for Dulcinea's sake even before being provoked into them by grief or jealousy. Or perhaps Tupra understood them—the various cases—even though they were pages as yet unwritten, and perhaps, for that very reason, forever blank. 'Life is not recountable,' Wheeler had also said, 'and it seems extraordinary that men have spent all the centuries we know anything about devoted to doing just that . . . It is a doomed enterprise,' he had added, 'and one that perhaps does us more harm than good. Sometimes I think it would be best to abandon the custom altogether and simply allow things to happen. And then just leave them be.' But the blank page is the best of all, the most eternally believable and the most revealing, precisely because it is never finished, on it there is eternally room for everything, even for denials; and, therefore, what the page might or might not say (because in a world of infinite talk—simultaneous, superimposed, contradictory, constant, exhausting, and inexhaustible—even when a page says nothing, it is saying something) could be believed at any time, not just during its one time to be believed, which, sometimes, lasts no time at all, a day or only a few fatal hours, and at others for a very long time indeed, a century, even several, and then it is not fatal at all because there is no one to check if the belief is true or false, and, besides, no one cares when everything is balanced out. So even if we abandon the custom altogether, as Wheeler said, even if we give up telling stories altogether, and never tell any ever, we can still not entirely free ourselves from telling. Not even by leaving the page blank. And even if there are things of which no one speaks, even if they do not even happen, they never stay still. 'It's awful,' I thought. 'There's no escape. Even if no one speaks of them. And even if they never actually happen.'

And so I got up and moved my chair slightly to one side and, without making my excuses to Manoia, without a word or a gesture, I set off briskly to the toilets, that was the first thing to do, as Tupra had indicated. The toilets were not that close and I had to walk quite a way to find them, I kept looking to right and left and straight ahead, just in case, en route, my eyes should catch sight of the escaped couple and I could thus complete my task without further delay, except that I was in too much of a hurry and too preoccupied—it quickly became very difficult to walk at all—to spot any one individual among the crowds I was trying to negotiate and who blocked my path, at that hour the disco was jam-packed, with the chic and the not so chic, the night becomes more heterogeneous as it advances, and our area—which included the Spaniards and the semi-fast dance floor—was far less congested, semi-slow music obviously didn't attract so many people (and so wouldn't be played for very much longer), and, on the other hand, the second stage or floor, or whatever they call these things nowadays, was absolutely frenetic, out of the corner of my eye I glimpsed the crushed and sweating masses a few metres or yards away, I skirted round them rather than plunging in, that would have taken me time and effort, and the urgent thing now was to get to the restrooms. Tupra knew that the greatest risks for the two escapees lay there, that is how it is from adolescence onwards, when you smoke on the sly at school.

There was a bit of a line outside the Ladies, which is not unusual, I don't know why that is, perhaps women take more time because they have to sit down and because each one, each time, gives the cubicle she is about to use a thorough clean; there were two or three women waiting at the door, whereas outside the Gents there was no one, and so I went in there first to have a look, or, rather, to inspect every nook and cranny, I didn't want to let Mr Reresby down, 'Bring her back. Don't linger or delay.' Those clear orders were still ringing in my ears. I saw three men standing up, two of them gravely or sullenly urinating, one beside the other, although they didn't appear to be friends and were not, of course, talking, it was odd that they should be standing so close when there were another six places free, one tends to keep a distance when engaged in such activities; the third man was standing at the mirror, combing his hair and humming to himself. Of the six cubicles, two were occupied, but beneath the truncated doors (given the shortened perspective, I had to lean right down) both revealed their respective pairs of trouser legs duly converted into bellows; I don't know why these doors, in public conveniences I mean, almost never reach the ground or even the ceiling, as if they were saloon doors in the Wild West, well, at least they're not swing doors and not quite so short (they're more raincoats than waistcoats). The urinators eyed me suspiciously, they turned their heads in one synchronised movement and their faces grew still more sullen, I pushed open the other doors to check that the cubicles really were empty, because if someone stands on the toilet bowl, you can't see their feet under the door and the cubicle appears to be empty, although if two people were standing on the bowl they would be in grave danger of falling in, especially if one of them was wearing fierce falsies made of oak or implants made of liquid lead or whatever. The comber, however, did not turn round, he was very carefully parting his hair with a wet comb and continuing his blithe, oblivious humming ('Nanna naranniaro nannara nanniaro', was what it sounded like), it was 'The Bard of Armagh', an Irish song, or 'The Streets of Laredo' if you prefer, which is from the American West (it's the same melody with different words and accompaniment), I recognised it at once, I've heard it hundreds of times in movies and on certain records, and the disco was at least not so unreasonable as to have loudspeakers in the toilets, so the music from the dance floors could be heard only as a distant echo through the double doors of those English toilets, and I immediately picked up that very audible ballad or perhaps lullaby, I knew most of the words of the cowboy version, which is far better known than the Irish original, '*I spied a young cowboy wrapped in white linen, wrapped in white linen as cold as the clay*', it's the very partial story of a dead man talking (although, in fact, it's a denial, a non-story), whose own violent death or, rather, the bad life that led him to that death, he wants to keep hidden from his mother, his sister, and his girlfriend, '*I'm a poor cowboy and I know I've done wrong*', that was one of the lines that surfaced in my memory, singly and in no particular order. He's probably not dead but dying, although in the glum lyrics this remains ambiguous and confused, or perhaps this depends on which version and which singer you hear. But I don't think so. As I remember it, the poor cowboy who speaks is already dead. I left the Gents before the other three or possibly five men who were already in there, I was very quick. There was still one woman waiting to go into the Ladies, there was a lot of coming and going, so I went into the handicapped toilet—painted on the door was the bizarre image of a hook, perhaps a wheelchair would have been too prosaic and sordid for such a posh place—or the toilet for cripples as Tupra had called it (I very nearly became one myself when I slipped on the ramp, which can be lethal to the still able-bodied) although he certainly did not do so out of any lack of respect, but because he must have thought that Manoia would be less likely to know the word 'cripple'. It was much bigger, positively spacious in fact, and strangely empty. Not that I thought it strange to find no handicapped person in there: the toilet was a courtesy, a considerate gesture or merely a hypocritical measure, or perhaps one made obligatory by the regulations for discos in these insistently demagogic times of ours. It is not the norm in these places for there to be an abundance of wheelchairs and crutches or even hooks. What I found odd, especially viewing the situation with the Spanish gaze I have never lost, was that other people did not just swan in there as cool and *sans façon* as you like and make use of the lavish facilities as if they were intended for them as well, especially if there were lines outside the other restroom. In my country no one would have taken the slightest notice of the sign on the door: they wouldn't even have seen it (I mean, no one would; we are an uncivilised race). I didn't understand the purpose of the cylindrical metal bars on the walls, perhaps they were supports for someone unsteady on their feet or barely able to walk, I touched them, there were four of them, solid rather than hollow and cold, one was fixed and the others could be moved to the right and the left, and so could be pushed out of the way against the elegant fake wall tiles, they weren't towel rails because there were no towels, however, I didn't have time to speculate further about them or to lie across one of them on my stomach (an exercise referred to by sports writers, I believe, as a 'front hip circle') as if they were exercise bars, to find out how much weight they would bear: they weren't very high, just shoulder-height. I had still not found De la Garza or Flavia, I had taken all these steps very swiftly, but my sense of urgency was growing with each second that passed without my sighting them. I had a good look, just in case, and I searched every corner of this luxury toilet for the disabled, and then I left, it was time to arm myself with determination and audacity and—there was nothing else for it—venture into the Ladies, I couldn't risk the bold duo having taken refuge in there in order to surrender themselves to lust ('It's not possible') and for me not to have found them there merely because I was too embarrassed. '*But please not one word of all this shall you mention, when others should ask for my story to hear,*' said another two lines from the song I had suddenly remembered, and which was now installed in my head, even if only in fragments, and despite the surrounding din. I hoped that I would not see anything that might displease me, that I would not be asked to hear any stories; I hoped that there would be nothing that I could or should recount later.

There was still one woman, a different one from before, waiting to enter the busy toilet reserved for women and, who knows, possibly for transvestites too (I had seen a couple of them around, and I'm not sure which toilets they're supposed to use when out in public). I walked past her so quickly and with such resolve that she could only have noticed my contravention of the rules when the first door was already closing behind me. 'Hey, you,' I heard her begin to exclaim, the second word almost abandoned as if she had suddenly run out of steam—so it was not an exclamation—and she certainly wouldn't follow me in. I pushed out my chest, took a deep breath, squared my shoulders and with the same apparent sangfroid (a complete act) opened the second door, the door that gave directly onto the toilet area and a sudden vision of a host of ladies standing before the mirrors or near them awaiting their turn or taking advantage of a space between two manes of hair to primp themselves from a distance; a kind of half-silence fell, there was a movement of heads turned in my direction, I caught the occasional perplexed or amused or frightened or even appreciative eye. I took the safe option of muttering several times the absurd word 'Security' and each time I tugged at or lifted one lapel of my jacket as if it bore an insignia which was not there: not that it matters, what matters is the gesture or the drawing of attention to something even if there's nothing to draw attention to, as when one points with one finger at the sky and everyone looks up, at the blue and the clouds, as empty and tranquil as they were a moment before; I had no idea if that repeated word 'Security' was plausible in English or if it would sound even more foolish than it did in Spanish, or if that was what a British policeman or hitman would say when pursuing someone or when engaged on some urgent mission.

I had a quick look round at the mainly attractive faces, if Rafita and Mrs Manoia had gone in there, they were not only stupid, they were imbeciles (he, of course, was a complete imbecile anyway, but not even he would be that imbecilic: in a crowded Ladies' restroom, when there was a deserted toilet for the handicapped right next door); but now that I was there, I had to make sure, so I strode over to the cubicles with the firm step of an inspector or a hired gun (following orders, doing something on someone else's say-so and not in your own interest or on your own initiative helps, it exempts you from responsibility, rendering a service to someone instils ease and thoughtlessness and even cruelty); there were eight cubicles, all, of course, occupied as was only to be expected given the permanent queue outside. I cast a panoramic eye over what was revealed below the abbreviated doors, two pairs of concertinaed trousers and six skirts, no—the skirts would be pulled up and therefore invisible—six pairs of legs festooned with tights and knickers (there was the odd thong and one of the women wasn't wearing tights at all, which is unusual in England, even in summer; she must have been a foreigner. 'What a palaver,' I thought, 'what a lot of minor complications, we men have it much easier'), there was nothing odd about any of the eight, the eight pairs of legs, I mean, they all appeared to be in the same normal posture, the expected, ordinary posture. It took only a moment, at most two, that sliding glance, but I couldn't help recalling the imagined image from a story my mother used to tell me when I was a child: one of the seven tests that a hero had to pass in order to rescue his beloved—a country girl or a kidnapped princess, I'm not sure which, imprisoned in a castle—consisted in recognising her by her legs alone, the rest of her body and face were hidden behind a long screen or a similarly truncated door, as were those of the six or thirteen or twenty other women lined up, an identity parade like the ones they hold in police stations except that the aim in the story was liberation rather than accusation and involved only legs, not sitting down like those in the cubicles, but standing up, the hero was thus able to see only the six, thirteen or twenty pairs of calves and thighs, and he had to guess which belonged to his shepherdess or damsel; if I remember rightly there was some trick, some detail—not a scar, too obvious even for the imagination of a child—that would lead him to give the right answer and so pass the test, even if that meant being set another far more difficult one. My mother was no longer in the world for me to ask her what that clue to recognition had been, and my father certainly wouldn't remember the tale, he might never even have heard it or asked for it since he was not her son but her husband, perhaps my sister or my two brothers would, although that was unlikely, I generally had a better memory for childhood things, and if even I couldn't remember . . . 'I'll never know, not that it really matters, most people fail to realise that not knowing everything doesn't matter in the least, because even then we always know too much, so much so that, unwittingly or deliberately, we forget most of what we know, but without worrying about it or regretting it, even if finding it out in the first place may have cost us tears and sweat and toil and blood.'

So there it was, that line of legs, and it seemed to me that Flavia's were not among those sixteen much younger legs, almost all of whose feet were very well shod—that I did notice: they were wearing party shoes—I was particularly struck by the elegant high heels of the woman who was not wearing tights or had taken them off along with her knickers before sitting down—there was nothing around her ankles, they were bare— obviously I only had a very quick look, the women by the mirrors were not protesting or hurtling out of the door, I sensed behind me more expectation or curiosity than indignation or alarm, the opportunistic people who govern us have made people so afraid that we have rapidly grown docile, especially when confronted by someone wielding the terrifying, omni- present word—'Security'—that justifies everything, even supposedly ironic uses and abuses of it and humiliations that pretend not to be humiliations, but, how can I put it, purely functional.

Perhaps I did not think this then, but only afterwards, when I finally went to bed much, much later that night or, rather, that morning, but the germ of those thoughts did surface then, during that urgent, absurd visit to the Ladies' room, sometimes such thoughts come to us in a flash and we put them off because we haven't time to consider them at that precise moment, and then we recover them afterwards and develop them at our leisure and in a spirit of false calm; and yet it could be said that such a flash is already the thought, concentrated or almost unacknowledged (or perhaps it is a kind of prescient prescience).

'I would have recognised Luisa's legs out of sixteen or twenty-one other pairs of legs, even though I haven't seen them for a long time now and they seem sometimes to fade and become muddled with other legs in the here and now that will certainly prove transient and will, in time, be forgotten,' I thought. 'I might also be able to pick out those of Clare Bayes, my former lover in Oxford, but it's years since I've seen them and they might have changed, they might be scarred or she could be lame in one of them like Alan Marriott or they might have become puffy and swollen or there might be only one of them, just as there were only three on the dog whose fourth leg was *not* cut off by the gypsy Jane—I have constantly to remind myself of that, that she did not cut it off, because whenever I recall her and the dog, that, initially, is what I always believe and what always assails me, for the hypothesis, the invented story with its horrific couple and horrible conjunction of ideas is more vivid to me than the true story with its train station and its drunken Oxford United fans—the young florist who was there when Clare Bayes used to visit me with her strange collection of purchases, with her constant need for fragments of eternity or her expansive notion of time about which there was always something utilitarian, I can say that now without feeling hurt by the word or the fact, for that was in another country and who knows, who knew, what might have happened to the wench (and that other country is once again this one), all it takes is a car accident and that can happen to anyone, the amputation would come later and then she would have to use the spacious, deserted toilet for the disabled. But it's hard to imagine Clare Bayes without a leg, because both were so very striking, with their feet always shod in Italian shoes or else barefoot, she took them off when indoors, a kick, one for each shoe, would send them flying, and later we would have to hunt for them.' I thought all this as I stood before the closed cubicles with their eight pairs of shining shoes peeping out from beneath the doors, and also before I went to sleep weighed down by the terrible unease I took with me to bed; I must have done both things—

relived the scene in the Ladies' room and recalled the story, so furled in mists, which my mother used to tell me—in order to drive from my mind everything that happened later and to ease the pinprick pressing into my chest. And I even managed to go on to think: 'On the other hand, I wouldn't recognise Pérez Nuix's legs, not yet, if that word "yet" has any intention or meaning.'

What I said next was quite unnecessary, it was clear that the disappeared couple were not there and that I should hurry off to look for them elsewhere, I still could not believe that they had left altogether, but neither could I risk angering Tupra, still less Manoia, 'Don't linger or delay', that had been Tupra's recommendation or instruction, and the order had been 'Bring her back here'. But I did linger a little, although only a little. I suppose the sight of those eight doors and those sixteen legs was too much of a temptation for me to abandon it as soon as I had discovered it, without even spending the necessary seconds looking at it in order at least to fix and retain it in my memory, like someone memorising a vital phone number or learning a few lines of poetry ('Strange to no longer desire one's desires. Strange to see meanings that once clung together, floating away in every direction. And being dead is hard work . . .' Or these lines: 'And indeed there will be time to wonder, "Do I dare?" and, "Do I dare?" Time to turn back and descend the stair, with a bald spot in the middle of my hair . . .'; and a little later comes the question that no one asks before acting or before speaking: 'Do I dare disturb the universe?', because everyone dares to do just that, to disturb the universe and to trouble it, with their small, quick tongues and their ill-intentioned steps, 'So how should I presume?'). Perhaps it attracted me because of that childhood reminiscence—there must be some reason why an image described to us but never seen, should remain with us our entire life—or perhaps there was in it also a prosaic element to do with secretions and humours, to use Sir Peter Wheeler's words after I had spoken out in praise of Beryl's unusual and very sexual smell and of her magnificent and amply displayed thighs that had so exasperated and maddened the same wretched attaché who had now slipped away with the person who had, that night, been placed in my extremely careless care.

And so I said unnecessarily, partly because I could not resist the minor or venial vice of making an impromptu joke, raising my voice as if I were some person in authority, police or governmental or lay, and addressing myself to the eight users of the cubicles, whose feet had something choreographic about them, as if they had paused momentarily in mid-dance, and as soon as they heard my incongruous, male voice, I saw seven pairs of legs instinctively and simultaneously press together or close, I mean each pair on its own account, the only legs that did not change position being the bare-legged pair with the ankles unencumbered by any item of clothing, their owner must be foreign and, possibly, given their perfectly depilated state, a compatriot of mine. There was a slight, not very penetrating odour of secretions and humours in that place (not, curiously and fortunately, of urine), doubtless sexual and, to me, unusual, mixed up with various female colognes and perfumes, women tending to be cleaner than men, although not always (and then they are as slovenly and dirty as the SMERSH agent Rosa Klebb, luckily she was only a fictitious character and so poor Nin would not, in reality, have been able to take her as his lover), and I found the whole scene not at all unpleasing. And so I said this, which was completely irrelevant to the search I was engaged upon, and I acknowledge that I said it purely in jest and for fun:

'Forgive the intrusion, my dear ladies,' it seemed to me that addressing them thus would calm them down, despite the fright I had given them, 'but we're hoping to apprehend a particularly skilful pickpocket.' 'A particularly skilful pickpocket', those were the ludicrous words I came out with, and as soon as I said them, I was struck by how antiquated they sounded, like something out of the 1930s or even Dickens (a pickpocket), but any mention of a maniac or a terrorist (still less of a hidden bomb) would have sown panic and the women would have rushed out, without pulling up their tights or trousers and would have risked staining them with some drop, and I had no desire to put them in such a humiliating position or to cause them any public embarrassment, even if they and I were the only witnesses. 'I'm sure he's not here,' I added with as much circumspection and neutrality as I could muster, films are invaluable to those of us who, from the moment we first sat down in that darkened auditorium, used them as a kind of apprenticeship, 'but I would just ask you to confirm to me that there is, in fact, no man hidden in any of the cubicles. I can see two pairs of trousers from here and the legs wearing them are not entirely . . .' I did not continue, for I was, I'm afraid, about to say something like 'unequivocal'. 'I would be extremely grateful if you would be so kind as to answer me, one by one, and I will then leave at once.'

I imagine that a real policeman would have waited until they came out to make certain, but I, of course, was not a real policeman, nor was I, in fact, in pursuit of a pickpocket. I heard one or two involuntary titters behind me, in the area by the mirrors, women, generally speaking, are more prepared to see the funny side of things that have a funny side, especially if they are matters that can be taken lightly and as if they were already over and done with and can thus be retold without fear of incurring any further consequences (not, at least, as regards the original events, of course, but retelling anything almost always brings consequences of its own). After a couple of seconds of what was, doubtless, some bewilderment, the female voices gradually responded from behind their doors, some more submissively than others, and only one angrily; but given that people now meekly allow themselves to be frisked at any airport or public building, and obediently take off their shoes or even get undressed at the orders of some grim-faced customs officer, it is little wonder that they should accept importunate demands and interruptions and impertinent questions even while engaged in the most private of occupations. 'No', 'Of course not', 'Are you mad? Get out of here', 'No, sir, there's no one else in here', came the answers, and only one departed from the norm of these simple denials: the woman who was apparently wearing neither tights nor knickers, the one who had not pressed her legs together when she heard my male voice, slowly pushed open the door, which emitted a faint creak, and, looking straight at me from where she sat, said:

'You come and see.' That's what she said. (English doesn't distinguish between formal and informal 'you', between '*usted*' and '*tú*', but in her mind she must have been using the latter.)

The phrase was too short and too unproblematic for me to be able to tell whether or not she had an accent, the 'k' sound of 'come' was perhaps not sufficiently aspirated, which would mean, therefore, that she was a stranger to England and even to the Commonwealth or to any of the other former British colonies, but I couldn't really pay close enough attention, I was in no state to make fine phonetic judgements, for I found the sight of her distinctly troubling, which was why the scene lasted almost as short a time as the phrase itself, I myself hurriedly closed the door, although not as hurriedly as, on that other morning, I had opened the door to the office shared by Pérez Nuix and Mulryan and found Pérez Nuix bare from the waist up and drying herself, I did not close it with brio or with gusto, I closed it rather as I had my colleague's door, after only a few seconds' delay, in one resolute movement, but nevertheless still looking and memorising the image, it lasted twelve seconds, seconds which I counted only later in my memory, the scene in the Ladies' room did not, I think, last even that long, for I promptly pushed the door shut as I stammered—although it was probably not my voice that stammered, but my thoughts: 'I can see well enough, thank you very much'; and it was true, I could see well enough that she was there alone and seated, she was not one of those prissy women who avoid sitting down on the actual seat and who urinate hovering above it so to speak— only a short distance above, but nonetheless poised in the air – any contact with the seats in public toilets fills them with disgust or revulsion, after all, they don't know who might have been there before them and there are all kinds of grubby, slovenly, dirty people in the world, not to say poisonous ones too, indeed, however chic a place may be, there is contagion everywhere and a great deal of grime. This woman was evidently not the prudent sort, given that she clearly didn't even bother with underwear: her knickers had not remained at garter level or barely been pulled down at all, there simply were no knickers, as I confirmed or discovered when she revealed her whole figure to my now elevated eyes, her thighs were as unencumbered with clothes as were her ankles, her tight skirt pulled up to groin- and hip-level and, therefore, wrinkled (not that there was a great deal of fabric, it would doubtless be on the short side), a straight white tube skirt, her shoes, with their slender but sturdy heels, were the same colour, like the summer shoes women wore in the 1950s, which was, generally speaking, the best and prettiest decade for female fashion, but they, like the skirt, were unexpected in London and worn outside of the season to which they were best suited, I saw, too, a yellow shape or smudge beneath which there was no bra, a blouse with a rounded neck and almost imaginary sleeves—sleeves like stumps, the upper part would cover only the tops of her arms, and the lower part, or so I deduced, would barely cover her armpits—most troubling of all were her strong, sturdy and very—very—bare thighs, not heavy, but compact and dense, as if the whole surface were filled to bursting, with not an ounce of excess fat, but making the most of every millimetre of skin, which was as taut as a tight wrapping, thighs which quite properly grew wider as they advanced up to her hips and groin and towards the dark triangle that I could see (at least I think I could), they looked vaguely Central American those hips or perhaps they, too, were reminiscent of the 1950s when curves were fashionable, or perhaps it was her mass of curly hair and the enormous earrings—huge hoop earrings—that lent her a tropical air which need not necessarily have been authentic, despite the golden colour of her bare skin—it could never have been British skin, nor from many places in the

Commonwealth—it might just be a choice she had made, a disguise chosen for a long night at the disco, just as De la Garza imagined he had got himself up as a black rapper, but had succeeded only in looking like some kind of alternative bullfighter or some absurd Goya *torero*.

My gaze was fleeting, but not veiled, it was not an English gaze or a modern-day Spanish one as it had apparently been on the morning when I found myself confronted by Pérez Nuix and her towel, she had been naked from the waist up, and this young woman—well, she seemed young to me, about thirty-five I reckoned—was naked from the waist down, I felt for a moment as if I had completed a jigsaw puzzle, but one of a rather Cubist bent, as if the two pieces were not an entirely harmonious fit (they were so different), and, besides, only their naked halves matched, not their clothed halves. And so my gaze lasted no time at all, but during that no-time-at-all my gaze was a truly searching one, I did not pretend that she was standing up, with her skirt pulled down, and that I did not know, therefore, whether she was wearing anything underneath or not. She too looked back at me when she spoke. Not defiantly, not coquettishly and not, of course, salaciously, not reproachfully or sarcastically, but with an amused expression on her face and, needless to say, without a flicker of embarrassment, as if she didn't mind in the least being seen in that rather inelegant position if she could manage to make a little joke of it and to discomfit or trouble me (although that last effect was purely incidental, she could not easily have predicted it without first having seen my face, I could have been a thug who might have responded by taking two steps forward), she more than any of the other women must have picked up on the comical, silly side of my explanation or question, addressed simultaneously, to eight women, no less, protected or hidden away, who, with an incredulous start, doubtless all stopped what they were doing, I was sure that as soon as my voice rang out all liquid ceased flowing into the eight toilet bowls, a collective retentive reflex reaction, a shutter, an eyelid, a contraction of the same controlling muscle, and this, fortunately, would have been equally unavoidable for the woman who continued to sit there with her legs imperturbably akimbo in that first moment and in those that followed—one, two, three, four; and five, that was how long it took for the door to creak open and for her four provocative words to be spoken, 'You come and see'—and in the moments that followed—five, six, seven, eight; and nine; or ten, that must have been how long they lasted, my shock, my photographic memorisation of the image, my grateful response and my resolute movement to close the door—and in those ten seconds I also had time to see the most troubling thing of all, a drop of blood fallen on the floor of the cubicle, or, rather, two, except that the second smaller drop lay, like a lentil, on her left shoe, it wouldn't be a problem, the shoes were so smooth and gleaming that, even though they were white, they looked like patent leather or like porcelain, it would be easy enough to remove that tiny stain from such a polished surface, always assuming she realised it was there.

I immediately thought what almost any man would have thought, for we tend to know almost nothing about menstruation—at most, we have seen the traces left behind on a bedspread or a sheet, I, at least, have always tried to know nothing beyond that—we don't even know if a drop or more than a drop *can* fall unnoticed onto the floor, if the woman is standing up and wearing a skirt but no knickers, and doesn't have easy access to sanitary towels or something similar, cotton balls, Kleenex, absorbent paper, or even blotting paper—no, that's ridiculous, idiotic, that was stiff and pink, I haven't seen it since I was a child, since the days when my mother used to tell me that story—I knew nothing about such matters despite having been married for many years which, now that they were over, seemed far fewer, just as I had never seen Luisa sitting down to urinate in the way that this unknown woman had shown herself to me, there are some things that do not necessarily come with cohabitation, or perhaps one's upbringing, at least my upbringing and that of Luisa, imposes natural, unspoken limits on familiarity, and always shies away from any form of slovenliness, and prevents one from becoming the idle and indifferent witness of things to which one should not be a witness.

Comendador—my former schoolfriend, who subsequently went so badly astray—had also immediately assumed it must be the result of the sudden onset of menstruation when he saw the blood of that young woman on the wooden floor and on the sheets and on her long T-shirt, the blood of the drug-dealer Cuesta's temporary girlfriend whom Comendador believed had died after she stumbled and tripped and hit her head hard on a wall—it had made a sound like wood being chopped—and he had discovered a gash on her head as she lay unconscious, or, as he thought, dead. And, later, he had doubted that he had seen anything at all and had even admitted the possibility that he had mistaken for blood what had perhaps been only brandy or wine or even a dark stain on the floorboards. I was currently experiencing a feeling of unease or a sense of a problem in the making because of another man so like Comendador that there were moments when they seemed to me to be one and the same, Incompara was his name, and there was something about those two surnames that automatically made me think of them both, or which my personal sense of language linked together: Incompara, Comendador; Comendador, Incompara, as if, I don't know, as if they were of the same calibre or somehow analogous, equally commendable and comparable (well, certainly as regards going about the world with aplomb and brio and making a big splash).

But what flashed into my mind was that other bloodstain, the one I saw on the stairs in Wheeler's house, the one I had painstakingly cleaned up in the middle of the night that I spent there, well, in the early hours of Sunday morning really, but which was, as far as I was concerned, still Saturday night, given that, for me, the day had been lengthened out by books and given that I had still not gone to bed, I finally went to sleep, soothed or lulled by the murmurings of the river, so late or so early that

I could already see a little light in the sky. I still did not know from whom or what it had come, that blood, for the following day over lunch I had finally asked Peter and Mrs Berry, but without success: I found their reply so disappointing that I began to doubt the existence of the large drop whose rim had resisted me the night before, reluctant to disappear and to be erased (and I had, up to a point, already foreseen that future uncertainty: one can always doubt anything that ceases and does not persist, which means that one is always in a state of doubt about everything, because nothing is ever constantly present, apart from the stars and the seasons, that is, but nothing human); and so, in a way, the same thing happened to me as happened to Comendador, who distrusted the reality of the various stains which, in his panic, he had seen in that apartment. But I felt no panic when I discovered mine, at the top of the first flight of Wheeler's stairs, although I had been drinking and was slightly feverish with words and my long hours of wakefulness, with my many tangential night-time readings, all interleaved with memories of my father, more his than mine: 'an assiduous collaborator on the Moscow newspaper, *Pravda*; contact, willing companion, interpreter and guide in Spain to the bandit Dean of Canterbury; and privy to the whole web of red propaganda throughout the conflict', he had been accused of all those things, accusations dreamed up by his best friend whose face he had failed to recognise, the face of a tomorrow that arrived all too soon, almost when it was still today. But now they were my memories too, for sometimes we have memories that are only heard or inherited. Like the legs of my fairy-tale princess lined up with another six or thirteen or twenty other pairs.

I had to leave that busy and entirely inappropriate restroom, it was, after all, not my restroom, a long line would be forming outside, I had been in there for a couple of minutes now, during which time no one had entered or left, the women inside being occupied, while those behind me, in the area by the mirrors, were by now, most of them, laughing openly at my exchange of words with the seated Caribbean woman—Cuban, Puerto

Rican, Nicaraguan, or from further south, Colombian or Venezuelan or even Brazilian; or Spanish, that, too, was a possibility. But I could not possibly fail to draw the stain to the attention of this young woman with the powerful thighs which I knew then I would think about later, on other nights or days. She had very almond-shaped eyes, that much I did have time to see, although not the colour, and a rather broad nose, or perhaps her nostrils were flared or it was a combination of both things, she struck me as one of those beauties who look as if they had just breathed out, it's a common look in all races now, perhaps it's one of the more sought-after types of nose among women who go in for such operations, almost no one is content with the sum of their features. So I said to her through the now closed door, with my left hand still on the handle so that it wouldn't open again of its own accord (the bolt was on her side, inside, and I had not heard her slide it shut) or so that she would not try to open it again herself, who knows:

'You've got a red stain on your white shoe, madam. I just thought I'd tell you.'

She could have told me that it didn't matter and that it was none of my business anyway, in the same tone that Wheeler had used (or an even surlier one) when, very late on that Saturday night, just before he turned round and finally went up the first flight of stairs to bed, I pointed out to him that his socks had slipped down. But the woman said only 'Thank you', and again I did not notice any accent. A 'red stain', I said. I did not dare to say 'bloodstain', although I was sure that the drop on her shoe and the one on the floor were drops of blood, newly spilled, newly fallen.

I left the restroom as resolutely as I had entered it, muttering, 'No luck, no luck,' as if I were explaining or making excuses to myself, I didn't even look at the women inside or, when I strode past them, those waiting outside (there were once again three or four), I had to find Flavia and take her back to her husband's table, not that my mind wasn't on the job or that I had lost sight of my mission, it had simply got mixed up with a few other things: lines of poetry, images and inherited memories as well as a story, none of which managed to fill my mind entirely, because none was particularly pressing, but they were all floating around in there, perhaps waiting to be picked up later by idle thought—that is, by thought at its most active—at the end of the day, when I finally went to bed.

The song from Laredo and from Armagh was still going round and round in my head despite the blaring music, which once again grew deafening as soon as I walked through the double doors and found myself back in the main room, I hadn't been gone very long and yet the crowd had grown, things were moving towards their apogee. But when a tune we used to know reappears and lodges itself in our brain, there is no way of getting rid of it without the mediation of something from outside, something entirely different (perhaps, as with hiccups, a shock), 'And when Sergeant Death's cold arms shall embrace me', that was the Irish version from Armagh, in English the idea still survives of death as a masculine being or figure although—with the exception of 'ship', I believe—ordinary nouns lack any grammatical gender; it was not always thus, however, at least not for everyone, the related language of German does have genders and there is no doubt at all that death is masculine and that it is always shown as a man, as in the classic subject of Death and the Maiden, so often seen in paintings and engravings, in which he is depicted as a knight with helmet and armour and spear, or perhaps with a sword, or with both, Sir Death he was called in more than one English medieval play, and he also turned up disguised as a white-coated doctor in certain pictures from the Nazi era, watching and waiting with his lamp on his forehead and with a predilection for half-naked young women like Pérez Nuix on that other day and like the woman with her skirt hitched up that night in the Ladies' room, just like his fierce antecedents from the Middle Ages and the Renaissance, who pursued maidens through woods and over fields; the poor, desperate women, according to the fantasies illustrated in the pictures, tore their clothes in their futile flight. While for us Latins, whose words are more or less obliged to have a gender, death is a feminine being and old too, the decrepit old lady with the scythe of so many paintings and so many illustrations, and perhaps that is why her victims are more often men than women, although she visits and hunts us all or literally cuts us down with her rustic tool, it makes sense for her to be old, she's been working furiously for a long time now and hasn't stopped for a single hour, day or night, since she made her debut with that first remote, unknown dead man who is still waiting for the world to end and for no one else to be left, in order finally to be judged and to tell his story and to set out his case, 'when all those legs and arms and heads, chopped off in a battle, shall join together at the latter day, and cry all, "We died at such a place."' And it makes sense, too, that in the Germanic imagination he should be a knight in his prime, a strong, spirited warrior, capable of relentlessly snatching lives, a skilled professional with the cold arms of a disciplined sergeant, because no other being could cope with such an infinite task in those ancient times: and many centuries later, the Nazi leaders faced the same problem and sought faster, cheaper, less tiring methods of mass extermination, and so resorted to the intelligence of the men in white coats, physicists and chemists and biologists, as well as doctors wearing head-lamps, killing is not so easy, it takes time. And, of course, it's tiring, even exhausting.

'We died at such a place,' Wheeler had said to me in his own language, quoting from Shakespeare, and one assumes that this Final Judgement foreseen by the steadfast faith of the times, with the whole of the world's history recounted at once and in detail by all those people who had made and composed it, from the powerful emperor who left a more enduring mark to the newborn baby who departed this earth with his first cry and never traversed it or set foot on it and did not leave in anyone's memory even the image of his perfectly formed face, one assumes that on that final day, with all time and all space transformed into a madhouse and an uproar, as I had suggested to Wheeler—perhaps that day would already belong to eternity, and thus would have existence but not duration—the condemned and those who'd condemned them, the betrayed and their betrayers, the persecuted and their persecutors, the tortured and their torturers, the mutilated and their mutilators, the murdered and their murderers, the victims and their executioners, along with those who urged them on or issued the order, would also all meet up and gather together and once more see each other's faces as they stood before that Judge to whom no one lies (a judge lenient or wrathful, implacable or kindly, that is something no one knows). And all of them would have great difficulty justifying their respective causes and thereby their innocence or the attenuation of their guilt, that was what the soldiers were saying to Henry V (now I knew which Shakespeare king it was) when he joined them incognito, wrapped in a cloak, on the eve of battle, as Wheeler remembered and described, all of them ready for combat; and one of them even said: 'If the cause be not good, the king himself hath a heavy reckoning to make.'

All those dead would exchange reproaches, accusations,

charges: 'You killed me and I had done you no harm at all.' 'I died because of you and your flippant comments.' 'You sacrificed me in order to destroy another who was your enemy, you didn't even know of my existence, but that didn't stop you cutting it short, after the bombardment, I was just a number to you, or not even that, a mere unit of that number then hidden away in your secret files.' 'I died by my own hand because I could no longer live with the deaths I had caused; believe me when I say that the harm I did by killing myself cost me great effort and much fear and terrible anticipatory remorse; but I could no longer carry on as if it had never happened and as if those deaths were not mine.' 'You fired a bullet into the back of my neck in the gutter of a street I had never seen before, although it could not have been far away, we took no time at all to get there from the detention centre in Calle Fomento from which you dragged me at night and into which you had thrown me that morning after stopping me in the street, because I was wearing a tie, you said, and was carrying a membership card to some club you didn't like, "A lot of Falangists go there," you said, and to which I had foolishly applied in order to be like my elder brother, who was in hiding at the time, I was seventeen and didn't even know what it meant, and you didn't allow me time to find out or to go back to my comic books which were my great joy and passion, I knew nothing about politics,' my Uncle Alfonso would say when he met up again with the forgetful militiamen who had killed him: they would scarcely remember him, still less the young woman who was with him and who shared the same fate, a bullet in the temple or perhaps the back of the neck, or perhaps in the ear. 'You showed no mercy and I felt such pain as you could never imagine all the days of your life or of your death in infinite waiting for this final day, and you falsely accused me even though you were perfectly aware of the absolute falsity of your accusation, and you demanded that I give you names and confess to betrayals I never committed, knowing that I could not do so,' Nin would say to those two or three men—all of them former comrades: Orlov certainly, possibly Bielov, perhaps Contreras—who exasperatedly interrogated and tortured him in Alcalá de Henares and, according to one grim source, flayed him alive. 'You fired poisoned bullets at me, but didn't smear them with enough poison to kill me at once, with the botulin they brought you from America and which gnawed away at me for seven whole days without actually killing me or bringing to an end the suffering and the fury, and if you had been better shots, there would have been no need to wait for it to take effect and I would have been spared that long, wretched period of dying,' the Nazi Heydrich would say to the two Czech resisters or students who machine-gunned his car in Prague and hurled grenades, and who were trained and equipped by the British Special Operations Executive, the SOE, whose director, Spooner, planned the attempt. 'Yes, you committed a grave and frivolous crime by not honing your marksmanship and ensuring that the Nazi was blown to bits at once, because every night that he lay dying, they took a hundred of us out to be shot, and he survived for one long, bloody week,' those same resisters and those in charge of the SOE would be told by the seven hundred hostages who continued to be executed until the slow-acting poison finally overcame both Heydrich's powers of endurance and his rage. 'We died on June 10, 1942, in Lidice, you didn't leave a soul alive in the whole village, you killed us all regardless of age or sex, you killed the men right there and took the women to the camp at Ravensbrück to die more slowly, simply because it was our bad luck to live in the place where the agents who were behind the Reich Protector's slow death parachuted into our occupied lands of Bohemia and Moravia, it wasn't enough for you just to loathe us and to punish a few of us as possible collaborators, why waste time finding out or checking anything, you simply hated our entire line and you destroyed it so that no memory of it would exist or survive, and you murdered us all so that there wouldn't even be anyone to remember what no longer existed,' the Nazi occupiers would be told by the 199 men and the 184 women of that Czech village who were victims of the reprisals for Heydrich's eventual death, down to the last old man and almost the last child, for there were three of the latter, very young and 'of Aryan appearance', who, it was judged, would be capable of being re-educated as Germans and so were saved; they could not, however, save their memory. 'You killed me so that I would write no more poetry after my twenty-ninth year, you've stolen my manhood, I thought as I fell to the wine-spattered floor that later became soaked with my blood; but I was careless, you were quicker than me, and I would have done just the same to you, your life was as valuable as mine then, even though you had written nothing, but it's quite another matter for these other selfish men to come along and hate you simply because you cut short my art and deprived them of further enjoyment; but I, your dead victim, have no complaints, nor anything to blame you for,' the dramatist and poet Marlowe would say in the inn at Deptford to his knifer Ingram Frizer, if, of course, that is his definitive name, a name that has changed or remained unknown over the centuries. 'You had two henchmen plunge me head first into a butt of your disgusting wine and drown me, poor me, poor Clarence, held by the legs, which remained outside the butt and flailed about ridiculously until my lungs' final intoxication, betrayed and humiliated and killed by the black, opaque cunning of your hideous, indefatigable tongue,' George, Duke of Clarence would say to the murderous English king who was also one of Shakespeare's kings.

Oh yes, on that last day, when all times, perhaps suspended and unmoving, are brought together, these words would ring out again and again until they made the dead retch, even those who had murdered (but none of them had ever imagined the final result of the final addition, because when things end they have a number), and even the Judge to whom no one lies, who might perhaps feel tempted to forget his promise and his plans and cancel for ever that eternal, pestilential assembly: 'I died in such a place and on such a date and in such a manner, and you killed me, you placed me in the path of the bullet, the bomb, the grenade or the torch, of the stone, the arrow, the sword or the spear, you ordered me to step out and meet the bayonet, the scimitar, the machete or the axe, the dagger, the club, the musket or the sabre, you killed me or you were the cause of my death. May it all now sit heavy on your soul and may you feel the pinprick in your breast.' And the accused would always answer: 'I had to do it, I was defending my God, my king, my country, my culture, my race; my flag, my legend, my language, my class, my space; my honour, my family, my strongbox, my purse, and my socks. And in short, I was afraid.' (That last was a line from a poem too, and I repeated it to myself later out loud, when I was in bed: 'And in short, I was afraid'; several times, because that night I was applying it to myself or endorsing it: 'And in short, I was afraid.') Or else they would resort to this excuse: 'I had to do it in order to avoid a greater evil, or so I thought.' Because before that weary, nauseous Judge they would not be able to claim: 'I didn't intend to do it, I knew nothing about it, it happened against my will, as if befuddled by the tortuous smokescreen of dreams, it was part of my theoretical, parenthetical life, the life that does not really count, it only half happened and without my full consent.' Any judge hearing the case would say: 'Overruled, case dismissed.' No, they would not be able to make such claims before the judge who was now going to hear their case, and yet there would be some who would: they're always unmistakable, I've known them myself in my own lifetime. There is never any shortage of them.

How comforting it must have been, that distant hope or postponed reward or deferred justice, that prospect, that vision, that idea, for those people of steadfast faith during the many centuries when they believed it to be true and imagined it and nurtured it, as if it were part of a knowledge common to everyone, the illiterate and the learned, the wealthy and the needy, and when it was more like a kind of prescience than a promise or a desideratum. What a consoling idea, especially for all those who were forever subjugated, for those who knew they were destined to suffer in life—throughout their entire meek life, with no escape and no respite—injustices and abuses and humiliations that would go unpunished, with no hope of any possible reparation for their grievances nor of any conceivable chastisement for the offending parties, who were more powerful or more cruel, or simply more determined. 'I won't see it here,' they would think, biting their lower lip or their tongue until it hurt, and then easing their bite, 'not in this stubborn, unequal world, not in its unchanging order which I cannot alter and which causes me such harm, not in the skewed harmony that governs it and that is already digging my grave in order to drive me out early; but in that other world I will, when time comes to an end and we are all gathered together, all invited, without exception, to the great dance of suffering and contentment, and I will be told that I was right and will be rewarded by that Judge to whom one cannot lie because he knows already what went on, the Judge who has been everywhere and seen and heard everything, even the most trivial and insignificant of things in the world as a whole or in a single existence; what happened to me today, the terrible insult which I myself will forget if I live a few more years and it doesn't occur again, or else occurs so often that I will get the different occasions muddled up and, for my own sake, become used to it and cease to see it as a crime, no, that will not be forgotten by the Judge who remembers everything in his all-embracing record or infinite archive of the history of time, from the first hour to the last day.' What an enormous solace to utter solitude it must have been to believe that we were seen and even spied upon at every moment of our few, miserable days, with superhuman perspicacity and attention and with every tiresome detail and vacuous thought supernaturally noted and stored away: that is how it must have been if it truly existed, no human mind could have stood it, knowing and remembering everything about each person from each age, knowing it permanently, without a single fact about anyone ever going to waste, however dispensable it was and even if it neither added nor subtracted anything: a real affliction, a curse, a torment or even heaven's version of hell itself, perhaps the Judge would come to regret his omniscience with all those goings-on, become resentful of that proliferation of boring, puerile, stupid and entirely superfluous events, or else would have turned to drink in order to grow forgetful (just a little snifter now and then), or else become an opium addict (leisurely smoking the occasional pipe, to empty himself of knowledge).

'There are many individuals who experience their life as if it were the material for some detailed report,' I had said to Tupra when interpreting Dick Dearlove for him, 'they inhabit that life pending its hypothetical or future plot. They don't give it much thought, it's just a way of experiencing things, companionable, let's say, as if there were always spectators of or permanent witnesses to their activities and passivities, even their most futile steps and during the dullest of times. Perhaps this narcissistic daydream prevalent among so many of our contemporaries, and sometimes known as "consciousness", is nothing more than a substitute for the old idea or vague perception of the omnipresence of God, who was always watching and saw every second of each of our lives, it was very flattering in a way, and a relief, despite the inconveniences, that is, the implicit element of threat and punishment and the terrifying belief that nothing could ever be concealed from everyone and for ever; in any case, three or four generations of predominant doubt and incredulity are not enough for Man to accept that his gruelling and unasked-for existence goes on without anyone ever observing or watching or even taking an interest in it, without anyone judging it or disapproving of it.'

Perhaps even the most atheistic of men would find that hard to accept, without doing himself rational violence. And perhaps the narrative horror or disgust I had mentioned to

Tupra—maybe all of us feel it to some extent, not just the Dearloves of this world—also came from the old days of steadfast faith, when a whole lifetime of virtue and good deeds and abiding by the rules could be destroyed by a single grave sin committed at the last moment—a mortal sin they called it, the record didn't mince its words—with no room for repentance or forgiveness, any proposed mending of ways being barely credible given the brief amount of time remaining to the sinner, the old must have felt in their final years as if they were walking on hot bricks, trying not to succumb to untimely temptations, or, which comes to the same thing, trying to avoid any narrative error or blot that might mar their end and see them condemned when the Day of Judgement came. It seemed an unfair system, whether or not it was divine, I don't know, but it was certainly not very human, relying too much on the succession or order of words, deeds, omissions, and thoughts, I could not help recalling one of the reasons my father had given me for never having done anything to get back at his betrayer Del Real, no settling of accounts or belated seeking of compensation, when he could have done so after the death of the tyrant, the now remote Franco for whom the traitor performed an early service and was subsequently rewarded with university posts and, as regards that early service rendered, with the assured protection of the former's barbarous laws for thirty-six and a half years. Thirty-six years of immunity, from May 1939 to November 1975: a few more years than Marlowe enjoyed, twice the number lived by my uncle Alfonso . . . 'It would have given him a sort of *a posteriori* justification, a false validation, an anachronistic motive for his action,' my father had told me when I asked him about his false friend. 'Bear in mind that when you look at your life as a whole the chronological aspect gradually diminishes in importance, you make less of a distinction between what happened before and what happened afterwards, between actions and their consequences, between decisions and what they unleash. He might have thought that I had, in fact, done him some harm, it didn't matter when, and then he would have gone to his grave feeling more at peace with himself. And that wasn't and hasn't been the case. I never wronged him in any way, I didn't harm him and I never have, either before or afterwards or, needless to say, at the time . . .'

Yes, my father and Wheeler were both very old now, and perhaps in their last years they, too, had the feeling that they were walking on hot bricks, not out of any sense of religious fear, but out of biographical dread; or perhaps not, perhaps they merely feared becoming besmirched. My father seemed quite contented and serene in his present, with a few surviving female friends and with his children and grandchildren who visited him and made him talk about the past, both personal and collective, and that is always a great solace (I had not been there much lately, what with my new departure for England and the deliberate daze in which I lived in order not to think too much about my own present, which was not, as yet, a source of solace; he never said as much to me, but when we spoke on the phone or wrote—the latter to please him: 'I hate it when the postbox is always empty, or full of nothing but advertising flyers and other rubbish'—I realised that he missed me, at least a little); he would surely not foresee any dramatic changes, or some harmful episode that would end up ruining a story whose essence had been set down in far more difficult times than the present day, and which he had already told to himself, if not with pride, at least without any feelings of disgust and with few embellishments, or so I imagined; nor was it likely that it would become besmirched in the eyes of others, even in the demanding eyes of a son, nor was it likely, therefore, that he would betray my trust, unless, one day, I were to make some unfortunate discovery, and something that was hidden ceased to be hidden. (I, on the other hand, was in a position to betray his trust and that of anyone else, this was the disadvantage of having lived only half one's life; and I would doubtless already have betrayed the trust of a few other people too, certainly that of Luisa and of my children.)

As regards Wheeler, maybe he was more at risk, because he was only the simulacrum of an old man and because behind his meek and venerable appearance he still concealed energetic, almost acrobatic machinations, and behind his absent-minded digressions an observant mind, analytical, anticipatory, interpretative, and one that was ceaselessly judging; he seemed disposed to not only intervene in the diminishing time that remained to him, dictating as far as possible its final contents, rather than leaving it in the hands of chance, but ready also to participate in and to influence the odd minor worldly matter, even if it was only through friends, through me or through Tupra, or someone else unknown to myself or to Tupra, who knows how many others went to visit him in his house by the river, or simply phoned him or spoke to him with Mrs Berry as intermediary, or even perhaps wrote him letters. He had, for a start, put me in touch with Tupra and with everything that flowed from that, this would have been a spontaneous move on his part, an intervention in my life and a helping hand to Bertram, at the very least an offer, for only he could have offered me to the group and to the building with no name to which I now belonged, almost without realising it, although at the end of that night, I realised more clearly that I did belong. Wheeler had not given up plotting, manoeuvring, manipulating, and directing, and in that sense he risked not only becoming besmirched with ashes or coals, but getting burned too. He did not seem to feel he was being in any way reckless, nor, of course, did my father, each had his own distinct and even opposing brand of recklessness: but it might be that Juan Deza considered himself prepared, ready, and with everything in order, while Peter Wheeler, on the other hand, felt hopeless and unfinished, even his own name had been substituted, cancelled out, at least that was how I saw it with my imperfect perception; it would have been risky, excessive, unjust to say that the former felt himself to be saved and the latter damned, even if only in narrative terms, and not at all in moral ones. I don't know, perhaps Wheeler was able to apply to himself his own conviction that individuals carry their probabilities in their veins, and time, temptation, and circumstance will lead them at last to their fulfilment; and he knew his own probabilities well, possibly he always had, but now he knew from experience too; and he knew that he had enjoyed all three of those things in abundance, especially time, in order to be persuasive and to make himself more dangerous and more despicable even than his enemies, and to develop superior and more deadly powers of invention; to take advantage of the mass of people, who are silly and frivolous and credulous, on whom it is easy to strike a match and start a fire, and for that fire to spread like the worst of epidemics; to have others fall into the most appalling and destructive of misfortunes from which they never emerge, and thereby transform those thus condemned into casualties, into non-persons, into felled trees from which the rotten wood could be chopped away; time to spread outbreaks of cholera, malaria, and plague, and, often, to set in motion the process of total denial, of who you are and who you were, of what you do and what you did, of what you expect and what you expected, of your aims and your intentions, of your professions of faith, your ideas, your greatest loyalties, your motives . . . He knew that everything could be distorted, twisted, annulled, erased. And he was aware that at the end of any reasonably long life, however monotonous it might have been, however anodyne and grey and uneventful, there would always be too many memories and too many contradictions, too many sacrifices and omissions and changes, a lot of retreats, a lot of flags lowered, and a lot of acts of disloyalty, or perhaps they were all just white flags of surrender. 'And it's not easy to put all that in order,' he had said, 'even to recount it to yourself. Too much accumu-lation . . . My memory is so full that sometimes I can't bear it. I'd like to lose more of it, I'd like to empty it a little. No, that's not true . . . I only wish it wasn't quite so full.' And then he had added some words which I remembered well (ever since then they have kept coming back to me like an occasional echo, or perhaps not that occasional): 'Life is not recountable, and it seems extraordinary that men have spent all the centuries we know anything about devoted to doing just that . . . Sometimes I think it would be best to abandon the custom altogether and simply allow things to happen. And then just leave them be.'

Yes, perhaps Wheeler would have declined to speak on that famous last day: he would have scorned setting out his case and overwhelming the weary Judge with his carefully honed arguments and a list of his most notable deeds or with his entire history since birth, he would have scorned asking for or expecting justice or a mercy that he would doubtless find offensive, had he lived and died in a time when the majority of people still believed in such a day. Perhaps he would have preferred to avail himself of the Miranda law applied to anyone arrested in America (it was once recited to me, albeit imperfectly), I mean to create it *avant la lettre* and, of course, give it a different name in the midst of that great dance, so that its benefits or disadvantages would not, in any case, have spread beyond the living (although, on that day, I realised, there would be no one living, and everything would be *après la lettre*). Wheeler might have kept silent and thus saved the Judge a drink or two, or half a pipe of opium, leaving him, instead, the task of ordering and recounting, after all, he had seen everything and heard everything, why bother telling him your story and enduring the inevitable shame and effort, it would be a waste of time even though there would be no time or only a kind of absurd time that would have a beginning but no end. And had he been questioned, or if the Judge had urged him to defend himself or make some kind of allegation—'What have you got to say to that, Peter Rylands and Peter Wheeler of Christchurch in New Zealand?'—he would not even have answered 'Nothing', but would have remained silent, avoiding until the very end any careless talk, even his own and even when surrounded by it, because that would be the supreme day of careless talk and imprudent conversation, of loquacity and verbiage and full-scale confessions, a day made for reproaches and total justifications, of accusations and defences, excuses, appeals, furious denials and biased testimonies, for the odd bit of naive perjury and much telling of tales ('I didn't want to, I had nothing to do with it', 'You can search me if you like', 'It wasn't me', 'I only did it under duress', 'They put a gun to my head, I had to do it', 'It was his fault, her fault, their fault, everybody's fault but mine'); the ideal day to offload all those infinite deaths and to blame them on someone else. Yes, perhaps Wheeler would have refused to participate in that worldwide chattering, and decided not to play any trump card in that unequal game: 'Keep quiet and don't say a word, not even to save yourself. Put your voice away, hide it, swallow it even if it chokes you, pretend the cat's got your tongue. Keep quiet, and save yourself.'

That is what Sir Peter Wheeler had done, kept silent from the start, when I finally asked him and Mrs Berry, over Sunday lunch or, rather, afterwards, just before I got up from the table and left for the station to catch the train back to London, about the bloodstain at the top of his stairs.

'Before I forget,' I had said, taking advantage of a pause, the kind that heralds or brings about farewells, 'last night I cleaned up a bloodstain on the stairs, at the top of the first flight, when I went up to my room.' And I pointed backwards with my thumb at the first few stairs. In fact, it had happened when I was coming downstairs, carrying *From Russia with Love* as if it were a treasure, the copy dedicated to Wheeler by the former Commander Fleming of the Naval Intelligence Division ('. . . who may know better. *Salud!*'), but that didn't matter and I didn't want Peter to take me for a tattletale, or a *chafardero*, as they say in the Castilian spoken in Catalonia. 'I don't know where it came from, but it wasn't a small drop. Do either of you have any idea?'

It was Mrs Berry who answered, the odder the question is,

the more immediately a reply is required, although this one consisted only in repeating a word:

'A bloodstain?' she said, and her eyebrows arched of their own accord and not apparently in response to any previous command. And then she added, slightly annoyed: 'How could I possibly not have seen it on my way up to my room, especially if it was a large stain,' and thus she appeared to deflect the matter and turn it into a possible act of negligence on her part. 'At the top of the stairs, you say, Jack? How odd.' And she eyed with disgust the lower steps I had pointed to, as if the thing I had told her about were still visible—although I had also told her that I had cleaned it up—and in such an unfortunate place too. 'I'm so sorry to have put you to all that trouble, Jack.'

I glanced at Wheeler, who had opened his eyes very wide and his mouth just a little, a look of sufficient surprise to warrant the expression 'left speechless'. Or was it merely a look of partial incomprehension, as if the occasional slowness of his years were processing my question or news with bewilderment and even difficulty; as if he were thinking: 'Did I hear correctly, did he say blood? Did he mispronounce it, or did he actually say bloodstain? He may be foreign, but his pronunciation rarely lets him down, except in the case of strange or unusual words that he has perhaps never heard and only seen written down, but then he is conscious of his own uncertainty, and he hesitates and asks before saying them. Or was it me, perhaps I wasn't concentrating and didn't understand.' Those, at least, seemed to be his thoughts, but they couldn't have been because Mrs Berry had immediately repeated 'A bloodstain?' and there could be no doubts about *her* pronunciation.

'Don't worry, Mrs Berry, it was no trouble at all, besides, I wasn't tired,' I replied. 'It's just that I can't understand where it could have come from. I thought it must have come from me, that I had inadvertently cut myself, but I felt myself all over and I hadn't. So you've no idea either?' I insisted somewhat hesitantly.

Mrs Berry looked at Wheeler in perplexity, as if asking him

a question with her eyes, or, it occurred to me, that glance might merely have been one of consultation or even of concern for me, because there I was claiming to have cleaned up some peculiar and highly improbable stain in the middle of the night. Peter, however, remained silent, with his metallic or mineral eyes very wide (in the daylight, they were like chalcedony) and his lips still parted (but not so much as to merit the description 'open-mouthed').

'Not really,' she replied. 'Perhaps a guest cut himself when he went up to the bathroom on the second floor, I saw several people go up there during the evening . . . Where was it exactly?'

I stood up and so did she ('I'll show you'), I led her to the stairs, went up the first flight two steps at a time, and she followed more sedately behind.

'Here,' I said, and pointed to the approximate place. I couldn't be more exact because spatial memory is imprecise unless there is some established, unchanging reference point, and not a trace was left, you couldn't even see where I had rubbed, everything was smooth and immaculate, I had done a good, thorough job, I would have made an excellent servant in another life, or a conscientious, although probably not very illustrious, janitor. 'It was more or less here,' I added, 'about an inch and a half in diameter, perhaps two. And what's so odd is that there was no trail, just that one drop. Like a single footstep.'

Mrs Berry bent over to study the floor more closely. I had crouched down and was tapping on the wooden boards with my five fingers, my hand in the shape of a claw, as if trying to summon up something from the wood, only there was nothing to invoke and nothing that could burst forth from it. 'I knew it,' I thought fleetingly, 'I should have left a bit of the rim, there was a reason why it resisted being erased.' Peter had also got up from the table now, rather more calmly, and had followed us to the foot of the stairs, but he did not come up. He stood there with his hands resting on his walking stick as if it were a sword stuck in the earth in a moment of temporary rest, looking up, looking at us with that gaze one often sees in the old even when they are in company and talking animatedly, the eyes become dull, the iris dilated, staring far, far off back into the past, as if their owners really could physically see with them, could see their memories I mean, sometimes even the old and blind have this gaze, like the poet Milton in his dream, and it is not an absent look, but a very focused one, focused on something a very long way off. And Wheeler was still saying nothing.

'That big? But there's nothing here,' said Mrs Berry. The wood was, indeed, polished, shining, waxed, as if it had never been touched. 'What did you use to clean up the stain?'

'I got some cotton balls and rubbing alcohol from the bathroom downstairs. I did it very slowly and carefully. I didn't want to dirty one of your cloths or leave a mark.'

'Well, you certainly succeeded, Jack,' said Mrs Berry approvingly, still staring hard at the blank floor, but I thought I noticed just a hint of irony in her words. She was possibly beginning not to believe me. 'Are you sure it was blood, Jack? It couldn't have been a drop of liqueur or wine that someone spilled? Or some juice from the roast beef, from a slice that slipped off someone's plate? I'm afraid Lord Rymer wasn't the only one who was a bit unsteady on his feet last night. And the meat was *très saignante*, and some people had gravy with it. Could you have mistaken the juice or the gravy for blood? That would explain why there was no trail, a piece of meat falls from a plate and leaves just one mark. It doesn't drip.' I thought: 'She thinks I was drunk and that I imagined it all; true enough, a rare steak would just fall onto the floor, plop, but they weren't steaks, they were slices of beef.' And then I remembered that I couldn't even retrieve the bloodstained cotton balls to show her, I had put them down the toilet, not in the waste paper basket, and, naturally enough, had pulled the chain; besides, it would have looked very odd if I had gone and rummaged around in the waste paper basket, it was fortunate I couldn't really, she would have taken me for a fool, a maniac.

'I didn't taste it, if that's what you mean, Mrs Berry,' I said and there must have been a touch of disappointment in my voice, or hurt pride. 'But I know blood when I see it, believe me. I can tell the difference.'

'Well, then, that's very odd indeed.' That is what Mrs Berry said, as if bringing the inspection and the whole matter to a close; it was as if she had said: 'Don't go on, Jack, what more do you expect of us? I don't know anything about it and I didn't see it, neither did Peter. And it's not like me to miss a stain like that, certainly not on the way up to my room. Don't you see how difficult it is?'

I removed my fingers from the floorboards, I got up, I turned more towards Wheeler, I regarded him from above. He had not said a thing, but it seemed to me that this was not another oral blockage like the one that had afflicted him shortly before in the garden, after the episode with the low-flying helicopter, or the previous night, when we were alone and he could not get himself to come out with the ridiculous word 'cushion'. It did not seem to me that any kind of prescience was involved at all, his elderly gaze was no longer staring into a future that was as uncertain and, therefore, as blank and smooth as the floorboards, I was sure of that, rather, in his current state of amazement, it reached much further, to something beyond my head and Mrs Berry's head, at which his gaze was directed, although without actually focusing on that either or not entirely, and his wide eyes gave him a contradictory expression, almost like that of a child who discovers or sees something for the first time, something that does not frighten or repel or attract, but which produces a sense of shock, or else some flash of intuitive knowledge, or even a kind of enchantment. He was looking at something that was rough in texture, with a design or a figure on it, unlike the floor, but it wasn't clear to me at all whether its outline was firm and distinct or if it belonged to the past. It was as if he were gazing into limbo, that enviable place, the only one, on that final day, which, according to ancient speculations, would be free of judgements and calculations and to which the Judge would withdraw now and then for some peace and quiet and to take a breather from all the atrocities and all the perfections, from the wild excuses and the overblown aspirations, perhaps to enjoy a small snack to restore strength and patience for the interminable sessions, and even to take a sip from the divine hip flask, a little trip to perk him up, before returning to the great ballroom where he would continue listening to those millions and millions of imbroglios and confused, pathetic, ridiculous stories.

'And you have no idea what it could have been either, Peter.' I spoke directly to him now, it was more a statement than a question, but also, I realised, an attempt to elicit some verbal response from him about the blood or not blood that I had seen or not seen, something spoken in his own voice and not through the intermediary of Mrs Berry, who had commandeered the conjectures and responses. In a way, there was nothing strange about that, it was only logical, she was in charge of the upkeep of the house, of its spotlessness or cleanliness as well as of its imperfections and stains. She was what is known in English as the housekeeper, literally the person who tends or looks after the house.

'No.' Wheeler's negative was immediate, he wasn't miles away, he had, after all, been listening to what was being said. His gaze may have gone off travelling, but it had not got lost. 'That's very odd indeed,' he repeated, although he did not say this in the same categorical tone as his housekeeper. 'That's very odd indeed,' he said in English, as if it were just a conventional phrase, a more or less acceptable and inoffensive way of leaving the matter hanging in the air, or of packing it off to limbo, where everything is overruled and there is never any case to be answered, because no one cares what happens there. He picked up his sword, held it for a moment in both hands as if about to deal a two-handed blow, and then turned to go back to the table and finish dessert. For me this was a sign that I had better stop there, give up, resign myself. I came down the stairs, letting Mrs Berry go first, and as we followed him in, I made only one more comment on the subject:

'I had to use a lot of cotton balls to clean up the stain. There won't be many left, so you'd better buy some more. The same goes for the rubbing alcohol too.' That is what I said. I felt it was only fair to warn them, so that they would not go thinking that I had imagined or invented that too.

I thought of another possibility then, yes, another one occurred to me as I left the Ladies' room or, rather, afterwards, that same night, but some hours later, when I was trying in vain to get to sleep, managing at most a kind of meditative doze during which I was thinking how much had been revealed to me in the course of events and how much I had pushed to one side. Yes, it was probably afterwards, because when I left the toilet I was in a hurry and my attention was focused on what was happening outside, although I must have had some inkling of it while I was in the Ladies' room, it was an idea that would never have crossed Wheeler's mind or Mrs Berry's for that matter, indeed, it didn't even cross mine until that moment, after I had seen the woman with the abundant thighs sitting on the toilet, no, abundant makes them sound fat, but they weren't, they were, how can I put it, magnificence, formidability, pure presence. A summons. 'A woman is wearing no panties,' I thought, 'although she is wearing tights, possibly the sort you can get nowadays that come halfway up the thigh like stockings, but which are held up by elastic, a graceless substitute for old-fashioned garters, the kind worn by that imminent heiress-cum-spouse—the one who stayed the night and for breakfast as well and whose husband-to-be and cuckold-that-was appeared to be obsessed with her cell phone or to consider it a military objective—at least she wore them on the one occasion when I saw her take them off or when I took them off for her, I can't really remember the incident in any detail.' I remembered and thought this while lying in bed, when I wasn't, in fact, particularly interested in remembering, it was entirely involuntary. 'A woman decides not to wear panties to Wheeler's cold buffet, some women take a pride in doing without this particular item of clothing in order to feel terribly avant-garde and radical, or they do so only occasionally and provocatively in order to risk being seen if they wear a short or very short skirt and there are going to be a lot of witnesses present (a meeting, a banquet, a premiere, a class if they're students and the male teacher always stands in front), or to annoy a husband whom they inform of this intimate detail on the way to the party and who is troubled by it, or to provoke an outbreak of fleeting and very basic desire where it did not exist or perhaps never would have existed—a glimpse, a glimmer—and which might then become persistent or pro-longed—a condensation, an increase—quite a few women learned this from that famous film starring Sharon Stone and Kirk Douglas's witch-faced son.

This woman goes up to the bathroom on the second floor, the one downstairs is occupied, or perhaps she goes up in search of an empty room in which someone is already waiting or where someone will join her after a minute or never does, an arranged meeting, but snatched and hurried, what is graphically and vulgarly known in Spanish as 'un mete y saca' and in English as a quickie (very vulgarly: not that it matters, the thought is more vulgar than the word, or it is for those of us who tend to avoid verbal vulgarity so that it at least has some meaning when we do resort to it), an absence of panties in such situations is perfect, not that they need be an impediment, they just have to be pushed delicately aside with a couple of fingers—mind you don't pinch anything—at the right moment. This woman in the skirt goes upstairs, her high heels make a noise on the floor-boards or no noise at all on the carpeted part, and as ill luck would have it—although, depending on your point of view, the host or the unusually sharp-eyed guest has the worse luck—just at the moment when she gets to the top of the stairs and pauses for an instant looking for the most suitable door or the one agreed upon, her period suddenly starts—she had doubtless had a feeling that it would, but not much or not a strong enough feeling—in the form of a drop that falls to the floor, there being no fabric to prevent it; but it's still in the very early stages and is only a drop, the first, a single drop, there's no trail because it isn't as yet a steady flow and does not immediately continue, and so she might not notice its arrival until a little later, when she has already gone into the bathroom and can improvise a temporary solution or when the man waiting for her notices this different, warmer moistness and has already stained himself, the stain on the wooden floor remains there unnoticed, which is why it's not cleaned up until much later that night, when I go upstairs in search of a book and when I come down again carrying that book, I find the stain, I see it, and think that I mustn't leave it there now that I know it exists: it is up to me to remove it, otherwise Wheeler might slip on it in the morning—although, by then, it will have dried—and he can't be allowed to fall over at his age, best to avoid any risk and save him.'

My former schoolfriend Comendador had thought of this menstrual possibility more quickly than I had, but he could actually see the young woman there before him when he saw the blood, and had noticed some minuscule red drops on her T-shirt and another larger one on her sheets, so it was easier for him to come up with the idea, and, besides, we—he certainly and I very probably—would never know if that was the correct explanation for those respective stains, although it would be for the stains left on a tile and on one white shoe by the woman in the toilet cubicle who had carried herself with such aplomb. But who knows.

Suddenly I found myself trying to recall which of the women at Wheeler's party had been wearing a skirt (this was half involuntary too, or perhaps it is simply that any kind of inventory brings on partial sleep): Beryl had, of course, been wearing a skirt and a very eye-catching one at that, and she might well have dispensed with any underwear, judging by the eagerness with which De la Garza was trying, from his position on a very low pouffe, to keep his gaze fixed pretty much on a level with her long legs (thighs you could toboggan down, he had said, the freak); and it would have been just like her to want to embarrass Tupra by such an audacious move (she wouldn't have told him until they were in the car and nearly at Oxford), or else, for all her apparent disdain, she had been trying to re-seduce him in that rough and rudimentary way, barely touching and keeping a certain distance, with no need for any personal, psychological, sentimental or biographical effort, only animal, which requires no effort at all. Mrs Fahy, the wife of the soporific Irish historian, Professor Fahy, had also been wearing a skirt, as had the tragic (by dint of marriage) Labour mayoress of the unhappy towns of Eynsham or Ewelme or Bruern or Rycote, or perhaps of that most ill-famed of places in Oxfordshire since the far-off days of Marlowe, Hog's Norton; but both ladies were long past the age of such regular occur-rences, as was Mrs Berry, who was clearly much younger than Wheeler, but not four decades younger or even three or two and a half, indeed, I immediately felt ashamed to be thinking of her or of them (but especially of her, for I had known and respected her for such a long time, ever since she had worked for Toby Rylands) in such circumstances and at her age, I mean in society and with no panties, I rejected the idea out of hand, largely because it seemed so irreverent, and partly out of hypo-thetical compassion, I reproached myself for such thoughts. As for the Deaness of York, who had aroused such coarse passions in De la Garza ('Shit, get a load of that,' the idiot had said), it seemed hazardous to make any pronouncement on the current influence of the moon on her body, widowhood blurs age and can be most deceptive, it makes the very young seem older and rejuvenates those no longer in the first flush of youth; nevertheless, she had been wearing a skirt, plus, I would have said, a vintage petticoat and an even more vintage girdle, and I could not, therefore, believe that the unassailable dowager of a clergyman would ever have renounced her more intimate garments (possibly not even alone in her bed, and certainly not in someone else's house and with a lot of other people present). Some of the women present had been wearing trousers, but not Harriet Buckley, the newly divorced medical doctor, who, according to Tupra, might have been more interested that night in making investigations in that area than Beryl or Mrs Wadman (not, of course, her real name); I had paid no attention to her nor spoken with her beyond the introductions, but she was not lacking in a certain basic attractiveness, indeed, it was a miracle she did not burst out of her skirt, not because she was fat, but because her skirt was so tight, so close-fitting, so figure-hugging (these apparent redundancies are necessary to give an idea of just how tight it was), and she kept her glasses on throughout the evening, which gave her a vaguely lascivious air, like a spry, young secretary out of a 1950s American comedy (a pure fantasy figure); the pantie-less doctor seemed to me an acceptable idea, well, at least it didn't set my teeth on edge or prick my conscience (or only slightly), nor did the idea of an equally naked Beryl or a young woman who had drifted around all evening looking bored and whose identity I never discovered, she was doubtless the student daughter of one of the guests, possibly even of Buckley herself: at any rate, I had judged her from afar to be capricious and bold and had noticed a hint of licentiousness about her mouth (wide-spaced incisors; lips that never managed entirely to close nor, consequently, to conceal those lewd teeth); I did not feel it was unfair of me to imagine her to be flighty, I mean, when it came to what she wore or did not wear under her skirt.

One of these three women must have chosen an unfortunate moment to go up to the first floor and must have lost or released without noticing that one drop of blood, as had the Central American woman who had thanked me, which meant that she had not noticed the drop on her shoe until I had pointed it out to her. It was, however, an unlikely conjunction of factors at Wheeler's party, and I did not even know if such unpreparedness and the consequent stain on the floor were technically possible (technically or physiologically, if I can put it like that). I realised that in London I had no close female friend or regular lover whom I could ask about this, no one I knew well enough; in Madrid I had, and in my normal life I would immediately have consulted Luisa, then there was my sister, and old female friends and former girlfriends, 'old flames' as Beryl was to Tupra, or Tupra was to Beryl, she being more indifferent to their past. 'My normal life': I could not get used to the idea that it was no longer normal, I had been expelled from it or else my tomb was there, dug down deep inside it; I still had the illusory feeling that this other country was just a parenthesis, that my second sojourn in England was a life not entirely lived, a life that does not really matter and for which I was barely responsible, or only when the time came to hold that ever more improbable great dance—it has doubtless been abolished now, cancelled until further notice or, more likely, until further belief—a time that is no longer time or is frozen and motionless. ('*Cuán largo me lo fiáis*'—'I'll believe it when I see it'—we Spaniards used to exclaim ironically when confronted by such a prospect, paraphrasing Don Juan in a line written by a contemporary of Marlowe; people say it less often now, but it's still used, when the times are not too fearsome and when it seems that what has been predicted is so far off it will never arrive.) Perhaps that period of my life would, in the end, prove merely provisional, but nothing is ever provisional nor is it even a period until it is finished and closed, and until that happens, the parenthesis becomes the main, dominant clause, and when you read it, you forget that there ever was an opening parenthesis.

Two days later, regardless of the untimeliness and even eccentricity of my question, I phoned Luisa. It's more embarrassing talking about such things to a sister: our sister may be our first girlfriend, but that is when there has as yet been no blood, a sister is only ever our child-bride. I phoned Luisa and found her at home, I had no need to feel anxious; she sounded a bit surprised (after all, it wasn't a Thursday or a Sunday), but not put out. I asked a few routine questions about the children, about their health and hers, and immediately justified my call by saying: 'I'm phoning to ask you something.' 'Ask away,' she replied good-humouredly. And so I asked her, after a brief preamble and a few words of apology, if a drop of blood could fall from a woman wearing no undergarments and whose period had come on unannounced while she was standing up or walking ('Yes, or else going up the stairs,' I added pointlessly, to complete the already absurd image). There was a brief silence during which I was afraid she might simply hang up on me or suggest I go in search of my lost wits, but what I heard next was a friendly chuckle, I knew that laugh well, amused and genial, the laugh she always laughed when something really tickled her. At that moment, I could see her face clearly, and what a pleasant face it was (I saw it in my mind's eye, there in London, or, rather, in my memory's eye, as I stared out through my window).

'What kind of question is that?' she said, still laughing. 'Are you writing a novel or something, or maybe a Kotex ad? Or are you keeping very trashy company now? I hope not, because a woman would have to be very trashy indeed for what you're describing to happen.' And her merry laughter rang out again.

I had time to wonder if the reason she seemed so happy was because she had not been expecting to hear my voice or because the figure who would replace me was now clearly delineated— the kindly flatterer who wheedles his way in, the irresponsible raver who stays outside, the suspicious authoritarian who ends up imprisoning her; I preferred the second, hypothetically speaking, despite his bird-brain; but one thing was sure, she wasn't going to ask my opinion on the subject. I never questioned her about it, just as she never asked me what I was up to, only once had she said: 'I hope you're not too lonely there in London,' and that had not really been a question. 'No more than can be expected,' I had replied at once, answering neither yes nor no, and in any case making light of the whole thing. And I had time to wonder if her mention of 'trashy company' could mean that she was curious to know if I mixed with women in situations intimate enough for them to walk around in my presence without their panties on (although I could, of course, be totally oblivious of any such manoeuvre). And that could, in turn, mean either that she was not entirely indifferent to this news and found it a little irksome, or that she couldn't care less, which is why she could speak so blithely, perhaps urging me to frequent or to recruit a few such trashy women, of whom she was sure there would be no shortage. I no longer had the slightest idea what her feelings for me were, if she merely harboured a quiet affection or if there was still some lingering passion there, or what place she assigned me, if she was still waiting for the smell of me to disappear entirely and for me to become a ghost (one with whom she got on well, or the sort who remains friends and makes no demands and agrees not to appear too often) or if the process was already complete and my sheets torn up to make rags or dust cloths. The truth is that we almost never know anything about what touches us most directly, however much we interpret and conjecture, as I did endlessly, perhaps I was wasting my time in the building with no name, I thought I was making a contribution there, but perhaps I was unwittingly doing harm: perhaps I was working in a vacuum. And in short, I was afraid, afraid of Tupra and afraid of failing him, and I was filled, too, with self-distrust (I had discovered all this only a couple of nights before, the night spent with the Manoias). I was paid to make guesses about the future behaviour of people and their probabilities, and I could not even see the face—today's or tomorrow's; I saw only yesterday's face with my one mind's eye—of the person I knew best, I had lived with Luisa for quite a number of years and, through my children, continued to receive further complementary information, they were a prolongation of her, and children are transparent as long as they are still our children, later, they grow a shell or run away or wrap themselves in their own mists. I didn't even know what her hair was like now (and the way a woman's hair is combed or cut says so much about her), indeed, I could not even see myself; but that was of less importance, because the report about me that I had read half secretly in the filing room was quite right: this had never interested or worried me in the least. A rather unworthy enigma, a waste of time.

I could not resist joining in her laughter, nor did I want to resist, on the contrary: I had missed it intensely and therefore made the most of this opportunity; she had long since withdrawn her laughter from me, but, before, we used to set each other off, or would burst out laughing almost simultaneously, that laughter—when she laughed with me and I with her—was of the kind that is never forced and never preceded by a decision or a calculation, although this time I did join in afterwards, I had lost the habit and had not even noticed the comical nature of my enquiry, I suppose I was too sunk in myself, especially during the days that followed that night of new fear and not-so-new distrust; but she had found it funny at once or almost at once, after a few seconds' disbelief, unable to credit that I would phone her up to ask such a question. (An old but far from ephemeral flame from Italy, someone from my now remote past, to whom I largely owe my knowledge of Italian, used to exclaim: '*Che vanto ridere insieme.*' I don't know quite how I would say that in English: 'What a glorious thing it is, laughing together' or perhaps 'What a joy.')

'You are silly,' I said, 'you really are,' and while I was saying it, we laughed together, and I felt something like *vanto*. 'I'm not quite so stupid as to devote myself to the advertising world or, like everyone else, to writing novels. Although, who knows, more ridiculous things have happened, and I never rule anything out. But, honestly, you are so silly, even after all these years, you're just as silly as you always were.'

'All right, then, perhaps you could tell me why you're asking me this perfectly natural, perfectly normal question. A question, of course, that my colleagues at work ask me daily.' And she continued or we continued laughing that easy laugh, there is nothing like a bit of mutual leg-pulling, the sort that never offends and always gives pleasure, to show one's affection for someone, I mean that preliminary affection, when she and I were still together, and when, after a few such phrases, we would touch and kiss and embrace, lying down and wide awake. But we wouldn't have wanted to do that now, if we had really been able to see each other. 'What's wrong? Has someone made a mess of your floor? Surely not.'

I finally stopped laughing, just for a moment.

'No, it's not my floor. It was Wheeler's. But it's too long a story to go into now. Is it possible, do you think? Could that happen?'

'Peter's floor? At his age? I'm going to have to tell him off. I can understand the temptation, but I really don't think it's right. Why doesn't Mrs Berry put a stop to it, why doesn't she chase the filthy creatures away?' And she gave another gust of laughter, she was clearly in a good mood. This both pleased and displeased me, it might be because of me or because of some other man who had, perhaps, just left, or was about to arrive, or whom she was getting ready to go out and meet, or else he was already there in my house, listening to the conversation and waiting impatiently for it to finish, listening only to her side of it, to Luisa's, not mine. I didn't believe this last possibility, she sounded as if there were no witnesses and as if she were free of constraints or threats. But who knows, no one ever does, it could be a foreigner who didn't understand the language, and when you're sure you won't be understood, you do speak as if there were no witnesses or even do so on purpose to make yourself appear attractive or to make someone fall in love with you, at least that is what you conceitedly hope, to show yourself as you supposedly are, to allow the person watching to admire the way you are with others, so nice and jolly, there is in it just a pinch of pretence and another of exhibitionism, I've done it myself, in times of weakness of course, and I was beginning to think that this was one of those times. Besides, it wasn't my house. These embryonic thoughts made my laughter abate and allowed me to insist, not in a serious tone of voice, but in one of obvious haste:

'All right, I'll warn them both that you're going to tell them off and that they're in big trouble. But is it possible, the drop of blood, I mean, the stain?'

She knew me well, she was probably the person who knew me best, she realised that it was time either to answer my eccentric question or to drop it altogether, to forget about it, that was easy enough, we were not as close as we used to be and she owed me nothing, not even a polite answer. At least, I didn't feel she was in my debt, and in these matters (whether one feels oneself to be a debtor or a creditor), it is what one feels that counts and is important, much more so than facts or money, or than favours and damage done.

'Yes, it could. But it would be a tiny amount, I should think, a small drop; the thing would have to be in its very early stages to catch a woman offguard like that.'

'In the region of a couple of inches, or one and a half? The stain I mean. Is that possible?'

This again provoked her laughter, although it wasn't quite as it had been before, when we had laughed together; it was a mere remnant, lacking in gusto.

'Inches?' she said, amused. 'What do you mean, "inches"? I would remind you that we don't have inches here, and we don't understand them either, so enough of your anglicised ways. Anyway, did you take a tape measure to it? Or was it just a rough guess? What is all this about? Have you turned detective? Have you joined Scotland Yard? What *has* got into you?' There was surprise in her voice now. In Spain, no one ever remembers that it is New Scotland Yard and has been for years.

'Sorry, I meant centimetres, four or five. In diameter. You get used to these English measurements here.'

'I know, I know. But I really haven't a clue, Jaime. I don't usually carry a tape measure around with me, and, besides, something like that has never happened to me. I'm too careful and I still wear my undergarments as you put it. I've never heard you call them that before, by the way: it's rather nice.' And she gave a snort of genuine laughter. It was only a snort, as if the expression really had struck her as funny, but she couldn't be bothered to laugh out loud.

'Could the woman be unaware of it?'

'Yes, she could, although it wouldn't be long before she did become aware of it, if she's normal, of course, and not crazy. Or drunk or something. But initially, yes, she might not be aware of it, I suppose. Tell me what this is all about, go on, if it isn't anything to do with Kotex ads or a novel. You're starting to worry me.'

'In that case, she presumably wouldn't clean it up, then?' I asked. 'If she doesn't see it, there it stays.' And this was not a question but a statement.

The laughter had dissolved, vanished, ended. I had asked one too many questions, perhaps two, but certainly one, I had realised this before I even asked it, that last question. But it's hard not to try and ascertain whether or not something is possible, and the remoter the possibility, the harder it is.

'I've no idea, you presumably know just how trashy the person you're talking about is. But seriously, what is all this about? What's happened?' There was no anger in her voice, nor, I think, any jealousy, I'm not that naive. But there was a slight abruptness, perhaps she had grown tired of this game and was no longer playing.

'Wait, there's one more question I want to ask you, you probably know more about these things than I do, because I haven't got a clue. Have you heard of a beauty product, some sort of artificial implant or something, an injection apparently, although, frankly, I find that hard to believe, something called Botox?'

I wanted to know even if the information were purely anecdotal, and this way I could avoid answering her, she had asked me quite seriously ('But seriously,' she had said, and she did seem serious) and I wasn't going to tell her, not just because it was a long story and nothing to do with her, but because she would find the story disappointing and, above all, because once she knew about it, she would no longer feel intrigued. And she had seemed slightly intrigued, not quite worried, although that would have been still better, so that for a few days I would drift into her thoughts now and then. Yes, I had aroused her curiosity and her impatience, that hadn't been my intention when I phoned, but that's how it had turned out. And suddenly she was interested in my life, just like in the old days. It had been brief, only a minute (there is always more to come, there is always a little more, one minute, the spear, one second, fever, another second, sleep and dreams, and a little more for the dance—spear, fever, my pain, words, sleep and dreams, and still a little more, for the last dance), she had wanted to share my researches, or my exploits, without even knowing what they were, just as she used to. Poor me or whoever I was at the time, it felt to me like a triumph, however brief. Or, rather, like a glory, a gift, a joy, a *vanto*. She would certainly drift into my thoughts for some days following that conversation, and not just now and then, but all the time. But I could not return home, or even think about it, and so, necessarily and fortunately, these days would be few. They would last only until the disappearance once more of my renewed realisation that Luisa was not going to say to me: 'Come, come back, I was so wrong about you before. Sit down here beside me, here's your pillow which now bears not a trace, somehow I just couldn't see you clearly before. Come here. Come with me. There's no one else here, come back, my ghost has gone, you can take his place and dismiss his flesh. He has been changed into nothing and his time no longer advances. What was never happened. You can, I suppose, stay here for ever.' Yes, that night would pass too, and she would still not have said these words.

I first heard the word 'Botox' from De la Garza while we were waiting for Tupra in the spacious handicapped toilet, where Tupra had ordered me to take the attaché; I had to escort him there and wait while Tupra restored Flavia to her husband, I had to take Rafita off to that empty room and keep him or hold him there until Tupra could rejoin us, he clearly preferred to take full charge now, he must think me stupid and slow and completely impractical in an emergency and perhaps, also, lacking in courage. It had not, I think, taken me more than five minutes to enter and leave the three toilets one after the other, but this doubtless seemed far too long to someone whose response to any setback was unyielding.

Once out of the Ladies' room, I went over to the busiest and most frenetic of the dance floors and saw Tupra or Reresby leaving his table and coming towards me, pushing his way nimbly through the throng of night-owls—he slipped past them without touching them, thus avoiding being soiled by their perfumed sweat—he must have left Manoia on his own, something that would not have pleased Tupra at all, obliging him as it did to interrupt his persuasions and proposals, his gaze was alert, as alert as mine, and when we simultaneously caught sight of each other, I saw in his a glint of mingled annoyance and incomprehension ('Why haven't you brought them back? Why haven't you even found them yet? I asked you not to delay,' he said to me just with his pupils, which were sometimes almost as pale as his irises, or did he say it with his eyelashes, so thick and lustrous that they immediately became the predominant feature in any situation where there was more darkness than light); but there was no time to ponder this at length: we instantly joined eyes so that there were now four eyes doing the looking, and his were the first to spot them, Flavia and De la Garza, he pointed them out to me with one irritated finger, like someone pointing the barrel of a gun.

They were in the thick of the crowd on the fast dance floor, gyrating wildly, each seemingly in urgent need of an exorcist, and both were scaring the life out of the people nearby, who doubtless saw them as foreign elements (she because of her age, he because he was dangerous), the music did not allow for any normal dance-hold or even for proximity, and so De la Garza was not subjected to torture by the erect cones or horizontal ice picks that he and I had both experienced already, indeed it was he—and this was what most alarmed Tupra and myself and obliged us to intervene without further delay or ceremony—who was now flailing Mrs Manoia, almost literally, no, literally, and the most surprising thing was that she evinced no pain—that, at least, was my impression, I've no idea what Tupra thought—from the unintended lashes that the prize prick kept dealing her as he danced, I mean, you had to be a complete prick to dance in that crazy way, only a short distance away from his partner, performing Travolta-like turns, presenting Flavia as often with the back of his neck as with his face, completely oblivious to the fact that, with all these fast, abrupt movements, the empty hairnet, with no ponytail, no long hair to fill it and no weight to constrain or hamper it, could easily turn into a whip, a lash, an unruly riding crop; if there had been some metal ornament on the end, it would have been just like the *bolas* a gaucho uses to catch cattle or the knut deployed by cruel Cossacks, but, fortunately, he had not adorned it with aglets or bobbles or bells or spikes, any of which would have made mincemeat of Flavia; I shuddered nonetheless, because such ornamental ideas could so easily have entered his vacant head, it would have been just like an idiot of his calibre, disguised as he was as a rapper, as a Napoleonic bullfighter, as the painter-cum-*majo*, Meléndez, in his self-portrait in the Louvre, and as a fortune-telling gypsy with the obligatory hoop earring tinkling and bobbing (all these things at once, a total mishmash). 'I'd like to smash his face in,' this, at that instant, was my one brief, simple thought. Every time he spun round, the wretched hairnet would whip across whichever part of Flavia happened to be at the right height and within range, fortunately, most of the time, because De la Garza was taller, the scourge merely skimmed the top of her hair or, perhaps, hair extensions, but we had time to notice that, on a couple of occasions, when the attaché crouched down a little in his febrile whirlings, the hairnet cut across Mrs Manoia's face from ear to ear. It made me wince just to see it, which is why it was so incomprehensible that she should appear not to notice, regardless of however many layers of make-up there might be to deaden the impact of the lashes: I had a fleeting recollection of those boxers who can take an enormous amount of punishment, who do not even blink when they receive the first onslaught—a real rain of blows—although it all tends to be a question of whether their opponent is attacking—and, ultimately, opening up—a cheekbone or an eyebrow.

We did not wait for the ferocious piece of music to end. We immediately rushed onto the dance floor and, grabbing them firmly and carefully by the shoulders (Tupra grabbed Flavia and I grabbed the moron, we did not need to discuss who would grab whom), we brought them both to an abrupt halt. We saw the look of bewilderment on their faces and saw too—now that we were closer—that Mrs Manoia had a line across one cheek, a welt left by the rope, a weal left by the whip, it was not bleeding but it was, nevertheless, noticeable, like a scratch, it reminded me of Westerns I had seen, of the mark that remained on the neck of a hanged man (one who had been reprieved, of course; well, it wasn't perhaps that bad, the mark on her face would soon fade). Manoia wouldn't like it one bit when he found out, I saw from the expression on Tupra's face that he was thinking the same thing and heard him click his tongue, she had not even noticed, perhaps she was too caught up in the excitement of the dance, I just couldn't understand it.

'I'll take her to the Ladies' room and see if she can do something about that or at least conceal it,' he said to me, pointing at the mark. Then he turned to her: 'You've hurt your face, Flavia.' And he drew his finger across his own cheek. 'Let's go to the Ladies' room, I'll wait for you outside. Make sure you wash that scratch and see if you can cover it up with some make-up, all right? Arturo will be worried if he sees it. He wants you back over at the table. Does it hurt?' She raised her hand to her cheek and shook her head, she seemed pensive or perhaps she was merely stunned. Tupra then turned to me again and gave me this order, he spoke rapidly but calmly: 'Take him to the cripples' toilet and wait for me there, I won't be long. Let's hope we can do something about that wound, it doesn't seem to be an actual cut, and then restore her to her husband. Hang on to this cunt meanwhile, I'll be five minutes at most, well, say, seven. Keep him there until I come back. This moron has got to be neutralised, stopped.'

He referred to him first as 'cunt' and then as 'moron', at the time I only knew the first word in the sense of *coño*, the crude name for the female sexual part when spoken or merely thought, that night I only inferred its other meaning and confirmed it later in a dictionary, a slang dictionary. It wasn't so very different from the way I referred to him mentally, as *capullo*, 'cunt' probably meant pretty much the same, while *mamón* was less exact and possibly more aggressive. But what you think and even what you say are not the same as hearing someone else saying it; with an insult that you yourself think and even utter, you know exactly how serious it is, that is, usually not very serious at all, you know that it serves largely as a way of letting off steam, and most of the time you don't worry about it or think it important because you know how little importance it has; you are in control of your own vehemence, which, generally speaking, can be pretty artificial, if not entirely false: a rhetorical exaggeration, a performance for your own benefit or for that of other people, a form of bragging. On the other hand, an insult proffered by someone else is always troubling, whether it is directed at us or at a third party, because it's difficult to gauge its true intention—the intention of the person doing the insulting—the degree of anger or resentment, or if there is any real likelihood of violence. And that is why it made me uneasy to hear Tupra use these words, especially, of course, because I had never heard him use them before and because we do not like to discover in others what we carry within ourselves, our worst potentialities, things which, in us, seem acceptable (what can you expect); what we want is to believe that there are men and women who are better than us, people who are beyond reproach and who might, furthermore, be our friends, we would like, at least, to have them near, but never confronting us, never in opposition to us. Obviously, I don't often say the word *capullo*—to seek no further examples—and yet I had thought it that night over and over, just as I had during supper at Wheeler's and afterwards, when we were alone. But I did not, I think, actually say it, not in his presence, because, again, it is not the same to think something but keep it to yourself, to think it strenuously and yet remain silent, as it is to say it out loud before witnesses or to the person at whom it is directed, even if only because by doing so you are allowing others to attribute certain words to you and for those words ever after to be held as typical of you or as something you might well say ('I heard you, you said it, you've resorted to precisely that kind of language before'). That involves giving far too much away, showing far too many cards.

The order seemed so impossible to carry out that I said to Tupra straight out:

'What do you mean, take him there? On what pretext? And what for, what are you going to do?'

'Tell him you're going to suck him off.' Reresby had lost

patience with me, but only for a second: the look of surprise on my face must have been so intense (my anger would have shone through, irrepressible, immediate) that he doubtless read it as potential rebellion or even as a possible threat. And so he immediately added, suppressing his previous crude words (perhaps Reresby was the only foul-mouthed one, not Tupra or Ure or Dundas, and maybe each night he was who he was, to all intents and purposes and regardless of the consequences): 'Ask him if he wants a line of cocaine, top-grade stuff. He'll be bound to wait for me then, with his nose watering. He won't mind at all.'

'How do you know?' I asked. Then it occurred to me that this was a pointless question to ask Tupra, one to which any answer would be redundant. He devoted his life principally to knowing, or so I thought, and to knowing in advance, to recognising future faces; and unlike myself or Mulryan and Rendel, or possibly, occasionally, Jane Treves and Branshaw (although probably not Pérez Nuix), he did not need to be guided towards that knowledge or to have the path ahead pointed out to him. He was the one who led us, who decided which aspects of people were of interest or concern to us, the person who questioned us about those particular areas: for example, if the singer Dick Dearlove would be capable of killing and in what circumstances, or if an anonymous man had any intention of returning a loan, all kinds of situations on all kinds of occasions. He had never asked me if I thought De la Garza was into cocaine or glue or opium, in fact, I couldn't recall his ever asking me anything about him. It was only now, therefore, that I stopped to consider. And when I thought about it, it seemed to me probable that De la Garza would be into everything: he was so eager, so arrogant and impetuous, as well as highly excitable.

'Yes, just tell him and you'll see,' Tupra answered, while he delicately offered his arm to Mrs Manoia and they set off together for the Ladies' room. They would doubtless find a line. 'I'll be back within about seven minutes. I'll join you there. Keep him entertained until then.' And with that same finger, like the short barrel of a gun, he pointed at the hook painted on the door, and I could not help thinking of Peter Pan.

So I told Rafita, who, like Flavia, had been rendered temporarily speechless. My words made him recover, revive; he seemed interested, or, rather, somewhat over-eager.

'All right, let's go,' he said at once, and off we went through the door bearing the sign of the hook. Once we were inside the toilet for the mutilated, which was as deserted as it had been a short while before, he could not conceal a certain impatience at the prospect, he must have thought the cocaine might mitigate his drunkenness, he had started feeling slightly dizzy, fortunately nothing very grave, he was unlikely actually to throw up, but he was not in full command of his feet during the short walk with its many human obstacles, I put this down in part as well to his demented dancing and, of course, to his consequent breathlessness, then I realised that his shoelaces were undone, both of them, he could have had a really nasty fall and been left for dead on the dance floor, the hordes would have finished him off and saved us a few problems. 'So you haven't got it, then?' he wanted to know.

'No, Mr Reresby has it,' I replied, and it occurred to me that Reresby could as easily have some as none at all; it wouldn't be difficult for someone like him to get hold of it, being able to hand around a bit of cocaine can prove very useful these days and he knew how to handle himself in any territory. 'He said he wouldn't be long. He was going to see if he could do something about the whipping you gave our bit of pussy with that whacko string bag you've got on your head, that basket.' At this point, I had no hesitation about telling him off, besides, when abroad one acquires a rapid and baseless intimacy with one's compatriots, usually to ill or even worse effect, but it has the advantage that, when necessary, you can come straight to the point. De la Garza was causing me too many problems, all of which, and this was the worst of it, had been entirely avoidable. I had instantly adapted my speech to his customary brand of fake slang (normally, I would never myself use words like 'whacko' or 'pussy'); in terms of gaining familiarity, this was the equivalent of the hundred-yard dash. 'I mean imagine wearing a ridiculous thing like that and then whipping your dance partner across the face with it, I dread to think how her husband will react when he sees that welt on her face.' Horrified, I suddenly remembered one of the words Manoia had asked me about—'*uno sfregio*'. 'We're going to return her to him with a kind of *sfregio*, if, that is, I understood his gesture correctly, the thumbnail drawn across his cheek; this could be very tricky, he's not going to like it one bit, although it would have been worse if the scratch had been on her *bazza* rather than on her *guancia*, then Manoia might have taken it as an allusion, a joke, a revenge on my part for his rudeness, although poor Flavia's chin isn't at all protuberant and so isn't properly speaking a *bazza*.'—'He'll crucify you, De la Garza. I told you the guy had a lot of influence at the Vatican, well, in the whole of Italy really, including Sicily.'—I myself was surprised to find myself using that expression (about crucifying), one I would never normally use, it must have been an association of ideas with the Vatican, I suppose, which must be crammed with crucifixes, at least one in every room—'You wouldn't want to rub him the wrong way, he's a real snake in the grass'—I was clearly still making associations, and slipping into the mode of speech, part crude, part high-flown, of that terrible perfumed boor—'I just hope Reresby can explain it away: that it wasn't deliberate, that you didn't realise. You didn't do it on purpose, did you, Rafita?'—I had never before, it seemed to me, addressed him like that directly; in fact, I had first heard Peter use the diminutive form of his name only after the attaché had left his house that night empty-handed and without dipping his wick, to drive off and crash his car on the road somewhere, along with the Mayor and Mayoress of Thame or Bicester or Bloxham or Wroxton (except that we did not have such luck).

'Of course I didn't do it intentionally, don't be stupid, it's just that I don't want to miss out on dipping the old wick, you know, I don't want to ruin my chances of a quick fuck. I hope you two haven't screwed things up for me, you've broken my concentration, you have, all that hard work down the drain, you assholes. I was just going in for the kill too.'—That's what he said, he had a real knack for mingling vulgarity and prissiness, 'dipping the old wick' and 'broken my con-centration', and 'down the drain' and 'going in for the kill', that terrible jumble of registers and references so typical of Spanish nowadays, and much in vogue with many Spanish writers, including certain depressingly old-fashioned young people, who positively reek of the old days, perhaps because contemptible traditions are so easy to adopt, they're very tenacious. I wasn't prepared to go that far, to adapt to such a fashion, to join in: imitating such an affectation would be a concession too far.

'What quick fuck are you talking about? God, De la Garza, you're obsessed with dipping your wick. Just forget it, will you? It doesn't make any difference to you who it is, does it? It could be your old aunt, for all you care—and I warned you that her husband was watching. Why don't you just go to a prostitute now and again, I'm sure your salary could cover that. I mean the idea wouldn't even have occurred to her. And then, to top it all, you lash her face with that hairnet of yours. She won't even want to say goodbye to you.'

'Bah,' he said disdainfully, 'of course I didn't mean to, in fact, I think I'm going to take this snood off, it's no good if you're dancing, a drag, really.' He ran his whole hand over the hairnet from top to bottom, as if squeezing out a cloth. 'Not that she'll have noticed anyway, not with her face packed with Botox like that. In any case, I don't know what you're talking about, she's there for the taking, man. It was just a question of manoeuvring her into position and then in I'd go, the *coup de grâce*, in with sword, up to the gunnels. Two ears and a tail to me and fuck everyone else.' He mimed a bullfighter driving the sword in. He was beginning to string together total non sequiturs, a sign that he was recovering. I wondered if he actually knew what 'gunnels' meant, but I had no intention of asking him.

'Botox?' That was when I heard the neologism for the first time. 'What's that? What kind of word is that? Botox,' I said it again to get used to it, as one tends to do with words one doesn't know. De la Garza had referred to his dangling hairnet as a snood, although I bet he had never seen one in his life. What with that and his enigmatic 'gunnels', I held out little hope of his offering me the etymology of Botox. He insisted on the bullfighting analogy, with gestures and everything, something typical of our home-grown fascists—I use the word in its colloquial sense, and, indeed, in the analogical. The gestures in themselves, of course, are not necessarily fascistic (even I can manage a fair imitation, as well as a pass made with two hands and a pass made only with the right—when on my own, needless to say), but the sheer presumption of comparing (shall we say) the labour involved in seducing a woman with entering an arena and facing an enraged bull in front of a crowd of spectators definitely was fascistic. Perhaps he was, after all, a fascist at heart, analogically speaking.

'You mean you don't know?' And he said this with the puerile sneer of a hard-bitten thug, as if my ignorance were proof of his greater worldly wisdom (I had no argument with that, there are worldly-wise louts by the thousand, and their numbers are on the increase) and of his permanent place in the land of chic that was so precious to him (he could stay there until the last day for all I cared, I had no intention of disputing the territory with him, or even setting foot in it). 'You mean you don't know,' he repeated. He was delighted to be able to teach me something, if you can call it teach. 'Rich chicks have it injected all the time, and some guys do, too. Your friend's a likely case, if you ask me, he looks like he's had it in his cheekbones, his chin, his forehead, and his temples, to ward off crow's feet. Yeah, that Reresby guy's skin is suspiciously tight and smooth, he probably has a hypodermic stuck in him every

165

few months, and the Italian woman every few weeks I would think, assuming they let her.'

It was true that Tupra's skin was disturbingly lustrous and firm for a man of his probable years, and was the lovely golden colour of beer, almost peachy sometimes, but it had never seemed to me that this was due to artifice or to some special treatment, rather, it would simply never occur to me that men would resort to such things, or not then at least. Who knows, though. I was becoming old-fashioned in some respects: I knew nothing about the existence of Botox or, doubtless, about other products, that was just one example. In fact, I still didn't really know about it, and Rafita was hardly the best person to explain it to me.

'A hypodermic? You mean they inject it, real injections, with a needle and everything? What is it? Some sort of liquid presumably. Against wrinkles.' My last sentence was a statement, another way of getting myself used to the idea. It seemed to me inconceivable that anyone would have a needle stuck in their forehead or their chin (I couldn't believe they would inject it into their temples) unless they had some pressing reason to do so, and, besides, that word . . . If I have a feeling for anything it is for languages and etymologies, I suppose I got used to having to be alert to them and to deducing them when I taught at Oxford, and the students (who were, generally speaking, malicious and mischievous) were always asking me about the most outlandish words, I often had to improvise, inventing etymologies on the spot; I mean, how, in the middle of a class, is one supposed to know the origin of *papirotazo*, or *moflete*, or the roots of *coscorrón*, *esgrima* or *vericueto*? Now I could not help but suspect that 'Botox' was a contraction (soothing and camouflaging, as well as comfortable and practical) of 'botulinum toxin', that is, a feared and highly dangerous substance, which, according to what Wheeler had told me, had been brought *ex profeso* by the SOE from America in the middle of the war in order to impregnate and poison the bullets that were fired at Heydrich in the attempt on his life in 1942 in Prague, and which was, in the end, what caused the death he struggled—his will refusing to give in—so hard against. 'Botox,' I thought, 'it must be that, it's too much of a coincidence. But if it is, it's madness to have yourself injected with poison in order not to grow old, or, rather, not to look old, it must be administered in very measured, minimal doses. But it would be so easy for a *practicante* or visiting nurse to make a mistake. And how old-fashioned that term *practicante* seems now, yet it was normal in my childhood.'—'I hope Botox isn't the same thing as botulinum toxin,' I said to De la Garza. When I saw the look of brute ignorance on his face I realised that he had no idea, but the utter idiocy of his reply took me by surprise, so much so that I wondered if he wasn't pretending or if his state of semi-intoxication and his recent jigging up and down to that violent music had perhaps exacerbated his usual stupidity. But he wasn't such a mule, despite everything, to make a mistake like that unintentionally.

'It's got nothing to do with bulimia,' the idiot replied. 'No, it's nothing to do with bulimia or anorexia.' He had rested one hand on one of the strange cylindrical bars in the spotless, spacious toilet; on the only bar that was, fortunately for him, fixed: it doubtless helped to keep him from collapsing while he waited for his promised line of cocaine.

'Not bulimia, man, botulin. You know, as in botulism.' He continued to stare at me blankly. 'Botulism, an illness you get from eating food that's gone off, or from canned food that hasn't been properly prepared, haven't you ever heard of it?' This was one etymology I did know and so I let him have it, possibly to repay him for the lecturing tone he had used on me. 'It affects meat or fish, possibly fruit; but it was especially common in sausages, that's where the name comes from: *botulus* means "sausage" in Latin.'

'I've no idea what you're talking about, not a clue, so don't ask me what it is or where they get it from. But as far as I remember it certainly didn't involve sausages or chorizos or anything. They inject people with this substance and it paralyses the nerves, I think, so that they can hardly move their face, all their wrinkles disappear while the effect lasts and they don't get any new ones either, at least, not in the places where they've had the injections. Anyway, that's what it is, I know several women who've had it, I mean, say some woman's forehead is like piece of old parchment, a little injection in one corner and her forehead's as smooth as a marble statue's. Cheeks like an accordion? Give her a few doses of paralysis and they'll be as fresh and firm as you like. The only downside is that when the nerves are paralysed, the whole area becomes completely desensitised, that's why the Italian woman didn't notice it at all'—he touched the hairnet as if it were a mane— 'and they get a funny, slightly crazed expression too. They can't really move their face at all, so although their skin appears very youthful and firm, there's something stiff and doll-like about their face, they look a bit stupid or a bit touched. Haven't you seen that actress, she's the ex-wife of that guy who's hitched up now with one of our Spanish actresses, oh, fuck, I've forgotten her name, the one with the face of someone very tall, well, I reckon that fixed look in her eyes is from the Botox, her eyes have gone all kind of pointy-looking, haven't they? It makes her look slightly unhinged, don't you think? They must inject it into her cheekbones and into her crow's feet by the pint, I'd be surprised if she can even close her eyes, she probably sleeps with them wide open. Just like this Flavia woman. I mean, depending on the angle, she looks like some kind of sprite.'

He stood there giving me this absurd speech, apparently recovering without too much difficulty from his slight dizziness, and dressed in what he had obviously intended to be an original, modern get-up, but which was, in fact, merely laughable, he was nothing but a clown, a character out of a farce; having announced his intention of removing his snood, he hadn't even attempted to do so, and then there was his vast, stiff jacket and his untied shoelaces. I couldn't help smiling, and I felt a pang of pity. De la Garza was, from every point of view, unbearable, a complete waste of space, an embarrassing one at that, but he wasn't unpleasant, like others of his ilk, I've known so many of them from childhood on, they appear to be jolly and even affectionate, but they're basically inconsiderate and obscene, and even when they're being obsequious or servile they're only out for themselves; deep down, though, they can't stand not to get on with anyone, even with people they detest, they aspire to be loved even by those they hurt, and, in general, they manage it, they have no idea how annoying they are, no sense of when they're in the way, they're too vain even to conceive of the possibility, they live in a permanent state of smugness, they would never pick up a subtle hint or even a rude, unsubtle one, which means it's very difficult to shake them off. And then again what he had said about the accordion and the pointy eyes of the cinema diva and the sprite-like features of Mrs Manoia (it was true that, however pleasant, there was something sharp and stylised about them), I had found all that rather funny, which made me think that there might be some cracks in his stupidity; in practice it's hard to find a person who never has anything interesting to say—or who does not have some quality peculiar to them alone—people are always coming out with images or expressions or comparisons which are comical in the best and most enjoyable sense and which make us smile or laugh, even if only because they're wrong or crude or inappropriate, there are few things as funny as blunders and gaffes, even if you're the butt of them. Perhaps that's why everyone talks so much and why it's so hard to remain silent, because in almost any speech there's nearly always some amusing remark, it isn't only keeping silent that saves, sometimes it's the opposite and that, indeed, is the general belief, a legacy from *The Thousand and One Nights*, the inherited idea among men that they must never let anyone else have the floor or finish a story, but ramble on endlessly and never stop, not even in order to tell anecdotes or to persuade with reason or discord, which often proves unnecessary anyway, it can be enough just to keep someone else's ear busy as if you were pouring music into it or lulling it to sleep, and thus prevent them from leaving us. And that might be all you need to do to save yourself.

Suddenly I wanted to hear more from him, from De la Garza, more chatter and more nonsense and more comical similes (perhaps I was missing my own language more than I realised), despite the fact that his chauvinistic side kept reappearing like a stigma, without his necessarily intending it to: 'one of *our* Spanish actresses' he had said—that terrible sense of belonging. I wondered if how I was feeling about him was similar to how Tupra felt about me (although obviously there was no real comparison): I amused Tupra, he enjoyed our sessions of conjecture and examination, our conversations, or even just listening to me ('What else?' he would demand. 'What else occurs to you? Tell me what you're thinking and what else you noticed'), perhaps he liked the sound of the Canadian accent he had attributed to me on the night we first met, or, to be more precise, the accent he thought came from British Columbia, the man had been everywhere. It's all a question of suddenly seeing the funny side of someone, even someone who really gets on your nerves, that, too, is possible, but dangerous, seeing in the person you most detest a smidgeon of previously unsuspected wit (most people's solution—or, rather, precaution—is not to admit the tiniest spark, and to pretend to be blind). Tupra doubtless saw my funny side, almost immediately; it was unexpected and much stranger that I should find a funny side to Rafita after just two infuriating encounters, but it might, of course, be only a short-lived illusion.

As for the Botox, I decided it must in fact be what I had deduced, because botulinum toxin did, indeed, produce muscular paralysis, it attacked the nervous system, you ended up unable to speak or to swallow (ah, an illness that could suppress speech) and, later, unable to breathe, and the idea of a death like that, from asphyxia, brought back familiar warnings from my childhood, when you still feared the tiniest dent in a tin, or any gases that might escape when you opened it, or a can that gave off even a minimally questionable smell when still sealed, canned goods were in no way a novelty then, but neither were they particularly widespread, and all grandmothers distrusted them, mothers no longer did or, under the influence of *their* mothers, only a little; I had never, in my entire life, heard of a single person in Spain (or perhaps only in some very backward rural area) who had been struck down by botulism; however, a phrase expressive of the prevailing anxiety had remained with me, for what impresses you as a child never really fades, it was something my maternal grandmother used to say, I think, and what impresses the child is always remembered by the adult who replaces him, right up until the final day, and it was one of those threats which, at the time, you take absolutely literally, terrified by the instantaneous effect attributed to the poison, dazzled by the glamour of anything so devastating and so extreme, which allowed one unlimited scope for fantasy and from both sides of the trenches too, as victim and as murderer: 'Under no circumstances must you ever eat the contents of a can or tin which looks even slightly dubious, which is to say most of them,' the four of us had heard her warn the maids, 'because if the contents *have* gone off, the toxin is so strong that sometimes it can take fatal effect even if you only touch it with the tip of your tongue.'

We imagined something as normal and trivial as a spoon whose edge or tip is carried to the tongue of the woman stirring the stew, to see if it needs more salt or if it's warmed up and hot enough to eat, and she does this so calmly, as she softly sings or hums to herself or even whistles (although only men used to whistle then, or girls who were so young that they were still almost children), perhaps without even looking at the casserole or pot, but, instead, peering through the window and down at the courtyard where other women or other maids are leaning out over windowsills, shaking rugs or pinning up the damp clothes (with always at least one clothes pin held between the teeth), or indoors lazily flicking a feather duster around or standing on a stool unscrewing a burnt-out light bulb. When you heard the warning, which was also directed at us in the future ('Don't even touch the suspect contents, just in case. Not until they've been thoroughly boiled'), you imagined the contaminated spoon touching tongue or lips and the woman being instantly felled as if by a lightning bolt or a bullet, and lying lifeless on the kitchen floor while her stew continued to simmer, and then you feared for your own mother if she was the one who did the cooking, because when you heard the word 'fatal' it never occurred to you to think of something deferred and slow, something not immediately perceptible and whose effects would appear later, but a kind of spectacular, murderous electrical charge, a flash, children can only conceive of the immediate and the very swift, if something is fatal it is fatal now, never in the long or medium term, like a blow from a tiger's paw or a musketeer's sword-thrust to the head or a Moor's arrow piercing the heart, we played at these fictions, and if a danger wasn't imminent, then it wasn't truly a danger, 'I'll believe it when I see it', that is the motto of the child when something does not arrive immediately or fails to happen today or even tomorrow—that mere prolongation of today—of course there is no irony in the child, nor does he say it in those words, but in a more childish version: 'That won't be for ages yet', more often than not in the form of a repeated question when faced by any wait or delay: 'Will it be much longer?' 'Will it be much longer until summer?' 'Christmas?' 'My birthday?' 'The start of the movie?' 'Tomorrow?' followed, five minutes later, with the impatience that denies or eats up time, with: 'Is it tomorrow yet?' 'No, dear, it isn't tomorrow yet, it's still today, which takes a long time to pass.' 'And will it be much longer until I go back home to Madrid and the children, until I go back to Luisa?' Or the question that becomes more common in adulthood and keeps nagging at us, although without ever formulating itself quite so clearly: 'And will it be much longer until my death?'

That is why I asked her, when I phoned her two days after that night with the Manoias and Reresby and De la Garza, before she could angrily hang up on me, I asked her about Botox, in case she knew about it, Luisa had loads of female friends and acquaintances and some, to use the attaché's expression, were rich chicks, although it seemed to me both incredible and ironic that a solution or dose of that once-feared toxin with which they smeared the most fatal of bullets, those destined for the very few Nazi tyrants whom they tried to lay low, should now be used to the advantage of the wealthy, to pander to their every caprice and luxury, to postpone their wrinkles or eliminate them for a few months, using the same elements of muscular paralysis or anaesthetised or damaged nerves—whichever was required, or both, or one as a consequence of the other—the same elements which in days gone by brought on dizziness and growing immobility and a lack of co-ordination and double vision and serious intestinal problems, followed by aphasia and then asphyxia and total paralysis and which, in the end, killed. Yes, everything is painfully ridiculous and subjective and partial, because everything contains its opposite and depends entirely on the moment and the place and the virulence and the dosage, delivering either sickness or vaccination, either death or beautification, just as all love carries within itself its own staleness and every desire its own satiety and every longing its own ennui, so the same people in the same position and place love each other and cannot stand each other at different moments in time, today, tomorrow; what was once a long-established habit becomes slowly or suddenly unacceptable and inadmissible—it doesn't matter which, that's the least of it—and the merest contact, a touch once taken for granted, becomes an affront or an insult, what once gave pleasure or amusement becomes hateful, repellent, accursed and vile, words once longed for would now poison the air or provoke nausea and must on no account be heard, and those spoken a thousand times before are made to seem unimportant (erase, suppress, cancel, better never to have said anything, that is the world's ambition, whether it knows it or not, whether or not it realises this). And even to phone home you have to come up with a reason to present or put forward.

'Have you heard of a beauty product, some sort of artificial implant or something, an injection apparently, although, frankly, I find it hard to believe, something called Botox?' With that almost last-minute question, I was also trying to distract or quash her incipient irritation, the sudden seriousness that had followed her laughter, her annoyance at my other—too insistent—questions about the absence of panties and a bloodstain that I might well have imagined, or to which, having erased it entirely, thoroughly, completely, including its sticky, resistant rim, I could at last say what has been said to so many events and objects and to so many dead, always assuming anyone still bothers to do so: 'Since there is no trace of you, you never occurred, you never happened. You neither strode the world nor trod the earth, you did not exist. I cannot see you now, therefore I never saw you. Since you no longer are, you never were.' It was possible that Luisa said this to me in her thoughts, when she was alone or asleep; even though she spoke to me from time to time, and there was, of course, the permanent trace of our two children, and I had not yet died. I was simply 'in another country', expelled from her time, the time that wraps around the children and steals them away and which is already very different from mine, outside her time which advances now without including me, allowing me to be neither participant nor witness, whereas I don't quite know what to do with my own time, which also advances without including me, or perhaps it is just that I have still not worked out how to climb aboard (perhaps now I never will catch up), and in which, nevertheless, this parallel or theoretical life in England is taking place, and which will have little to tell when it ends and closes like a parenthesis, and to which it will also be possible to say: 'You are no longer moving forwards. You have become a frozen painting or a frozen memory or a dream now over, and I cannot even see you now from this adverse distance. You no longer are, therefore you never were.'

Luisa did not answer me at once, she remained silent, as if she perceived this second request for information as something it only very minimally was (that is, a diversionary tactic, a way of avoiding responding seriously to her question), or as if it seemed to her as unlikely a question for me to ask as the first one and thus only contributed further to her perplexity or to her sense of intrigue.

'Botox? Yes,' she repeated the word after a pause of a few seconds. 'But what *are* you up to, Jaime? Panties, menstruation, and now this. You're not about to have a sex-change, I hope. I'm not sure how the children would take it, but I imagine it would frighten them. It certainly frightens me.'

'Oh, very funny,' I said, and I did find it quite funny, or perhaps I was just glad that her sense of humour had returned, if Luisa was making jokes it meant that she was feeling friendly and, besides, her jokes were never aggressive, at most slightly acerbic like this one, and she always made them in a kindly or clearly affectionate way, cheerfully and without seeking to wound. She had amused herself by her own silly comment, because I heard her laugh again, and she could not resist carrying the joke a little further.

'What would we call you, do you think? It would all be a bit confusing. Please, Jaime, consider carefully before taking the final step, an irreversible one, I presume. Think of the problems, and the embarrassing situations. Remember the college bursar Wheeler told us about. There he was, a terribly proper gentleman, and suddenly his colleagues didn't know whether to address him as "sir" or "madam"; his more intimate friends spent months addressing a be-skirted, matronly lady as "Arthur", after all, she still had Arthur's face, apart from the painted lips in place of the usual moustache, and the short, untidy bob of hair, which she had no idea what to do with, well, she wasn't used to it, they said.' Hearing her recall this anecdote, I found that the image of Rosa Klebb crossed my mind again, the slovenly, lazy, 'dreadful woman of SMERSH', a disciple of the implacable Beria who had infiltrated her into the POUM as the lover and right-hand woman of Nin, whose murderer she may also have been, at least according to Fleming; or was it, rather, Lotte Lenya in her interpretation of the role: trying to kick Connery with those poisoned blades, possibly tipped with the same toxin? No, it would have to have been something faster-acting if she wanted to kill him by kicking him with her lethal shoes. 'It won't be an easy job softening your features, however stuffed with hormones you might be, and whatever you've had removed. I don't know, you'll have to see, but you've quite an athletic build and pretty heavy stubble, you'd make a very imposing, not to say alarming, woman. You certainly wouldn't get any women pushing in front of you at the market.' And this time she laughed out loud.

I had to bite my lip in order not to join in, even though I found my description as a woman somewhat troubling; but some telltale sound nevertheless escaped my lips.

'Yes, I remember Vesey the bursar,' I managed to say, once I could contain myself. 'In fact, I knew him by sight during my time in Oxford. When he was still Arthur, of course, not Guinevere. I must ask Peter what's become of him or her. He'll be getting on a bit now, and men age differently from women. After a certain age, you get the upper hand again.' And when Luisa's laughter had subsided, I returned to my question: 'So you *do* know about Botox. Is it true what I was told, about the injections?' This was all very familiar to me: it was what normally happened, she would stray off the point when she was talking to me and intersperse her own jokes. But unlike me or Wheeler, and Tupra too, she did not usually, of her own accord, return to the point.

'Yes, I've heard a few women talking about it. When it first appeared and it wasn't yet on offer here at beauty salons or beauty clinics or whatever you call them, there even used to be parties apparently, where you could have it injected.'

'Parties?' Now I was the one to repeat a word, the one that had most disconcerted me.

'Yes, I heard María Olmo talking about it once. It's something that ladies with a bit of money go in for; they would get together for tea or whatever, and a *practicante*, a visiting nurse, paid for by all the participants, would come in and inject each woman as required. I mean, those who wanted to have it done, of course, and who had contributed, I suppose, to buying the stuff, which would be the expensive part. No, it was probably the hostess who paid the nurse.' And I thought to myself: 'She's not that much younger than me, which is why she, too, uses the word "*practicante*". But it would have to be someone who specialised in Botox injections,' or so I imagined; I didn't want to interrupt her to ask. 'It was the in thing at the time, people said the results were spectacular, although I don't know if they thought it was quite such a big deal afterwards. I believe lots of salons do it now, but to start with, about a year or so ago, they had to import it specially from somewhere or other, from abroad. Now I assume everyone has it done individually.'

'From America,' I murmured, thinking of Heydrich and Colonel Spooner of the SOE, who organised the attempt on the former's life. 'They'd import it from America.'

'No, actually, I think it was from England, or else Germany.' There was no reason why she should know what I was thinking, she hadn't been there when Wheeler had spoken to me about Lidice and about spatial hatred, the hatred of place suffered by Madrid and by London during those years of bombardment and blockade; and Madrid still suffers from it now, since all its governors, without fail, hate it or have hated it. Now she was never in the same place I was. Before, she often had been; that's why we both knew the story about the transsexual bursar.

'Why is that? Wasn't it illegal, like melatonin? It was

melatonin, wasn't it, that was banned in Europe? Didn't they ban it or something?'

'Not as far as I know. It must just have taken a while to arrive. As soon as people find out about something new, they get all impatient and then, when they do finally get hold of the stuff, they pretend they're way ahead of the crowd. You know the type, the idiots who get in a state if they don't fly to New York at least once a year and then insist on telling you all about it, I mean there are more and more of these pretentious hicks; frankly, I'm up to here with stories about New York. And, of course, if they find out that over there or in London, people are shooting up some new, rejuvenating product as if it was heroin, they immediately rush out and buy some needles, just in case.'

'But do they really have injections in their forehead and cheekbones and chin and temples?' I found this in itself shocking, the needle being stuck into the face and the liquid slowly penetrating, all the more so—and this was what really horrified me—if Botox was what I feared it to be. So my tone of voice must have been one of scandalised amazement because I noticed that Luisa's response deliberately brought it all back into perspective, although not with the intention of lecturing me, that wasn't her style.

'Yes, they do, and in worse places too, I understand. In their eyelids, in the bags under their eyes, in their neck, and doubtless in their lips too and, of course, above their lips, in those little vertical lines that are the banc of quite a few of my women friends, that and thcir ncck. It seems pretty horrific to me as well, but I'm probably more used to all these implants and inoculations than you are, as well as to various other forms of butchery. I know more and more women who go for periodic sessions of nip and tuck, just as if they were going to the hair-dresser's. And, you know, quite a lot of men go in for it too, and not just vain bachelors and depressed divorcés, I know of more than one husband as well. If, that is, I can believe what I'm told, which, of course, one never should.' She said this so casually that it made me think: 'That's good, it doesn't even occur to her to include me among the depressed divorcés, I don't inspire her pity, at least not yet, and, besides, I don't like to play the poor sap as so many boyfriends and husbands do. Also, we're still not divorced. But that will come, I suppose, when she wants it.' I felt that such an initiative was unlikely to come from me. But you never know. I did not, however, share these thoughts with her. 'I mean look at that clown Berlusconi, he must be entirely made of latex by now, have you seen him, he looks like a papier-mâché doll. Now there's someone who should perhaps consider changing sex, to see if it improved him, or rehumanised him and turned him into a grandmother.' And she laughed again, as I knew she would when she used the word *caricato* or 'clown': we knew each other far too well for us ever to stop. The danger now was that we might set off along that tangent and start imagining other politicians transformed into portly matrons; and so I led her back to the subject:

'And what exactly is Botox? Do you know?'

'Someone told me at the time, but I didn't really pay much attention. It's a toxin, I think, or an antitoxin, I can't remember to be honest.'

'Botulinum toxin? Could that be it? As in botulism. It was used as a poison in the past, you know.' And I told her about my intuited etymology.

This apparently failed to shake her. Through her various female acquaintances, or from the occasional insecure girlfriend, she really must have grown used to the most bloody and venomous remedies against ageing.

'I can't remember. Possibly. It wouldn't surprise me, half of these cosmetic surgeons are completely irresponsible, if not criminal. María told me about one man who had helped her lose an enormous amount of weight. They happened to go into a pharmacy together one day and he claimed to have left his prescription pad at home and the only way he could think of convincing the pharmacist he really was a doctor was to run back to his car and bring her the stethoscope he happened to have lying on the back seat. Can you imagine: "Look, I've got a stethoscope, I'm a doctor," and he waved it around in front of her. María deduced from this that, despite the fact that he ran a clinic, he wasn't a member of a professional association or certified or anything. She was horrified. Which is why now I can believe anything.'

'Could you find out for me if it *is* botulinum toxin?'

'I suppose so. María is sure to know, or else Isabel Uña will, she's involved in things like that too, I can ask them. But why this interest of yours in Botox? Are you thinking of turning yourself into a Berlusconi or is that careless girlfriend of yours considering Botox? You don't need it, you haven't got a single wrinkle, it's not fair really.' She hadn't forgotten my first question about the drop of blood, she was still thinking that someone might have stained my floor, some chance or not-so-chance visitor. The prospect of Luisa carrying out a bit of research for me cheered my innocent heart. It was the first time in ages that we had shared something in common, something new (not the children or money or practical matters), even if it was a trifle. And it would mean that we would phone each other again soon, that she would phone me or I her, to share the information she had gathered. There were matters pending between us, and that, now, was a novelty.

'Thank you, you're very youthful-looking yourself,' I replied with equal parts of humour and gallantry, and added: 'No, it's just curiosity. Someone mentioned it to me, and I'd like to know if it's the same substance that was used in 1942 to kill a Nazi bigwig Wheeler told me about. Do you know what effect it has? The process I mean.'

'I think it paralyses the muscles in the injected area and so smoothes the skin out and plumps it up, don't ask me why or how. Apparently the people who have the injections look a bit expressionless afterwards, although I haven't noticed that with María or with Isabel, who are the two women I know who've tried it. Although, of course, I may just not have seen them when they were under its first effects, I think it lasts for a few months and then after a break they have it done again, but the breaks get shorter and shorter. Although now that I come to think of it, they did look a bit stiff and somehow tauter, more compact . . . It's odd this obsession,' and she sounded more thoughtful now, 'it's not just prevalent among rich people, nor, as I said, only among women. We'll all be at it soon. You've no idea the things people do to themselves nowadays, the putting in and taking out that goes on, the injecting and slicing, and all the other tortures they submit themselves to. It would make your hair stand on end if you knew the details. But you wait, we'll all end up the same way, and those of us who won't join in will be told: "How can you bear to go around looking like that," they'll say, "with all that flab and those folds of skin and those bags under your eyes; with those lines and that fat and that sagging flesh, how can you stand to go around looking so neglected?" Some people compare it to going to the dentist. "After all, we go to the dentist when we have a chipped tooth, and because it looks unsightly we have it capped. Well, all these other things are just the same." As if growing old were a defect or a vice we tolerated, the result of negligence on our part. As if you could choose and were guilty of allowing yourself to grow old. Or, of course, as if you were poor, with no means to conceal the fact. That's what looking old will mean eventually, that you're a pariah. It will be another division, another difference, as if there weren't enough already. It will be equivalent to walking around in threadbare clothes. I hope we don't live to see it.'

And then she fell silent, as if she were suddenly considering her own case. I had never noticed in her the slightest concern or temptation in that regard: I used to hear her talk about the female acquaintances and friends who were most preoccupied with the passing of time, she would laugh indulgently at their extravagances and their experiments, she didn't really give it much importance, or else thought it a good thing if her friends were then happy with their supposedly improved appearance, even if it were only borrowed or false or bought or were sometimes downright monstrous. She had never been like that.

But Luisa was no longer so very young and she had never before mentioned my lack of wrinkles—on a par with Tupra's firm skin; a family legacy—as a comparative reproach, not even in the joking tone she had used now. 'Perhaps she's starting to worry, under the effect or influence of everyone else,' I thought. 'She certainly has no reason to, not judging by the last time I saw her; although my criterion would be of little use to her if she's invented reasons (no one is safe from that) or someone has instilled them into her (no one is safe from that either), she thinks I look at her with too kindly an eye.'

'You're not considering resorting to such things yourself, are you?' I asked. 'You certainly don't need to.'

She laughed for a moment, thus emerging from her brief brooding silence.

'I might not need them today, but tomorrow, rather than the day after tomorrow, I certainly will,' she said. 'Not that I'll be able to afford it, I'll be one of the pariahs, one of the threadbare ones.' And she laughed again, it had amused her to say this. 'Even though you are sending us an awful lot of money since you've been in that job of yours that you keep so quiet about,' she added. 'I'd like to thank you, Deza; we're living in the lap of luxury here—or very nearly. There's really no need to send us quite so much.' It was as if she wanted to apologise for accepting it; that is why she called me Deza and not Jaime, she wasn't trying to worm anything out of me nor was she angry with me.

'You thank me every time I send a bank transfer. I only send you what's fair, after all, you've got the kids to take care of, and, besides, I'm earning good money now and don't have that many expenses. I'll only send less if my expenses go up.'

'Yes, but you could be putting some aside. The kids have been asking when you'll be coming to see them.'

'Not in the immediate future I shouldn't think. I've got a trip with my boss coming up, but I don't know exactly when yet, it might be in a week's time or in a month or later, so I'm tied up until then. Perhaps I'll make it over after that, on a bank holiday weekend.' That is what public holidays are called in England, they usually fall on a Monday, apart from Christmas and New Year. 'Anyway, I've still got enough to put some aside. And I'm buying some really good antiquarian books, better and more expensive than ever.'

'Well, hang on to that job. Who knows, perhaps you'll tell me about it one day, what you're doing, I mean.' I didn't think she was really interested, it was just a way of being friendly. She had shown no interest in it in other conversations. Or was it just that those conversations had always been much shorter?

'There's not much to tell,' I said and here I lied, especially considering what had happened two nights previously. 'Diplomatic and commercial translation is pretty routine stuff, although you do get to meet some interesting people now and then. But, as you know, I won't hang on to the job if I get bored with it.'

She waited a couple of seconds before replying:

'Yes, I know. And, as *you* know, that's fine with me too.'

I saw her smile when she said this, with the wide-awake eyes of my mind. She was in another city, in another country. But I could see her very clearly from London.

I thanked her and said goodnight, we said goodbye, I put the phone down. But not so my thoughts. I glanced up, got out of my chair, went over to the sash window and opened it to air the room, I'd been smoking while I was talking. It wasn't raining, nor was it cold, or so it seemed to me at first, and it could have been an early-spring night, except that it wasn't very late, not even for England, and yet it had got dark some hours before, outside I could see the pale darkness of the square, barely lit by those white street-lamps that imitate the always thrifty light of the moon, and a little further off, the lights of the elegant hotel and of the houses that shelter families or men and women on their own, each enclosed in their own protective yellow rectangle, as was I for anyone watching me. I also thought I could hear faint music, so faint that any movement I made covered or smothered it, and so I stood quite still—another cigarette in my hand—and tried in vain to hear and identify it, but it was so tenuous that I couldn't even make out what kind of music it was or even its rhythm. Then, as I usually did, I looked across beyond the trees and the statue to the other side of the square, in search of my carefree, dancing neighbour.

There he was, as always, and the night must, indeed, have been warm, because he, too, had flung open two of his large windows, two of the four, and it was likely that the music was coming from his long room, bare of furniture, like a dance floor cleared of all obstacles; it wasn't late and so he must, for once, have dispensed with his headphones or with the cordless con- traption he used, and this time the tune would not be playing in his head alone—as well as in the deductive ears of my mind, as I watched him dance—but throughout the house and outside too, until it died like a shadow or a fraying thread where I stood at my window. He wasn't alone, but with the two partners I knew from before, the two women I had occasionally seen, usually separately I seemed to remember: the white woman in tight trousers who had not, as far as I knew, stayed the night (she had got on a bicycle and pedalled briskly off into the dark), and the black or mulatto woman with the full, swirly skirt who appeared not to leave afterwards. Both of them were now wearing rather short, tight skirts (about mid-thigh-length, and possibly not very comfortable to dance in), and none of the three was as yet dancing, not properly, it was more as if they were deciding or agreeing on the exact steps they were going to take, doubtless in unison with the music that was just failing to reach me, and which I would, therefore, never recognise.

'He's brought them together,' I thought, 'perhaps he's going professional and wants to rehearse with them what in America they call a "routine", that is, movements and steps that are not improvised but agreed and coordinated, that country and this era are always spoiling words, everything is always being usurped, always becoming more imprecise, more oblique and fictitious and often incomprehensible, words and customs and reactions; but it may be that only one of them is his lover and there is, therefore, nothing odd about the three of them getting together to dance, or maybe neither of them is; if, on the other hand, both of them are, that would be a bit strange, I suppose, despite the artificial liberalism of these times in which, according to many people, nothing is ever very important, not even violent actions, which are so easily forgiven or regarding which there is never any shortage of imbeciles equipped with an imbecilic—or should I say monkish?—moral authority and ready to delve with infinite patience into the utterly unmysterious causes of that violence and which, naturally, they understand, as if they were above such things (they may pretend to be secular, but the old question that priests used to ask is always on the tip of their tongue, a permanent temptation: "Why are you like this, my son?"), until someone gives them a smack in the mouth and knocks them off their ivory tower and then they no longer understand; for example, I know that I could be violent in certain circumstances, apart from in self-defence, that is, but I know that it would be for the basest of reasons about which there would be no mystery at all, out of frustration or envy or revenge or in response to my own petty fears, and so it is best simply to avoid those circumstances: I couldn't meet up with a boyfriend or lover of Luisa's for some unthinkable activity involving all three of us, not at the moment, but in a few years' time who knows, when not a centimetre of my skin still smarts and if he turns out to be a really great guy, which I doubt; nor could she, I think, with a girlfriend or lover of mine, who will, at some point, inevitably exist, and given that she and I are neither that nor anything else at the moment, what, I wonder, will we be or what are we already, perhaps just a past, each other's past and one so long and enduring that it seemed to us it would never become the past. She can't be so very distracted these days—although she did sound happy at the beginning and also at the end of our conversation—if she has time to worry about how she will look in the immediate future,' I thought. When speaking of using those poisonous brews and blood-stained bits of plastic, she had said: 'I might not need them today, but tomorrow, rather than the day after tomorrow, I certainly will,' and that is not so very different from what Flavia Manoia must think when she wakes each morning from her last anguished and already diurnal dream, at least according to Reresby or Tupra, who described her to me beforehand, as he did her husband, thus skilfully determining my subsequent perception of them both: 'Last night, I was still all right, but today I'm another day older,' thinks Mrs Manoia when she opens her eyes, bare of make-up, and then, for a few minutes, unable to stand the thought of submitting herself to another test, she wants simply to close them again. How hard it is for me to imagine Luisa with such fears, I am used to her being young.

Or, rather, when I think about it, it isn't so very hard: such fears are not unknown to me either, I suppose. Such feelings are felt not only by women, but probably by anyone who suffers some setback late in life or experiences a first real sense of weariness, I myself believe I feel it every day, that fear or some inkling of it, especially in this foreign time in which I am without a partner and a little alone here in London, not greatly alone, as Wheeler believes, only a little and only sometimes; 'But women recognise it, they confront it without ennobling it or looking for some meaning in it, while we men, most men, think of it with a more deliberate and therefore somewhat phoney bleakness, our way of thinking being both sadder and more definitive, but, on the other hand, we thus manage not to see ourselves as either frivolous or fearful of solitude—which is incidental—nor of the loss of love—which is fundamental, but, at the same time, insignificant.' And so we ask ourselves, in order not to blush: 'And how much longer until I die?'

I listened more closely because it seemed to me that the music was clearer now, they must have turned the volume up, and when I looked again—really looked this time, rather than while absorbed in thought—I saw that the three of them had finally begun their much-discussed dance. It was an elegant dance, they weren't jumping or running around, instead, they were taking short and, how can I put it, sinuous and, yes, synchronised steps, the same steps at the same time, all the movement was in their feet and hips, heads nodding in time, arms accompanying those movements only lightly and minimally, slightly bent and held out to the side, as if each pair of hands were holding an open newspaper. They, the trio, travelled swiftly across the floor, but the impression they gave with their tightly controlled steps was that each of them maintained their position, as if their respective positions or allotted areas of floor moved with them, and each of them were stepping always on the same boards; I said to myself—or perhaps it was because I could hear more clearly now, in the distance—that they must be dancing to some Henry Mancini tune, it could be the famous 'Peter Gunn', hardly anyone remembers now that it was originally written as the theme tune for an old TV detective series, I don't know if it was ever shown in Spain, I think it was on in the 1950s (that is, almost prehistoric) and, of course, in black and white, but the music has not aged and has gone on to become an elegant modern-dance classic, assuming people know how to dance it elegantly, as these three did. Otherwise, it might be the beginning of the soundtrack to *Touch of Evil*, a film from the same period made by Orson Welles, in which Charlton Heston, no less, played a Mexican, it was astonishing that anyone could possibly believe he was a Mexican however large the moustache he sported from the first frame to the last, but people did. But that music is much less famous, and so I decided it must be 'Peter Gunn'. There are a few essential pieces of music that always travel with me if I'm well prepared (I wasn't when I left Madrid, I brought very little with me) or which I buy again if I'm staying in a country for any length of time, and among them are three or four pieces by Mancini because they almost infallibly cheer up even the gloomiest of days, and so I got it out and programmed the machine to repeat the first track, which is what the three people opposite must have done (the track lasts only two minutes and their dance was going on for much longer than that), and I played it in my apartment, as I had with other melodies on other occasions when I thought I could guess the music my dancing neighbour was dancing to, partly to amuse myself, partly to save him from the ridiculous fate of flailing around and moving and making absurd leaps before a spectator who cannot hear the music provoking them, who hears nothing, not that he would care anyway, for he was oblivious to the fact that he had any spectators, but one should show even more respect than normal to those who cannot demand it.

'Luisa's interest may mean,' I thought, 'that she hasn't been out much lately and hasn't received any stimulating visitors, that she hasn't got much to do, and this in turn may—just possibly—mean that she has not as yet entirely replaced me, otherwise she would have some distraction or would nurture some small, more or less daily hope, even if it was only a phone conversation with one particular person at the end of the day, if, for whatever reason, it wasn't easy for them to see each other—I don't know—perhaps because of his wife or his children, or our children. I realise that this is a baseless deduction to make, without foundation. But it may perhaps mean, at least, that no one has as yet entered her life to the extent that he has also gained access to the apartment, I mean not on a daily basis and not frequently enough for her to expect it, or for her not to be surprised if he turns up without warning, simply phoning from downstairs and saying "Luisa, it's me, I'm here, open the door", as if "me" were his unmistakable name, and for her, moreover, to be glad if he should decide to appear there as night falls or as evening comes on. No, he cannot yet have arrived, the flattering, sibylline man, diligent and even hard-working to begin with, the one who wants to help with supper and take out the trash and put the children to bed in order to seem—how can I put it—domestic, and then gradually move in on a permanent basis, restricting himself to filling a gap and trying not to upset whatever arrangements he already finds there. Nor has that other fellow, the jolly, laid-back one, the restless type who is terrified of leaving the landing and coming inside, of going in and meeting my children or even catching a glimpse of them in their pyjamas from his position at the front door, where he stands leaning while he waits for Luisa to finish giving instructions to the babysitter before she can finally leave to go out partying, the one who hopes, little by little, to remove her from there, night after night to lure her away or, by force of habit, to distance her from all that, so that she can then follow him everywhere and in everything, without ties. Nor has this third type as yet entered the apartment, the one who pretends infatuation, the weak tyrant in disguise, who will gradually isolate her from the external world with his melodramatics and his guile, in order to enclose her and keep her to himself, with only him as final horizon, the one who plays the poor sap in order, later, to possess and dominate her totally, the one who always finds a justification for his deep feelings and his intense suffering and who, in that respect, is like almost everyone else, so many people believe that strong feelings or, indeed, suffering and torment, make them good, deserving individuals and even give them rights, and that they should be compensated for these feelings incessantly and indefinitely, even by those who did not arouse the feeling or cause the suffering, who had nothing whatsoever to do with either, because, as far as they're concerned, the whole earth is always in their debt, and they never stop to think that one chooses a feeling or, at the very least, agrees to it, and that it is almost never imposed on one, nor is fate necessarily involved; nor do they think that you are as responsible for your feelings as you are for whomever you fall in love with, contrary to the general belief which, over the centuries, declares and tirelessly repeats the old fallacy: "I can't help it, it's not in my power to stop it", and that merely exclaiming "But I love you so much" as an explanation for one's actions, as an alibi or an excuse, should always be met with the words that few dare to utter even though it is the only fair response when love is unrequited and, perhaps, when it is requited too: "So what, that's got nothing to do with me." And that sometimes—yes, it's true—even unhappiness is an invention. No, no one is obliged to concern themselves about the love someone else feels for them, still less about their depression or their spite, and yet we demand attention, understanding, pity, and even impunity for something that concerns only the person who has those feelings, "It's understandable really," we say, "he's having a really hard time at the moment, that's why he's being so horrible to everyone," or "He's really hurt, he's at odds with the world because his heart is broken, he just can't live without her," as if not loving someone or ceasing to love them were an attack on the person who does love or continues to love, a plot or a reprisal, a desire to harm them, which it never is. So I can't really complain, indeed I mustn't: when Luisa wanted me by her side, I benefited from a grace that she renewed in me each day, just as I renewed in her an equal amount of grace; and if, one morning, that grace was no longer confirmed, there was no question of my throwing it in her face or seeing it as a wilful act of hostility or even dislike—that never even occurred to me—what I felt was more a sense of surrender, and great sorrow. Nor was there any question of appealing to those despicable modern notions which meddling laws use to protect the millions of opportunists who nowadays travel and populate every path and field of life: acquired rights, the years invested, cherished plans, force of habit or custom, standard of living reached, the future on which we were counting and the amount of love given, everything becomes measurable. And then, of course, there are the children born and the contracts signed. Or those not signed, but only verbal. Or those that were not even verbal, but merely implicit, those outrageous implicit contracts which, according to our pusillanimous world, the mere passing of time prepares and draws up behind our backs and even takes it upon itself to sign, as if time could ever be accumulative, when, in fact, it begins again from zero with each dawn and even with each moment . . .'

I suddenly felt lighter, possibly for the first time since—two nights before—I had got up from the table occupied by Manoia and Tupra at the disco to carry out the latter's orders and go in search of De la Garza and Flavia, I had stood up and pushed back my chair with an instantaneous, overwhelming feeling of heaviness, of uneasiness and foreboding, the pinprick in the chest and the sense of impending doom, all of which was emanating from Tupra rather than from myself, as if just by issuing that order he had transferred to me the caught breath or feigned breathlessness of someone about to deal a blow, or as if he had poured lead into my awakened soul and thus plunged it into sleep, and it had not left me since, that heaviness which I had sensed beforehand and experienced afterwards, that burden which had been growing in me hour upon hour, so much so that I had asked myself over and over, during the forty-eight hours which had passed so slowly (no, not even forty-eight hours), if I should resign and leave, give up, abandon that very attractive and comfortable job in the building with no name, working for the group with no name which, more than sixty years before, had been created by Sir Stewart Menzies or Ve-Ve Vivian or Cowgill or Hollis, or even the celebrated traitor Kim Philby or the loyal Winston Churchill himself, little would remain of them and of the mettle or intention or courage with which they conceived it; or perhaps that mettle and that courage have survived without diminution, and it is simply that the group was, at its foundation, as radical and unforgiving as it has seemed to be since the day before yesterday or as I sensed it was only two nights ago: perhaps all of them, the original group as a whole, including Peter Wheeler and his younger brother Toby Rylands, carried their probabilities in their veins, and time, temptation, and circumstance had led them at last to their fulfilment. Perhaps those circumstances and temptations, perhaps that undesired time, had arrived now, only a short while ago, when most of them continued to live on only in their disciples and heirs (Tupra, for example, was Rylands's heir), in the recent empty years of disintegration and apathy, or of compromise and confusion, orphanhood and idleness, for those private private individuals, as young Pérez Nuix had called them when she was telling me about them and describing them to me on that night of eternal rain when she visited me with her dog, having trailed me for far too long. Those circumstances and temptations had simply coincided with my arrival on the scene, that was all. Or they had, perhaps, merely proved more enduring. Pure chance, nobody's fault; not mine, that's for sure, not at all. Perhaps everything that had happened, everything I had seen and heard, at the disco and later on at Tupra's house, in reality and on screen, was not yet reason enough for me to withdraw or to leave.

I realised that I felt lighter, in part thanks to the music, to 'Peter Gunn' which never fails and works in all situations, and at the same instant I saw that it was also—or even more so— thanks to the dance into which I had unconsciously slipped, doubtless in instinctive, mechanical, almost unthinking imitation of the three carefree individuals on the other side of the square: sometimes your feet move of their own accord, or as we say in Spanish with more metaphorical exactitude, *cobran vida*, they take on a life of their own, they just won't keep still, and you barely notice. I had started dancing, it was incredible, there I was alone in the house, as if I were no longer me, but my agile, athletic neighbour with the bony features and neat moustache, a clear case of visual and auditory contagion, of mimesis, encouraged, in fact, by my own musings. I found myself (in a manner of speaking) moving around my living room, which was encumbered with furniture and much smaller than the one opposite, taking short, quick steps, although whether or not they were sinuous, I don't know, furiously jiggling feet and hips and with my head keeping time, my arms accompanying these movements only lightly and minimally, slightly bent and held out to the side, and in my hands an open newspaper which, of course, I wasn't reading, I had picked it up, I suppose, to provide an element of balance required by the dance. And then I felt embarrassed, because when I turned to look properly at the original dancers, when I looked again—really looked this time, rather than while absorbed in my own thoughts—I had to assume that they, in turn, had heard my music during a brief pause in theirs—my window was open as were two of theirs—and they would have located me without difficulty, by tracing where the music was coming from; and, of course, they were amused to see me (the watchman watched, the hunter hunted, the spy spied upon, the dancer caught dancing), because now not only were the four of us dancing absurdly and wildly according to their choreography, there had been another contagion too, from me to them: they must have found my idea ingenious or imaginative, and so each of them was now holding an open newspaper, as if they were dancing with the pages, with the newspaper as partner.

I stopped at once, I felt my face grow hot, fortunately, given the distance, they would not be able to see that, they weren't using binoculars as I occasionally did to spy on their dance studio. They too immediately stopped, they came over to the windows and signalled to me, waving, in fact they made explicit gestures to me to go over there and join them, to go to their apartment and not dance alone any more, but to form part of a jolly quartet. That made me feel even more embarrassed: I slammed the window shut, stepped back, switched off the light and turned the music down. I made myself invisible, inaudible. From now on, it would not—alas—be so easy for me to watch them or, rather, him, since, more often than not, he was alone. But it made me smile too, and I saw that it had one advantage: I thought that if ever a day or night should seem so desolate that even one of those infallible Mancini melodies, or another of those tunes that had the same effect, should prove incapable of raising my spirits, I at least had the possibility of going in search of company and dancing on the other side of the square, in that happy, carefree household whose occupant resisted all my deductions and conjectures, and inhibited or eluded my interpretative faculties, something that happened so infrequently that it bestowed on him a slight air of mystery. The prospect of a hypothetical visit, of his possible or future support, made me feel lighter still. I picked up my racing binoculars and looked across at them from behind the window, safe inside, safe from their eyes, and it seemed to me, judging from the way they were moving, that they had changed the music (they had gone back to their own dance, after my eclipse and flight), and so I altered the track on my machine as well and replaced it with a tune from *Touch of Evil* called 'Background for Murder', not as sombre as its title would suggest. But I made a mistake when trying to programme it in the dark or lit only by the thrifty light of the lunar street-lamps, and in its place another unexpected and entirely different tune began to play, it wasn't jazz this time, but a pianola, 'Tana's Theme' by name, as I later saw on the back of the disc, a tune I barely remembered from the soundtrack and from the film (I had a still fuzzier memory of the film, I should buy myself a DVD player without delay, in London I hardly ever went to the movies), although gradually, through those notes so like a hurdy-gurdy, emerging from the mists, came the figure of a mature Marlene Dietrich with black hair, dressed as a fortune-teller or something of the sort, also playing the role—even more improbably, and yet one believed in her too—of a Mexican woman I suppose, or perhaps a stateless gypsy in the eponymous frontier town of Tana.

It was a melancholy tune, difficult to dance to on your own, a valedictory melody, and bore no relation—indeed it was utterly incongruous—to the long strides and leaps my neighbours were performing over there in the distance, although I could see them close to through my lenses. However, I let the music play, I stood listening to it; hurdy-gurdies always bring back memories of childhood, they were common in the Madrid of the time, you still occasionally see one now, but it's not the same, they're not part of the natural landscape, but an intentional lure for tourists; and hearing the hurdy-gurdy music which I had accidentally programmed on my CD player, which was repeating slowly and calmly over and over (as if it really were a pianola, whose keys move on their own, as if played by ghostly fingers), images of those childhood streets appeared before me, Génova and Covarrubias and Miguel Ángel, the image of four children walking along those streets with an old maidservant or with my young living mother (both of them now ghosts), my siblings and me, three boys and a girl, she by my side, holding my hand, she was the youngest and I was the second youngest, and that had doubtless drawn us together.

'It seems odd that it should be the same life,' I thought. 'It seems odd that I should be one and the same, that boy with his three siblings and this man sitting in the half-darkness, with his own distant children whom he never now sees, a little alone here in London.' 'How can I be the same man?' Wheeler had wondered out loud in the garden of his house beside the river, just before lunch on that Sunday. How could that old man—he said to himself and to me—be the man who was married to a very young girl who had stayed forever young because she had died when she was still that age? Peter had preferred to leave the story for another day ('How did your wife die, what did she die of?' was my question), doubtless a day that would never arrive, at least not on earth but, with any luck, on Judgement Day, if that ever took place: it was clear that he found it hard to talk about her, or preferred not to. I, on the other hand, could still recognise myself as the man who married Luisa, on my return from my stay in England, and which I now had to call my first stay, the wedding took place not long afterwards. Years had passed, but not so very many, and unlike what had happened to Wheeler with his wife Val or Valerie, Luisa had kept me company through almost all the days of my slow ageing, at least until my expulsion and exile. I realised that my lightness that night was due less to the music or to my unpremeditated dance than to the whole of my conversation with her, especially the latter part, with that optimistic suspicion of mine, possibly without foundation, that no one had yet entered her life, not fully, and had not therefore yet installed himself in my house to rest his head on my pillow and to occupy all those places that had once been mine.

'Perhaps I should hang on to this job for a while longer, despite everything, despite Pérez Nuix, despite Tupra,' I thought as I began to doze off, sitting in my chair again, still dressed, my binoculars on my lap, in almost total darkness, lulled by the hurdy-gurdy or pianola which was playing out its melody in a series of endless farewells (Farewell, wit; farewell, charm; farewell, laughter and farewell, insults), convinced that I would at last enjoy a night without insomnia or unpleasant surprises, without any crushing nightmares, without that sense of something sitting heavy upon my soul. 'That was her advice to me, that I should hang on to this job about which she knows nothing, absolutely nothing. It wasn't because of how much I earn, she wasn't serious about that, and I do send her more than I need to, as she said with her usual honesty, she hasn't changed now that she's alone. But it's good that they're living in the lap of luxury, or nearly, that's what she said, it pleases me to be able to make that possible, although she's probably exaggerating, and it's all thanks to this job of which there is still more to come, there is always something, just a bit more, and so why not continue, one minute, the spear, one second, fever, another second, sleep and dreams (but afterwards there is always pain and the sword, and days and weeks and months and possibly years will have passed). What happened the night before last, what I saw and heard, is already beginning to grow blurred on this other night and will doubtless fade with the passing of the days, thanks to our ability to erase all things, we have an enormous capacity for that, as we do for temporary denial and transitory forgetting, and it will end up perhaps like the drop of blood at the top of the stairs, which I can no longer swear that I saw because by cleaning it up so very thoroughly, I opened the way to doubt, however contradictory that may seem: if I know I got rid of it, how can I doubt it; and yet that is how it is, you erase or delete something and what was erased or deleted no longer exists; and if it no longer exists, how can you be sure that it did actually once exist or if it never existed at all; when something disappears without leaving a rim or a trace, or someone vanishes without leaving a corpse, then it is possible to doubt their actual existence, even an existence that happened and had witnesses. It is therefore possible to doubt the existence of my uncle Alfonso, of whom my mother found only a photo of him dead, which I still have, but not his body. It's possible therefore to doubt that of Andrés Nin, for no one knows where he is buried or, indeed, if he was buried (perhaps in a little inner garden in the palace of El Pardo, and there, for thirty-six years, his bones would shudder whenever they felt the leisurely steps of his enemy above his anonymous or, rather, unrecorded grave). It's possible to doubt the existence of Valerie Wheeler, who, as far as I am concerned, has neither death nor life if no one tells me about them, she's just a name and might well be an invention and perhaps it would be better if she were (and maybe that's why her eternal widower gave me that warning: "One should never tell anyone anything"). What happened the night before last, and in which I participated, in this country which for me will one day revert to being "other", will become increasingly hazy, unreal, especially if it doesn't happen again or if I don't tell anyone else and don't keep thinking about it, then it will come to be remembered as, at most, a bad dream, and after every dream in which some appalling or violent act occurs, caused by me or which I did nothing to prevent, I can always say: "I didn't want it, that wasn't my intention, I took no part, it had nothing to do with me, I didn't choose it, what can I do about it . . ." That is what the dreamer thinks and what we all think, and who, from time to time, hasn't done the same? While the illusion lasts, we are safe, and it isn't a question of truncating the illusion, but, rather, of allowing it to have its full time to be believed.'

Suddenly—no, that isn't true, it took me a while to realise—I saw that the lights opposite, the dancers' lights, had gone out and the windows were now closed. They had, at some point, brought the session to an end, while I was drowsing or dozing to the sound of 'Tana's Theme', the pianola would not stop until I stopped it with my remote control, if not, it would never cease saying goodbye (Farewell, dear, delightful friends, for I am dying; I will not see you again, nor will you see me; and farewell, passion, farewell, memories). I had not been aware of what was going on outside, I had not gone back over to the window to see who came out, which of the two women, if one or both or neither, I could still peer out now and see if a bike was parked there, but if there wasn't, it wouldn't mean anything anyway, its owner might not have brought it tonight, she might have come by bus, Underground or taxi, there's no reason why what happens once should necessarily happen again, although we have the foolish tendency to believe otherwise, especially if what happens pleases us; and if there was a bike there, it wouldn't mean anything either, since it could belong to anyone. It really didn't matter to me at all, I wasn't going to go out and scan the square, all I cared about, at least a little, was who did or did not leave my house, that is, Luisa's and the children's house in far-off Madrid, or who did or did not enter it, and who stayed; and that was something I could not see, the eyes of the mind were not enough, they have limits. 'It's none of my business, I should get used to the idea once and for all,' I thought. 'Just as it's none of my business how Luisa spends my unnecessary money, the "excessive amount" I send without her asking me to, she knows what asking entails, for both parties involved, and now that we're no longer together, she prefers to wait and to avoid asking: nor is it my business if she succumbs to the same temptation as her female acquaintances and friends, deciding not to run the risk of ending up a pariah or one of the careless, and not wait until tomorrow or the day after tomorrow to have some treatment or other were she to want to, and submit herself to incisions and implants or to plump herself up like Mrs Manoia with those vile Botox injections if that makes her happy, although I can't see her taking that route, not yet, not the person I left behind, the person I know, she can't have changed that much, not enough to betray her own face; anyway, I probably should hang on to this job, so as to continue earning what I earn now and even a bit more, to defray or cover the costs of any more serious needs or emergencies, although it's no longer my role to try and protect her or try and make her happy, but how do you free yourself of that tendency, that habit; how do you expunge it from your thoughts?'

I pressed the remote-control button and silenced the hurdy-gurdy or pianola, it was high time, I had got carried away, I had opened myself up too much to evocations, although without ever becoming bored, hearing the same tune over and over. If I stayed in the armchair and went to sleep there fully dressed, I would wake in the night oppressed by leaden dreams, stiff-limbed and feeling grubby and cold. But I couldn't muster the energy to get up and go to the bedroom and at least lie down. And I thought this without the benefit of music, in total silence, it was late now, not by Madrid standards, but for London and that was where I was, one more inhabitant of that large island which was home or *patria* to some people, like Bertram Tupra, but not to me, to me it was simply that other country where there are no blinds or shutters and often no curtains, and so, if the sky is clear, the moon slips into all the rooms, or the lunar street-lamps do if it's cloudy, as if you always had to keep one eye open as you fell asleep: 'I must get used to the idea that I have no role now and that I am nothing in that apartment, between those sheets that no longer exist because they've been torn up to make rags or dust cloths long before they grew old and thin, or, indeed, on that pillow. I am just a shadow, a vestige, or not even that. An aphasic murmur, a dissipated smell and a vanished fever, a scratch without a scab, the scab came off long ago. I am like the earth beneath the grass or even deeper down, like the invisible earth beneath the still more sunken earth, a dead man for whom there was no mourning because he left no corpse, a ghost whose flesh is falling away and who is only a name for those who come afterwards and who will never know for sure if that name was invented. I will be the rim of a stain that vainly resists removal when someone scrubs and rubs at the wood and cleans it all up; or like the trail of blood that is so hard to erase, but which does, in the end, disappear and is lost, so that there never was any trail or any blood spilled. I am snow on someone's shoulders, slippery and docile, and the snow always stops falling. Nothing more. Or rather this: "Let it be changed into nothing, and let it be as if what was had never been." That is what I will be, what was and has never been. That is, I will be time, which has never been seen, and which no one ever can see.'

4
Dream

'Apart from that, it seems to me that time is the only dimension in which the living and the dead can talk to each other and communicate, the only dimension they have in common', that was the exact quotation, as I discovered later on in Madrid, and which I had murmured to myself when I was with Wheeler in his garden by the river, just after he had said: 'Speaking, language, is something we all share, even victims and their executioners, masters and their slaves, men and their gods . . . The only ones who do not share a common language, Jacobo, are the living and the dead.' I have never really understood that first quotation, and Wheeler, with his broader knowledge, might perhaps have been able to explain it, but he didn't hear me say it or chose not to, or assumed it was merely some idea of my own and so ignored it, but those words belonged to someone far more deserving of respect than me, the words of a dead man spoken when he was alive, he wrote them in 1967 and died in 1993, but now he was as dead as the poet Marlowe, although the latter had a four-hundred-year lead over him in death, for he was stabbed in 1593, that son of a cobbler born in Canterbury (the city of the bandit-Dean Hewlett Johnson, who was the absurd and indirect reason why my father could so easily have been shot long before I was born), and who had studied, in fact, at Bene't's College in Cambridge, which was later called Corpus Christi. Perhaps not talking any more has an equalising effect, perhaps that immediate levelling out and becoming alike is a consequence of being definitively silenced, which binds one with a strong and previously unknown bond to the already silent from every age, to the first and to the last, who will immediately become the second to last, and the whole of time becomes compressed and does not make divisions or distinctions or create distances because time ceases to have any meaning once it is over—once each person's life is over—even though those left behind continue counting, their own time and the empty time of those who have departed, as if one day the latter might be able to undo their leaving and be absent no longer. 'It's twenty-six years since my mother died,' we say, or 'It's nearly a year since your son died.'

When the person who wrote these lines wrote them that was more or less what he was talking about, he was a compatriot of mine, a *madrileño* like me, from that same hated city of Madrid, and, indeed, had lived through the blockade. Once, on a visit to Lisbon, he went to the leafy cemetery of Os Prazeres, with its avenues flanked by tiny mausoleums, a small fairyland of strange, low, grey, miniature houses, with ornamental pitched roofs, silent, immaculate and arcane—at once inhabited and uninhabited—and he began noticing the bare little living rooms which you can just make out through the glass-paned door which is set into so many of these tombs, each room furnished with 'a few chairs or two small upholstered armchairs next to a table covered by a lace shawl on which lies open some pious book, a silver-framed photograph of the deceased, a vase containing everlasting flowers and, on occasion, an ashtray'. In one of those small living rooms 'which are intended to look cosy', the traveller saw a pair of shoes, some socks and some dirty laundry peeping out from beneath one of the coffins; in another, some wine glasses; and in another, he thought, a deck of cards. 'It seemed to me,' my fellow countryman wrote, 'that the purpose of this décor was to give a familiar, ordinary, comfortable feel to any visits made to the dead, so that it would not be so very different from visiting the living.' He could see no relationship with the customs of the ancient Egyptians, who tried to ensure that the dead person, in his eternal isolation, signed and sealed, did not go without any of the things he had enjoyed and loved in life—although this, of course, applied only to those who were considered important—he related it, rather, 'to a desire not so much to make the dead person's stay in that place pleasant and homely, but to the need of the living to feel they will receive a warm welcome there'. And he added, clearly aware of the grave irony: 'One imagines that in this case it is the living who seek the company of the dead, who, as Comte would suggest, are not only in the majority, they are also a more influential and more animated majority.'

But what most shocked this traveller was the 'perfect composition' which he observed, 'with a degree of indiscretion', in one of these sepulchral rooms: as well as the small rug, the two armchairs and the table bearing the family photograph, the crucifix and a few artificial flowers, he saw 'an alarm clock, of the kind we used to see in our parents' kitchens, round in shape, with a bell like a spherical skullcap and with two small balls for feet'. He and his companions all, naturally, pressed their ear to the door to hear 'a loud tick-tock which was to a normal tick-tock what a shout is to the spoken voice'. And it was seeing this scene and hearing that loud ticking which sparked the reflection that culminated in the quotation I have never quite understood, which is why I remember it and why it makes me think. 'Was it,' he wondered, 'that, like the people buried alive in Poe, the clock was trying to remind the living of the macabre act of forgetfulness that had left it there? Or did it need that extra volume in order to keep the deaf people around it aware of time being measured out?' Then he went to the heart of the matter, to the real question provoked by that antiquated clock, apparently the most pointless and superfluous of alarm clocks: 'What was it actually measuring, I wonder?' wondered the man from my own city; yes, that was the main question, 'was it the amount of time they had been dead, or was it the countdown, as they call it now, the time yet to elapse before the final judgement? If it was measuring out the hours of solitude, was it counting those that had passed or those still to come? No other clock—and such a humble clock too—has ever seemed better placed or provided more food for thought. It occurred to me, with some surprise, that a religion which has always placed such emphasis on that precarious waiting time has not taken the trouble—not even the person who put the clock there—to give the soul the relief of knowing how long its anguish will last; for if the soul is waiting for the resurrection of the flesh, what better than a clock to give an idea not so much of how long the wait will be, but how much time has already been spent in waiting?' And it was here that the enigmatic words appeared or were inserted: 'Apart from that, it seems to me that time is the only dimension . . .' as given in full above. The passage continues, but does not help to elucidate these words, not that it really matters, it is often impossible to understand Shakespeare, to understand him exactly that is, and yet whenever he produces some obscure metaphor or dazzling ambiguity, he opens up ten paths or turnings down which one can plunge further (that is, he opens up these paths if you continue looking and thinking beyond what is merely necessary, as my father used to urge us to do, and you drive yourself on and say 'What else' at the point where you would normally say that there can be nothing more); 'in that sense,' added the traveller, 'within the confines of that comfortable, musty little living room, that troubling alarm clock is the only *deus ex machina* which allows the celebration of the mysterious dialogue which exists between the living and the dead'. There was no further comment, or, rather, there was: as is compulsory after these incursions into ghost time or dead time, before bidding farewell to his text, the traveller returned for a moment to the living and recalled how, 'as they were leaving', he had asked these two questions of one of his companions (someone, by the way, who bore the name of a character straight out of Edgar Allan Poe, Valdemar, no less): 'What happens, do you think, if it rings at night? Do the people sleeping here stir?'

One might ask those same questions now of him, my fellow countryman, who died twenty-six years after that visit or that piece of writing, although he was not buried in the small, leafy world of Os Prazeres, but, as he had wanted, in the tidy cemetery of La Almudena in the city of our birth, where my mother has been for twenty-six different years, her years. And one might well ask the same question of all of them: what if, instead of remaining silent, they talk among themselves while they wait, and the strong, unknown bond that places them on the same level and makes them alike and joins them together is not a definitive descent into silence but that indefinite counting throughout the interminable time which the stubborn clock measures and measures with its loud tick-tock, and during which its extravagant bell never rings even once? More than enough time to tell each other what they recall of their private dream—rather than of their consciousness—what they did and what happened to them and what they said, over and over, until they know everyone's story by heart, that is, each individual knows everyone's story and everyone knows each individual's story. Time enough for every man who has trodden the earth since the earth began and every woman who has traversed the world to tell the others their whole story, from beginning to end, the end being what carried them to the tomb or drove them from the living to join this other more numerous and influential company, more animated and perhaps also wittier and jokier, and certainly more indolent and more light-hearted, with fewer worries and responsibilities. Time, even, to contribute information and invent stories about beings that never existed and to recount deeds that never happened, fictions and fantasies and games with which to pass that long waiting time, and without ever once repeating themselves. And thus we would be back to our normal state, to not knowing what is true or, rather, what really happened.

And we might ask then how would the dead who died a violent death speak to the dead who killed them or who had issued the order to finish them off—they might never even have seen each other—once they were all on a level and all alike, although only in one respect, that of having died, which, in reality, is nothing, therefore the deceased, no less than the living, would be able to tell each other apart. And one might ask which version they would give, not to the Judge who has not yet appeared and to whom no one lies, and who is perhaps taking so long to arrive because there is no Judge nor ever was and never will be, mass suggestion will not summon him up nor mere insistence (or it may be that he does not dare to confront such a vast, querulous or possibly offended or, even worse, mocking multitude, and so he himself puts off until tomorrow, always tomorrow, the ghastly experience to which he committed himself out of pride; he places it infinitely on hold out of a sense of invincible fear or idleness), yes, which version would they tell each other and what would the two of them tell everyone else, martyr and executioner or instigator and victim, knowing that the present time, if I can call it that and as I have been calling it for a while now, would be too long, too unbearably long for that which did not happen, but was said to have happened, to be believed.

I only had time to say a few things in reply, I had time to smile to myself and to feel a pang of pity, to be amused by his comments on the sharp, stylised features that Botox gave certain faces, the faces of both divas and earthlings, and to think that there might be some unexpected cracks in De la Garza's global stupidity; and even to want to hear a little more from him, more chatter and more nonsense and more comical descriptions, and even to wonder fleetingly if how I was feeling about him was similar to how Tupra felt about me (although obviously there was no real comparison): I amused Tupra, and he enjoyed our sessions of conjecture and examination, our conversations or merely listening to me. ('What else?' he would demand. 'What else occurs to you? Tell me what you're thinking and what else you noticed.')

This lasted almost no time at all, or perhaps everything happened at once, which meant there was time for everything, or maybe I retrieved and rethought it later on, in the pause provided by my doze in the chair or by the sense of unease that persisted when I did finally go to bed, once that long, erroneous, disagreeable night was over. De la Garza had, in his own way, enlightened me about that product which once was poisonous, but was now possibly innocuous, and he had come out with a few amusingly impertinent remarks about its users or addicts with their wild expressions, the last thing he had said was this: 'It makes her look slightly unhinged, don't you think?' referring to someone he had called 'the ex-wife of that guy who's hitched up now with one of our Spanish actresses', I had understood him perfectly, one of the drawbacks or advantages of compatriotism, a tall woman who also had the face of someone very tall; it was a problem, having that kind of face, regardless of whether one was tall or short. 'They must inject it into her cheekbones and into her crow's feet by the litre, I'd be surprised if she can even close her eyes, she probably sleeps with them wide open. Just like this Flavia woman. I mean, depending on the angle, she looks like some kind of sprite.' There he was in his carnival get-up and with his shoelaces untied, long shoelaces too, they could easily get wet, even in a toilet that wasn't used very much, the floors in public toilets are always wet. It was a miracle he hadn't had an accident, especially during the last dance, when he had danced almost like one possessed, and which we had interrupted in order to save Mrs Manoia from the flailings of his fake hair and, according to what Tupra told me later on at his house, to save De la Garza himself from something far worse.

'Perhaps all sprites sleep with their eyes open.' That was all it occurred to me to say in response, as a preparation for a joke or a quip; I could feel laughter bubbling up inside me, and I didn't want him to take it as a pardon or a homage (he was a very arrogant attaché), and so I looked for and improvised another outlet for it: 'Well, you should know, Rafael, seeing as how you know such a hell of a lot about literary fantasy—including the medieval stuff.' And I pretended to laugh at my own comment, when in fact I was laughing at his outrageous remarks. Nevertheless, I immediately introduced another element to dissipate the possibly wounding effects of my sarcasm (so I obviously had time to say four or five things to him): 'By the way, your shoelaces have come undone.' And I pointed at his feet.

Without changing his posture, De la Garza looked down too; he had got over his dizziness or frenzy or vertigo, he must have thought it somehow chic to stand there, half leaning and half hanging onto a strange, cylindrical metal bar, despite the prosaic nature of the place and the complete absence of spectators (he could hardly imagine that I was likely to be impressed). He gazed at his shoes from afar, with an inexplicably commiserative look on his face, as if they were not his, but someone else's—mine—and he did not make the immediate movement one would expect, that of crouching down and tying them up. He had an ability to surprise, as does every major idiot, and, of course, to irritate, all in the space of a single second, and to erase at a stroke my open laughter, my inner smile, my incipient sympathy and that tiny pang of pity.

'Tie them up for me, will you, I'm still a bit too drunk to crouch down like that, and anyway, where's that fucking friend of yours fucking got to with his fucking vest and the fucking line of cocaine he promised me. And maybe make it a double knot, just in case. Go on, it won't hurt you.'

Perhaps the worst thing was that final remark, 'Go on, it won't hurt you'. His childishness, his rich-kid manners enraged me. The very idea that I would kneel down on a toilet floor, however clean and luxurious the toilet might be, and tie the shoelaces of a great dickhead like him who made an entirely artificial show of being foulmouthed (four 'fuckings' in one sentence is too much, it's bound to seem put on) and had blithely landed me in all kinds of trouble; just because the idea occurred to him or presented itself to him as something perfectly natural and possible, and he saw nothing unseemly or unusual about it; and he said it as if it were a whim of his or almost as if it were an order, and in that chic, idiotic place, I had already been given quite enough orders by others, by those who paid me and were allowed to give me orders, or not, or only up to a point; and he wasn't even disabled or crippled or anything, he just couldn't be bothered to crouch down . . . There are people who have no sense of boundaries and who always catch you unawares, however forewarned you might be, such people are simply impossible. I don't know what I would have replied or done, or done to him, I don't know because I didn't have time to do anything; although perhaps, after a few seconds of initial stupefaction, who knows, I would simply have laughed even more, at his sheer nerve. I didn't have time, though, because, at that moment, Tupra came in, or Reresby as he was that night. I think that when he came in, I had, at most, the same brief, simple thought that had filled my mind when I saw De la Garza's flailing hairnet in action on the dance floor: 'I'd like to smash his face in,' and that is what I must have been thinking when the door opened.

Seven of the minutes announced by Tupra must have passed or perhaps ten or even possibly twelve, he would have had various things to deal with, sorting out Flavia and cleaning her up, restoring her to her husband, offering him some kind of explanation, apologising for having to absent himself again and, since I was occupied elsewhere, leaving the two of them alone, he would, I thought, take over from me now and stay with the attaché—but what would they talk about—and send me back to the table to look after the Manoias. I saw at once, however— his whole figure appeared, as if we could see both the front and the back of him—that he was carrying his overcoat, he did not have it on, but wore it draped over his shoulders like an Italian or a particularly vain Spaniard or perhaps a wealthy Slav, and that he had another slung over his arm, there were two over- coats, his light one and a dark one, it occurred to me that the latter was mine, and so I thought that perhaps we were leaving and that he had picked them up before keeping our absurd ad hoc appointment in the handicapped toilet, so that we would not waste time at the coatcheck on our way out ('Don't linger or delay', perhaps that was Reresby's motto).

'Are we leaving?' I asked.

He did not reply at once, but did not take long to do so. I saw him remove something from his pocket and jam the door shut with it, a much-folded sheet of paper, a wooden wedge, a small piece of cardboard, I couldn't see what it was at first, he did it in a matter of seconds, as if he had been jamming doors shut since he was a boy. No one would be able to open it until he removed the wedge, I saw him testing it by pushing and pulling hard at the door, two rapid movements one after the other, I noticed a particular firmness and confidence and even economy in each and every movement he made.

'No, no one's leaving just yet,' he said.

He seemed distracted, or, rather, still preoccupied, he was very business like in his attitude. He slung the darker coat over one of the metal bars, a low one at about hip-height, while he hooked his own coat carefully over the end of another higher one, he took his coat off as if it were a cape, not that it was particularly full, it did, however, seem to me somewhat heavy and stiff, like the filthy coats worn by beggars or as if it had been starched. But no one uses starch any more, certainly not on overcoats. His was clearly very new and expensive, of the kind that underlines its owner's respectability, possibly too emphatically, to the extent that one begins to doubt it.

'At last,' De la Garza said in a whining voice. And he added in his hideous English accent, addressing Tupra directly (it was provoking and positively incendiary that he should have passed comment on the latter's vest given how extreme or, rather, offensive he himself was to the eye): 'It's about time too, you know.' Set phrases were always the only recognisable words in his mouth, precisely because they were so fixed and set, and he was one of those people who add 'you know' to everything, which is always a sign of someone who knows nothing at all; and as I knew all too well, the oaf was incapable of holding a conversation in English, he would get lost at the first subordinate clause, if not before, and he was only comprehensible to a fellow Spaniard, which it was my misfortune, and not my only one, to be. It was as if he had forgotten the real reason he was there, as if he had forgotten that we had separated him from Flavia to prevent him from turning her face into a holy shroud, that he was indebted to us and had, in a sense, insulted us as her companions and guardians; I, after all, had been the one to introduce her to him. That is the good fortune of the arrogant, they never feel responsible or have a bad conscience because they have no conscience and are totally irresponsible, they are bewildered and taken aback by any punishment or slight, even one they have determinedly brought on themselves, they are never at fault, and often convince others, as if by contagion, of that spontaneous conviction of theirs and end up getting off scot-free. I wasn't sure that this time he would. Tupra would not, I thought, like that carping tone; De la Garza had been offered a line of cocaine, not even directly, but through a third party (his compatriot and, very nearly, his interpreter), and in his happy, fatuous mind that meant he could justifiably demand to have it seven minutes later, or ten or twelve, it was tantamount to registering a complaint about a favour done or a gift given.

The feeling of heaviness that had overwhelmed me when I first got up from the table and headed for the toilets increased at that moment; I hadn't lost it, but now it grew stronger, became almost oppressive; various combinations triggered it: alarm and haste, the sense of tedium experienced at the prospect of having to carry out some cold-blooded act of reprisal, or the invincible meekness one feels in a threatening situation. That third blend would not apply to Rafita at the moment, he was unaware of any threat. I, on the other hand, was aware more of the second than the first, there was no alarm or haste now as there had been when I stood up and pushed back my chair in order to go in search of him and of Flavia, but a presentiment (I wouldn't go so far as to use the word 'prescience') of some near-inevitable act of reprisal hovering over us, as if the arrow had been placed in the bow and the latter, however lethargically, was now drawn tight, even if the arm drawing it tight was yawning. All this was emanating from Tupra, even though I was the one feeling it: the malaise, the pinprick and the sense of menace and of some impending misfortune. Yes, Reresby was clearly the kind to give no warning or only when it was of no use at all, how can I put it, when the caveat was just part of the punitive action already being taken.

'Don't worry, I'll reward you for the wait,' he said affably, he was still sending out no message, not verbally at least. I don't know if the attaché understood, but it didn't matter because, at the same time, Tupra slipped two fingers into the breast pocket of his reprehensible vest and drew out a neatly folded sachet. With those same two fingers, index and middle, he held it out to De la Garza; or, rather, he did not take a step forward or extend his arm, he merely showed the little packet to him, dangling it in mid-air, pincered between his fingers, the way an adult displays the prize a child has won, so that the undiplomatic diplomat was obliged to come and take it; and Reresby invited him to do so: 'Help yourself,' he added, and that can be understood by any fool who has ever set foot in England. 'But don't take too much. It's got to last all night.' He still sounded distracted, like someone going through the motions or else gearing up to something. And although there is no indication of this in English, I sensed that he was addressing De la Garza as '*tú*'.

'So it was true, he does have some,' I thought, without feeling it was in any way strange: indeed, there was nothing unusual about a man like him having one or two grammes or more, possibly even obtained from the police, confiscated goods; and it wouldn't even necessarily be for his personal consumption, it might serve for just such a situation as this, using the substance as a lure or as a symbolic reward, in order to get something in exchange. 'Comendador, in his day, used it as a bait for getting some pussy,' I suddenly recalled, 'they'd get into his car or go back to his apartment with him and in one of those two places he would frequently, but not always, end up getting it on with them, even though they might not have foreseen that when they first got into his car. This was the kind of language—"getting some pussy" and "getting it on"—that Comendador normally used, and although very different, it coincided in part with the slang of this imbecile here, and it had been my language too in other, younger, more subjective times and still can be on odd occasions—one never forgets a way of speaking, I can recall all the ones I've known and used—when a woman decides to be just pussy and nothing else and to let you screw her without more ado and without any sudden, subsequent show of affection, or if she screws you, it comes to the same thing, most women have known a night in their life when they felt like playing the role of pure, mindless flesh, of being either plunderer or spoils, it makes no difference, even Luisa had known such nights in her youth, although I don't know the details, and she might know such nights again now, just as I occasionally have here, perhaps, indeed, Luisa is experiencing such a night tonight; and Pérez Nuix must have known such nights too, she isn't old enough to have called a halt to them for good, that is, a temporary or apparent halt, because nothing is ever definitively over. With his cocaine Tupra has managed to have me lure this cunt into a handicapped toilet, and it's quite something to have got him to stay in here for ten or twelve minutes without complaint. So for the moment, he has managed to achieve his most urgent aim, to neutralise him, to prevent his making the situation with Mrs Manoia still worse and thus reassuring her Arturo or, still more important, assuaging his anger, that is doubtless the main thing.'

But now that he was offering him the little packet, I wondered what else he wanted in exchange for handing it over, perhaps it was a bribe (he would say afterwards: 'No, it's OK, you keep it') to make him disappear for good, so that he would go straight from that toilet out into the street with no stopovers en route, but that would be impossible, he would have to go and collect or warn his partying companions, unless they had left without him when they saw his wild behaviour on the dance floor. Reresby had also said: 'This moron has got to be neutralised, stopped,' which meant, *sensu strictu*, rendering him null and void, something not dissimilar to annihilating him.

De la Garza took it from his hand, the neatly folded packet, possibly as yet untouched, it looked quite plump. He did not even say 'Thank you', he merely used the edge of his bejewelled fist to check that the door was closed, securely jammed shut, and then set about preparing the cocaine beside the various taps, on the flat black marble that surrounded the concave porcelain. But he changed his mind as soon as he took out his wallet (perhaps he didn't quite trust Tupra's wedge after all, it didn't strike him as providing a strong enough padlock), and he went into one of the cubicles, still holding the packet in one hand; obviously he didn't close the door, we would have found that insulting, or as indicating a possible intention to take more than he should. I had not had a proper look during my first rapid visit—just a quick glance round in search of the fugitives—and had failed to notice that as well as bars at shoulder-height, there were also three or four bars at hip-height as well; on one of these lay my overcoat, if it was mine; nor had I noticed how large the cubicles were, there were only two of them, but they were almost like small rooms, everything about the toilet was spacious, doubtless to facilitate the movements of disabled people and to allow wheelchairs to make all kinds of turns (even sudden ones); equally generous was the excellent lighting, intended, I assumed, to avoid the possibility of any stumbles, everything was new and spotless, gleaming and even welcoming, without any of the sordid elements so frequent in public toilets. It was admirable that people should show such respect for the disabled of Britain, that they did not cheerfully invade it and soil and besmirch it, as is the norm among men and optional among women. Anyway, there the three of us were, still all able-bodied, not just making improper and semi-criminal use of the toilet, but also preventing any legitimately handicapped person who might need it from entering, although that would have been an unlikely coincidence; but two of we three intruders were Spanish, and you know what we're like, or most of us: you only have to forbid us from doing something for us all to rush in and disobey whatever orders or instructions or requests have been issued. The original idea, however, had come from the English member of the trio, the idea of meeting there or of profaning that place; regardless of whether his surname was Finnish or Czech, Turkish or Russian, he was a real and possibly patriotic Englishman and, besides, that night, he answered to Reresby. The truth is that I found it hard to remember when he was using one of his other names: I always thought of him as Tupra and that was what came to my tongue, not even Bertram or Bertie after he had repeatedly urged me to treat him in that more familiar way.

De la Garza lowered the lid of the toilet seat and placed the packet and the wallet on the tank behind, but immediately stopped when he realised that the tank top was white, and transferred them instead to the lid, which was ceramic or made of something similar, dark blue, polished and smooth, and he knelt down before it, almost resting his buttocks on his heels ('Ah, so now the little jerk doesn't mind kneeling down,' I thought bitterly, 'a moment ago, he didn't even want to bend down to tie his own shoelaces and wanted me to tie his knots for him, but he's happy enough to do it now in order to prepare his line of cocaine and sniff it up, well, I hope he steps on his laces afterwards and falls over; right now, I'd willingly tie a knot in his neck'). He pushed the hairnet out of the way with a toss of his head so that it wouldn't bother him, as if the hairnet were a full head of hair; it hung limply to one side; he took a credit card out of his wallet, it was, I noticed, Platinum, he must have a fair amount of money in his account, or else was in charge of administering embassy funds under various headings, they don't give Platinum Visa cards to just anyone. He opened the packet carefully and rather ineptly, he must be only an occasional consumer; with the aid of one corner of the credit card he scattered a small amount of cocaine directly onto the lid of the toilet seat, having nothing else to hand that he could use as a paten or tray, the white powder could be seen quite clearly, which would not have been the case had he used the white porcelain tank. With the stiff plastic card he formed the powder into a line, and he didn't take too much, he even returned a little of the powder to the sachet, which he pushed to one side, folded but not completely closed, as if suddenly aware that it was someone else's property. He did not manipulate the Visa card with great dexterity, he kept regrouping and shaping the line; I watched, perplexed, from the cubicle doorway and Tupra remained outside, behind me or so I assumed, I wasn't looking at him, only at Rafita on bended knee (he may not have been very experienced, but it was a brief operation, or should have been). The line did not seem to me either very long or very broad, at least compared with those I had seen Comendador and his friends prepare in earlier days, as well as other less nocturnal people at various parties and in the occasional toilet (the latter especially in the late 1980s and early 1990s, but not only then), including a minister, a tycoon, the president of a soccer club, a judge with a very stern reputation and even their respective wives in all their finery and from different backgrounds and of assorted ideas and ages, both in England and in Spain, as well as a couple of actresses and a couple of bishops (on separate occasions: one Catholic and one Anglican, but both incognito), a multimillionairess from Opus Dei or from Christ's Legionnaires, I can't quite remember now, and, more recently, Dick Dearlove at the end of his celebrity supper along with some of his supper celebrities; and one time in America, a Pentagon chief, although I can say no more than that, I mean, who or where or what the circumstances were; but it was pure chance that I was there, and, besides, that happened later, and at the time I'm referring to, I hadn't yet seen all this (I think it was the reason I escaped arrest, or else it immediately invalidated the arrest, more surely even than the faulty recital of the Miranda law on the part of the detective who had ordered me, the Pentagon chief, two women and another two men to be handcuffed, 'You have the right to remain silent . . .': the fact is that if I hadn't remained silent, I could have landed that high-up chief with all those troops at his command in a very tight spot indeed).

De la Garza patted his trousers and his giant jacket (the tails of which were brushing the floor) and he looked at me without really focusing or entirely turning his head; I was afraid he was going to ask me, or even Tupra, for a banknote, he was quite capable of doing so. 'If you're going to stick a note up your nose, use one of your own, you drone,' I thought, unwittingly falling into rhyme. But, in the end, he stuck his hand in one of his pockets and brought out a five-pound note which he rapidly rolled up—he was more dexterous at that—to make the tube through which to inhale the powder that looked rather like talc. 'Yes,' I thought, 'it does smell a bit like talcum powder in here. They're so clean, the handicapped,' although I was becoming increasingly convinced that it had been a very long time since any disabled person had visited that disco, perhaps the toilet had just been installed, a recent improvement. 'Or perhaps it isn't coke, but talc that Tupra's given him': that thought also occurred to me. I saw De la Garza bend his head and crane his neck forward, he was about to snort the line, or half of it, up his left nostril, he had closed his right nostril with his index finger. 'He looks like a condemned man in olden times,' I thought, 'offering his vanquished head, his bare neck to the axe or the guillotine, with the toilet-seat lid as stump or block, and if the seat was up, the toilet bowl would serve as a basket for his head as it fell—the way vomit does—into the blue water, that way, it wouldn't roll.'

Then I heard Tupra's commanding voice:

'Stand clear, Jack.' And at the same time, he grabbed my shoulder, firmly but not roughly, and drew me aside, removed me, I mean, from the doorway of that cubicle which was more like a small room, perhaps the same size as those minuscule mausoleums in the cemetery of Os Prazeres, summarily decorated and intended to be welcoming, at once inhabited and uninhabited. 'Stand clear, Jack' were his words, or perhaps 'Clear off' or 'Step aside' or 'Out of my way, Jack', it's hard to remember exactly something which, subsequently, disappears into nothing because of everything else that comes after, at any rate, I understood what he meant, whatever the phrase he used, that was the sense and it was, moreover, accompanied by that gesture, his firm hand on my shoulder, which allowed itself to be pushed out of the way; viewed positively, the phrase could have been understood as 'Step aside', more negatively as 'Out of my way, Jack, clear off, don't get involved and don't even think about trying to stop me', but his tone of voice sounded more like the former, a very gentle voice given that it was issuing an order that brooked no disobedience or delay, no hesitation in its performance, no resistance or questioning or protest or even any show of horror, because it is impossible to object to or to oppose someone who has a sword in his hand and who has already raised it up in order to bring it down hard, to deal a blow, to slice through something, when that is the first time you have seen the sword and have no idea where it came from, a primitive blade, a medieval grip, a Homeric hilt, an archaic tip, the most unnecessary of weapons or the most out of keeping with the times we live in, more even than an arrow and more than a spear, anachronistic, arbitrary, eccentric, so incongruous that the mere sight of it provokes panic, not just visceral fear, but atavistic fear too, as if one suddenly recalled that it is the sword that caused most deaths throughout most centuries—it has killed at close quarters and when face to face with the person killed, without the murderer or the avenger or the avenged detaching or separating himself from the sword while he wreaks his havoc and plunges it in and cuts and slices, all with the same blade which he never discards, but holds onto and grips even harder while he pierces, mutilates, skewers and even dismembers, never a bag of flour, but always a bag of meat that gives and opens beneath this skin of ours that resists nothing, which offers no protection and is so easily wounded that even a fingernail can scratch it, and a knife can cut it and a spear rip it open, and a sword can tear it even as it slices through the air—that it is the most dangerous and tenacious and terrible of weapons, because unlike something that can be thrown or hurled, the sword can strike again and stab repeatedly, over and over, again and again, each strike worse and more vicious than the last, it isn't an arrow or a spear which may wound, but which will not necessarily be followed by others that will hit and penetrate the same body, one may be enough, it may cause only a single gash or a wound that will subsequently heal, unless the weapon has been dipped in some deadly poison, whereas the sword slices insistently in and out and in and out, it is capable of slaying the healthy and finishing off the wounded and dismembering the indefinitely dead, only stopping when the person wielding it drops from exhaustion, but who will otherwise never let go or lose it, unless he, in turn, is killed or has his arm torn off; which is why the gesture of unsheathing was enough of a threat and never a vain one, it was best to leave it half unsheathed as a warning or a doubt or a signal that one was alert, a visual message that one was on guard, because once the whole blade was out in the air, once the tip was free and looking around, that was a sign that bloodshed would inevitably follow.

I hadn't seen Tupra unsheathe the sword, always assuming he had a sheath, yet, suddenly, as if by magic, there he was holding the bare blade, not a very long blade, certainly much less than a metre in length, but cruel and very sharp, the grip was not a medieval one, although, at a first glance, all swords look medieval apart from those that have a guard or a cup hilt, it was perhaps more Renaissance in style, it reminded me of a Landsknecht sword, at the time and later on too, when I returned home and remembered it in my state of half-sleep or sleeplessness, not that I'm an expert in these matters, but during my time teaching in Oxford I had to translate, among many a pretentious, ancient text with absolutely no practical application, one by Sir Richard Francis Burton—known as 'Captain Burton' to second-hand booksellers—about the different types of sword, an illustrated passage what's more, and the name and its corresponding image stuck in my head, as did a few others ('Papenheim', for instance), the Landsknecht sword also had a German nickname, *Katzbalger* or some such thing, a word that meant 'cat-gutter', a modest undertaking involving little risk, or else frankly profitable and base, after all, the Landsknechts were German mercenaries in the infantry, of whom my country nevertheless made full use in its imperial regiments, or perhaps that absurd translation had been from Spanish into English and not vice versa, *The Siege of Vienna by Charles V*, why else would that title by the infinite Lope de Vega ring a bell, why else would I know by heart these lines (although it was just possible that I had heard them spoken by my father, who loved reciting, as much as or more than Wheeler, they were almost contemporaries): 'I go, victorious Spaniard of lightning and fire, I leave you. I leave you too, sweet lands, I leave Spain and tremble as I go; for these men, full of rage, are like thunderless lightning that kills silently.' A highly patriotic, arrogant, eloquent passage, spoken by an invader put to flight, although this wasn't the case in that siege laid in order to destroy and put an end to another, the Ottomans' siege of Vienna under the command of Suleiman the Magnificent, there the 'cat-gutters' must have fairly burned in the hands of those mercenaries, more callous than angry, they appear in engravings by Dürer and Altdorfer, which show their weapons too, that not particularly long sword, seventy centimetres, worn diagonally across the belly, or sometimes they carry pikes, rather like the ones in Velázquez's painting of the surrender at Breda, had Tupra been wielding one of those as well he would have filled us with even more dread, me, of course, but especially his victim, De la Garza, against whom he had raised his sword, Reresby was holding it in one hand when he pushed me aside to get past, but he was gripping it now with both hands to raise it, ready to unleash the blow. I noticed that his vest rode up when he had both arms raised, he was creating as much momentum for himself as possible, underneath, above his belt, I could see his shirt with its very fine, pale, elegant stripes.

'He's going to kill him,' I thought, 'he's going to cut off his head, slice through his neck, no, he can't, he won't, yes, he is, he's going to decapitate him right here, separate his head from his trunk and I can do nothing about it because the blade is going to come down and it's a two-edged sword, he can't just deal him a blow, even a hard blow, with the blunt edge, just to frighten him, to teach him a lesson, because there is no such edge, but two equally sharp edges which would cut through him anyway, De la Garza will die immediately and then we will have to wait an infinite amount of time before we see him whole again, all in one piece, until the day when, out of respect, the two parts into which he is about to be transformed will be joined together, so that he can come to Judgement as he should, not like some freak-show monster, but with his head on his shoulders and not under his arm as if it were a ball or a globe of the world, and there cry: "I died in England, in a public toilet, in a handicapped toilet in the old city of London. This man killed me with a sword and cut me in two, and this other man was there, he saw it all and didn't lift a finger. It was in another country, the country of the man who killed me, but for me he was a foreigner, which is what he would have been in my country; on the other hand, the man who watched and did nothing spoke my language and we were both from the same land, further south, not so very far away, albeit separated by the sea. I still don't know why I was murdered, I hadn't done anything very bad, nor did I constitute a danger to them. I had half a life or more before me, I would probably have become a minister or, at the very least, ambassador to Washington. I didn't see it coming, I was left without life, without anything. They came like thunderless lightning: one did the destroying, while the other kept silent." But perhaps De la Garza would be incapable of speaking like that even on the last day, for on that day each man and each woman will continue to be exactly as they always were, the brutish will not become delicate nor the laconic eloquent, the bad will not become good nor the savage civilised, the cruel will not become compassionate nor the treacherous loyal. And so the likelihood was that Rafita would make his complaint in his usual coarse, affected way, and bawl at the Judge: "You know, the way I snuffed it was really nasty, I mean, along comes this guy and slices my head off on the lid of a toilet seat in a public lav for cripples, can you believe it? The great British bastard, the son-of-a-bitch. I was fucking innocent, I was, I hadn't a clue what was coming, I was pretty much out of my head and pretty much danced out too, and feeling distinctly under the weather, I was just minding my own business and hadn't a clue what was going down, but I hadn't done him any harm, I swear it, he just turned up there in psychopath mode, in inexplicable enigma mode, anyway, the brute produced this sword out of nowhere and chopped off my head with one blow, I don't know, the nutbag must have come over all Conan the Barbarian, or El Cid, or Gladiator, a guy in a vest for Christ's sake, a vest, and suddenly he goes and whips out this sword, and his little private fantasy cost me my neck, and my life ended right there and then, I mean, what a bummer. And the other guy just stood there like a statue, his face frozen in horror, a guy from Madrid, would you believe, a fellow Spaniard, one of us, and he didn't even try to grab the other guy's arm, well, his two arms, because the swine was holding this cutlass thing with both hands so as to bring it down on me with all his might, so much for world medieval literature, although it was probably better like that, you know, a clean cut, imagine if he'd only sliced halfway through and left me hanging, still alive and watching it all and knowing that I was being killed for no reason. I died in London, I died when I was out one night partying, I didn't even get to enjoy the whole evening, didn't even have time to drain it to the dregs, those two set a trap for me. And do you know the last thing I did, I knelt down, dammit. And then it was all over." 'No, there's nothing to be done,' I thought, 'he's going to kill him. The voice is the quickest thing there is, all I can do now is shout.'

'Tupra!'

I shouted his name, I didn't have time to do anything else, not even to add 'What are you doing?' or 'Are you mad?' or 'Stop!', as they do in old-fashioned novels and in comic strips, nor to come out with any kind of exclamation which would prove utterly futile in the face of something that is not just imminent but has actually begun, and is already happening and is an arrow flying. De la Garza turned his head for a fraction of a second—it would roll like a globe—just as he had done shortly before, when he had been on the point of asking me for a banknote so that he could roll it into a tube and stick it up his nose, that is, he didn't really turn his gaze on me, didn't focus, and would only have seen the blurred gleam of what hung or hovered over him, but he must have caught a glimpse or a glance of the steel, recognised the blade and the edge, but without recognising that recognition, not believing and at the same time believing, because you are always instantly aware of any real danger of death, even if, in the end, it turns out to be something that merely frightens you half to death. As when, in a dream, a life-threatening situation goes on for far too long, or there is a prolonged sequence of being chased and caught, then chased and caught again, and the sleeping consciousness succumbs to panic and to fatalism and, at the same time, knows that something is not quite right and that your fate is not necessarily sealed, because the dream is still going on without stop or respite or resolution, and the blow that began its descent some time ago has not yet fallen: it delays and lingers and dallies and loiters, the blow, the sword-strike, the dream, it pauses and waits and everything sits heavy on the soul, it freezes and plays for time while the conscious mind struggles to wake up and save us, to dissipate the terrible vision or to shatter it, and to drive away or staunch the pent-up tears that long to burst forth, but cannot.

I saw the look on his face, the look of someone who thinks or knows he is dead; but since he was still alive, the image was one of infinite fear and struggle, mental struggle, perhaps of desire; of childish, undisguised terror, his mouth must have dried instantly, as instantly as his face turned deathly pale, just as if someone had given his face a quick lick of grey or off-white or queasy-coloured paint, or had thrown flour over him or perhaps talcum powder, it was rather like when swift clouds cast a shadow over the fields and a shudder runs through the flocks below, or like the hand that spreads the plague or closes the eyes of the deceased. His top lip lifted, almost folded back on itself in a rictus, revealing his dry gums on which the inner part of his lip got stuck for lack of saliva, he would never be able to lower that lip, it would be fixed like that until the end of time on a tormented face separated from its body, he did lower his head as soon as he caught sight of the blurred gleam of metal overhead, above him and above me, up there, a double-edged sword, two hands, a grip, he pressed his head against the lid of the toilet seat as if hoping it would give way and disappear, and he instinctively drew in his neck, hunched up his shoulders as if in a spasm of pain, the deliberate or unwitting gesture made by all the victims of the guillotine over two hundred years or of the axe over hundreds of centuries, even those satisfied with their guilt and those resigned to their innocence, even chickens and turkeys must have made that gesture.

The sword fell with great speed and force, that one blow would be enough to make a clean cut and even splinter or split the lid, but Tupra stopped the blade dead, about one centimetre or two from the back of the neck, the flesh, the cartilage and the blood, he was in control of what he was doing, he knew how to gauge it, he meant to stop it. 'He hasn't done it, he hasn't decapitated him,' I thought with some relief and not in so many words, but this thought lasted barely a moment, because he immediately raised the sword again, in keeping with the terrible nature of weapons that are not loosed or thrown and can therefore be used repeatedly, and can strike over and over, can threaten first and then cut afterwards or pierce right through, a mistake or a sudden change of mind are not the same as the breathing space, the momentary reprieve or ephemeral truce one would get with a thrown spear that misses the target or an arrow that goes astray or gets lost en route to the sky or simply falls to earth, because it takes a few seconds for the archer to remove another from the quiver and place it in the bow and steady himself again to aim better and carefully pull the bow taut without straining a muscle, and that minimal pause allows you time to take cover or run zigzagging away, in the hope that the nervous archer who has flushed you out has only javelins left to throw, three, two, one, none. Every movement Tupra made continued to be or was resolute, not improvised, he must have planned and calculated each one before he even entered the toilet, when, on the dance floor, he ordered me to bring the attaché here and for us both to await his return with the promised cocaine, he had kept his word, he had brought it, always assuming it wasn't just talc, the powder that now lay scattered, swept aside by De la Garza's fleeing head, wishful thinking, for he had nowhere to flee to, nowhere to hide. But while Reresby might know what he was going to do, I did not, still less De la Garza, and so I didn't know how to interpret the half-smile—or not even that, only a quarter-smile, at most, or perhaps it was just his usual mocking expression—which I thought I saw on his fleshy lips, lips that were rather African or perhaps Hindu or Slav, when he stopped the sword and raised it again and thus once more appeared to be about to kill him, this seemed to me even more likely than the first time, because when one opportunity has been used up, that leaves one less chance that you will be saved, and the odds have narrowed. That is how it is, never the other way around.

'Tupra, don't!' Now I did have time to add a syllable, it would have been four in my own language, '*No lo hagas!*', although I could have just said, '*¡Tupra, no!*', I thought him both capable and incapable of doing it, both things, which meant, as I thought much later on in bed, that on this occasion he wasn't going to do it, but that he was certainly cold-blooded enough—or was it that he was cruel enough, or was it merely a question of mettle or nerve or character, or indifference, or was it something closely bound up with 'his line of work'—and that he might have done it before, in his youth and in the distant past, or in adulthood and only a short time before, perhaps only months or weeks or days before, and I knew nothing about it, could not even imagine such a thing; possibly in other countries and in the service of 'his line of work', even though everything he did was, more than anything, to his own advantage; in remote places where a blow with a sword is sometimes necessary to put out or stir up major conflagrations and to cover up or create large holes, to sort out messy pre-bellum situations and to calm down or urge on insurrectionists, invariably by deceiving them. And what was a blow with a sword compared to spreading outbreaks of cholera, malaria and plague, as Wheeler had done years ago, or so he said, or compared to a single act of treachery that takes hold and is passed on, that becomes an unstoppable, all-consuming fire, or an epidemic that eliminates all those in its path or merely close by and even on the very fringes, all those who cannot leave or seek refuge, so often there is nowhere to run and no shelter to be found, and not even a wing under which to hide your head.

De la Garza had resorted to both his wings, his two arms folded over his neck, as useless as an umbrella in a storm at sea, and he had closed his eyes tight shut, they were trembling or pulsating—perhaps his pupils were racing about madly beneath the lids—he must have understood the situation even without looking, the sword had fallen very fast, but stopped before it touched his neck and now had resumed its previous position, perhaps to correct its path by a millimetre and to check the trajectory, to make sure the blade kept to the perpendicular or else to hone its aim, the threat was not only still there, it was even greater (although if the first threat had been fulfilled there would have been no more, no more of anything). De la Garza preferred not to look again in any direction, not even with his gaze unfocused, or out of the corner of his eye, he did not want to see another blurred gleam or anything else, his final image was of a toilet with the seat lid down, and they are all alike, with his wallet on top and the Visa card he had used as a blade, he knew he was a dead man and considered himself still deader, he had been given a few seconds of awareness or life to feel the fear even more intensely and to understand that what was happening really was happening to him, that—unexpectedly, ridiculously, without, as far as he knew, having done anything to provoke such an extreme response—this is what he had come to, to this stopping-place, to this end. I thought that given a few moments more he could have dropped asleep, with his head pressed against the porcelain, however flat and uninviting it may have been as a pillow, sometimes it is the only way to escape from pain and to rest from despair, a form of narcolepsy, that's what they call it, but who has not experienced that sudden, unseasonable, inappropriate sleep, who has not fallen asleep or wanted to fall asleep in the midst of fear or in the middle of weeping, it's the same when you sit down in the dentist's chair or as you're being wheeled to the operating room, you try to anticipate the careful work of the anesthesiologist—irresistible sleep as the ultimate denial and flight—in the hope that dreaming what happens will transform it into fiction.

Tupra wielded the sword with such vigour that it sounded like a whiplash in the air, and this second time, he again displayed remarkable control, he stopped short so that the blade did not touch anything, animate or inanimate, fabric or skin or flesh or object, everything remained intact, the head, the lid of the toilet seat, the porcelain, the neck, he did not cut or split anything open, he did not dismember or sever, he did not slice. Then he held the blade for a moment very close to De la Garza's hunched neck and shoulders, as if he wanted him to feel its presence—the breath of steel—and even familiarise himself with it before the final blow, just as, after a while, we notice behind us agitated breathing or intense eyes that wish us ill or well, it doesn't matter which if they are as voracious as saws or axes or as penetrating as knives. As if he wanted him to realise that he was alive and was about to die in the next instant, in any one of those instants—one, two, three and four; but not yet; then five—and the attaché must have thought, if he was still thinking and not deep asleep and dreaming: 'Don't let him do it, please, he can hesitate and keep hesitating all he wants as long as he decides, at last, not to do it, make him raise that absurd weapon one more time and not lower it again, I mean, who does he think he is, a Saracen, a Viking, a Mau Mau, a buccaneer, let him take the sword away, let him put it back in its sheath and put it away, what is the point of this, and make Deza do something, for God's sake make him do something, make him take the sword off him, throw him to the floor or persuade him, he can't just let this happen, it won't happen, it won't happen to me, not to me, I'm still thinking so it can't have happened yet, time has ceased moving, but I'm still thinking, which means that my time has not entirely stopped.'

Something very similar must have gone through my head, perhaps equally supplicant and numbed—numbed by sheer incredulity perhaps, or simply dulled, even though I was only a witness or an involuntary accomplice—but to what: as yet nothing—and my neck was not on the block. Only a fool would consider trying to grab a sword from the person wielding it, he might well turn it on me, that double-edged blade, the Landsknecht or 'cat-gutter', and then my head would be the one at risk and might yet end up rolling around on the floor of that toilet, although there wasn't the slightest sign in Tupra of derangement or insanity, he was as he always was, concentrating on the job in hand, serene, alert, methodical, slightly mocking, even rather pleasant given that he was possibly about to kill someone, which is the worst and most unspeakably unpleasant thing anyone can do. It was unlikely that he would attack me, I was with him, I worked with him, we had gone there together and would leave together, he was a decent man, there was my overcoat, he had gone to fetch it for me and had brought it to me, why didn't he just abandon these shock tactics and let us get out of this vile place, I didn't want to see blood or to see De la Garza beheaded, headless like a chicken, what would we do with the body and what would the embassy say, they would launch an investigation in Spain, after all, despite his ludicrous appearance, he was still a diplomat, and New Scotland Yard would start their own, we had been seen with him on the dance floor, especially me, as had Mrs Manoia. I knew with absolute certainty then: Tupra would not kill him, because he wouldn't want to get her involved in a mess like that. Unless there was no corpse, because we would take it away with us. But how?

'Are you mad or what? Don't do it!' Now when I spoke, I had time to say more, although still not very much, the kind of superfluous, ineffectual, pathetic phrases that rush to our tongue when confronted by unexpected brutality, a mere verbal counterpoint to something that has dispensed with words entirely and is nothing but violent action, a stabbing, a beating, a homicide, a murder or a suicide, they are superstitious phrases, like interjections, I came out with them despite seeing no signs at all of any madness in Tupra, he knew perfectly well what he was doing and not doing, I saw no rage in him, or even anger, at most annoyance, impatience, irritation, and, doubtless, delayed censure: I would bear my fair share of that, I was sure, since, that night, I had been the link with De la Garza; Wheeler had dumped him on me, but that had been on another day entirely and only today counts. It was more like teaching someone a lesson or calling in a debt, a punishment that he was dishing out or was going to dish out in cool blood with that unlikely sword, I still didn't know where it had come from or why he should resort to such an unusual and impractical weapon—it took up a lot of space, it was a nuisance really—disconcerting nowadays. I found out the answer to the first thing at once; the second only much later, when we had left the club.

He raised the Landsknecht sword, removed it from the neck it had so nearly touched, and this was both a good moment and a bad moment, it could be the prelude to a final, fatal descent, it could be a new gathering of breath before the threatened strike and decapitation, or else signify the renunciation, withdrawal and cancellation of fear, the decision not to use the sword and to allow the head to remain united with its trunk. He rested the flat of the sword on his right shoulder, as if it were the rifle of a sentinel or of a soldier on parade. It was a thoughtful, meditative gesture. He looked directly down at the kneeling De la Garza, who was not moving apart from a few disagreeable, involuntary, spasmodic tremors, he must be holding his breath while his heart raced, he would not want to do anything to tip the balance, not speak or look or exist, like insects which, when faced with danger, remain utterly still, thinking that they can disappear from view and even from smell by changing colour abruptly and blending in with the stone or leaf on which their enemies found them perched. Then Tupra lowered his left hand, took hold of De la Garza's hairnet and pulled it hard, the attaché really should never have worn it. De la Garza felt the tug and squeezed his eyes still more tightly shut as if he were trying to burst them and hunched his neck still more, but, having no protective shell into which to withdraw, he could not conceal it.

'Don't do what, Jack?' Reresby said this without looking at me, he was still studying the figure at his feet, at his mercy, kneeling before the toilet. 'Who told you what I'm going to do or not going to do? I certainly didn't tell you, Jack. Tell me, what exactly is it that you don't want me to do?' He raised his eyes. He looked at me straight on, as he did at everything, focusing clearly and at the appropriate height, which is that of a man. And then he brought the sword down.

He sliced off the hairnet with one blow; a kitchen knife, scissors, a Swiss army knife would have been sufficient, a far shorter blade than that used by a bullfighter to cut off his pigtail when he retires from the ring, although that would have been slower and made less of an impression on the person being threatened as well as on the witness, nor would it have sounded the same, it wasn't like before, like a whiplash or a riding crop swishing through the air, but like a light slap or a soft, clear handclap or even the sound of a gob of spit hitting a tiled floor, it was, at any rate, audible enough for De la Garza automatically to raise his hands to his ears in another gesture of imaginary protection, it obviously didn't occur to him that if he could make that gesture, he must still be alive, it doubtless took him a while longer to tell himself that he had, in fact, survived the third lunge or pass or swipe of the terrible blade, that it had not severed or opened up any part of his body, or perhaps he could not believe it—and if that were the case, he was quite right— and was still waiting for the next blow, and the next, and another, from the weapon that remains in the hand and is not thrown away; of course, I, too, waited for a few seconds, although fewer than he, because I could see what he could not: during the minimal amount of time it took Tupra to walk a few steps, free up his hands and then retrace those steps, De la Garza remained still as a stone, like a strange imploring statue, anguished or, rather, vanquished, terrified, resigned to the sacrifice, with his eyes closed and his ears covered, and in that position he reminded me of Peter Wheeler—although only in that respect—when he had covered his ears in just the same way against the noise of the helicopter which he thought was a Sikorsky H-5 and against the winds that the helicopter kicked up, on that Sunday morning in his garden by the river, the day when he told me more about Tupra and the nameless group to which he too had belonged and to which I belonged now, and it was because of that tacit belonging that I was there, in that spotless, gleaming toilet, sharing in a man's terror.

The man who was Reresby that night moved away, holding his sword in one hand and the hairnet in the other, earned like a miserable little trophy, much less impressive than a scalp, a mere sweaty rag; he left the cubicle and winked at me—but it was not a reassuring wink, I took it to mean: 'That was just for starters'—and he went over to the overcoat he had left hanging up, and which now hung less stiffly, and then I realised that in the lining, at the back, there must be a very long inside pocket and inside it a sheath, because that is where he stowed his Landsknecht sword, and as it slid in, it made a metallic noise, and if there had been no sheath, the point would have torn the bottom of that long, narrow pocket, at least seventy centimetres in length if it was to hold the blade of the *Katzbalger* and with, perhaps, the grip protruding so as to make it easier to take it out, I couldn't quite see the actual pocket, but there was no other possible explanation. I gave a deep sigh—or perhaps more than a sigh—when I saw that deadly piece of metal disappear, at least for the time being. The fact that he had put it back in its sheath did not necessarily mean that he would not have recourse to it again—it was still to hand—and it might simply be a precaution typical of Tupra, not leaving the weapon within reach of the enemy, which was entirely the wrong word, for the poor nonentity of an attaché was certainly not putting up a fight, he was not even resisting; but if Reresby had placed the sword on the cistern or deposited it on the floor, there was no guarantee that, in a moment of desperation and panic, De la Garza would not have flung himself upon it and grabbed it, and then what, the tables would have been turned, the two-edged blade was fairly light and easy to handle, and danger lurks in the weakest and most insignificant of beings, in the most cowardly and most defeated, and you must never underestimate anyone or give him the chance to recover or pull himself together, to screw up his courage or muster a little suicidal valour, that was one of Tupra's teachings and that is why he immediately understood— he appreciated it, even made a mental note of it—a Spanish expression that so perfectly defines us and which I mentioned to him one day and translated for him: '*Quedarse uno tuerto por dejar al otro ciego*'—'To put out your own eye while trying to make another man blind'—he dreaded such a response like the plague. I was grateful that it did not occur to him to ask me to hold it, the 'cat-gutter', I would not have relished the idea, that is, of holding it, although I would, of course, have picked it up and brandished it while I had the chance. Or perhaps he didn't trust me with it either, he couldn't be sure that events wouldn't take a different turn, and that I might not end up using it against the wrong person, I never knew if I had his full trust or not, in fact, one never knows that about anyone. Nor should anyone ever entirely win our trust either.

And so he walked back to the cubicle, wearing a pair of gloves that he had taken from one of the ordinary pockets in his overcoat—good black leather gloves, perfectly normal—and he passed me again carrying the hairnet or spoils in one hand and with his right hand free; he maintained his resolute, pragmatic, dispassionate air, as if everything he was doing at each moment were programmed and, what's more, belonged to a programme that was tried and tested. He winked at me again, and again it was not in the least reassuring, these winks did not imply a smile, they were merely announcements or warnings that bordered on being instructions or orders, this time I understood it as 'Right, let's get down to business, it won't take long and then we'll be done', and that is why I found myself saying:

'Tupra, that's enough, leave him be, what are you going to do now, he's already half dead with fright.' But there was much less alarm in my voice than when I had only shouted out his name and little else, because I *was* feeling much less alarmed, now that the sword was out of the way; indeed, such was my relief, and so quickly had my feelings of anxiety and horror and heaviness abated, that almost anything that happened now seemed to me light, welcome, unimportant. I don't know, a few slaps, a few punches, perhaps the odd kick (even in the mouth): in comparison with my certainties of only a moment ago they seemed almost like manna from heaven, and to be honest, I didn't feel particularly disposed to stopping them; or only with my voice, I suppose. Yes, that was it: I felt grateful that he was going to hit him, as I imagined he would, with his gloved hands. Just hit him, that was all. Not cut him in two or into pieces or dismember him, what luck, what joy.

'It'll only take a minute. And remember who I am, that's three times now.'

I didn't grasp the meaning of those last words and didn't have time to think about it either or to reflect on my worrying feeling of gratitude and that anomalous sensation of a weight having been lifted from me, a near-criminal sensation of lightness, because Tupra went straight to work: he picked up the packet from the toilet-seat lid, resealed the top and put it back in his vest pocket—of his varied collection I will never forget that particular vest, intense watermelon green—then with the same two fingers he picked up the Visa card, placed it in De la Garza's wallet from which it had come and put that in his other jacket pocket along with the rolled-up banknote. With one hand he swept away what remained of the line of cocaine, or talc, and the dust scattered and fell onto the floor, Rafita had not even got a snort, had never had the benefit of it, after all his preparations. Then Tupra looped the hairnet around De la Garza's neck and tugged, and immediately my sense of relief went on hold—'He's going to strangle him, he's going to choke him,' I thought, 'no, he can't, he won't'—before I realised that this was not his intention—he didn't wrap it around De la Garza's neck, he didn't pull it tight or twist it—he was merely forcing him to lift his head, the attaché was still pressed so close to the lid that he was almost embracing the toilet bowl, and he would have embraced it, I think, if he had not chosen to keep his hands over his ears, he preferred not to see or hear anything in the vain hope that he would then not know much about what was being done to him, even though his sense of touch would be sure to inform him, and the pain and the hurt would tell him.

Once Tupra had lifted De la Garza's head high enough, he pushed up both lid and seat and plunged the latter's head into the bowl with such violence that De la Garza's feet lifted off the ground, I saw his loose shoelaces waving in the air, neither he nor I had got around to tying them. I did not, at first, fear that the water in the bowl would drown him, because it was too narrow at the bottom for his broad, full-moon face, which nevertheless got battered against the porcelain—and slightly stuck—every time Tupra pushed it back in again after pulling it up for a while, and he also flushed the toilet three or four times one after the other, the rush of blue water was so strong and so prolonged that I was once more briefly filled by terrible alarm—'He's going to drown him, he'll fill his lungs,' I thought, 'no, he can't, he won't'—and it occurred to me that, anyway, all it takes is two inches of water, a puddle in which to submerge mouth and nose and thus stop someone ever breathing again; and that the momentary rise in the water level, with each flush, would bring Rafita a sure sensation of drowning, or, at the very least, of choking; and in the toilet for the handicapped too: with luck there would be no remnants of fetid smells, and with even more luck, it would never have been used.

'I don't want to see Tupra as Sir Death,' I thought, 'with the cold arms of a disciplined sergeant, always brisk and busy; but that is how I'm beginning to see him, given his many abilities and the variety of his threats, decapitation, strangulation, drowning, to name but three, how many more are there, which one is he going to choose, if he does choose, which one will he select to finish his expert work or task, which one will become accomplished fact and not just a feint or an attempt.' He did not hold De la Garza under the water for very long, therefore that would not, it seemed, be the definitive form, although he might at any moment change his mind and all it would take would be for him to allow the seconds to pass, a few more, just a few, the seconds that normally pass so quickly that we don't even notice them, time's crumbs, he would only have to let those seconds pass while my compatriot's face was in the water—nose and mouth, that was all it would take—and life and death often depend on those scorned, wasted seconds or on a few centimetres that are often given away, or conceded to our rival for nothing—the centimetres that the sword declined to travel. 'You had two henchmen plunge me head first into a butt of your disgusting wine and drown me, poor me, poor Clarence, held by the legs, which remained outside the butt and flailed ridiculously about until my lungs' final intoxication, betrayed and humiliated and killed by the black, opaque cunning of your hideous, indefatigable tongue.' But this was not stagnant wine in a butt, it was blue water falling in torrents, and he was not George, Duke of Clarence, but the idiotic De la Garza, and we were not two henchmen, still less those of a murderous king. Or perhaps I was Tupra's or Reresby's henchman, I received small-scale orders from the former every day, and those issued by the latter that night were on a larger scale and of an unforeseen nature, utterly different from the kind of work I was paid to do, they had either released me from my normal commitments or had violated my contract, not that anything had ever been set down in writing or clearly stipulated. Or perhaps we were both henchmen, even though I didn't know it, of the State, of the Crown, of MI6, of the army, of the Foreign Office, of the Home Office, of the navy, I could be at the service of a foreign country and not even be aware of it in my foreign dream, and in a way, perhaps, that I would never have agreed to had it been my own country. Or we might be the henchmen of Arturo Manoia (according to Pérez Nuix, our employers, at the time, varied) and there we were beating Rafita to a pulp on his orders, wreaking revenge on his behalf, I had no idea how Manoia had reacted to his wife's return to the table with, on her cheek, a *sfregio* or scar, she had gone off to have fun and to dance and come back with a mark on her face, Manoia would not have liked that at all. And make-up could only do so much.

Suddenly, I heard the sound of squeaky, tinny music, like the tone of a cell phone, it took me a while to recognise it—it wasn't easy—the hackneyed notes of a famous and terribly Spanish paso doble, it was probably that tired old tune 'Suspiros de España' which is so often used in my country by novelists and film-makers in order to create a certain tacky, ersatz emotion (people with left-winger stamped on their foreheads love it as much as cryptofascists do), a ghastly thing, he must have chosen it for his cell phone out of pure racial pedantry, De la Garza I mean, poor De la Garza, and to think only a while ago I had thought 'I'd like to smash his face in', I had thought it on the dance floor and afterwards too, with that business of the shoelaces, and perhaps before as well; but it was just a manner of speaking, a figurative use of words, in fact, it's very rare that anyone actually means, literally, what he or she is saying or even thinking (if the thought has been sufficiently clearly formulated), almost all our phrases are in fact meta-phorical, language is only an approximation, an attempt, a detour, even the language used by the most ignorant and illiterate, or perhaps they are the most metaphorical of all, maybe only the technician and the scientist are safe from it, and even then not always (geologists, for example, are very colour-ful in their use of language). Now I was watching as he was being beaten—not slapped, Tupra had not once attacked him directly with his hands, not even now that he had his gloves on, they were getting wet, they would have to be thrown away— and I was very frightened and shaken, not only because I didn't know just how much harm Tupra was going to inflict on him— if he would be transformed before my eyes into Sir Death or if he would remain plain Sir Blow, which was quite enough, or Sir Wound or Sir Thrashing (he was, in any case, already Sir Punishment), it was unpleasant to discover any of these characters in someone who was a close acquaintance, and even more so to have to observe his actions—but also because the long habit of seeing violence on screen, and of hearing every punch and kick as if it were a thunderbolt without the lightning or a dynamite blast or a collapsing building, has led us to believe in a rather venial form of violence, when there is nothing venial about it at all, and seeing it for real, perceiving its emanations from close to, feeling it physically throbbing beside you, smelling the immediate sweat of the person getting angry and hitting out and of the person who shrinks back and is afraid, hearing the creak of a bone as it dislocates and the crunch of a broken cheekbone and the tearing of flesh, seeing fragments and slivers and getting spattered with blood, isn't just horrifying, it simply makes any normal person feel ill, physically sick, apart, that is, from sadists and those who are used to it, those who live with it every day or every so often, and, of course, those who make a profession of it. I had to assume that Tupra belonged to this latter category, having seen how determined and expert he was, his movements almost routine.

My father had spoken to me about it once, during one of our conversations about the past or rather about his past and not mine, about the Civil War and the way people were trampled upon during the initial Franco era, which lasted so very long and, indeed, seemed eternal because we weren't really sure when it had finished and because, now and then, it came back.

'Your generation and the generations after you,' he had said to me, using, as he often did, the second-person plural, always aware that he had four children, and when he spoke to one of us, it was, more often than not, as if he were addressing us all, or as if he were sure that his current interlocutor would later pass on his words to the others, 'have been fortunate enough to experience very little real violence, it's been absent from your day-to-day existence, and if you have encountered any, it's been the exception and never anything very grave, someone getting beaten up at a demonstration or during a brawl in a bar, the kind of thing that always comes to a natural halt and is never given free rein and doesn't tend to spread; a mugging perhaps, or a robbery. Fortunately, and I very much hope this continues, you haven't been in situations where violence was unavoidable, I mean, where it was certain, where you knew it was bound to surface at some point during the day or the night, and if there happened to be one day when there was no violence or you didn't yourself come face to face with it and only heard about it—no one was free from that, from stories and rumours—you could be sure that this was a gift that would not be repeated the following day, because the law of probabilities did not allow for such excellent good fortune. The threat was always there, as was the state of alert. For example, one afternoon, my room was shelled, a direct hit, a huge hole in the wall and the interior completely destroyed. I wasn't in, although I had been shortly before and was about to return. But it could have fallen on me somewhere else, walking down the street or travelling in a tram, in a café, at the office, while I was waiting for your mother outside her house, at the radio station or in the movie theatre. During the first months of the War, you saw arrests everywhere, people being pushed around or hit with rifle butts, or else there were raids on houses, they would take away whole families along with anyone who happened to be visiting, on any corner you could come across a chase or a shooting, and, at night, on the outskirts, you'd hear the so-called *paseos*, the random executions, or a few isolated shots from the *pacos* (the sharpshooters I mean) on the rooftops in the evening or very early in the morning, especially during the first few days, and any shots you heard at dawn would be shots fired point-blank into the head or the back of the neck of a victim who, sometimes, but not always, would be kneeling in the gutter, if you were very unlucky, you might actually witness this and see someone kneel down and have their brains blown out, and I don't mean that metaphorically, you'd actually see their brain matter spill out. It was best just to keep walking and not to look, to get away from there as quickly as possible, there was nothing you could do, and if you did only see it out of the corner of your eye, you could count yourself lucky. Other executioners started work at nightfall, they couldn't be bothered to go very far if they didn't have a car available or were short of fuel, and so they would slip down an alleyway where there wasn't much traffic and finish people off there, they were impatient and couldn't wait until the city had half fallen asleep, because it never did entirely fall asleep, not during those three long years of siege, hunger and cold, nor afterwards either, because from 1939 onwards, Franco's police would burst into people's houses in the middle of the night, just as their first cousins, the Gestapo, were doing in the rest of Europe. Others were more organised and carried out their shootings in cemeteries when they were closed or when they themselves had closed them for that purpose; and so for a long time afterwards, when peace had supposedly been declared, there were some areas where you would go on hearing shots late into the night. There wasn't a great deal of peace or only for those on the other side, they could sleep peacefully enough. I'll never be able to understand how they could do that, with so much killing going on. There were a few decent people among them, but most were just really proud and smug.'

I remember that my father paused at that point or, rather, only afterwards did I realise it was a pause. He had fallen silent, I wondered if he had forgotten what he wanted to talk to me about or tell me, although I doubted that he had, he, too, always used to pick up the thread, or it was enough for me to give the thread a short tug for him to return to the subject. He sat staring straight ahead of him at nothing, his clear, blue eyes gazed back at that time, a time he could doubtless see with absolute clarity, as if he were able to observe it through a pair of supernatural binoculars, it was very like the gaze I had noticed on occasions in Peter Wheeler, or, to be precise, on the occasion when I went up the first flight of his stairs to point out to him and to Mrs Berry where I had found the nocturnal bloodstain that I'd taken so much trouble to expunge and for which neither he nor she had any explanation. It is a gaze one often sees in the old even when they are in company and talking animatedly, the eyes become dull, the iris dilated, staring far, far off, back into the past, as if their owners really could physically see with them, could see their memories I mean. It isn't an absent or a crazed look, but intense and concentrated, focused on something a very long way off. I had noticed it, too, in the bi-coloured eyes of the brother who kept his surname, Toby Rylands. I mean that each of his eyes was of a different colour, his right eye the colour of olive oil and his left that of pale ashes. One keen and almost cruel, the eye of an eagle or a cat, the other the eye of a dog or a horse, meditative and honest. But when they adopted that gaze, his eyes became the same, as if they were, somehow, above mere colour.

'It fell to me to see what went on here in Madrid,' my father continued, 'and I heard more than I saw, much more. I don't know which is worse, hearing an account or actually witnessing what happened. Perhaps, at the time, the latter is less bearable and more horrifying, but it's also easier to erase it or blur it and then deceive yourself about it, convince yourself that you didn't see what you saw, to think that you anticipated with your eyes what you feared might happen and which, in the end, did not. A story, on the other hand, is closed and fixed, and if it has been written down, you can go back and check; and if it's spoken, it can be told to you again, but even if it isn't, words are always less equivocal than actions, at least as regards the words you hear compared with the actions you see. Sometimes actions are only glimpsed, like a flash that lasts no time at all, that dazzles the eyes, and which, afterwards, can be manipulated or cleaned up in your memory, which, however, does not allow such distortion with things heard or told. Of course, it's a bit of an exaggeration to describe as an account what, for example, I happened to overhear one morning on a tram, a few words spoken quite casually, in the weeks after the War broke out, weeks of murderous intensity and utter chaos, many people simply gave in to it and were just seething with rage, and if they had any weapons, they did whatever they liked with them and took advantage of the political situation to settle personal scores and wreak the most terrible revenge. Well, you know what it was like, the same in both sectors: in ours, later on, they did at least try to put a stop to all that, but not hard enough; in the other sector, they made almost no attempt at all for the three years the War lasted, nor afterwards either, when the enemy had been defeated. But I was so shocked by the violence described to me—well, not to me, but to anyone within earshot, that's the awful thing—that I can remember precisely where the tram was at that particular moment, the moment when those words reached my ears. We were coming down Alcalá and turning into Calle de Velázquez, and a woman sitting in the seat in front of me pointed at a house, at an apartment on one of the top floors, and she said to the woman she was travelling with: "See that house. Some rich people used to live there. We took them out one day and finished off the lot of them. And the little baby they had, I took it out of its cot, grabbed it by its legs, swung it around a few times and smashed its head against the wall. Killed it straight off. We didn't leave a single one of them alive, wiped out the whole damn crew." She was a rather brutish-looking woman, but no more so than many others I'd seen hundreds of times in the market, at church, or in someone's living room, poor and wealthy, shabby and smart, dirty and clean, you get brutes like that everywhere and in every class, I've seen equally brutish women taking communion at midday mass in San Fermín de los Navarros, wearing fur coats and expensive jewellery. The woman talked about the atrocity she'd committed in the same tone as she might have said: "See that house. I worked there for a while, but after a few months I couldn't stand it any longer, so I left, just like that. I walked out on them. That showed them." Perfectly naturally. Without giving it any importance. With the complete sense of impunity that people felt in those days; she didn't care a bit who heard her. She was even rather proud of it, and certainly boastful. And she had nothing but scorn for her victims, of course. And obviously it would have been naive to have expected any remorse from her, even a hint. I went cold with disgust and got off as soon as I could, one or two stops earlier than I needed to, so as not to have to look at her any more or risk hearing her recount more such exploits. I didn't say anything, you simply couldn't in those days if you wanted to survive, you could be arrested for the slightest thing and bumped off, even if you were a Republican; or like your uncle, Alfonso, who was nothing, just a boy, and the girl who was with him when they picked him up, who was even less than nothing. I glanced at the woman's face as I got off, an ordinary woman, with coarse but not ugly features, quite young, although not young enough to put it all down to the frequent callousness of youth, she might have had children of her own or had them later on. If she survived the War and suffered no reprisals (and she certainly wouldn't have been punished for the thing I heard her describe; although she might have been had she gone on to play a significant part in activities that could be more easily traced and reconstructed at the end of the War or if someone high up turned against her and denounced her just like that, or on some intuitive whim; because all those early atrocities were just left in limbo), she probably led a normal existence and never gave much thought to what she had done. She'll be like a lot of women, possibly even cheerful and friendly and nice, with grandchildren she's devoted to, she might even have been a fervent Francoist throughout the dictatorship, and yet none of that will have caused her a flicker of doubt. Many people who were responsible for barbarous acts and crimes against humanity have lived like that quite happily for years; here, and in Germany, in Italy, in France, all of a sudden no one had been a Nazi or a Fascist or a collaborator, everyone had convinced themselves that they hadn't been and would even explain themselves by saying: "No, it wasn't like that for me," that's usually the key phrase. Or else: "Times were different then, you would have to have been there to understand." It is rarely difficult to save yourself from your own conscience if that is what you really want or need to do, still less if that conscience is a shared one, if it's part of a large, collective or even mass conscience, which makes it easier to say: "I wasn't the only one, I wasn't a monster, I was just like everyone else, I wasn't unusual; it was a matter of survival and almost everyone did the same thing, or would have if they'd been born." And people who are religious have it even easier, especially Catholics who have priests to wash clean their sublime regions, their innermost selves, and believe me, the priests here were readier than ever to absolve, to rationalise and to justify whatever vile or cruel deeds their protectors or comrades had committed, bear in mind that they were equally belligerent and egged them on. All that may help, of course, but it isn't even really necessary. People have an incredible capacity willingly to forget the pain they inflicted, to erase their bloody past not just in the eyes of others—their capacity then is infinite, unlimited—but in their own eyes too. To persuade themselves that things were different from the way they actually were, that they did not do what they clearly did do, or that what took place did not take place, and all with their indispensable co-operation. Most of us are past masters at the art of dressing up our own biographies, or of toning them down, and it's astonishing how easy it is to exile thoughts and bury memories, and to see our sordid or criminal past as a mere dream from whose intense reality we escape as the day progresses, that is, as our life progresses. And yet, on the other hand, after all these years, every time I pass the corner of Alcalá and Velázquez, I can't help glancing up at the fourth floor of the building which that woman on the tram pointed out one morning in 1936, and thinking about that small, dead baby, even though for me the child has no face and no name and even though all I know about him or her are a couple of sinister sentences that chance brought to my ear.'

My father fell silent again, and this time I had something to say during the pause. The blue of his eyes seemed to have intensified. I said, in fact, what I had been thinking just before:

'From now on, I might also look at those buildings when I pass that corner, even though I don't know precisely which building it is. Now that I've heard you tell that story, I mean.'

He made a gesture with his hand in the air, or, rather, with three fingers, index, middle finger and thumb—the latter accompanying the other two with a slight delay and purely imitatively—as if I had touched on some very ancient matter, long since debated and resolved. Almost as if he were pushing it away or rejecting it as beyond further comment.

'Yes, I know. Perhaps one should never tell anyone anything,' he said. 'I mean, nothing bad. When you children started to arrive, your mother and I asked ourselves the question: how were we going to tell you about what had happened right here, in the country where you lived, only fifteen or twenty years before you came into the world, or even more than that in the case of your sister? It seemed to us that it wasn't something we could tell our children, still less explain, it wasn't explicable even to ourselves who had witnessed it from start to finish. There hadn't been enough time for us to begin to forget, and besides, it was still all too fresh in our minds, the regime made sure of that. There was never any process of psychological healing, no attempt at assuagement, the regime showed a consistent and thoroughly totalitarian lack of generosity, which was evident in every order and in every sphere of life, even the most intangible. I left the decision to her, to your mother, who spent more time with you than I did; you were always more her children than mine, which is why it seems so dreadfully sad that she ended up knowing you far less than I have, for fewer years and only when you were young and, how can I put it, less finished than you are now, although you're all still fairly unfinished, especially you, but don't take that the wrong way. And then there are your children, your siblings' children and yours, whom she never even knew. Anyway, I always felt her decision was the right one. She believed that you should never feel threatened, personally anxious, fearful for yourselves, afraid that something terrible might happen to you, insecure about your daily lives and your actions. That you should all feel protected and safe. But she didn't think it prudent or right that you should know nothing about how the world works, about the kind of thing that can happen or has happened. She thought that if you found out gradually, without going into gruesome, ugly, unnecessary detail, you would be forewarned and better prepared and have more resources with which to deal with life. It also depended, of course, on the questions you asked. She always hated lies. I mean she really did, she couldn't bring herself to tell you that something that was true wasn't. She could tone down or disguise the truth a little, but not deny it. The tendency today is to enclose children in a bubble of foolish happiness and false security, by not bringing them into contact even with the mildly disquieting, and by keeping them ignorant of fear or even of its existence, indeed, I understand that nowadays you can buy—and that some people actually give or read these to their children—censored, doctored or saccharine versions of classics like Grimm or Perrault or Andersen, stripped of all the darkness and cruelty, of anything that's threatening and sinister, and probably with all the upsets and deceptions removed. Rank stupidity in my view. Namby-pamby parenting and irresponsible teaching. I consider that a crime of neglect, really, and a dereliction of duty. Because being exposed to other people's fears provides children with a lot of protection; they can imagine it serenely from the background of their own security and can experience it vicariously, through others, especially through fictional characters, like a short-lived contagion which, while only borrowed, is nevertheless not pure fakery. By imagining something you are starting to resist it, and that applies to things that have already happened as well: you can withstand misfortunes more easily if, afterwards, after experiencing them, you can manage to imagine them. And, of course, the way most people do this is by talking about them. Not that I think everything could or should be told, far from it, but neither is it admissible to over-falsify the world and send idiots and dimwits out into it who have never known the slightest disappointment or anxiety. Throughout my life, before telling something, I have always tried to gauge what could be told. To whom, how and when. You have to stop and consider what stage or moment in their life the person listening to you has reached, and to bear in mind that what you tell that person will stay with them for ever. It will become incorporated into their knowledge, just as the murder I heard about on a tram became incorporated into mine, even though it was just one of many. And, as you see, I haven't managed to dislodge that story from my knowledge, nor another story from the War which, for example, it never occurred to me to tell your mother at the time, even though she was accustomed to horrors and even though I was in quite a state when I returned home after hearing it. But what is the point, I thought, what is the point of upsetting her with yet another story, now that the War has ended, I'll get over it, I'll forget about it in time without having to share or pass the burden on to her. And I did slowly get over it, because one does get over almost everything. But I've never forgotten it, that would be too much to hope for, how could I? This particular gift was given to me by a notorious Falangist writer who later ceased to be a Falangist, as most of them did, and, can you believe it, during Franco's latter years, never mind after his death, the man had the gall to pretend he was a veteran of the Left, and people swallowed it too. They weren't ignorant people either, but journalists and politicians. And so, with Spain's characteristic ethical superficiality, he was always celebrated, under two different flags.'

He stopped for a moment, but this time he was not remembering with particular intensity or sharpness, he was thinking, or hesitating, or perhaps biting his tongue. He had reined himself in.

'I can't really say whether I believe it or not,' I put in, 'if I don't know who you're talking about and you haven't told me the story. What was the story? Who was this man?'

'You reproached me just now with having told you the story I heard on that tram,' he replied, and I thought he seemed just a touch offended. 'I don't know if I should go on.' And he sounded to me as if he were asking my permission. He sounded strange.

'I certainly didn't intend it as a reproach, that would be absurd. That would be like reproaching historians for writing down what they have found out or what they know at first hand. We spend our lives adding to the catalogue of horrors that have occurred, there are always more being uncovered, always more surfacing. My listening to you telling the story can't possibly have the same effect on me as it did on you hearing it from that woman. She was the one who had done the deed, and she was proud of it too. Plus it had only just taken place. It was still taking place, here and everywhere, that's very different. Don't worry, you can tell me anything, it can't be any worse than all the other things I've read about or that we see on television every day. I don't want you turning into one of those namby-pamby parents, not at this stage in my life. Really! Besides, I would have to denounce you then and accuse you of neglect and, what did you call it, dereliction of duty.'

He gave a short laugh, it amused him that I should dismantle his improvised objections with the very arguments and terminology he had just used. But before replying, he once more addressed me using the plural 'you': including all four siblings was another way of softening a reprimand intended for only one of us.

'You're a silly lot sometimes,' he said. And then he went back to addressing me as 'you' singular. 'All right. I won't tell you who he was, his name. I can't be sure that if you knew it you would keep quiet about it, as I have always done. From your point of view, you would have no reason to. You wouldn't feel obliged to, not even if I asked you to say nothing, and I would rather not take the risk, Jacobo. It's not out of consideration for him, because ever since I heard him tell the story, I've felt nothing but contempt and resentment for him. No, something stronger than that, more like disgust and loathing. Not, I think, a desire for revenge, mainly because of the way unfulfilled desires eat away at you, besides, there was I a victim of reprisals and there was he on the winning side and wielding considerable influence. But, you know, for fifty years he kept publishing books and receiving prizes and being praised to the skies and appearing in the press and on television, and for about half or more of those fifty years I don't think I read a single line of his, and I would quickly turn the page of any newspaper that carried an interview with him or a review of one of his books, I simply couldn't bear to see his face or his name in print. Later on, though, I felt curious to see just what he was capable of, how far he would go in the biographical fiction he had shamelessly started to weave about himself in public. But above all, purely by chance, through my work, I met his wife and got to know her. She was a really nice, cheerful person, who clearly knew nothing of her husband's more repulsive side, or the more repulsive facts about his behaviour during the War. She was quite a bit younger than him, ten or twelve years, they must have got married in about 1950, when he was thirty-five or more, fairly old for the time. And not only was she an extremely nice, cheerful, capable woman, on one occasion she was very helpful to us, and to your mother in particular. That's all by the bye now, but I've always had a sense of enormous gratitude towards her, and any consideration I've felt has always been for her, not for him.'

'Is she still alive? Are they still alive?' I asked.

'No, he died a few years ago, and she died not long afterwards.'

'So?' What I meant to say was 'So why maintain the consideration and the silence?' and my father understood.

'There are two daughters, two very sweet, pretty girls, I saw them a couple of times. And they were and are her daughters as well, not just the daughters of the important man. Well, he was important while he was alive and could work his corner, and he used all available means to do so, but even though only a few years have passed, he barely merits a mention now, and his memory will continue to fade, he was a very overrated figure. But I wouldn't want to upset her daughters, whom she adored almost as much as she did her loathsome husband, she was devoted to them all and especially to him, one of those steadfast loves that remains undiminished and unquestioned, untouched by time or even infidelities (very minor infidelities, because, in his superficial, egotistical way, he loved her very much and couldn't have coped without her; he was even lucky in that respect too, in dying before her), the kind of love that is above such things. No, I would never bring such shame down upon her daughters, and even if they hadn't existed, I wouldn't bring down posthumous shame on someone so affectionate and compassionate. It seems to me that your generation, and the younger generations too, don't care much about the good or bad name of the dead, but for us it still matters. Besides, given that he was a man in the public eye, one day someone will probably reveal all anyway and, who knows, no one will so much as bat an eye or see it as shameful, or even as a stain, and his apologists will just ignore it as if it were purely anecdotal: this country is not only superficial, it's also arbitrary and partisan, and once someone has been issued with an indulgence, it's rarely taken away. But I won't be the one to tell the story, nor will it come out because I was foolish enough to tell you, no, it won't come out through me or because of some slip of mine. Most of the other men who were present must be dead by now, there were five of us round the table when I heard him tell the story, and I'm sure it wasn't the only time he had told it so brazenly, quite a few people must know it (although there can't be many of us left alive). But I wouldn't be in the least surprised if that was the last time, if after that little gathering he tried to keep quiet about it and even began the meticulous cover-up job of later years. It's quite likely.'

'What little gathering? What was it he told you?' I asked, although without emphasising the interrogative tone. I realised that I did want to know, despite the fact that, generally speaking, I did not try to worm information out of my father even if I was really curious, I left him and his memories alone unless he summoned them up on his own account and of his own accord—and despite having lied to him a little and having, in passing, lied to myself a little too, albeit only momentarily: it wasn't true that he could tell me anything, with no consequences, I mean, for my state of mind or my sorrow, nor that the unpleasant events related by him were more bearable or less awful to know about than the worst atrocities read about in history books or the contemporary atrocities seen on television. What he told me was not only as real and true as the siege of Vienna in 1529 or the terrible fall of Constantinople to the Turkish infidels in 1453; as the slaughter in Gallipoli of Wheeler's compatriots and the three battles or bloodbaths at Ypres during the First World War; as the devastation of the village of Lidice and the bombing of Hamburg and Coventry and Cologne and London during the Second World War; it had, moreover, happened here, in the same bright, peaceful and, nowadays, prosperous cities and streets, the 'sweet lands', where I had spent the larger part of my life and almost the whole of my childhood; and it had not only happened here—as had the executions of May 3, 1808, during what the English call the Peninsular War, as had the siege of Numancia between 154 and 133 BC, and so many other incidents of unspeakable cruelty—

they were things that had happened to him and which his blue eyes (dull now and with the iris dilated) had seen and which they now saw again, or which his defenceless ears had heard and now heard again (with stomach churning, with a weight on his chest as in murky, agitated dreams, all of it lying like lead upon his soul). What made his bad experiences more painful to me than almost any past misfortune or act of cruelty, or even present-day ones that take place somewhere far away, was that they had affected him personally and had cast a shadow over his biography, that of someone so close to me and who was there before me, still alive, still present—who knows for how much longer—with his mind still perfectly clear. No, you don't take in or receive first-hand testimony from a stranger—a journalist, a witness, a newsreader, an historian—in the same way as you do from someone you have known since birth. You see the same eyes that saw and, to their grief, found in a filing cabinet the photo of a young man who had been killed by a bullet in his head or ear; and you hear the same voice that had to tell the dead man's sister, or had to remain silent with horror or sorrow or suppressed rage when those same ears heard involuntarily, in a tram or a café, what they would prefer never to have heard ('Keep quiet and don't say a word. Put your voice away, hide it, swallow it even if it burns you, pretend the cat's got your tongue. Keep quiet, and save yourself').

'One morning, I went to the publishing house of Gómez-Antigüedad,' that voice told me, 'to see if they had any translation work for me to do, even though I wouldn't be able to sign it with my own name, or if there were any other anonymous, occasional jobs, reports on foreign books and so forth. The son, Pepito, was pretty much in charge of the company at the time, and I knew him slightly from university and from the famous Mediterranean cruise we'd been on as students, and he was one of the few people on the winning side who, as you know, behaved with great decency and generosity: he helped quite a number of people who were being singled out for reprisals, those whom he considered to be the most able, and he did that during the early years, when it was almost impossible for us to find any kind of work at all, things were really difficult up until 1945 and not a great deal easier between then and 1953. Your mother and I had only been able to get married thanks to the French classes she gave, a small loan from her godmother, who had money and had managed somehow to hang on to it, and to occasional commissions from the *Revista de Occidente*; but in order to keep going, I had to be constantly looking for more work, because three-quarters—or more—of the things I went after didn't come to anything. Antigüedad, the son, agreed to see me, and I explained my problem.' ('Whenever we ask for something, we are exposed, defenceless,' I thought, 'at the almost absolute mercy of the person giving or refusing.') 'Despite our political differences, he felt that I was being treated unfairly and gave me a couple of books to translate, I can still remember what they were, one from German, by Schnitzler, and the other by the French writer Hazard. At the time, this felt to me like winning the lottery, being able to get paid work, even if I wasn't getting paid very much. You just grabbed whatever there was, and as I've always told you, there's no such thing as a bad job if there's no better job in view. He was a very friendly man and, in order to celebrate our collaboration, he suggested having a drink at what used to be the Café Roma, in Calle de Serrano, close to his office in Calle de Ayala.'

'Oh, I remember the Café Roma,' I said, 'it was still there during my first year at university.'

'Possibly,' he replied, not wanting to pause. I felt that it was best not to interrupt him again, he had embarked on a story that was very hard for him to tell, and it was best not to give him time to have second thoughts or doubts, as he had with my mother, when he returned home after hearing the story and decided to keep it to himself. 'As soon as we went in, some friends or acquaintances of his called him over to their table and asked us to join them. I don't know if they knew who I was, I mean, if my name meant anything to them when I was introduced, but I certainly knew who two of them were, although not the other two. One was the writer I've told you about, and who, at the time, was still a shiny new Falangist, and the other was a monarchist, of the kind with infinite patience and in no particular hurry, that is, a Francoist through and through. Both were already safely ensconced in their respective cushy jobs. The writer was really only beginning to be talked about as such: he had published a volume, or possibly two volumes, of rather old-fashioned verse, much praised for obvious reasons; later on, he abandoned poetry and devoted himself to the novel, which is where he made his name; he also wrote a few dull plays and the odd dull essay as well. These two men appeared not to have seen the others for a very long time, and people then were still in the habit of recounting to each other what had happened to them during the War, what they'd suffered or made other people suffer. And this was the case with them. They were swapping experiences, stories, the occasional exploit, the occasional hardship, the occasional atrocity. Gómez-Antigüedad contributed a little, I not at all. And in the middle of all this, the writer mentioned a name which I knew and admired, that of a former university friend. We hadn't been close friends, he was a year below me, but I'd enjoyed talking to him from time to time, and he was just a very nice man: Emilio Marés, an Andalusian, very friendly and bright, he was rather vain, but in a funny, self-consciously frivolous way, he made out he was an anarchist, but there was nothing solemn about him at all; even when he got on his high horse about something, he did so with a degree of self-mockery, and he always looked immaculate, impeccably dressed, certainly not the kind of anarchist you read about in novels; a really lovely man, always in a good mood. He was in Andalusia when the War broke out; by 18 July a lot of students who weren't from Madrid had gone back home to spend the summer with their families, and he was from a village near Málaga or Granada, I'm not quite sure where, but his father was, I think, the socialist mayor, in Grazalema or Casares or Manilva, somewhere round there. We had heard, when the War was already in full swing, that he'd been killed in Málaga by the Nationalists, and we assumed that he'd been killed there in February 1937 when the Italian blackshirts moved in, more than ten thousand of them. We imagined that he would have been summarily shot. The repression or, rather, revenge was particularly ferocious there, because the city had resisted for seven months and the people of Málaga had committed a lot of barbarous acts themselves, random shootings, indiscriminate looting, the burning of churches, the settling of personal accounts, just as happened at the beginning of the War here. It was said that when the Nationalists took the city, under the Duque de Sevilla, they corrected the imbalance and went still further, and that in the first week alone about four thousand people were shot. It may have been fewer than that, but it doesn't matter, they certainly served up plenty of coffee, because that, as you know, was the euphemism used by Franco and his cohorts for ordering executions, "*Dadles café*"—"Give them some coffee"—they would say, and the prisoners would be put up against the wall and shot. In Málaga, a lot of them were taken to the beach to be shot. The Italians protested such brutality, they felt splattered by all that spilled blood, so much so that the ambassador, Cantalupo, spoke to Franco about it and went there himself to stem the violence. I read somewhere that he was stunned at the furious cruelty that had been unleashed, and how even wealthy matrons, all of them good Catholics, were busily desecrating Republican graves.' My father stopped and drew one hand across his forehead or, rather, almost squeezed it with his four fingers, as if he were trying to remove something, images perhaps, perhaps stories. He was then in his eighties. But it was a very brief pause and he immediately resumed his account: 'I can't remember exactly how the episode came up in the conversation, in the old Café Roma, but what was said about Marés is engraved on my memory. I think one of them remarked in offended tones that many Republicans, when they surrendered or were detained, "got very hoity-toity", he said, or something along those lines. And it was more or less then, spurred on by the mention of such arrogance, that the writer decided to describe the lesson they had taught just one such Republican. He told how once, in Ronda (Ronda had fallen long before Málaga, in September or October of 1936), they took three prisoners out at dawn to shoot them, and how, as was the custom, they ordered them to dig their own grave (it was the custom on both sides, and I fear it may still be so in any war). One of them, "a dandified little fellow called Emilio Marés", those were his words, "the son of a Commie mayor from some village around there" refused and said to his executioners: "You can and will kill me, I know that, but I'm not a bull to be baited." He wasn't prepared to do their work for them, let's say. The comment was just what I would have expected from the man I had known, who had, on that particular day, unsurprisingly lost his usual good humour: a final impudent remark, he obviously didn't want to spend his last moments digging and sweating and getting himself dirty. "The fellow got really uppity," the writer went on, "as if he was in a position to impose conditions. However much of a red he claimed to be, you could see, straight off, that he was just a little rich kid, done up to the nines, quite the young master. And he even urged his two companions to refuse as well. Luckily for them, though, they were too frightened, and kept on digging. He must have assumed we would just shoot all three of them afterwards beside the open grave. One man in our group, a local chap who clearly had it in for him from the start, struck him in the face with a rifle butt, knocking him to the ground, and told him again to start digging. But the fellow still refused, and repeated that we could kill him if we wanted to, beat him to death if we liked, but that he wasn't going to be our plaything, a bull to be baited 'as sure as my name is Emilio Marés', he said. That's how he put it, with his name and everything—conceited little man. Well, all I can say is that it was a most unfortunate turn of phrase to choose because, do you know what we did?" And the writer waited a moment, as if for dramatic effect, to arouse our expectations, as if he really needed us to say "No, what did you do?", although he didn't, in fact, wait that long, because it was a purely rhetorical question, pure theatre. Then he brought his index finger down through the air, stopping just short of the table, as if he were pointing something out or underlining it, as if he were proud of the answer, and at the same time as he made this gesture, he gave the answer, gave us the answer: "We baited him," he said smugly, pleased with the lesson they had taught the man. I remember that this was followed by a shocked, uncomprehending silence. I don't think any of us could grasp what he meant, because up until then it had been clear that the man had been speaking figuratively, and, of course, the whole thing was utterly inconceivable. Surprised and slightly apprehensive, Antigüedad was the one to ask him: "What do you mean?" "Precisely what I said, we took him at his word and we baited him like a bull. We played matador to his bull," replied the writer. "It was the chap from Málaga's idea, the one who'd had it in for him from the start. 'Oh, so you're not a bull to be baited, eh?' he said to him. 'I don't think you've quite got the measure of us.' And he climbed into the van and drove into town and in less than half an hour, he was back with all the stuff. We stuck banderillas in him, stood on the roof of the van and drove very slowly past him, jabbing at him like picadors, and then the *malagueño* delivered the *coup de grâce* with the sword. He was a nasty piece of work, a real bastard, but he obviously knew what he was doing, and he went in for the kill with genuine style, straight in, through the heart. I only stuck a couple of short banderillas in him, round the neck and shoulders. Oh, Emilio Marés got the measure of us all right. The other two men were our audience and we forced them to cheer and clap. We didn't shoot them until the show was over, as a reward for having dug their own graves. That way they could see what they had escaped. The *malagueño* insisted on cutting off one ear as a prize. That was perhaps going a bit too far, but we weren't going to stop him." And that was the story that the famous, celebrated writer told over drinks,' added my father, and as soon as he stopped speaking, his voice sounded suddenly weary, 'although he never told it again later on, when he was really famous. A solemn funeral mass was held when he died. I think one very democratic minister even helped carry his coffin.'

He fell silent for longer this time, his gaze again that of an old man remembering, as if he really had returned to the long-since disappeared Café Roma on Calle Serrano or to Ronda where he had not been, at least not in September 1936, when they baited his friend like a bull in the ring and delivered the *coup de grâce* with a sword. It was on the 16th of that month I found out later, when that 'heroic and fantastical' city, with its huge precipice or gorge, fell into the white-gloved hands of General Varela—or perhaps he was only a colonel then: it was said that he slept with his medals on—a far crueller man than the head of the Italian blackshirts, Colonel Roatta, who advanced on Málaga and was nicknamed 'Mancini'—like my musical protector—following the norm set by many others who passed through that war, when names were routinely renounced or lost; but no less cruel, at any rate, than the person who took over and controlled Málaga once it had fallen, the Duque de Sevilla was his somewhat inappropriate title: ah, these rapacious Spaniards, some silent, some verbose; ah, 'these men full of rage', as so many of them so often are.

The poet Rilke had stayed in Ronda for a couple of months twenty-four years before, at the end of 1912 and the beginning of 1913, when not even Wheeler had yet arrived in the world—in the Antipodes and as Peter Rylands. And there is a statue of him, of the poet, a very black, life-size one, in the garden of a hotel from whose long balcony you can see the broad, sweet lands of Spain, perhaps one of those fields was the scene of that brief one-man *corrida*: it's unlikely, but not impossible, because at dawn, there would be no one standing there contemplating the fields, or else the area would be occupied by victorious troops who would have had no objection to such sport should some guard have spotted it: perhaps among them would be some of the *requetés*, the Carlist militiamen trained up by Varela as he travelled around the villages of Navarra, disguised as a priest and going by the colourful sobriquet of 'Tío Pepe'; as well as legionnaires and Moroccans, a grotesque 'crusade'—Varela's favourite word—of fanatical Catholic volunteers and Muslim mercenaries engaged together in destroying and laying waste this secular land. That hotel is, I believe, the 'Reina Victoria', which, as Rilke put it, 'the devil persuaded the English to build here'; you can even visit the room in which he stayed, a kind of mini-museum or minuscule mausoleum, adorned with a portrait and a few bits of furniture, some old books, some jottings by him in German, possibly a bust (it's been years since I visited it, so I can't be sure). It may have been there that he began to conceive these lines, or, rather, fragments, which I often recall: 'Of course it is strange to inhabit the earth no longer, to give up customs one barely had time to learn; not to be what one was and having to leave even one's own first name behind. Strange to no longer desire one's desires. Strange to see meanings that once clung together floating away in every direction. And being dead is hard work . . .' Perhaps, who knows, this is what Emilio Marés thought, although not in these words.

'But what happened, what did you do, how did you react?' I asked my father, not just to draw him out of his silence and away from his long journey. I was intrigued to know what, if anything, he could have done or said. At that time, he could have been arrested on the slightest pretext and returned to prison, and probably with far worse luck, for he had had exceptional luck before, and in 1939 too, a year when anyone on the losing side had hardly any luck at all.

With some effort, he returned from far away. A sigh. One hand on his forehead, with the wedding ring he had never taken off. A clearing of the throat. Then he focused his gaze. He looked at me and answered me. Slowly at first, as if with sudden caution, perhaps the same caution he had had to use then, in the Café Roma.

'Well,' he said, 'the moment I heard Marés' name I feared the worst, and I was even more on my guard. I didn't at all like the turn the conversation was taking. But I did nothing while he was telling the story. It didn't even occur to me to interrupt him. I felt sick and angry as I listened, the two things at once, rather than alternating between them. I would have preferred not to be there, not to know what he and others had done to a former university friend whom I had liked and admired. I knew that Marés had been killed for no reason, and that was enough, that was bad enough, but he had not been such a close friend that I would not occasionally forget this fact. On the other hand, I realised that, once the horror story had begun, there was no stopping halfway. I must have turned very pale or very red, I don't know, I felt cold and hot, again both at the same time. Whatever colour I turned, however, no one else would have noticed, it wouldn't have aroused suspicions or given me away, because every other face round the table looked equally distraught, deathly pale, even though all four men present were Francoists and had doubtless witnessed similar acts of brutality or even committed them themselves.' My father stopped for a second and looked around him—we were in his living room, at the end of the twentieth century or possibly the beginning of the twenty-first, in the late morning: he was bringing himself back to the present—then he continued, more easily this time: 'I think the writer had miscalculated. He started telling the tale almost proudly, boastfully, but as he continued, and even though it didn't take him long to tell it, he must have realised that his story was going down very badly indeed, that it went too far, that it had shocked us all. Amid the sound and fury of the Civil War it might have amused someone (if I can put it like that), but not now. It was entirely inappropriate to describe such an episode seated around a café table, on a sunny Madrid morning, over a few beers and some olives. The silence which had fallen when he said "We baited him" and brought his index finger down like a banderilla or a lance or a sword, continued until the end of the story, and remained unaltered at its conclusion. And when it became embarrassing, and since the writer was probably the most influential person there, one of the other men whom I didn't at the time even know by name, the most deferential among them, broke the silence with a joke in the worst possible taste, one he was incapable of keeping to himself, or perhaps, being a rather stupid man, it was the only thing that occurred to him to fill the void and applaud the anecdote: "How come, while he was at it, he didn't award himself *both* ears *and* the tail?" he asked, referring to the *malagueño* and the ear he had cut off. And the writer again miscalculated, or perhaps the icy atmosphere left behind by his story made him feel, I don't know, uncomfortable, awkward, and in situations like that, any attempt to put things right almost only ever succeeds in making matters worse, it's best just to keep very still and quiet. He smiled as if he saw his chance. Perhaps he was still clinging to the idea that his story had had the effect he was hoping for, a slightly delayed effect given the shocking nature of the lesson dealt out, or perhaps he considered it an exploit to be proud of. He wasn't an intelligent man, only clever. And vain to his boot-tips, too, as tends to be the case with people who know their talents are overvalued, for spurious reasons or by dint of their own pushiness and sheer insistence. They can't bear to look bad or to feel they've been caught out, and everything about them is so fragile and so false that the slightest lack of enthusiasm, the smallest reservation upsets them. And so he replied, half coy, half derisive: "No, well, I didn't want to shock anyone. And I'm not saying he didn't cut the lot off. He was a dangerous man, our comrade. You should have seen him, doffing his red beret like a hunter and displaying his three trophies." I don't know if that was true or not, or if, goaded by the other man's comment, he simply made it up in order to show off; he probably felt he hadn't gone quite far enough and that this was the reason for his audience's cool response. I didn't care either way; or, rather, it was almost worse that he should have invented it on the spur of the moment, to flatter us, according to his criteria, or to make us shudder. I couldn't take any more. I couldn't before either, but I was suddenly assailed by a vague image of a mutilated Marés after he had been tortured and killed, of the amusing man I had known before, so delightfully full of himself, converted into mere mangled remains, more animal than human. I got up and, addressing only Gómez-Antigüedad, murmured: "I have to go, I'm late already. I'll pay for this round." And I went over to the bar to ask for the bill. I made my exit in two stages because I felt it would attract less attention and seem less abrupt than if I headed straight for the door. I couldn't really afford to pay for anything, as you can imagine, and it was, as far as I was concerned, a very expensive bar, I wasn't even sure I had enough money on me; and I can't tell you how it disgusted me having to buy a round of drinks for those four men. But I considered it would be money well spent if I could get away from them there and then, and not have to listen to their affected, mocking laughter or to the voice of that murderous thug; and to get out of there, of course, without any mishap. With my record, the last thing I wanted was to be arrested. I was standing not too far from them, with my back turned, while I waited for a barman or waiter to appear, and I heard the writer say to Antigüedad: "What's got into him? His name's Deza, isn't it? Where's he from anyway? Did I say something he didn't like?" It's always a bad thing when someone takes your name and notices it and remembers it, whether it's the authorities or a bunch of criminals, let alone when the authorities *are* the criminals. I thought I wasn't going to be able to escape, that the writer would not simply let me leave in peace, that he would want to find out what was wrong with me, and I was sure, then, that I would no longer be able to contain myself. If he demanded an explanation from me, I was likely to hurl myself at him without another word. He certainly wouldn't have come out of that very well, but I would have come out of it even worse. I would have got a sound beating in a prison cell that night, and they might well have decided to haul me into court again, on whatever charges they fancied. Fortunately, Antigüedad's response was immediate, and that's another reason I remained grateful to him for the rest of his life: "The same thing has got into him as into me, for fuck's sake, what a sickening story," he said. He was not a man who normally resorted to bad language, but, depending on who one is talking to, it's useful to know how to use it if necessary. Sometimes, it's just a question of authority. And he used that authority to rebuke the writer, to knock him down a peg: "Do you honestly believe it's all right to speak so lightly about an atrocity like that? Do you really believe it's a joking matter? Think about it, man, think about it. It's high time we put all that bad blood behind us." The writer may have been better placed within the regime, but Antigüedad was from a very influential, staunchly right-wing family, he had ended the war with the rank of captain and was entirely above suspicion; besides, he would one day be the owner of a publishing house and already pretty much called the shots there, and that is something any new writer must always bear in mind, because he never knows when he might need a publisher. So he swallowed his pride and accepted this dressing-down. "There's no need to get so worked up about it, Pepito, it's not that big a deal, is it? We could all of us tell some pretty ugly stories, I'm sure. But I agree, it probably isn't a suitable tale for peacetime." And Antigüedad immediately softened. He gave the writer a fatherly pat on the back and said: "Oh, that's all right, let's get together for a chat when we've got more time. See you, gentlemen." He said goodbye to the others as a group, without shaking them by the hand, and joined me at the bar, just as the waiter who had served us came over. "Give me that, Deza, after all, I was the one who invited you for a drink," and he grabbed the bill before the waiter could hand it to me. I was already anxiously counting my money out into the palm of my hand, worried that I wasn't going to have enough. We left together, he turned at the door and raised one arm in the direction of the other four men, as a gesture of goodbye. Then, once out in the street, he apologised to me, even though none of it had been his fault. "I'm so very sorry, Deza, I had no idea," he said. "You were friendly with Marés, weren't you? I only knew him by sight myself." He was one of the few on the winning side who tried to mitigate the situation, one of the few who did not blindly follow Franco's instructions to mete out constant humiliation and continual punishment to the defeated. And you've no idea how glad I was to be able to reciprocate later on in a not inconsiderable way: in the 1980s, I managed to keep him out of prison over some matter to do with company accounts, with the illegal transfer of funds, well, it doesn't really matter now what it was. Obviously, I would have preferred him not to have got into trouble in the first place, but for me it was a real blessing to be in a position to throw him a line and pull hard on it until I'd got him out. When someone helps you when times are really bad, for no real reason (you children have never known what really bad times are), well, you never forget it. If you're a decent person, that is, and don't take that help as a kind of personal humiliation or as a public insult.'

It occurred to me that when he made that last comment, he was thinking of Del Real, the treacherous friend whose future face, that of 1939, he had failed to foresee throughout the 1930s.

'And did you ever meet the writer later on, in person?' I asked.

'Only very belatedly, thirty or forty years afterwards, at a couple of public events to which we were both invited. The first time, he was with his wife, and, of course, I shook his hand then so as not to wound or worry her in any way, and the three of us spoke briefly, about nothing really, just a polite exchange. The second time he was on his own, or, rather, with his usual entourage of admirers, he never went anywhere alone. He saw me and avoided me, avoided my eye. Not that I, heaven forbid, was trying to catch his. But just in case. You can always tell these things. He knew exactly who I was. I mean, not only what I did, or the fact that his wife and I had a very civilised friendship based on great mutual respect, I mean that he remembered my name from that morning in the café, and had, ever since then, been conscious that I'd heard his story. He must have regretted time and again letting his mouth or his smugness run away with him in that café. That's why I think it was perhaps the last time he revealed it to anyone, his disgusting contribution to that "bullfight". Antigüedad's reaction must have provided a warning. That and the ensuing silence. So you won't be surprised to learn that I never told your mother, however much I wanted to share the state of despondency in which I arrived home that day, even though I'd just received commissions for two translations. She had known Marés at university too and really liked him, well, almost everyone did, he was one of those people who light up any gathering and make it seem more promising and more worthwhile. Why bring her more grief, why afflict her with some new horror that could not be changed and for which there could be no solace and, of course, no compensation. Especially since she really liked bullfighting, much more than you might realise, a liking she inherited from her father, but one that she preferred not to pass on to you children. On more than one occasion, when we told you we were going to the theatre or the movies, we actually went to the bullring.' And my father chuckled briefly to remember and to confess that small, innocuous deception. 'I didn't want to ruin bullfighting for her, because it doubtless would have. I myself didn't particularly enjoy bullfights, they left me pretty cold really, but it took a long time and a lot of effort on my part to prevent the story of Marés' death spoiling them for me entirely: at first, every fight we went to reminded me of him, and that cast a pall over the whole event, I felt his shadow slip in between me and each stage of the corrida. It's just the same, I suppose, as when I pass the corner of Alcalá and Velázquez, and I always think of the little child whom the militiawoman claimed to have killed by slamming against the wall.' My father had grown tired, as I saw when he paused again; he closed his eyes as if they ached from having gazed for too long into the far distance. But it was not yet time for lunch; I glanced at my watch, it would be another twenty minutes before the woman who did the cooking came in to call us to the table or before my sister arrived, she'd said she would drop in and have lunch with us if she managed to finish what she had to do early. And he had not yet taken up the thread again; then, after a while, he decided to continue talking, although without immediately opening his eyes. 'I saw many things, we saw possibly worse things,' he said, using an ambiguous plural after that unequivocally singular 'I'. 'Many simultaneous deaths, people I knew and didn't know, suddenly, during a bombardment, and then you don't have time to think about any of them, not even for a second, what tends to prevail is a sense that it's all over, a desire simply to give up, a feeling of being on the brink of extermination, that is what you feel then, and you're full of contrary impulses, wanting to survive at all costs, to simply step over the surrounding corpses, to seek shelter and save yourself, but also to stay with them, I mean to join them, to lie down by their side and form part of the inert pile of bodies and stay there; it's a feeling almost akin to envy. It's odd, but even in the din and the collapsing buildings and the chaos, as you're racing to help someone who's wounded or to protect yourself, you know at once when someone's a hopeless case. Not a threat to anyone, but at peace, at rest, gone in a flash. It's likely, in fact, that if you followed the second impulse, you would unintentionally achieve the same effect as the first, because the next bomb would never fall in the same place as the previous ones: the besiegers didn't squander their bombs, the safest place might well be alongside the already dead. But, as you see, I've told you about two things that I didn't see, that we didn't see, but which were recounted to me or, rather, which I happened to hear, in neither case were the words addressed to me personally, or at least not exclusively; and yet they've stayed in my memory as clearly as if I had seen it myself, possibly more clearly, it's easier to suppress an unbearable image than it is to suppress someone's account of an event, however loathsome those events might be, precisely because narrative always seems more bearable. And in a sense it is: what you see is happening; what you hear has happened already; whatever it is, you know that it is over, otherwise no one would be able to tell you about it. I believe that the reason I have such a vivid memory of those two stories, those two crimes, is because I heard them from the mouths of the people who had committed them. Not from a witness, not from a victim who had survived, whose tone would have been one of justifiable reproach and complaint, but also, therefore, of a more dubious veracity, there is always a tendency to exaggerate any description of suffering, because the person who endured it tends to present it as a virtue or as something to be admired, a noble sacrifice, when sometimes that isn't the case at all and it was just bad luck. Both of the people who told the stories did so unhesitatingly and boastfully. Yes, they were showing off. To me, though, it was as if they were accusing themselves and without even having been asked to do so, the Falangist writer and the woman on the tram. That, at least, is how my ears reacted, they were not amused, they did not admire the cruel acts described, but were horrified and disgusted; and my judgement condemned them, passively of course.' ('With my tongue silenced,' I thought.) 'It gives you an idea of how other people experience violence; of how simpler, more superficial people—although they're not necessarily more primitive or less educated—grow accustomed to it and then see no need to place limits on it and consequently don't; and it gives you an idea of just how much violence there was. So much, and so taken for granted, that the people who perpetrated the most brutal and gratuitous acts of violence, committed out of a senseless, baseless hatred, could talk about it in public with perfect aplomb, could boast about it. I mean what possible need was there to bash a baby's brains out; what need was there to stick banderillas and lances into a condemned man and then mutilate his body. But there were others among us who never got used to it, you never do if you keep your sense of perspective and don't fall into the lazy way of thinking that says "What does it matter, after all . . ." which lay behind the comment that other man made to the writer when he asked if the *malagueño* had claimed the other ear and the tail too "while he was at it", if you refuse to allow the concrete to become abstract, which is what happens today with so many people, starting with terrorists and followed soon after by governments: they don't see the concreteness of what they set in motion, nor, of course, do they want to. I don't know, it seems to me that most people in these societies of ours have seen too much violence, fictitious or real, on the screen. And that confuses them, they accept it as a lesser evil, as not being of great importance. But neither fictitious nor real violence is real on screen, as a flat image, however terrible the events we're shown. Not even on the news. "Oh, how terrible, that really happened," we think, "but not here, not in my room." If it were happening in our living room, what a difference that would make: feeling it, breathing it, smelling it, because there is always a smell, it always smells. The terror, the panic. People would find it unbearable, they would really feel the fear, their own and other people's, the effect and the shock of both are similar, and nothing is as contagious as fear. People would run away to take shelter. Look, all it takes is for someone to give someone else a shove, in a bar, say, or in the street or in the subway, or for two uncouth motorists to come to blows or to grapple with each other, for those nearby to tremble with shock and uncertainty, for them to grow tense and filled with often uncontrollable alarm, both physical and mental, it happens to most people. Worse still if there's a crowd. And if you punch someone really hard, you'll probably do them quite a lot of damage, but your own hand will be a mess too and will be inflamed for several days afterwards. After just one blow with the fist. It's no joke.' ('That's true,' I thought, but didn't say anything so as not to worry him, 'it happened to me once, and I could hardly move my hand afterwards.') 'Anyone who, at some stage in his life, has lived with violence on a daily basis will never take any risks with it, never take it lightly. He'll administer it not just with care and with extreme caution, but in as stingy and miserly a way as he can. He won't allow himself to be violent, not as long as he can avoid it, and it almost always is avoidable, although he'll be able to withstand it better should violence ever return.' Then my father opened his pale eyes again, and they were once more serene; they had been troubled by all those memories. 'Apart from in fiction, that's different, although people should be more aware of that than they are. Exaggerated violence is even funny, watching film violence is like watching acrobatics or fireworks, it makes me laugh, all those bodies sent flying, all that blood spattered about, you can see a mile off that they're wearing springs and bags of liquid that they puncture and burst. People who are shot in real life don't leap into the air, they just drop and cease moving. That kind of violence is perfectly innocuous or, at least, it would be if there hadn't been such a decline in people's general levels of perceptiveness. For someone as ancient as me, it's astonishing to see how stupid the world has become. Inexplicable. What an age of decline, you have no idea. Not just intellectual decline, but a decline in discernment too. Oh well. That kind of violence is not much different from the beatings described in Don Quixote or the ones shown in those Tom and Jerry cartoons you enjoyed so much as children, when you know deep down that no one has been badly hurt, that they'll get up afterwards unscathed and go out to supper together like good friends. There's no need to get all puritanical about it, or prudish for that matter, like those people who reduce the classics to pure saccharine. With real violence, on the other hand, you must take no chances. But look how things have changed, and attitudes too: when war was declared on Hitler, and it may be that there has never been an occasion when a war was more necessary or more justifiable, Churchill himself wrote that the mere fact of having come to that pass, to that state of failure, made those responsible, however honourable their motives, blameworthy before History. He was referring to the governments of his own country and of France, you understand, and, by extension, to himself, although he would have preferred that state of blameworthiness and failure to have been reached at a much earlier stage, when the situation was less disadvantageous to them and when it would not have been so difficult or so bloody to fight that war. ". . . this sad tale of wrong judgements formed by well-meaning and capable people . . .": that is how he described it. And now, as you see, the same people who are scandalised by the rough and tumble of Tom and Jerry *et al.* unleash unnecessary, selfish wars, devoid of any honourable motives, and which sidestep all the other options, if they don't actually torpedo them. And unlike Churchill, they are not even ashamed of them. They're not even sorry. Nor, of course, do they apologise, people just don't do that nowadays . . . In Spain, the Francoists established that particular school of thought long ago. They have never apologised, not one of them, and they, too, unleashed a totally unnecessary war. The worst of all possible wars. And with the immediate collaboration of many of their opponents . . . It was absurd, all of it.' I realised that now my father was thinking out loud, rather than talking to me, and these were doubtless thoughts he had been having since 1936 and, who knows, possibly every day, in much the same way as not a day or a night passes without our imagining at some point the idea or the image of our dearest dead ones, however much time has passed since we said goodbye to them or they to us: 'Farewell, wit; farewell, charm; farewell, dear, delightful friends; for I am dying and hope to see you soon, happily installed in the other life.' And in the thought that followed he used a word which I heard Wheeler use later on, when talking about wars, although he had said it in English, and the word was, if I'm not mistaken, 'waste'. 'And what a terrible waste . . . I don't know, I remember it and I can't believe it. Sometimes, it seems unbelievable to me that I lived through all of that. I just can't see the reason for it, that's the worst of it, and with the passing of the years, it's even harder to see a reason. Nothing serious ever appears quite so serious with the passing of time. Certainly not serious enough to start a war over, wars always seem so out of proportion when viewed in retrospect . . . And certainly never serious enough for anyone to kill another person.' (And then even our sharpest, most sympathetic judgements will be dubbed futile and ingenuous. Why did she do that, they will say of you, why so much fuss and why the quickening pulse, why the trembling, why the somersaulting heart? And of me they will say: Why did he speak or not speak, why did he wait so long and so faithfully, why that dizziness, those doubts, that torment, why did he take those particular steps and why so many? And of us both they will say: Why all that conflict and struggle, why did they fight instead of just looking and staying still, why were they unable to meet or to go on seeing each other, and why so much sleep, so many dreams, and why that scratch, my pain, my word, your fever, the dance, and all those doubts, all that torment?)

That squeaky, tinny music immediately distracted me from the apocryphal lines from 'The Streets of Laredo' that were going round and round in my head, for despite my fear and alarm, the tune had barely left my mind for a single moment, and now, seeing De la Garza gulping down that blue water, a third version had, I feel, become intertwined with it: people put whatever words they want to ballads and I had heard the Laredo or Armagh ballad converted into 'Doc Holliday' on the whim of some forgotten singer, who had the good doctor recount his story to that same tune, the man who had been with Wyatt Earp at the OK Corral, at the famous duel or, rather, pitched battle between gangs, the tubercular, alcoholic gambler and medical doctor (or was he an odontologist like Dick Dearlove?) and connoisseur of Shakespeare, or so at least he was presented to us in the best film about them certainly I have ever seen, about Earp and Holliday in the town of Tombstone, and not in Laredo nor, of course, in that unknown place, Armagh in Ireland: 'But here I am now alone and forsaken, with death in my lungs I am dying today', and that might well have been what Rafael de la Garza would have been saying in his own inevitably racier and coarser language, although he was not dying from a lung disease, with his handkerchief pressed to his mouth and coughing up bloody sputum, but from inundation or flooding.

The squeaky paso doble bothered Reresby, even annoyed him, and this didn't surprise me in the least, because it irritated the hell out of me as well.

'What's that shit?' he said, while I, at the same time, was thinking: 'Oh no, not that again.'

The insistent sound made him interrupt his beatings and immersions of De la Garza in the toilet bowl. He rudely and rapidly frisked De la Garza in search of the impertinent cell phone, and when he found it in one pocket of that rapper-style jacket, he took it out, stared at it in perplexity and rage and slammed it with all his might against the wall, the phone broke into pieces and the clichéd Spanish music ceased at once. 'At least he's not going to drown him now,' I thought, 'for the moment,' and I realised that I was beginning to think that nothing was as dangerous or as deadly as the sword, perhaps this was only because strangulation or drowning take time, however brief, and that brief amount of time allows time for someone else to intervene and that someone else would have to be me, but how, there was no one else there and no one was trying to get in, they would have found the door wedged shut and assumed the toilet was out of use; whereas a decapitation or an amputation requires no lapse of time, and if Tupra hadn't checked the fall of the blade, the attaché's head would have been lopped off and be lying on the floor, De la Garza would be in two parts now or, rather, he would not be at all. And so while I kept an apprehensive eye on what Reresby was doing, I also cast occasional glances over at where his coat was hanging, I knew now that it was there that he kept the fearsome weapon of the Landsknecht soldiers and that, should his temper flare up or boil over, he could easily go back for it and unsheathe it and brandish it again.

Tupra grabbed Rafita by the lapels or, rather, by the shirt-front and did with him more or less what he had done with the mobile phone, that is, he slammed him against the wall, and one of the strange cylindrical bars attached to the wall, I noticed, thudded into his back. Fortunately, the bars did not have sharp edges, but even so it must have hurt him badly, Tupra's violence had not abated. After this, De la Garza collapsed, with a defeated, breathless howl. His shirt had come out of his trousers, and I discovered to my amazement—to my embarrassment and almost sorrow too—that the diplomat had a jewel encrusted in his navel, like a small diamond or perhaps a pearl, doubtless cheap imitations, fakes. 'Good grief,' I thought, 'he's obviously really desperate to keep up with trends, and the gypsy earring and the hairnet just weren't enough, I wonder if he always wears it, even in the embassy, or only when he gets dressed up to go out on the town?' Tupra dragged him to his feet again, still gripping his shirt-front, pulled him close and then again flung him against the metal bar placed there for the handicapped, the fixed bar, I had the sense this time that it caught him in the shoulder blades. De la Garza was a puppet, a sack, he was drenched and stained with blue, with gashes on his chin and forehead and a cut on his cheekbone, *uno sfregio*, his clothes all dishevelled and torn, and his cries very feeble now, only an irrepressible groan each time his back hit the bar, because Reresby continued in the same vein, repeatedly and rapidly: he would pull him to his feet, draw him a little away from the wall and then hurl him against that battering ram, he must have been breaking several of his ribs, if not causing more dangerous internal lesions, the attaché's whole ribcage resounded and his insides crunched, and with every impact it was if his breath dried up in him. Reresby did this a total of five times, as if he were counting them, in a patient, disciplined way, like someone who has it all planned out. De la Garza did not defend himself at any point (he could not even shrink in on himself or cover his ears now), I suppose you know when there's nothing you can do, when the other person's strength and determination—or the sheer numbers if there are several of them, or the weapons if you yourself are unarmed—are so much greater that all you can hope is that they will grow tired or decide to finish you off; during these attacks, during the beating, Rafita would also be thinking of the sword with a mixture of fear and something like hope, as perhaps Emilio Marés would have done in the fields of Ronda once he saw them coming for him first with the banderillas and then with the lance: 'They're going to do it. They're really going to do it, the bastards, the brutes,' he must have thought then. 'They're going to bait me like a bull, it would be better if they just killed me now and did a good job of it, rather than give me the *coup de grâce* with whatever they have to hand, because they're capable of doing it with a nail.'

When Tupra had finished, he turned to me and said: 'Jack, translate this, will you, I want him to understand and to be quite clear about what I'm saying.' And before he began, he added: 'Have you got a comb?'

De la Garza was slumped on the floor, he seemed incapable of movement and would not, in my presence, be hauled to his feet by Sir Blow or Sir Punishment or Sir Thrashing, well, at least he wasn't Sir Death. Reresby looked in the mirror while he was talking, he tucked in his shirt, tugged at his jacket, smoothed his vest, otherwise he looked exactly as he always looked, even his hair had remained relatively unruffled. He straightened his tie, adjusted the knot, and did this without his sodden gloves, which he had deposited, with a grimace of disgust, next to the toilet. When he'd had the gloves on, he had not once used his fist or even the flat of his hand—or his foot either—every blow dealt had been made by another interposing object, the toilet bowl, the cylindrical bar and even the hairnet and the flushing water, he must have known all about what my father had told me years before, that a punch can shatter the hand of the person doing the punching. In Spain we have always known about these tricks of the trade as regards violence: in 1808 (to give but one example), during the Peninsular War or the War of Independence, Filanghieri, the governor of La Coruña and, more suspiciously still, Italian by birth (and not 'a Spaniard of lightning and fire'), was judged by his troops to be a traitor because he delayed slightly before rallying to the cause of Independence (he lingered, he claimed, only out of strategic prudence, but, by then, it was too late); and so they stuck their bayonets in the ground, points uppermost (this happened apparently in Villafranca del Bierzo, although I've no idea what they were doing there), and threw their Captain-General onto the spikes a few times, until some vital organ was finally pierced and there was no point in continuing, thus saving the mutineers the energy and effort involved in sticking their bayonets into him themselves and leaving the not-yet-dead Filanghieri to do all the work for them. This was not apparently the first example of such idleness, and was started perhaps by the Carthaginians who deployed spears in a similar way against the Roman general Atilius Regulus in the third century BC; and an English traveller in Spain remarked that murdering the unjust, despotic, incompetent and generally appalling generals and leaders who have, on the whole, ruled over our Peninsula throughout history (good vassals, but bad lords) was 'an inveterate Iberian trait'. He also remarked: 'Help from Spain comes either late or never'—the person who would succeed Filanghieri did eventually come to his aid, but only long after the latter had been tested to destruction as a fakir and been found wanting, as I remembered when I bent down over De la Garza to enquire vaguely and ineffectually about his battered state, there was little I could do then, the fatuous fellow lay there crushed and half conscious, he might perhaps be crippled for some time to come, not for ever I hoped, otherwise he would have to grow used to frequenting toilets like this one. And I wondered, too, if the surname Tupra did not perhaps have its remote origins among certain ancient, idle compatriots of mine.

'A comb?' I replied, somewhat annoyed. It reminded me of Wheeler's comment about Latins, in his garden by the river, after the helicopter had had its little joke. A reputation for being vain. 'What makes you think I'd have a comb on me?'

'You Latins usually have one, don't you? See if he's got one.' And he jerked his head in the direction of the fallen man.

It made me squirm inside, it seemed outrageous to me that Reresby should use the comb that De la Garza was bound to have on him, assuming he had not lost it in that one-sided scrimmage or during the furious dancing beforehand. I felt ashamed at the very idea of frisking the beaten man, that all too easily defeated man. And so I took mine out, even though this meant admitting that Tupra had been right.

'Very clever,' I said to Tupra and handed it to him. It was clearly a widespread idea on that large island, about us Latins and our combs.

Not that I cared particularly if I did corroborate his theory: I suddenly felt extraordinarily relieved, because it was over and De la Garza was still alive and I had already imagined him dead. Very dead indeed, sliced in two, transformed into head and trunk. The greatest danger was over, or so it seemed, however recently it had occurred, it was nonetheless over, it is amazing and also irritating how cessation brings with it a kind of false, momentary cancellation of what has happened. 'Now that he's not walloping the hell out of him any more, it's almost as if he hadn't done it at all,' we think in our excessive adoration of the present moment, which is madly and permanently on the increase. 'Now that it isn't burning any more, it's almost as if it had never burned. Now that they're not bombing us any more, it's almost as if they had never bombed us. Yes, there are the dead and the mutilated, and the charred houses reduced to rubble, but that's how it is now, it's happened, it's already past and there is no one who can change or undo it, and now, at least, they're not killing or mutilating or destroying, not while I'm here and breathing and with things still to do.' These thoughts pass through our heads whenever one of the present-day, more or less televised wars is going on—the Gulf War, the wars in Kosovo and Afghanistan, the Iraq War based on dishonest motives and spurious interests and which was totally unnecessary except as a way of feeding the limitless arrogance of those who were the driving forces behind it—wars which are held in such scorn by older people, like my father or Wheeler, who had been involved in the non-frivolous variety. As long as there are battles and as long as there are bombs falling on soldiers and civilians, we are gripped by a terrible anxiety, we watch the news every day with our hearts in our mouths; this phase doesn't usually last very long nowadays, sometimes only a matter of weeks or, at most, months, and so we don't have time to get used to it nor, therefore, to become sufficiently desensitised, to accept that this is the nature of any war, be it treacherous or righteous, and that it is something that can be lived with on a daily basis, without giving it too much importance or worrying about other people all the time, especially about distant people unknown to us; not even about ourselves and those close by, once the slaughter has begun, if your time is up, it's up. If a bullet has your name on it, as Diderot said—long before anyone else did, if I'm not mistaken. Nowadays, we don't have time to become accustomed to living in a state of war, a state which, as Wheeler remarked, makes peace inconceivable and vice versa ('People don't realise to what extent the one negates the other,' he had said, 'how one state suppresses, repels and excludes the other from our memory and drives it out of our imagination and our thoughts'), and thus the sense of emergency remains intense for the brief duration of the horror seen on screen, and when that phase ends, we are filled by a strange conviction that it is all over and has, to some extent, disappeared. 'At least it's not happening now,' we think, sometimes even with a sigh; and that 'at least' implies a real injustice: what happened loses in gravity and impact simply because it is not happening now, and then we almost lose interest in the wounded and the dead who so distressed and affected us while it was going on. They are the past now, someone is taking care of things, reconstructing, healing, burying, adopting, preferably the same people who caused the war, so that they can then be seen as righters of wrongs, the very height of absurdity and an out-and-out lie. It's yet another symptom of the infantilisation of the world, mothers used to soothe their children by saying: 'It's over now, it's all right, it's over,' after a nightmare or a fright or some unpleasant incident, trapped fingers or some such thing, almost as if they were saying: 'What no longer is never was', even if the pain persisted and an itchy scab formed afterwards or the fingers became bruised and swollen and even if, sometimes, a scar was left behind so that, later, the adult could stroke it and continue to remember that injury and that day.

To experience a sense of relief after having watched as some cowed, unwitting, half-drunk person was roundly beaten and having myself lacked both the courage or the ability to stop it, after having believed that my colleague was about to slice someone's head off, was going to strangle him with a hairnet and drown him in the toilet bowl, was not at all reasonable nor, of course, noble. And yet that was how it was, Tupra had stopped, and I was pleased, he had removed a much greater weight than he had placed on me, and that was no small thing. De la Garza was no longer in danger, that was my main, grotesque thought, because danger had already taken a brutal toll on him. It had not, it's true, killed him, but it seemed ridiculous to be satisfied with that, with seeing him still alive, and even feeling glad, when the last thing I had imagined as I led him to the Disabled toilet was that he would leave it so badly injured, doubtless with, at the very least, several broken bones. If, that is, he did leave it, because while Reresby was readjusting his dress and trying to tame his dark hair, thicker and curlier than one normally finds in Britain (with the exception of Wales), and which was probably dyed, particularly at the temples where the curls were almost ringlets (he combed it through a few times and tidied it, although it didn't look much different afterwards), he again ordered me to translate the following:

'Translate this for him, Jack,' he said once more, 'I don't want there to be any misunderstandings, because he, not us, will suffer the consequences, make it quite clear, tell him, tell him what I've just told you.' And I did, I told De la Garza in my own language about those possible misunderstandings; his eyes were half closed and puffy, but he was doubtless able to hear me. 'Tell him that you and I are going to leave here quietly and that he is going to lie there, where he is, without moving, for another half an hour, no, make that forty minutes, that gives me a bit more leeway, I've still got some things to deal with out there. Tell him not even to think of leaving or of getting up. Tell him not to shout or call for help. Tell him he's to stay here during that time, the cold floor will do him good and it won't do him any harm to spend a bit of time lying still, until he gets his breath back. Tell him that.' And I did, including the part about the restoring coolness of the floor. 'There's his overcoat,' Reresby went on, pointing to the second coat he had brought with him, the dark one, which he had left hanging on one of the lower bars, and then I realised how carefully my transitory boss had planned it all: it wasn't my coat, but Rafita's, which he had gone to the trouble of fetching from the coatcheck before coming to the toilet, he presumably had some influence in that chic, idiotic place or else a talent for deception, they would have fetched it and handed it to him without asking any questions and even with a bow. 'With that on, no one will notice the state he or his clothes are in, he won't attract attention. If he finds walking difficult, people will just assume he's sloshed. He can always pretend, unless, of course, he really is still a bit pissed. When he leaves, he's to go straight out into the street without stopping in the club for any reason, he's to go straight home. And he must never come back here, ever. Go on, translate that for him.'—And I did so again, translating Tupra's English word 'sloshed' as '*mamado*'.—'Tell him not even to think of going to the police or kicking up a stink at his embassy, or making a complaint through them, of any kind: he knows what could happen to him. Tell him not to phone you to demand an explanation, but to leave you alone, to forget he ever knew you. Tell him to accept that there's no reason to demand an explanation, that there are no grounds for complaints or protest. Tell him not to talk to anyone, to keep quiet, not even to recount it later as some kind of adventure. But tell him always to remember.'—As I gave these instructions to De la Garza, I thought again: 'Keep quiet and don't say a word, not even to save yourself. Keep quiet, and save yourself.'—But Tupra added a few more, in quick succession, as if he were reciting a list or as if they were the known consequences of a plan successfully carried out, the known effects of a treatment.—'Tell him he's probably got a couple of broken ribs, three or possibly four. They'll be very painful, but they'll heal, they'll mend eventually. And if he finds something worse wrong, then he should just think himself very lucky. He could have been left with no head, he came very close. But since he didn't lose it, tell him there's still time, another day, any day, we know where to find him. Tell him never to forget that, tell him the sword will always be there. If he has to go to hospital, then he should give them the same line drunks and debtors do—that the garage door fell on him. Tell him to wet his hair before he leaves, to clean himself up a bit, although I shouldn't think anybody would find that particular shade of blue out of place here. Actually, he looks less odd and less ridiculous than he did wearing that string bag he had on. Go on, tell him all that, then we can leave. Make sure he's understood everything. Oh, and here's your comb, thank you.'

He handed it back to me. Unlike Wheeler, he hadn't taken the precaution of holding it up to the light to see if it was clean when I gave it to him. I, however, did do so when it was returned to my hand, but there were no hairs caught on it. I translated that last list of orders to the attaché, but I left out the bit about the sword; that is, I mentioned his head and its possible, perhaps only postponed, loss, but not the sword. You cannot ask someone to translate everything, even insane, obscene or nasty remarks, even curses and calumnies, without their questioning or judging or rejecting some of it. Even if you are not the person doing the speaking or the saying, even though you are the mere transmitter or reproducer of someone else's words and sentences, the truth is that these do in large part become yours when you make them comprehensible and repeat them to another person, to a far greater degree than might at first seem likely. You hear them, understand them and sometimes have opinions about them; you find an immediate equivalent for them, give them a new form and let them go. It's as if you endorsed them. I had approved of nothing that had happened in that toilet, nor of anything that Tupra had done. Nor of my own passivity, or bewilderment, or was it cowardice or perhaps prudence, perhaps I had prevented worse calamities. I was even more displeased with Reresby's improper use of the plural, 'we know where to find him', it troubled and upset me that he should include me in that, without my consent and when he knew me so little. What he could not ask me to do was to play an active role and to threaten De la Garza with the weapon that arouses most fear, an atavistic fear, the weapon that has caused most deaths throughout most centuries, at close quarters and face to face with the person killed. And the one that I had feared so much while it was unsheathed and ready for use.

I finished, and added in Spanish on my own account:

'De la Garza, you'd better do everything he says, is that clear? I mean it. I honestly didn't think you were going to get out of here alive. I don't know him that well myself. I hope you recover. Good luck.'

De la Garza nodded, just a slight lift of the chin, his eyes dull, his gaze averted, he did not even want to look at us. He was not only in pain, he was, I think, still terrified, and the terror would not pass until we were out of his sight, and even then a remnant would always remain. He would be sure to obey, he would not dare to make enquiries or seek me out or phone me. He might not even phone Wheeler, his theoretical mentor in England, to have a moan about it. Nor his father in Spain, Peter's old friend. His name was Pablo, and he was, I recalled, a much better man than his son.

Tupra picked up his own pale coat, so stiff and respectable, and put it over his shoulders, there was no difference now between the man who was leaving the toilet and the man who had entered it. He picked up the sodden gloves and put them in one of his overcoat pockets, having first wrung them out and wrapped them each in several pieces of toilet paper. He removed the wedge from beneath the door and held the door open for me.

'Let's go, Jack,' he said.

He did not so much as glance at the fallen man. De la Garza was just that, one of the fallen, no longer of any concern to him, he had done his job. That was my impression, that he viewed him probably without hostility or pity. That must be how he saw everything: you did what you had to do, you took care of things, sorted them out, defused them, set fire to them or restored them to balance ('Don't linger or delay'); then they were forgotten, relegated to the past, and there was always something else waiting, as he had said, he still had some things to deal with out there and needed thirty or forty minutes; with all these interruptions, he wouldn't have had time to close the deals or agree the bribes or the blackmailing scams or the pacts with Mr Manoia. Or he would not have convinced or persuaded him, or he would not have had sufficient opportunity to allow Manoia to persuade or convince him about whatever it was. Nor did he give a farewell kick or flourish as he passed by De la Garza's fallen form. Tupra was certainly Sir Punishment, but he was not perhaps Sir Cruelty. Or maybe he simply never ever hit anyone directly with any part of his body. As he left, only the tail of his overcoat, which swirled like a matador's cape, brushed the face of the fallen man.

Before going through the second door, the one that gave onto the disco itself, another line from 'The Streets of Laredo' came into my mind, with its insistent, repetitive melody. I found the line unfortunate, because I couldn't be sure that I did not, at that moment, endorse it slightly, as one does when one translates or repeats an oath, or that Tupra could not adopt the line as his own that night, after what had, in his eyes, been my entirely unsatisfactory behaviour from start to finish: 'We all loved our comrade although he'd done wrong,' it said, '*Todos queríamos a nuestro camarada aunque hubiera hecho mal.*' Although, of course, it could also be translated as '*aunque hubiera hecho daño*—'although he'd caused harm'—and perhaps that version was the more accurate one.

Reresby knew his timings, we spent thirty-five minutes at the table before the four of us left the disco, Mr and Mrs Manoia, him and me. We had left the couple alone for far less time than that, the business in the handicapped toilet, that is, Tupra's violent intervention, had lasted barely ten minutes, and before that he had first solicitously accompanied Flavia to the Ladies' room and then back to the table: he had neglected neither her nor, indeed, him, so there could be no great complaints about our absence. Manoia did not, therefore, seem particularly impatient or ill-humoured, or perhaps lo sfregio on his wife's face had so incensed him that this could only be followed by an abatement of the fever, a relative calming down, while we (I included myself in that plural now) were busy punishing the dickhead, possibly in Manoia's name and possibly on his orders.

Tupra, at any rate, did not return his overcoat to the cloak-room, he sat down with it over his shoulders, allowing it to hang straight, like a cloak, as he was obliged to do given the rigidity of the concealed weapon, he seemed used to doing so (the hem must have got dirty, since it was dragging on the floor). I wondered if Manoia had any idea as to what my boss had hidden about his person, he might not have liked it at all. It was not impossible either that the sword had not been there from the start, that Tupra had not always had it with him, that it had been handed to him in the cloakroom when he went to ask for his coat; that, at a signal from him, they had slipped it into the long pocket-cum-sheath, that it was held there for him, so to speak, and given to him whenever he needed it. He was probably a regular customer, a favoured client, and must have been so in all the places we went to, at least that is how he was treated, as a familiar figure, someone to be flattered, respected and even slightly feared, he was known as Reresby in some, Ure in others and Dundas in the rest. But not all of those places would keep a store of weapons to be handed over as and when. Long, sharp weapons.

During those thirty-five minutes he immersed himself in conversation with Manoia, having first made a gesture which I took to mean 'It's done' or 'You can consider yourself avenged' or 'Problem solved, I'm sorry it ever happened'. I heard them mention some of the same names that had cropped up earlier: Pollari, Letta, Saltamerenda, Valls, the Sismi, although I still had no idea what the latter was. Manoia did not so much as glance in my direction, he must have formed a very bad opinion of me and decided to avoid all contact, even visual. It again fell to me to keep Flavia amused, as if nothing had happened; but she seemed dejected, almost depressed, with little desire to talk, she kept glancing vaguely about her, as if she were bored and killing time, she tapped her foot to the music, languidly and discreetly, she had carefully applied more make-up to her cheek, but it still looked raw, there was still a visible mark, her hair had become dishevelled during the dance and, in her case, a comb, her own or someone else's, would not have been enough to restore order to a complex arrangement of what were doubtless various forms of false switches and plaits. She had aged a few years, she might even have wept a few artificial, childish tears, which is something that immediately accentuates the age of someone intent on delaying or concealing it (but only fake tears do this, not real ones). Then, after some moments had passed and while her husband was busily engaged in whispering into Tupra's ear, she asked me in Italian:

'And your friend?' She had suddenly reverted to the formal mode of address, a further indication of her low spirits.

I cast a sideways glance at those penetrating nipples, those *brutali capezzoli*, fancy arming yourself with such ice picks. They had been indirectly to blame for almost everything, notably my negligence.

'He's left,' I said. 'He got bored. Besides, it was getting late, he's a very early riser.' My second comment was spiteful, because I myself was feeling miserable and found her presence unbearable.

Then I looked round for the group of noisy Spaniards who had come with De la Garza; I couldn't hear them, so it was logical to think that I wouldn't be able to see them either, their table was empty. They had left or scattered, without waiting for him or going in search of him, they would have assumed that he was either in full or partial copulatory mode somewhere; there was, therefore, no need to worry about them, to worry that they might rescue their friend and prevent his complying with Reresby's implacable orders and deadlines.

I had more than enough time—contemplative or dead time—to become retrospectively angry. How could it have happened? I asked myself, and with every second it seemed more like a stupid, disturbing dream, of the sort that will not go away, but which lingers and waits. Why hadn't Tupra contented himself with merely giving De la Garza the slip, with all four of us leaving and making sure that he wasn't following us? Why was it so important to continue the conversation there, in that noisy, pretentious place, rather than somewhere else, where there would be no hold-ups or interruptions? The city was full of such places, there were several in Knightsbridge itself, and Tupra would have been perfectly at home in any of them; I couldn't understand the need for the thrashing either, still less the sword. And why hadn't I grabbed his arm? (When I thought he was about to bring the sword down on living flesh.) The answer to this last question came to me at once, and it was very simple: because he might have cut my head off instead, or sliced through one of my shoulders and punctured a lung. With a single two-handed blow. ('And in short, I was afraid.') And given that answer and what I had seen, I interrogated myself about Tupra as if Tupra were interrogating me in one of our sessions spent interpreting lives in the building with no name, and he might well have asked me questions such as these— almost impossible to answer at first, until you plunged in—the day after any meeting or outing, after any encounter or observation, about anyone with whom we had spoken, or even been with, or whom we had merely observed and heard:

'Do you think that man could kill, or that he's just a braggart, the sort who looks as if he's going to do something, but never dares? Why do you think he stopped short of decapitating him with the sword?'

And I could have replied:

'Perhaps we should start by asking why he took the sword out in the first place. It was melodramatic and unnecessary and, in the end, he didn't even use it, except to cut off the hairnet and frighten his victim half to death, and the witness too, of course. One has to ask oneself whether he brandished that sword purely so that I would see it and feel alarmed and shocked, as indeed I did, or, I don't know, so that I would believe he was capable of actually killing, without giving it a second thought, in the most brutal manner and for no reason. Or perhaps he stopped short so that I would believe quite the opposite, that he wasn't capable of doing it despite having every opportunity to do so or, how can I put it, despite being already halfway there. Or perhaps he wanted to test me, to see my reaction, to find out whether or not I would back him up or if I would confront him over such a violent act. Well, he knows the answer to that last point. He knows that I wouldn't, not when unarmed. Not that this tells him very much: he would have got a clearer idea if I had been wielding a weapon as well.'

'So what do you actually believe? You haven't given me an answer, Jack, and the reason I ask you a question is because I'm interested in your answer; whether you're right or wrong doesn't really matter, because most of the time we'll never find out one way or another. Do you think this man Reresby could kill or would ever really kill? Don't just consider this one situation, think of the man as a whole.'

'Yes, I think he could,' I would have said. 'Everyone could, but some are more likely to do so and the majority far less so, and as regards the latter, infinitely less.' And I would have added to myself: 'Comendador could, I've always known that, Wheeler could and I could, although I've only known that very recently; Luisa couldn't, but I don't know about Pérez Nuix, I can't tell, and Manoia and Rendel could, although not Mulryan or De la Garza or Flavia, or perhaps De la Garza could accidentally, treacherously, in a moment of panic; Beryl couldn't nor could Lord Rymer the Flask—he doesn't get aggressive when he's drunk, although, of course, he might when he's sober, but no one can ever remember seeing him sober—and, on the other hand, Mrs Berry could, as could Dick Dearlove, but for very different horrific reasons, I don't know quite what, but not out of narrative or biographical horror, which only affects celebrities. My father and my sister and my brothers couldn't, and my mother couldn't have, nor Cromer-Blake or Toby Rylands, well, Toby could have killed in battle and probably did. Alan Marriott with his three-legged dog couldn't, but Clare Bayes, my former, clinging lover from Oxford, could. My son wouldn't be capable of killing, but my daughter might be, as far as one can tell, which is, as yet, very little. Incompara certainly could, even though I have stated the contrary.' And I might have continued that train of thought: 'When I think about it, I know this about nearly all the people I have ever known, or pretty much, and I believe I also know who would come and kill me, take me out and finish me, as they did with Emilio Marés and so many others: if they had the chance, if another civil war broke out in Spain, if there were enough confusion and enough excuses and a way of covering up their crime. I'm better off in England.' And then I would have continued interpreting for Reresby: 'He has probably killed before. Sometimes with his own hands, but far more often by using intrigue, subterfuge, defamation, poison, by dint of innuendo, laconic orders and condemnatory silences. He has doubtless spread outbreaks of cholera and malaria and plague too, and then pretended to be either surprised or in the know already, depending on the circumstances and what seemed appropriate, depending on whether he wanted to leave his mask on or take it off. Take it off to instil fear, leave it on to instil confidence. Both things bring great benefits, they never fail.'

'So you have to be very careful with him, then,' Tupra would have said of Reresby. 'He's dangerous and, of course, to be feared.'

This was almost the conclusion reached by the somewhat vague report about me which I had discovered among some old files in the building with no name, an anonymous report, but which had referred to particular people, although I had no idea who they were (or perhaps they were merely archetypes) and was clearly addressed to someone: 'He may not care very much what happens to anyone . . .' it said in that English text someone had devoted to me. 'Things happen and he makes a mental note, not for any particular reason, usually without even feeling greatly concerned most of the time, still less implicated. Perhaps that is why he notices so many things. So few escape him that it's almost frightening to imagine what he must know, how much he sees and how much he knows. About me, about you, about her. He knows more about us than we ourselves do.' And further on: 'He makes no use of his knowledge, it's very odd. But he has it. And if he did one day make use of it, he would be someone to be feared. He'd be pretty unforgiving, I think.' And it concluded, as if to emphasise this point: 'He knows he doesn't understand himself and that he never will. And so he doesn't waste his time trying to do so. I don't think he's dangerous. But he is to be feared.'

The first statement might be true, that I rarely gave much importance to what was going on around me (perhaps that is why I had not grabbed Reresby's arm, when he was wielding the Landsknecht sword). The second was, I felt, an exaggeration: however much I might think I knew, I didn't know *that* much, there is always an enormous difference between those two things which are constantly being confused—

thinking you know something and really knowing something. And who was 'I', who was 'you', who was 'she' in that report? Was 'I' Tupra? Was 'you' Pérez Nuix, or was she 'she'? It suddenly occurred to me that 'I', the person writing and pondering, the person who had observed me, must have known me for longer and in greater depth than my colleagues (although this was to forget for a moment what they did, what we did, with great arbitrariness and audacity). Was it Wheeler, was it Mrs Berry or was it even Toby Rylands himself who had written or dictated and prepared it years ago, just in case, at a time when I was still living in Oxford and wasn't even married and when it was unlikely that I would return to England once my university contract ran out? Did they really file away such useless stuff? Would he really have thought so far ahead? That would mean that the 'you' was his brother, Wheeler, whom I hardly knew during my stay there. And who could 'she' be but Clare Bayes, who was my only 'she' at the time. 'He knows more about us than we ourselves do.' Perhaps that was a way of referring to the Congregation, which is what the assembly of dons at the university call themselves, following the strong clerical tradition of the place, and of which both brothers were members. Peter had told me that Toby was the first person to talk to him about me and my supposed gift, which in fact was why we met: 'he aroused my curiosity. He said that you might perhaps be like us . . .' That was a different 'us', not an Oxonian one this time, he was referring to what both of them were or had been, interpreters of people or translators of lives. 'That's what he had given me to understand, and he confirmed it later when we happened to talk about the old group.' These had been his words while I was having breakfast, and later he had been even more explicit: 'Toby told me that he always admired the special gift you had for capturing the distinctive and even essential characteristics of friends and acquaintances, characteristics which they themselves had often not noticed or known about . . .'

All these things were possible, it might even have been

Rylands's voice from beyond the grave reporting on me to Wheeler or to Tupra himself, who was, after all, a former student of his, I mustn't forget that. (We never know to what extent and in what way we are observed by those who surround us, by those closest to us, our most loyal supporters, who appear to have long ago renounced objectivity and to take us for granted, or to consider us permanent or inviolable or non-negotiable, or to have bestowed on us their eternal clemency; we don't know what silent and constantly changing judgements they are making, our wives and our husbands, our parents and our children, our best friends: we consider them utterly and definitively safe, as if they were going to remain like that for ever, when it is clear that their faces change as ours do for them, that we might love them and end up hating them, that they might be unconditionally on our side until the day they turn against us and devote themselves to seeking ways to ruin us, wreck us, drown us and bring us pain. And even to expel us from the earth and from time itself, that is, to destroy us.)

As for the third statement, that I was not dangerous, but that I was to be feared, and that I was unforgiving (although this was offered only as an opinion), that seemed even more of an exaggeration. I'm not sure that anyone knows whether they are to be feared or not, unless they set out to be feared, unless they work at it, dominating minds and laying down rules or calling the shots, as part of a plan or strategy, or, when I think about it, as a fairly common way of going about the world. Otherwise, how can I put it, you never see yourself as someone to be feared because you never fear yourself. And of those who struggle hard to be dreaded and feared, only a few actually manage it. Tupra and Wheeler, each in his own way, were good examples of this, and if there were links between them and if there were, in turn, links between each of them and the teacher or the friend or the dead brother, if among those three there were similarities and bonds of character, or, rather, of capability, the shared gift which, according to their wise view, I also had, then it was not impossible that I too, however unintentionally, must also be feared, and the report was therefore right. I had already been less than honest with Tupra on one occasion, in my interpretation of Incompara: I had agreed to Pérez Nuix's request, and so had kept silent or said too little or lied. And perhaps that alone made me someone to be feared or, which comes to the same thing, someone not to be trusted or, which is very similar, a traitor. (Asking favours is, after telling tales, the most common curse; let us hope that no one ever asks us for anything, but only gives us orders.)

'Oh, yes,' I would have said to Tupra about Reresby. 'Even though he doesn't appear intimidating, not initially, or make you feel you should be on your guard, rather, he invites you to lower your sword and remove your helmet in order to be more easily taken captive by him, by his warm, enveloping attention, by those eyes of his which plumb the past and end up making the person they're looking at feel really important: even though, to begin with, despite being a native of the British Isles, he seems a cordial, smiling, openly friendly man, whose bland, ingenuous form of vanity proves not only inoffensive, but causes you to view him slightly ironically and with an almost instinctive fondness, he is, nevertheless, infinitely dangerous and, I believe, to be infinitely feared. He is certainly a man who takes it very badly if someone fails to do what he himself considers to be just, right, appropriate or good, especially when it's perfectly do-able.'

And Tupra would then have asked me the most difficult question of all:

'Do you think he could have killed you, Jack, there in the Disabled toilet, if you had grabbed his arm, if you had tried to prevent him decapitating that loudmouth? You believed he was going to kill De la Garza and that seemed to you wrong, very wrong. Even though you loathed the individual, it horrified you. Why didn't you stop him? Was it because you thought that if he was capable of killing one man, he was capable of killing two, and then you would all end up losing still more? Two deaths instead of one, and one of them yours? I mean, do you believe him capable of killing you, not a friend exactly, but someone in his charge, an employee, a hired man, a workmate, a colleague, an associate on the same side as him? Tell me what you think, tell me now, just say whatever comes into your head. Have the courage to see. Be irresponsible enough to see. This is the kind of thing that one believes one knows.'

And I would have succumbed to the habitual temptation of those first sessions when he used to question me about famous or unknown people scrutinised on video or in the flesh from the stationary train compartment or face to face, and often he would ask me very specific things about aspects of people that are usually impenetrable at first sight and even at last sight, even with those people to whom you are closest, for you can spend a lifetime by someone's side and watch them die in your arms, and, at the hour of their death, still not know what they were or were not capable of, and not even be sure of their true desires, if they were reasonably content in the knowledge that they had achieved such desires or if they continued to yearn for them throughout their entire existence, and that is what most frequently happens unless the person has no desires at all, which rarely occurs, some modest desire always slips in. (Yes, you can be convinced of something, but not know for certain.)

So I would have preferred to answer 'I don't know', the words no one ever wanted to hear and which were deemed almost unacceptable in the building with no name, in that new group, which, as I was becoming increasingly aware, was the impoverished heir of the old group, the words that never found favour, but met with scorn and blank rejection. And it wasn't just Tupra to whom they were unacceptable: they were unacceptable to Pérez Nuix, Mulryan and Rendel as well, and probably to Branshaw and Jane Treves too, who although they were only occasional collaborators would doubtless not allow such words to be spoken by their lower-ranking narks and informers. 'Perhaps' was allowed—it had to be—but it made a bad impression, it wasn't much appreciated and, in the end, was ignored as if you had made no real contribution or suggestion at all, it had the same effect as a blank vote or an abstention, how can I put it, the attitude with which it was received almost never had a verbal correlative, but was equivalent to someone muttering: 'Well, that's a fat lot of use. Let's move on to the next subject'; and sometimes they would frown or pull an exasperated face. At that stage of my induced boldness and my carefully elaborated or developed powers of penetration, it would have been extraordinary for me to give such a reply to that final question about Reresby, shrouded, as he was, in his unending night: 'Perhaps. It's unlikely. It's not impossible. Who knows? I certainly don't.' And so I would have had to take a risk and, after considering for a moment, would at last have given my most sincerely felt verdict or wager, that is, the one I most believed to be true or, as people like to say, as I believed in my heart of hearts:

'I don't think it would have been easy for him, it would have been hard for him to do it, he would have tried to avoid it, that is, he would have given me at least one or two opportunities before unleashing the blow, the opportunity to desist. Perhaps a wound, a cut, a warning or two. But yes, I think he would have been capable of killing me if he had seen that I was determined and serious, or if it meant that I was stopping him doing what he had decided to do. He would have been capable of killing me because I was in his way and would not give up. Except that, as we have seen, he had not yet decided on an execution.'

'Do you mean you would have so enraged him that he would have lost control and lashed out murderously in a burst of impatience, pride or anger?' Tupra might have asked, perhaps offended by such a possibility.

'No, no,' I would have said. 'It would have been for the reason I gave before, because he takes it very badly if someone fails to do what, according to him, they should and could do. Something on which he has already reached a reasoned decision, based on his own or other people's reasons, which sometimes emerges after long reflection or machination and at others very quickly, in a flash, as if his all-seeing eyes saw at once what there was to see and knew at a glance what would happen, with just one clearly focused glance, with no going back. I don't know how to explain it: he could have killed me for reasons of discipline, which is something the world has relinquished; or out of determination or haste, or as part of a plan; because he was used to overcoming obstacles and I had suddenly, gratuitously, superfluously, become an unplanned and, from his point of view, unreasonable obstacle.' But then I would have had to give voice to a last-minute doubt, because it was a real doubt, and added: 'Or perhaps not, perhaps he wouldn't have been capable of killing me, despite everything, for one reason only: perhaps he likes me too much and has not yet tired of that feeling.'

When we got up and went to fetch the overcoats, the Manoias' and mine, Tupra went back to the handicapped toilet. He didn't tell me he was going to, but I saw him do so. He indicated to me that I should accompany Flavia to the coatcheck, he gave me the tickets for the coats, and I saw him and Manoia head off in that direction, go through the first door and, I assumed, through the second door too, but I have no idea what happened next. I didn't have the energy to become alarmed and angry all over again: what had happened was bad enough, and the fact that De la Garza had not died—I realised—only made things marginally better. I had seen the expression on his face, the look of a dead man, of someone who knows he is going to die and knows he is dead. There were three or four or five times when his heart could have burst. 'Reresby is probably going to kill him now,' I thought without believing it, 'he's still got his sword with him. Or perhaps he's merely going to check that De la Garza has obeyed his orders. Or perhaps he wants to show his work to Manoia, to give Manoia or himself that satisfaction. Or maybe it is Manoia who has demanded to see the results of his labours and to give or withhold his approval, a "*Basta così*" or a "*Non mi basta*". Or, more likely, this Sicilian, Neapolitan or Calabrian isn't going there to check anything, but is going to finish him off in person.' They did not take long, they were in and out in a trice, and when they rejoined us, our coats, Mrs Manoia's and mine, were still lying across the coatcheck counter. The fourth or the third possibilities were the most likely, either a case of accounts rendered or of pure vanity; I doubted it was the second possibility, Tupra knew as well as I did that De la Garza would not have moved an inch from his place on the floor. In that idiotic place, no one seemed to pay for anything, at least I didn't and I saw no one else pay either. Reresby must have an account there or else everything was always on the house or perhaps he was a member with a share in the profits. Or, who knows, perhaps De la Garza had paid already behind our backs, before his last, interrupted dance, in order to seduce Flavia by that generous gesture. But that would have been most unlike him, nor would that dickhead have thought she was worth such a gesture.

The four of us got into the Aston Martin used on nights when the aim was to make a good impression or to toady up to someone, that night it had been the former; it was quite a tight fit, but we couldn't send the couple off in a taxi, we were the hosts, and, besides, it was only a short ride. We took them to their hotel, the opulent Ritz no less, near Hatchard's bookshop in Piccadilly, which I had visited so often following in the footsteps of past notables, Byron and Wellington, Wilde and Thackeray, Shaw and Chesterton; and not far from Heywood Hill, which I frequented more when I lived in Oxford, and not far either from the shops of Davidovich and Fox in St James's Street where Tupra probably bought his Rameses II and where I obtained my rather less magnificent Karelias cigarettes, from the Peloponnese.

When I said goodbye to Flavia, I had a presentiment—or was it prescience—that if she were still disappointed or disconcerted by the incident and the removal of the young man, after a while, in the darkness, when she and her husband were lying silently in their respective beds or together in their double bed, what she would remember most were the compliments paid to her during the evening and she would fall asleep feeling calmer and more contented than when she had woken up that morning; and this meant that she could still wake up the next day thinking: 'Last night, I was fine, but will I be all right today?' So at least, in that one respect, I had done my job and had, indirectly and extravagantly—the best way—given her a further extension. (How she would love to have known that she had been the cause of violence.) One more extension before the day on which her first thought would be: 'Last night, I wasn't fine, so what will happen today?' She kissed both Tupra and myself and went inside, not noticing the man who held the door open for her and not waiting for her husband to finish saying his goodbyes. He wouldn't tell her off for that, and she must have been eager to study her *sfregio* in a magnifying mirror and in a better light, and to start summoning up the more pleasant moments of that long night, when she had still been in such excellent spirits that she could urge me in mock-reproachful tones: '*Su, va, signor Deza, non sia così antipatico. Mi dica qualcosa di carino, qualcosa di tenero. Una parolina e sarò contenta. Anzi, me farà felice.*'

As for Manoia, he shook Reresby's hand in what passed for effusiveness in such a mild, anodyne, Vaticanish man—the mildness, of course, was phoney—and I assumed that they had, in the end, reached some mutually convenient agreement, or had got from each other what each of them had asked for or proposed or had imposed by dint of some unspoken threat.

'It has been a great great great pleasure, Mr Reresby,' he said in his heavy Italian accent: he probably didn't know how else to translate '*grandissimo*'. 'An evening full of incident but no less of a pleasure for that. Be so kind as to keep me informed.' In contrast, he was extremely cold with me, indeed, he left the hand I held out to him hanging in mid-air and merely inclined his head slightly, like an old-fashioned diplomat (and 'inclined' is something of an exaggeration). He did not even look at me, or, rather, I could not see his dull, zigzagging eyes behind his large, reflecting glasses. He pushed his glasses up on his nose with his thumb one last time, although they had not in fact slipped down, and said: '*Buona notte.*'

Then he scuttled off after his wife, he probably found separation from her painful. He looked then more like a diligent civil servant than a rapist, not so much Mafia or Camorra or 'ndrangheta as Opus Dei or Christ's Legionnaires, or perhaps Sismi, whatever that was. But Flavia was nowhere to be seen in the lobby, not at least from the street, from Piccadilly. She must be in the elevator, on her way up to their room, where she would lock herself in the bathroom for a while alone and thus postpone her husband's private reproaches. She would have warned him not to speak to her through the bathroom door, and in such matters he would doubtless have obeyed her.

He had not even added: '*E grazie.*' Nor was there any reason why he should, he was unaware of my growing anger or my unease. He may even have believed that I had been responsible for handing out the beating whose result must have pleased him when he visited the toilet to check. He may have taken me for a mere henchman, an underling, a flunkey, a thug. And the truth is that, at that moment, I did feel like a henchman and an underling, and even like a flunkey too: I had placed Tupra's victim precisely where he had wanted him to be. But not a heavy or a hitman or a goon, not a thug, because I hadn't laid a finger on anyone and had no intention of doing so. Just as I hoped no one would lay a finger on me, with or without the benefit of a sword, even with or without a comb.

Anything I sensed or knew about him and anything he knew or sensed about me—since you cannot, at will or with impunity, crouched or invisible like someone watching from a house or like a ghost, decipher another person who is, in turn, studying and deciphering you—came from observing someone who was also continually observing me, someone equipped with identical faculties and with the same or similar or possibly superior weapons; or perhaps all that can emerge from such a situation is a kind of sterile, reciprocal neutralisation, an impenetrability, a blockade, a cancelling out and a blindness— a sort of Cold War peace and détente—the mutual defusing of curses or gifts, paralysed and rendered useless when confronted by another mind that also suffers or enjoys them, if he and Wheeler were right and were not lying and I really did live up to their predictions. I was still so unconvinced of this that I did not quite believe it, despite Wheeler having persuaded me— invoking the authority of Rylands which there was now no way of refuting—that I did possess such a gift, and despite having grown bolder with each day spent on our one-eyed task in the building with no name, goaded by the faith of the others or by their demands: 'Tell me what else, don't stop, what else do you see, just say whatever comes into your head, don't delay or linger, the next to last thing we want is for you to keep quiet, to hesitate, to watch your back, we don't pay for your prudence, that isn't why we employ you, and the very last thing we want is for you to know nothing and to say nothing. Everything has its time to be believed, remember, so never keep silent, not even to save yourself, there's no room for that here and there's no cat either to get anyone's tongue, any of our five tongues, and you can't swallow it, not even if you wanted to choke yourself . . .' Or else: 'Why, you haven't even started yet. Go on. Quickly, hurry, keep thinking. The really interesting and difficult thing is to continue: to continue thinking and to continue looking when you have the feeling that there is no more to think and no more to see, that to continue would be a waste of time. In that wasted time lies the truly important, at the point where you might say to yourself there can't be anything else. So tell me, what else, what else occurs to you, what else can you offer, what else have you got? Go on thinking, quickly now, don't stop, go on.' That was what my father used to say to us during any discussion, even from when we were very young.

And that possible situation of stalemate or of a draw and of resignation, of an absence of any duel, of holding back among one's peers, could happen not only with Tupra and, of course, with Wheeler, but with the other three, with young Pérez Nuix and Mulryan and Rendel, and who knows, even with Branshaw and Jane Treves, if it came to that. And possibly with Mrs Berry too.

When Manoia had disappeared (at a trot), Tupra looked at me very seriously, almost ominously, outside on the pavement by the lights of the Ritz Hotel, Ritz Restaurant, Ritz Club. Then he smiled broadly and said:

'Shall I give you a lift? It's Dorset Square, isn't it, or a square near there? In that area, anyway.'

I knew, for example, that he knew the precise details of my address and that all these approximations were a pretence, he would have memorised the floor and the number and the letter of my apartment, as he did with all his collaborators. I also knew that he *wanted* to give me a lift, for some reason that went beyond mere thoughtfulness. He wanted to talk, to comment on the events of the night. Or to warn me about something. Or to give me advice and perhaps instructions for other such occasions, after my baptism of fire, as a witness and in the presence of a sword. I didn't think he intended giving me an explanation or apologising, smoothing away any rough edges. But he wanted something. I assumed, therefore, that he would end up giving me a lift in his Aston Martin, *velis nolis*. And that if I declined his offer, he would insist. And that if I refused, he would insist further.

'There's no need, I'll take a taxi,' I replied, and he must have realised that my indignation had not abated.

The two of us were standing on the pavement outside the Ritz, underneath the colonnade or arcade; he had left the car door open while we were saying our rapid farewells to the Catholic couple, the nearside door, the co-pilot's door, from which I had emerged. The doorman kept shifting from one foot to another, as if his feet were cold. He was keeping an urgent eye on us, we weren't supposed to park there, of course, or even to stop.

'Oh, come on, it's no bother, besides, this whole business has woken me up. It'll only take ten minutes; it's the least I can do, you deserve it. Come on, get in, we're in the way here.'

I would have taken a taxi and that would have been an end to it, but no taxis were passing at that moment, and the hotel taxi rank must have been down a side street, I couldn't see it, or perhaps that was it, right there, and it was deserted. However, I knew now, very clearly, that he wanted to or, rather, intended to give me a lift.

The prospect didn't please me. I would have preferred to see no more of him that night and not to run the risk of confronting him and reproaching him and demanding an explanation, and it seemed to me impossible not to do this if we were to go in the car alone. The following morning—we would start late, that was the norm when we had had a late night because of work, and our timetable was, anyway, fairly flexible—I would feel calmer, I thought, and might have come to terms with it more. And although he knew exactly where I lived, I didn't much like the idea of his encroaching on my territory, not with my knowledge and in my company. When someone drops you off or follows you or tails you or spies on you, and sees you open your front door as night falls or evening falls, they have seen much more than they appear to have seen or should have seen: they have seen you—how can I put it—in retreat, probably tired and even on the point of succumbing to passivity after the long day of pretence and effort and of false alert; they have, moreover, seen something that we repeat every day, perhaps the most everyday event of our external lives. People allow themselves to be accompanied or given lifts without a qualm, they even expect it and are grateful, as is often the case with women, but from then on it is as if someone knew where to find us—as if they knew it with their own eyes and had stored away the image, which is different from merely knowing something—and at approximately what time too. (Indeed, this is the first thing that burglars and kidnappers, rapists and murderers, spies and policemen find out and observe, what time you come home, when you are at home or when the house is empty, depending on their intentions and whether or not they would prefer you to be there or safely out of the way.) Yes, it makes a lot of difference being seen in our own territory or environs, even more so being seen going up the four or five steps that separate the street from our front door in London, opening the latter with our key, going in and closing it behind us with the involuntary slowness of the weary. After a couple of minutes, they will be able to identify our lights and our balconies, from the sidewalk below, or from behind the trees and the statue—except the window on that side has no balcony; and then they are better able to imagine or to guess at our domestic interiors, to know what kind of lighting we like, and even make out our silhouette if we go over to the window or observe us in our personal frame if we lean out to smoke a cigarette or to admire the twilight or to take the air or water the plants, or to see who it is ringing our doorbell on a rainy night, who it is who has been following us for ages now, she and I both with umbrellas and she with a white dog, tis tis tis the dog went, its footsteps almost flying. And someone in the square, from a distance, or, more precisely, someone from one of the houses opposite, the house of the proud dancer, for example, could have watched the two of us while we were talking, while young Pérez Nuix was asking me a bothersome and awkward favour, and was explaining why it is that our clients are no longer always the State, the army, the navy, a ministry or an embassy, New Scotland Yard or the judiciary, Parliament, the Bank of England, the Secret Service, MI6, MI5 or even Buckingham Palace, the Crown; and also while she was answering my numerous questions, sometimes without my even having to ask them and sometimes once I had asked them, 'What do you know about criminals?', 'Who are these "wet gamblers"?' and 'Who do I have to lie or keep silent about in order to please you?' and 'You still haven't asked me the favour, I still don't know what it is exactly' and 'How long have you been working here, how old were you when you started, who were you or what were you like before?' and 'Which private private individuals do you mean, and how is it that this time you know so much about this particular commission, its origin and provenance?' It could no longer be, nor was it, 'a moment', as she had announced after saying 'It's me' from down in the street. (Everything immediately grows longer or becomes tangled or adhesive, as if every action carried within it its own prolongation and every phrase left a thread of glue hanging in the air, a thread that can never be cut without something else becoming sticky too. Everything persists and continues on its own, even if you yourself decide to withdraw.)

And whenever I've brought a woman home, before, when I was single, or during that time in London (I mean brought someone back to spend the night or at least spend some time in my bed), I have always feared that she might later revisit the place uninvited and unsolicited: precisely because she had once set foot there and had seen me inside my apartment, seen how I lived and then stored away the image. And sometimes I have been quite right to fear this. And if someone has returned to this territory because I wanted them to and with my permission, or even because I summoned them and desired their presence, then, if we don't want them to move in, if we're not prepared for that, there is one room we must never allow them to enter, not even to keep us company while we fix a drink or prepare a snack, and that room is not the bedroom, where it doesn't even matter if they spend the night, nor the bathroom, a single man's bathroom is hardly a place to fire the imagination, but the kitchen, because if a woman enters the kitchen to continue the conversation while we're busy or to help us without our asking or suggesting that she does; if she follows us there on her own initiative, or almost instinctively, the way ducks do, she will probably want to stay by our side *sine die*—for a moment, she experiences or even smells what it would be like to live together—even though she may not know it and it is only her first visit, and even though she would genuinely deny it if someone were to predict it. This was perhaps one of the more trivial things learned from my gift or my curse, assuming I possessed either.

Tupra wasn't a woman and wasn't going to stay, he wasn't even coming upstairs to my apartment, he was merely going to drive into the square in his speedy Aston Martin and leave me at my door. Nevertheless, I didn't like the idea, because I could so easily imagine him afterwards, or on another night, another evening, another day or at dawn, spying on me from behind the trees or the statue, watching my window, or lying in wait in the hotel opposite, eyes trained on my lights or my window and on the possible woman who might have come to see me, although not necessarily to spend time in my bed. Waiting for her to leave. No wonder he had, from the first, struck me as a man who spent more time padding streets than carpets, more time out of the office than slaving away inside.

I opened the passenger door properly and got back into the car, without saying a word. He walked round to his side. I simply gave him my exact address, rather sarcastically I imagine, as if he were a taxi driver, and that was all. I knew I wouldn't be able to contain myself during the next few minutes that we would spend alone, but I wasn't sure how to begin, perhaps it would be best if I didn't rush things, despite my anger, by saying the first and possibly trivial words of recrimination that sprang to my lips, a mere detail in comparison with the real gravity of what had happened. I had not yet decided to leave this job for good, I needed to think about it more coolly and get myself used to the idea of going back to the BBC, with its ill-paid tedium. I waited for a few long seconds, with the car already moving off and accelerating, to see if he would say something and thus give me an opening. 'He won't do that,' I thought, 'he's very good at withstanding silences, especially those he initiates.' He was the one who had wanted to give me a lift, but perhaps it was not in order to lecture me or to tell me off (it was my fault that we had got stuck with De la Garza), nor to clarify anything to me, but to hear me venting my rage in the heat of the moment, and thus gauge my capacity for anger. After a while, the silence became that of two people who do not wish to speak to each other.

'It's not exactly a cheap area where you live,' he said eventually; the silence, therefore, was not, I judged, one he had decided upon and chosen, and he was not so good at withstanding those: his permanent state of vehemence and tension demanded that he fill every moment with some palpable, audible, recognisable or computable content. The whole car, free now from the interference of Flavia's rival fragrance, smelled of his aftershave, it was as if the lotion impregnated his skin or as if he were constantly, secretly, applying more. I hadn't seen him do so in front of the cripples' mirror. I wound down my window slightly.

'No, it's not cheap, in fact, it's rather expensive,' I replied almost reluctantly. 'But I prefer to spend my money on that, I avoid squalor like the plague.' Suddenly I realised that Tupra wasn't wearing his overcoat and hadn't been for a while, not even draped over his shoulders or over his arm, I hadn't noticed when he had taken it off or where he had put it, it must have been when we left the disco, or perhaps, unbeknown to me, he had switched coats in the cloakroom. I turned my head to see if the coat was lying on the shelf behind the back seats, but I couldn't see it, so where was the wretched sword? 'What about that sword?' I said.

Tupra—he was no longer Reresby, even though the night was not yet over—took out a cigarette and lit it with the lighter in the car, illuminating for a moment his smooth cheeks the colour of beer, he looked as if he had just shaved. This time he did not offer me one of his precious Egyptian cigarettes. To underline this, I got out one of my own Peloponnese brand, but did not immediately light it.

'It's in the trunk.'

'No, I mean what was it for? Why do you carry it with you? That was a monstrous, brutish thing to do, I thought you were really going to cut the guy's head off, I nearly died, you must be mad, I mean what is all this about, where do you think we are, you're nothing but an animal, and why did you need to—'

It all came out in a rush, in a torrent, despite the fact that his answer ('It's in the trunk') had been spoken in the same concluding or conclusive tone with which he had once answered me in his office ('Yes, I have') when I asked him if he had heard about the *coup d'état* against Chávez in Venezuela (and had added: 'Anything else, Jack?'). My tone was not yet furious, but if I had continued my disjointed litany, that tone would inevitably have come to the fore, we tend to generate our own heat, everything happens inside our head, especially if there is a pause, a condensation, an enforced wait between the events and the explosion. Tupra seemed unaffected, as yet, by my bitter outburst—he did not appear to feel uncomfortable or even moderately upset—and he dammed the current, only barely begun, with a calm, tangential sentence which I only partly understood. Not understanding is what most effectively brings us up short, and the need to understand is more urgent and more potent than any other.

'I learned it from the Krays,' he said, using that plural which is redundant in Spanish when used with surnames or the names of families (the plural is indicated by the article, for example, '*los Manoia*') and which more and more of our idiotic compatriots are transferring into our language out of pure copy-cat ignorance: they'll end up saying '*los Lópeces*' or '*los Santistébanes*' or '*los Mercaderes*'—but I didn't understand the word at the time, nor did I imagine it as having a capital letter or even know that it was a surname, still less how it was written ('crase', 'craze', 'kreys', 'crays', 'crease', 'creys', or even 'krais'? Most Spaniards have difficulty distinguishing the different kinds of 's' in English). That is why I abruptly stopped the deluge, at the same time as he stopped at a traffic light.

'From *what*?'

'From whom, you mean,' he replied. 'The Kray brothers, k-r-a-y.' And he spelled it out, as people so often do with English words and names. 'There's no reason why you should have heard of them, they were twins, Ronnie and Reggie, two pioneering gangsters from the 1950s and 1960s, they started out in the East End, they were from Bethnal Green or thereabouts; they took over the respective turfs of the Italians and the Maltese; they prospered and expanded and eventually ended up in prison at the end of the 1960s, one died behind bars and I think the other one is still in there, he must be pretty old by now and he'll probably never be let out. They were the most violent and the most feared and the most vicious of the lot, sadists really, and they did little to curb their cruelty, and to start with, they used swords. Obviously, in their first attempts at punishment beatings and intimidation, they did so out of necessity, because they didn't have the money for more expensive weapons. They provoked terror with those swords, they would slice their victim's face from ear to ear with a single cut, or slit them down the spine or lower still. They'd sometimes make a second cut too, and it's said that they sliced one woman in four. There are a number of books about them, and there was a film as well, I thought you were a movie-goer. Although it probably wasn't shown in Spain, too parochial to be of interest in other countries, a minor London story. I've seen it, though, and in one or two scenes they showed them sowing panic with their swords. I remember one scene took place in a pool hall. It wasn't a bad movie, well documented, and the actors were twins too. Biographical cinema, they call it.' I had never heard that term. I'd heard of 'biopic', but never 'biographical cinema', yet that was what he said.

He had defused me, at least for the moment. That was the way he usually talked, he went from one sentence to another and each one took him further away from whatever had given rise to the first, further away from the origin of the conversation or from his disquisition, if that was what it was. The origin in this case had been my anger, my resentment at the way he had involved me in his atrocities and made me witness them, in films and in novels anyone can get killed for no reason at all and no one so much as blinks, not the author or the characters or the viewers or the readers, it always seems so easy and so ordinary and so commonplace. But it isn't like that in real life, it isn't easy or ordinary or commonplace, not in the lives led by the vast—and I mean vast—majority of people, and in real life it causes enormous unease and alarm and sorrow, unimaginable to someone who has never been embroiled in such things. (As I believe I said before, it leaves you trembling and for a long time afterwards too. And then you feel depressed, and that lasts even longer.) Fortunately, we had not, as far as I knew, killed anyone, contrary to what had seemed likely when that sword first appeared (I might be the one to phone De la Garza later, behind Tupra's back—that would be best—to find out if the dickhead was still alive, and hadn't subsequently snuffed it because of some internal injury). After all, it had only been a few blows and shakings and a brief attempted drowning, pretty minor stuff really, very small beer in a movie or in one of those slow-witted novel-clones about body-busting psychopaths or analytical, almost arithmetical, serial killers, there are dozens of them, in imitative Spain as well. And yet that trifling incident— at least compared with fictional versions—had left me feeling feverish and nauseous and suffering from intermittent cold sweats, they did not last long, but nor did they entirely go away either, and every time the car stopped at a red light and no air was coming in, the sweats would return and I would be drenched again in a matter of seconds. This was during the car journey, which was indeed brief, especially at night, for we had nearly reached my square already.

Feeling troubled, but, even more than that, feeling both irritable and curious, I had said nothing after his explanations about the Kray twins, and had to backtrack mentally to recover if not the origin of that comment, at least the near vicinity: the sword.

'What do you mean when you say you learned from them? Do you mean the business with the sword? And where did you learn it from, from books, from the movie, or did you actually know the Krays?'

Tupra would have born around 1950, slightly before or slightly after. He might have known them in the role of apprentice, beginner or acolyte, before their imprisonment, in some spheres of activity people do start very young, almost as children. He had mentioned Bethnal Green on other occasions, it had been the poorest part of London during the Victorian era, and its poverty had lasted much longer than that very long reign. For decades, it was home to an insane asylum, the Bethnal House Lunatic Asylum, and the district around Old Nichol Street known as 'Jago'—the name by which Tupra sometimes ironically called me—was notorious for its high levels of deprivation and of crime. If he did come from an area like that—but had also studied at Oxford, thanks perhaps to his gifts—it might explain why he was equally at home among low-lifes and in high society: the latter can be learned and is within the grasp of anyone; on the other hand, the only valid training for the former is total immersion. It was possible, given his age. Tupra, however, did not answer me directly, but then he rarely did.

'The movie must be available on DVD or video. But it's

pretty gloomy stuff, and fairly squalid. If, as you say, you tend to avoid squalor like the plague, you'd better not see it,' he said, as if he hadn't heard my questions or merely found them superfluous; and I noted, too, a slight hint of mockery, taking my aversion to squalor so literally. 'An actor I know well, an old friend of mine, had a bit part in it and, one night, when they were filming, I helped him rehearse his scene. I think that's why I went to see it later on, he had picked up a lot of my style. In the scene, he was sharing an army cell with the twins, during their national service, when they were still very young; he was watching them and giving them a brief lesson on what they would have to do when they left the army and returned to civilian life. It's a very condensed lesson in how to get what you want, whenever, whatever. "I know your name. Kray," he said to them.' And this time Tupra pronounced the name in a cockney or perhaps it was merely an uneducated accent, that is, as if the word were 'cry', which, depending on the context, can mean 'a shout' or 'weeping'. As if, at that moment, he were himself playing the part: his bland, ingenuous vanity resurfacing. We had just driven into my secluded square, which was silent and tranquil now that night had fallen; he had parked opposite the trees and had immediately turned off the engine, but he wasn't going to let me get out at once, he still had things to say to me. And he had not yet revealed why he had wanted to give me a lift.—' "And I think to myself, George, I think," '—he continued his monologue, it was as if he had learned it by heart on that night, years ago, when he had rehearsed it with his friend the actor—' "these boys are special. These boys are a new kind. You've got it . . . And I can see it." '—That or something similar was also our motto at work, 'I can see it, I can see your face tomorrow'—' "And you've got to learn how to use it. Now these people, they don't like getting hurt. Not them or their property. Now these people out there who don't like to be hurt, pay other people not to hurt them. You know what I'm saying. 'Course you do. When you get out, you keep your eyes open. Watch out for the people who don't want to be hurt.

Because you scare the shit out of me, boys. Wonderful." '—
That is what Tupra said in a fake accent which was perhaps his
real accent, inside his fast car, in the lunar light of the street-
lamps, sitting on my right, with his hands still resting on the
motionless steering wheel, squeezing it or strangling it, he
wasn't wearing gloves now, they were hidden away, dirty and
sodden and wrapped in toilet paper, in his overcoat, along with
the sword.—'That's the thing, Jack. Fear,' he added, and those
words still sounded as if they belonged to the role he had been
imitating, or which he had usurped, or which perhaps he had
stolen, or which he felt he had actually played through the
intermediary of his friend. But it didn't really sound like his
style, not the usual style of the Bertram Tupra I knew, more like
the performance of a Shakespearian actor, although he did
sound sombre, not squalid perhaps, but definitely sinister,
ominous, so it was not surprising that along with the cold sweats
that came and went and my general sense of fever, a shudder
also ran through me.

My unease, however, had begun to subside since he had stopped the car. I could see the lights on in my apartment, I often left some or all of them on, to anyone watching from the building opposite or from the street, it would look as if I were always home, apart from when I was sleeping or on other occasions when I deliberately turned them off, to listen to music, for example.

'Are those lights yours?' asked Tupra, following my gaze, and he had to invade my space for a moment in order to lean across and peer through the open window on my side of the car, he liked to see things for himself, to scrutinise everything he saw with his insatiable eyes, blue or grey depending on the light.

'Yes, I don't like finding the apartment in darkness when I come home late.'

'It isn't because there's someone waiting for you upstairs, is it? And here I am monopolising your time down here.'

'No, no one's waiting for me, Bertram. You know I live alone.'

'You could have a visitor, a regular one, someone with a key. Perhaps an English girlfriend. Or would she have to be Spanish?'

'No one has my keys, Bertram, and tonight would hardly have been the best one to choose for a late-night tryst. When we go out with you, we never know what time we'll be back. We're not that late tonight, but if De la Garza had put up a fight or run away, or if we'd had to go to the police station for disturbing the peace or for possession of some very original weapons, we would have been out until the small hours, or even until the morning.'

I had recovered my slightly reproachful tone and that may have reminded him that he, in turn, had something with which to reproach me, either in order to crush or quash my reproaches or because he had been keeping it back, and which was his original reason for wanting to give me a lift home. Yes, that was probably it, he did not usually allow faults to go unnoticed, or his own discontents.

'He couldn't have run away, nor could he have put up a fight, you know that,' he pointed out. 'But seeing as how you're calling me Bertram now, there's something I want to say.'—And his face hardened, I really must have done something to annoy him. 'Three times tonight, three times if not four, you called me Tupra when we were with that imbecile friend of yours. How could you, Jack? Where's your head?' And he even struck me on my forehead with the soft, lower portion of his palm, as if he were a gym teacher. 'I'm Reresby tonight, Jack, tonight that's the only name I have—I'd made that perfectly clear—under any circumstances. You know that full well, no matter what the situation, that's an immutable rule, unless, of course, I tell you otherwise. How could you have been so careless? That cretin heard my name. Other people could have heard it. He doesn't matter, he's not important, it makes no difference to him what my name is, besides, the last thing he'll want to do is remember me, my face or my name. He'll want to forget the whole dreadful nightmare, he won't be looking for revenge. But imagine if you'd let my name slip in front of Manoia, for whom I've always been Reresby, ever since he's known me. And we go back years, Jack. You can't just chuck all those years down the drain, simply because you throw a fit and get all hysterical and act as if you know what I might or might not be about to do, you can't possibly know that until you actually see me do it, and sometimes not even then, do you understand? I wouldn't have done it anyway. Not that it's any business of yours. You'll be doing some travelling with me soon, Jack, abroad, and there'll probably be other trips too, if, that is, you stay with us and we continue working together. Regardless of what you see me doing, don't ever try to interfere again. It doesn't bear thinking about: with Manoia it's taken years to build the rather precarious, uncertain trust we've got and to see all that tossed overboard in a moment . . . How do you think someone would react to hearing a negotiator or a colleague suddenly being addressed by a different name from the one by which he or she has always known him?'

He was right in a way, indeed he was largely right: it had been a failure on my part. But it had happened when it had happened, each time that I believed he was about to kill the cretin, it wasn't exactly a normal situation. However, instead of immediately defending myself (to call him by the wrong name three times was quite a lot), I decided to ask a question of my own:

'So you've known each other for years, then, and yet he still thinks you're Reresby,' I said. 'I didn't know that, not that you ever explained. And may I ask what the Sismi is?'

Tupra laughed, on his own this time, a short, almost sarcastic laugh it seemed to me; or worse than that, condescending.

'You may,' he replied, 'although you may not need to. You'd probably find it in a dictionary, an Italian–English one, or Italian–Spanish in your case. It's the Italian Intelligence Service. The Military Security and Information Service, or something like that, it's an acronym, which in Italian gives you SISMI, s-i-s-m-i, there's no great mystery about it. You were paying more attention than I thought.'

'I see. Should I deduce, then, that Manoia works for them, that he's one of Berlusconi's vassals? Those poor Italian civil servants and soldiers, slaves to a man who has no taste in clothes at all. You can sense the sequins and the red satin jacket even when he's not wearing them. I wasn't paying much attention actually, it just happened to be a word I didn't know in any language.'

He didn't respond to my joke, but that wouldn't have been out of respect for that particular Prime Minister, I knew he shared my views, that Berlusconi was a man with no taste in clothes who was always implicitly wearing a sequinned satin jacket.

'That would be a deduction too far, Jack. So don't even ask. Mentioning the CIA or MI6 or MI5 doesn't necessarily mean that you work for them, does it? In fact, those who do rarely talk about them at all, just as many mafiosi have banned the word "Mafia", they can't bear to hear it being bandied about by other people, by civilians shall we say. Besides, you're not paid to make deductions or to ask questions, so you can save yourself some work, which you're doing for free anyway. So, if ever you're tempted, just keep any deductions and questions to yourself. But don't piss me off, all right, don't bother me with them.'

He suddenly turned rude and unpleasant and said those last words with great disdain. It was easy enough for me to recover my own anger, I wouldn't get over those deep feelings of rage for a long time and I would never forget the whole awful experience, the feeling of wretchedness and outrage he had instilled in me, of impotence and menace and even of analogical fascism. If it *was* analogical: it had reminded me of that gang of Carlist militiamen or Falangists who had baited a man in a field outside Ronda, in the remote October or September of 1936. Tupra had pissed *me* off, and so I responded in kind.

'You were about to explain,' I said, 'about that wretched sword. About the Krays and all that. What was it you learned from them that was so important, how to be Zorro perhaps? Or d'Artagnan, Gladiator, Conan the Barbarian, Spartacus? Or Prince Valiant, the Seven Samurai, Aragorn, Scaramouche? Or even Darth Vader? Which was your chosen model?'

He rested his hands again on the immobile steering wheel. He turned towards me, to his left, and in the faint light—the lunar light—his eyes seemed black and opaque, as I had never seen them before; or was it the dominant effect of his eyelashes, long and dense enough to be the envy of any woman and to be considered highly suspect by any man? Although I'm a man too, and my lashes are neither short nor sparse. He laughed briefly, although more wholeheartedly this time, my remark had amused him. Once again I had amused him, and that is the best safe-conduct pass you can have in order to step free from any situation (not where grudges or revenge are involved, but certainly from angry reprisals and threats, which is no small thing).

'Oh, you can laugh now, Iago,' he said mockingly, he always called me that when he wanted to annoy me. And then he continued in a more serious vein. 'You can laugh now, but an hour ago, when I had that sword in my hand, you were as petrified as Garza was'—he pronounced this in the English fashion, 'gaatsa'—'and if I were to get out of the car now, go to the trunk and take out that sword, you would be terrified all over again; and if I threatened you with it, you would race off to your front door, cursing the existence of keys, which have to be taken out of your pocket and fitted into that tiny slot, not so easy to do when your life depends on it and when you're desperate and can't catch your breath. You would never get the key in the lock in time. I would have caught up with you before you managed to open it. Or if you had managed to unlock it, leaving me outside with my sword, I would have jammed the blade in the crack so you couldn't slam the door shut. Even dreams know that your pursuer usually catches up with you, they've known it since the *Iliad*.'—He paused for a moment and glanced across at my front door, he pointed at it as if we could both see, in split-screen image, the hypothetical scene he was describing, a man running frantically to the door, taking the steps in one bound and fumbling with the key in the lock, completely panic-stricken; and behind him the other man holding a double-edged 'cat-gutter', wielding a Landsknecht sword. If I shuddered, I tried to conceal the fact. I was disconcerted by his mention of the *Iliad*.—'It's fear, Jack.

Fear. I told you once that fear is the greatest force that exists, as long as you can adapt to it, and feel at home and live on good terms with it. Then you can benefit from it and use it to your own advantage, and carry out exploits never dreamed of even in the most fatuous of dreams, you can fight with great courage or resist and even overcome someone stronger than yourself. As I said, mothers on the front line with their children nearby would make the best combatants in any battle. That is why you have to be so careful with the fear you provoke, because it could turn back on you. The fear you provoke has to be so terrible that there is no chance of the other person absorbing it or incorporating it, adapting to it or finding it bearable, there must be no point at which the fear stabilises, no pause so that the person can get used to it, not even for a second, or can assimilate and make room for it and thus, for a moment, cease the exhausting effort involved in fending it off. That is what paralyses and crodes and absorbs all their energy—incomprehension, incredulity, denial, struggle. And if the struggle (which is pointless anyway) stops, then the person's strength returns in spades. No one thinks they are going to die, not even in the most adverse of situations, not even in the bleakest of circumstances, not even when confronted by death's irrefutable imminence. Therefore, the fear you provoke or instil cannot be a known or even an imaginable fear. If it's a conventional, predictable or, how can I put it, common-or-garden-variety fear, the person feeling the fear will be capable of understanding it, of gaining time and, eventually, getting used to it, and perhaps, afterwards, even being able to tackle it. He won't stop feeling the fear, he won't lose it, that's not the point: that fear will remain active, plaguing and tormenting him, but he will be able, partly, to come to terms with it, he will be able to reposition himself and to reflect; and when you're in the grip of fear you think very quickly, the imagination grows keener and solutions appear, whether realisable or not, whether doomed to failure or not, but you at least catch glimpses of solutions, the mind becomes alert and with it everything else. You leap a wall that would have seemed insurmountable at any other time, or you run for hours as you make your escape when, before, you would have said you didn't have enough wind to run for the bus. Or you begin to speak, to ask questions, to discuss and to argue, to divert the person threatening you and to see if you can dissuade them, when all your life you have been at a loss for words and have never even been able to catch the eye of a waiter at a bar to place your order. People become transformed by fear if you allow time for the quick inventiveness of survival to prevail in them, rather than mere instinct.'

And Tupra fell silent, he was definitely not Reresby any more, his lecture was over, he must have studied fear first hand, must have experienced and lived it as well, presumably because he had made great use of it during his life, here and there, who knows, on his missions to various countries or on field trips, there are insurrectionists everywhere especially if one is working for an old empire that is in ruins and in retreat, which leaves behind it only a few sturdy outposts to take stock and to transfer powers and to organise not entirely dishonourable departures, future business deals and belated withdrawals. The dark thought crossed my mind that he might have been a torturer himself and witnessed as much panic as Orlov and Bielov and Contreras, who, in their day, had tortured Andrés Nin (the first man's real name was Nikolski and the third was really Vidali and later, in America, Sormenti: Tupra had his aliases too) in a cellar or a barracks or a house or a prison or a hotel in the Russian colony in Alcalá de Henares, the town where Cervantes had been born; one sombre and unspecified informant suggested that these three comrades had flayed him alive; but this version or idea filled me with such fear that I flatly rejected it for no other reason than my own incredulity or my struggle against that fear, just as I immediately rejected this dark thought about my comrade, Tupra; after all, I saw Tupra nearly every day, on workdays anyway, during that London time of mine.

He suddenly fell silent, as if he had run out of verbal rather than respiratory wind, his hands still on the wheel, as if he were a child playing in a pretend car or in his father's stationary, immobilised car. He was staring absently into space, at nothing in particular, he was certainly not seeing what his eyes were seeing, my front door, my square, the trees, the offices, the hotel, the street-lamps, the statue, or the scene that he had just invented, in which he was pursuing me in order to kill me—it was odd to see those eyes at rest, so to speak, eyes that were normally so aware and never idle—or the lights in my dancer-neighbour's windows, Tupra knew nothing of his existence, nor that he was my entertainment when I was alone at home, tired or depressed or nostalgic, and sometimes also a solace, the happy, carefree dancer with his two women, and an extra one now and then. The square was empty during almost all of this time, only the occasional car or passer-by, several minutes apart; and because it was a secluded place, a semi-oasis, the footsteps of the latter rang out loudly on the pavement. Some noticed this and tried to silence them, to muffle them, as if they suddenly missed having a carpet beneath their indiscreet feet. Not the cars though, cars are always inconsiderate everywhere. They didn't even slow down. Nor had we, in the Aston Martin, when we drove into the square.

'Anyway,' I said, because, like Wheeler and like Tupra too, I did not let go of my prey if I was interested in what I was being told. 'You were talking about your apprenticeship, about the sword.' I had dropped the wounding tone, or perhaps it had merely been one of friendly mockery.

He immediately emerged from his absent state, lit another Rameses II and this time he did offer me the open, predominantly red, Pharaonic packet; he did so mechanically, without, I think, realising that he had not done so before. We had carefully extinguished our previous cigarettes in the ashtray; in London people don't throw matches or cigarette butts out of the car window. He began talking again with the same vigour and conviction. He had clearly studied and weighed his methods, he had pondered them or else experts had pondered them for him and he had adopted them after listening to their explanations and fully conscious of the implications; almost nothing happened by chance, nothing was mere outlandish caprice, judging by what he said next (and for once he did not change the subject from sentence to sentence):

'Exactly. If I draw a gun or a knife on someone, they're bound to be scared, but only in a conventional, or, as I said, common or garden-variety way, yes, perhaps that's the word. Because it's the norm these days and has been for a couple of centuries, quite ancient really. If someone mugs us or kidnaps us, if they threaten us in order to make us talk or want to force us to do something or to teach us a lesson, in almost every case they will do so at gunpoint or knifepoint: those are the easiest weapons to get hold of and, besides, they're simple to use and practical, they fit in the pocket and can be pulled out quickly with one hand, and they're what we expect the other person to be carrying when we sense that something bad is going to happen. When, for example, we come across a gang of soccer hooligans or skinheads and we just have time to wonder whether or not to cross over to the other side of the road, almost always too late, if they've already seen us, it's not usually worth it and may even make matters worse. Or if someone is following us with suspicious intent, for example, the woman who suspects she's going to be raped both fears and assumes that the point of a knife will be pressed to her chest or her throat; the man who is home when his house is broken into expects the barrel of a gun pressed against his temple or the back of his neck, it's normal and predictable and, in a way, you get used to the idea. Getting used to the idea may not help much, but it does to some extent, because, almost unwittingly, you're already thinking about ways of escaping or of limiting the damage, even though, given the circumstances, such thoughts are pure fantasy; but at least you're one step ahead, and, more importantly, you're not quite so terrified or so surprised, or, rather, you're surprised to find yourself in this predicament because you never thought such a thing could possibly happen to you, that you weren't even in the running, our optimism is infinite when, confronted by someone else's misfortune, even that of someone close, you can still say to yourself after all the words of condolence and lamentation: "It's not me, it didn't happen to me." Nowadays, there are gangs, you'll have read about them in the press, most of them from Eastern Europe, Albanians, Russians, Ukrainians, Kosovans, Poles, who, without warning, burst into people's houses carrying machine guns, they kick the door down and make everyone lie on the floor and start beating them with their machine-gun butts, all very brutal, and sometimes they go too far and kill someone. The old KGB techniques, or those of the even older NKVD, and not so very different from the Gestapo's techniques.'—'Because they knew nothing of the machinations of Orlov and his boys at the NKVD': this quote surfaced in my memory, I had read it in Wheeler's house, during my long night of research into the mysterious disappearance of Nin.—'That already creates more fear because it's so unexpected, and the violence is seen at once as being totally out of proportion to that required to subdue and rob an ordinary, peace-loving family, who are not going to put up any resistance; and so they start to fear that something even more disproportionate might happen. I believe that in Spain, as well as these ungrateful Slavs, there are Colombians and Peruvians who do the same, the fact that they speak the same language helps enormously, well, it's what tempts them over there in the first place, and since language isn't a problem for them in your country, they're unlikely to move elsewhere. So at least here we're pretty safe from them for the moment. We get Arabs, Chinese, Rastas and Pakistanis, but that's another matter. But the fear provoked by a machine gun is still not that terrible, not what I would call terrible, the kind of fear that cancels out and overwhelms everything, leaving no room to think about anything but that, about the fear filling your whole being.

Because a machine gun is difficult to use, and they won't use it if they can avoid it. It's noisy and flamboyant, there's a lot of vibration and the recoil is so powerful that it shakes you and tires you, and the gun's very hard to conceal if you have to run away. Its function, then, is more to intimidate than anything else, and the victim knows or senses this from the very first moment and he takes comfort in that, and consoles himself thinking that his assailants will only fire if things start to go badly wrong for them.' Tupra paused again, only very briefly this time, as if to start a new paragraph, but not a new chapter.—'A sword, on the other hand,' he went on. 'Oh, you can laugh now and say it's theatrical or anachronistic or even rusty, but you didn't see the look on your face when you saw that sword in my hands. You saw the look on the monkey's face, though, and that should give you an idea.'—He used the word 'monkey' to describe De la Garza, and I translated this to myself as *macaco*, although the English equivalent *macaque* would sound ludicrous as an insult.—'It's probably the weapon that instils the most fear in people, precisely because it seems so out of place in a day and age when hand-to-hand fighting barely exists, or only as some curious sport. They hurl bombs and projectiles from unimaginable distances, it's as if the explosives simply fell from the skies, often you don't see the planes or even hear them, perhaps they don't have a pilot at all, or so it seems to the populations below. They suffer the appalling consequences, but rarely see who caused them, that's been the tendency ever since the invention of the crossbow, which Richard the Lionheart and others considered dishonourable, because it gave too much of an advantage to the crossbowman and exposed him to so little risk, much less than with the ordinary longbow, because that, at least, required a greater degree of skill and effort and didn't use any kind of mechanism, and it reached—if I can put it like this—it reached only as far as a man's arm, never much further or much quicker or with much more precision. For centuries now, everything has been tending towards the concealment and anonymity of the person doing the killing, and towards dishonour; and that is why the sword seems to be more in earnest than any other weapon. It seems impossible to wield it in vain; it seems impossible to do anything else but use it, and to use it immediately.'

And it was true that I had wondered about it when I saw it in his hand—or perhaps that was later on, when I finally got home (not then, not during that car journey or while sitting in the car) and it took me so long to get to sleep (therefore, he may have formulated it for me, may have put it into words for me in the car and my thought might have been a mere echo of those words)—and I had done so in these terms: 'Where did that come from, a primitive blade, a medieval grip, a Homeric hilt, an archaic tip, the most unnecessary of weapons or the most out-of-keeping with these times, more even than an arrow and more than a spear, anachronistic, arbitrary, eccentric, so incongruous that the mere sight of it provokes panic, not just intense fear, but an atavistic fear, as if one suddenly recalled that it is the sword that has caused the most deaths throughout most centuries; that it has killed at close quarters and face to face.'

Earlier, Tupra had alluded to Homer and now he was talking about the second Plantagenet king and the first of the Richards, born in Oxford of all places, although it is highly unlikely that he knew any English, even broken English, and during the ten years of his reign, he spent, altogether, no more than six months in the country of that language, the rest of the time being taken up with the Third Crusade or with familial wars in France, where he was killed as he was besieging Châlus in 1199 by—to add insult to injury—an arrow from a crossbow, as I was able to confirm later on in a couple of history books: another British foreigner, yet another bogus Englishman and another one who had his aliases: not just the famous 'Lionheart', but also 'Yea and Nay', which, understandably enough, tends to be forgotten; well, Richard Yea and Nay sounds rather comical, even if he was called that because of his sudden and continual changes of mind and plan, even in the midst of battle (he must have been infuriating, that cruel king). I inevitably found these cultural references coming from Tupra rather surprising, in normal conversation he didn't usually make such references, either historical or literary, although perhaps it was because there was no need for them at work: we were always talking about other people, most of whom were present and none of whom was fictitious, although the majority of them were strangers to me. Perhaps, for professional motives, he knew the entire history of weapons. Or, more likely, it was because he had studied at Oxford and been a disciple of Toby Rylands, eminent emeritus professor of English Language and Literature, and was more educated than he seemed. But sometimes I wondered whether Rylands's tutorship had taken place more within the group with no name, which provided a more practical training, rather than at the renowned university to which we had all belonged. Even I had belonged to it during those two now distant years of which barely a trace remained, as I had confidently predicted when I still lived there, conscious that I was just passing through and would leave no mark. Now, in this other London time, I thought the same sometimes, only more so, despite never being very clear as to where I would go if I left or whether I would return: 'When I leave here, when I return to Spain, my life during these real days—and some pass very slowly—will become a "Yea and Nay" or like a banal dream, and none of it will be of any importance, not even the gravest events, not even that temptation or that sense of panic, not even the feelings of disgust or embarrassment that I myself provoke, not even the sense of something sitting heavy upon my soul. A day will have arrived when I will have said a farewell to these days perhaps similar to that written by Cervantes and of which I tried to remind Wheeler, although without entirely daring to, in his garden by the river. Doubtless a less cheerful farewell, but definitely more relieved. For example: "Farewell, laughter and farewell, insults. I will not see you again, nor will you see me. And farewell, passion; farewell, memories." '

'What did you study at Oxford, Bertram?' I suddenly asked him, although it was probably not the best moment, especially when there had been (and would be) so many other moments, during our sessions and dialogues and pauses to ponder or consider, and idle moments too, in order to find this out. The fact is that I didn't know because I had never got as far as asking him, and in England that is always one of the first things one asks in order to break the ice between strangers and even between colleagues. That was how it was whenever I met some Oxford don outside of our teaching or administrative activities, having a coffee in the Senior Common Room at the Taylorian, between classes, or in between lectures or seminars; or at one of the hellish high tables held by one of the thirty-nine colleges (elevated and eternal tables), in which one might find oneself seated and immobile for several hours beside a young economist whose sole topic of conversation was a peculiar cider tax that existed in England between 1760 and 1767 and on which he had written his thesis (this is a true example from my previous Oxford experience, the name of this glorious individual was Halliwell), as I found out by politely asking the simultaneously fatal and inaugural phrase: 'What's your field?', literally, in Spanish, '¿Cuál es su campo?', but meaning 'What's your specialty?' or 'What do you do?', although in Oxford it could also mean 'What do you teach?' However, none of these variants was an appropriate way of interrupting Tupra in the middle of a discussion about swords.

If I still remember even Halliwell, obese and with a bright red face and a small, sparse military moustache, how could I not remember all the other people from then, the old, time-travelling porter Will with his clear, limpid eyes, and Alec Dewar—the Butcher, the Ripper, the Inquisitor, or the Hammer—a selfless Dickensian teacher beneath his proud façade and his unjustified nicknames; or the inebriated Lord Rymer—the Flask—who had since reappeared with his all too justified nickname, and Rook, the gossipy expert in Slavonic languages, a man with a large head and a slender body—an egghead, in short—who claimed to have been friends with Nabokov and who had, for about a thousand years, been translating *Anna Karenina* as it should be translated, although with no visible result; the Alabasters, who used to spy on me with bated breath via the closed-circuit television in their second-hand bookshop when I went down to their basement to snoop around in the dust; and the head of my department, Aidan Kavanagh, whom I saw once wearing a vest, as my boss Tupra always did, except that Kavanagh wasn't wearing a shirt underneath his or only some strange sleeveless variety; the fat girl called Muriel—who wasn't really fat—with whom I spent one night, and one night only, and who told me that she lived between the rivers Windrush and Evenlode, in an area which was once a forest, Wychwood Forest; the gypsy florist, Jane, with her high boots, and Alan Marriott with his docile, three-legged dog, who had visited me with his master one morning, just as, many years afterwards, late one night, the white pointer had visited me with his mistress, Pérez Nuix; my best friend Cromer-Blake, my guide in the city and who had sometimes been both father- and mother-figure to me, alternating between health and sickness during my time there and dead four months after my departure (I still have his diaries); and the great authority Toby Rylands so like Wheeler but, as far as I knew then, unrelated, and who might well have got me into all this by means of a report written then and filed away just in case; the young woman with the rhythmic, well-shod feet and perfectly turned ankles, to whom I had not dared to speak with sufficient emotion, the emotion I felt in her presence, on a late-night train journey from Didcot station, and Clare Bayes, my lover. All those people existed in my life before Luisa, whom I met only on my return. While I might not have left any mark on Oxford, my time there had certainly left a mark on me. As this other period of London solitude would too, even if, one day, it appeared to me like a daydream never lived and shorn of consequences, and I could misquote those lines from Milton each morning: 'I wak'd, time fled, and day brought back my day.'

No, it wasn't at all certain that what was happening now did not count, while I was working in a foreign country and in a building with no name and for whom I did not know, or only sometimes, as young Pérez Nuix had explained to me in my apartment. And at the same time as I asked Tupra that question in the car, about what he had studied at Oxford, I glanced up at my illuminated window behind which I was already yearning to be: it would have looked just like that while she was standing in the street wondering whether or not to ring the bell, and afterwards too, while she was inside on that night of heavy, steady, sustained rain, talking and even lecturing, and asking me for that awkward favour which I finally granted a few days later, and which now made me feel in silent debt to Tupra—or perhaps it was a secret, guilty debt—and which somewhat checked my anger or near rage, for I could still not come to terms with what Reresby had or hadn't done—what I had thought he would do—in that gleaming toilet for cripples, to use his term, in which he might, who knows, have left another cripple, and in which he had been about to leave a corpse, before my very eyes, a man decapitated in my presence.

'I read medieval history, in the Modern History department,' he replied. 'But I've never done anything with it, professionally, that is. Why do you ask?'

I had time to think, although not in as clearly articulated a form as follows here: 'What a shame I didn't know before. Instead of beating De la Garza up, he could have made friends with him, even joined forces, De la Garza being such a connoisseur of chic medieval literary fantasy. He might at least have shown him more mercy.'

What I actually said was this: 'Oh, so it's a kind of nostalgic throwback, the sword, I mean. Perhaps a youthful fantasy.'

He did not initially appreciate my irony, he pulled a face and I heard an impatient tut-tutting: after my triple blunder with his name, he must consider that I was in no position to criticise him or to make derisive comments.

'Possibly. I always liked medieval history, and the military history that I studied later on,' he replied calmly, he was, after all, a man capable of seeing the funny side of things where there was one. 'But never dismiss ideas born of the imagination, Jack, you only get to them after much thought, much reflection, and study, and considerable boldness. They're not within the grasp of just anyone, only those of us who see and who keep looking.'—'It's a very rare gift indeed nowadays, and becoming rarer,' Wheeler had explained to me over breakfast, 'the gift of being able to see straight through people, clearly and without qualms, with neither good intentions nor bad, without effort.'—'Like you and me, like Patricia and Peter.'—And Peter had added: 'That is the way, in which according to Toby, you might be like us, Jacobo, and now I think he was right. We could both see through people like that. Seeing was our gift, and we placed it at the service of others. And I can still see.'— Patricia, that is how Tupra referred to young Pérez Nuix, by her first name, or else by the diminutive form Pat, just as Wheeler would say Val sometimes, when he recalled his wife Valerie, whose early death he had preferred not to tell me about, as yet ('Do you mind if I tell you another day. If that's all right,' he had said almost in a whisper, as if he were asking me a favour, that of allowing him to remain silent). This was not the same as when Tupra or Mrs Berry called me Jack, that was because it was easier for them and a phonetic approximation of my real name Jacques, more than Jacobo and Jaime, although no one ever used it now. And then Tupra went on and concluded his explanation: 'That atavistic fear is so powerful, Jack, that if ever one of our contemporaries finds a sword hovering above his head or pointing at his chest, the moment the sword disappears from view and returns to its scabbard, he'll feel so grateful that anything that happens to him afterwards will seem good and he will accept it without resistance, not just without defending himself, but with immense relief, almost with gratitude, because he will have surrendered even before the first blow was struck, having given himself up for dead. And he will do whatever you want him to do: he will betray, denounce, confess the truth or invent a lie, he will undo what has been done and retract what has been said, he will disown his children, beg forgiveness, pay whatever is asked, allow himself to be mistreated and accept his punishment without a murmur. Without opposition and without haggling. Because, as I said, people today can only conceive of the sword as a weapon to be used, not merely brandished as a threat or as a way of keeping someone quiet. That's what guns are for or even knives, no one would bother taking up such an awkward object, such an encumbrance, if he were not going to make use of it, at least that is what anyone who sees a sword raised against them will believe. That is why the Krays provoked such fear, right from the very start, even when they lacked power or influence and were mere beginners, upstarts: because they would turn up with their sabres and they would use them too. They would cut and slash, you bet they did, and in London too. And that panic continued and remained for ever, it became legendary the panic they spread with that archaic brand of violence from a more barbarous age. Admit it, Jack, even you breathed more easily when I put the sword away. And everything after that seems almost welcome, isn't that right, Jack? Admit it.'

I had to admit he was right, but I did not do so out loud. The fact that he should boast about it struck me as intolerable.

'And what was the point this time, Bertram?' I asked instead. 'You didn't use it, damn it; fortunately, you only pretended you were going to use it, but I don't know what good it did you, taking the sword out and terrifying us both with it or with everything that came afterwards. I didn't notice you taking advantage of De la Garza's fear to interrogate him or to get something out of him, or to demand an apology, or to force him to undo something he had done or to get money out of him. What exactly were you after, may I ask? To frighten me? If so, what you did was gratuitous and entirely unnecessary. It was absolutely outrageous. There was no need for you to produce a double-edged Landsknecht sword. Nor to half drown him in the toilet. Nor to hurl him against that bar. Unless all you wanted was to punish him because he had got in your way. I agree the man is an asshole, but he's completely harmless. You can't just go around beating people up, killing them. Especially not if you're going to involve me.'

For a moment Tupra again invaded my side of the car with his curly hair, to look up at the window as I had done, perhaps he wanted to make sure that no figure had since appeared there, silhouetted against the light.

'That isn't what I do,' he said. 'And I see you know about swords. You're quite right, it is a Landsknecht or *Katzbalger*, a genuine one,' he added pedantically and with a touch of pride. 'But why, according to you, can't one do that?'

His question caught me off guard, so much so that I did not, for a moment, know what he was talking about, even though I had just said what it was that could not be done.

'Why can't one do what?'

'Why can't one go around beating up people and killing them? That's what you said.'

'What do you mean, "why"?'

My confusion was growing; sometimes we don't have an answer to the most obvious of questions. They seem so obvious that we take them for granted, and stop thinking about them, still less questioning them, and so literally decades pass without our giving them a thought, however paltry or vague. Why, in my opinion, can't one go around killing people, that was the idiotic question Tupra was asking me. And I had no answer to this idiotic question, or only equally idiotic, puerile answers inherited but never thought through: because it's not right, because it's immoral, because it's against the law, because you can get sent to prison, or in some countries to the gallows, because you should not do unto others what you would not have done unto you, because it's a crime, because it's a sin, because it's bad. He was clearly asking me something that went beyond all that. He did not reply at once. He saw that I did not know what to say, or at least not immediately. He took out another Rameses II, and did not offer me one this time, two in a row would have seemed to him an extravagance; he put it to his lips, but did not light it yet, instead, he turned the ignition key and started the engine. I did not for a second think that he was going to ask me to get out, to dismiss me and drive off. He did not let go of his prey either, whether dialectical or otherwise.

'I hope there really isn't anyone waiting for you up there, I hope so for her sake,' he said, and pointed up at the car roof, then glanced at his watch; in an almost reflective, mimetic response, I looked at mine too: no, it wasn't very late, despite everything, not even for London, and in Madrid the night, any night, would just be getting into its stride, the partying would be at its height—'because it's not yet time for you to go up and see her. Anyway, it's not that late, and you can have tomorrow off if you want. But we need to talk a bit more about all this, I can see that you've taken it all very much to heart, too much so really. I'll explain to you why it was necessary. We're going to go to my place for a while, it won't take more than an hour or an hour and a half. I want to show you some videos that I keep there rather than at the office, they're not for just anyone's eyes. And I'll tell you a couple of stories, one from medieval times in fact. I'll tell you about Constantinople, for example. Perhaps a bit about Tangiers as well, not quite so remote, although still a few centuries ago. And while we're driving, think a bit more about what you said, so that you can explain to me why one can't beat people up or kill them.'

I had said nothing since my failure to find an answer to his idiotic question. Or perhaps it wasn't so very idiotic and there *was* no easy answer. I didn't feel I could say no. And, besides, it made no sense, after all we had already been through that night.

'I know what happened in Constantinople in 1453,' I said, for lack of anything else to say. Many years ago, before I went to live in Oxford, I had read a marvellous book, *The Fall of Constantinople, 1453* by Sir Steven Runciman, who was not from Oxford, but from Cambridge. Nor was it true that I knew what had happened, I couldn't remember, you read and learn and immediately forget, if you don't continue reading, if you don't continue thinking.

'I see,' replied Tupra. 'But I'll tell you a bit about what happened shortly before as well.'

He drove around the square in order to leave it and head north. I didn't know where he lived. 'Perhaps in Hampstead,' I thought. I looked back once more at the lights in my windows, and at those of the trusting dancer. Tupra caught these two glances out of the corner of his eye. Everything was still lit, the large dancing windows, my silent window. Mine would have to remain silent, and would stay like that until I returned, with Tupra you could never tell what time you would be back. And however much he insisted, there was, fortunately, no one waiting for me in my apartment, no one to turn off any lights in my absence, while I was not there. No one had my keys and no one was ever waiting for me.